Tyler Anne Snell lives in South Alabama with her same-named husband, their artist kiddo, four mini 'lions' and a burning desire to meet Kurt Russell. Her superpowers include binge-watching TV and herding cats. When she isn't writing thrilling mysteries and romance, she's reading everything she can get her hands on. How she gets through each day starts and ends with a big cup of coffee. Visit her at tylerannesnell.com

Julie Anne Lindsey is an obsessive reader who was once torn between the love of her two favourite genres: toe-curling romance and chew-your-nails suspense. Now she gets to write both for Mills & Boon Heroes. When she's not creating new worlds, Julie can be found carpooling her three kids around northeastern Ohio and plotting with her shamelessly enabling friends. Winner of the Daphne du Maurier Award for Excellence in Mystery/Suspense, Julie is a member of International Thriller Writers, Romance Writers of America and Sisters in Crime. Learn more about Julie and her books at julieannelindsey.com

DANGEROUS RECALL

TYLER ANNE SNELL

UNDER SIEGE

JULIE ANNE LINDSEY

MILLS & BOON

First Published in Great Britain 2024
by Mills & Boon, an imprint of HarperCollins*Publishers* Ltd
1 London Bridge Street, London, SE1 9GF

www.harpercollins.co.uk

HarperCollins*Publishers*
Macken House, 39/40 Mayor Street Upper,
Dublin 1, D01 C9W8, Ireland

Dangerous Recall © 2024 Tyler Anne Snell
Under Siege © 2024 Julie Anne Lindsey

ISBN: 978-0-263-32229-3

0524

This book contains FSC™ certified paper and other controlled sources to ensure responsible forest management.

For more information visit: www.harpercollins.co.uk/green

Printed and Bound in the UK using 100% Renewable Electricity at CPI Group (UK) Ltd, Croydon, CR0 4YY

DANGEROUS RECALL

TYLER ANNE SNELL

This book is for everyone who loves love.
I hope you enjoy Mack and Aiden as much as I did.

Chapter One

The nameless park a mile past the town crossroad was hands down the quiet pride and joy of the town of Willow Creek.

It wasn't much—there was no playground equipment, no intricate flower beds, no fountain or centerpiece that sparkled or stood out—but the greenery surrounding the half-acre plot of land more than earned the love of the town. It was called magic by most, a godsend by a few, because no matter what was happening in a person's life, the park always seemed to spare a moment of peace to those who visited. There was no rhyme or reason to it. No town lore or rumor that made it so. Yet, there wasn't a local who hadn't gone there at one time or another looking for some slice of soothing.

Which made the body found buried next to the big, knotted and knobby oak tree near the end of the simple walking path a shocking discovery. And, honestly, a shame to boot.

The park's peace had been invaded.

That was to speak nothing of the man murdered and hidden there.

Malcolm Atwood squatted down to get a better view of the makeshift grave. He was wearing the clothes he'd come from the airport in and was regretting not changing into something more comfortable before his way-too-early morning flight. He'd been in town less than a half hour and now he was staring at a dead man while wearing slacks and shining shoes.

It made an already not-right situation feel even more so.

Mack sighed out long and drew the attention of the young deputy standing a few feet from them. He'd already caught her flinch at the blood-soaked earth. It was her first homicide, he'd guessed. It was not Ray Dearborn's first. Medical examiner by day, childhood friend of Mack's since first grade, Ray had been at the feet of a dead body before. However, what was a first was calling Mack in to see it, too.

"Usually when I come back into town you're offering me a drink, not the dead," he said, crouching to get a better look at the partially uncovered man between them. Mack guessed he might not have been found so soon had it not stormed the night before. The ground around them had been washed out by the rain. "I also think you've forgotten that my job revolves around protecting the living. This is a little out of my bounds."

Ray stopped whatever notes he'd been taking on his clipboard and tried to be cheeky.

"Maybe this is my way of forcing you to be social," he said.

Mack snorted, because it wasn't exactly outside the scope of what Ray might do. The saying that introverts don't make friends, they only get adopted by extroverts was an accurate way to describe how their relationship started. Now in their early thirties, that dynamic hadn't changed.

"Considering you know where I live and what time I was coming in today, I'm guessing this isn't a social call." Mack met his friend's eye. "Tell me."

Ray let out a sigh that rivaled Mack's. He at least managed to look apologetic before he spoke again.

"The almighty Sheriff Boyd told me to reach out," he admitted. "He was with me when I first got on scene and kind of got squirmy when I said I didn't recognize this victim. This is the first murder in Willow Creek since he took over. I think he wants us to wrap this up before anyone else gets word of it."

"And why did he want *me* here?"

Mack still wasn't getting how the dead one and his one made two.

Ray put up his gloved hands in defense. He'd never been a man to be sheepish, but he looked close to it.

"He knows about your face thing," he answered. "And before you go throwing rocks, it wasn't me who spilled the beans. I mean, seriously, how many times have I heard you complain to me that you're not some kind of computer or personal database? Why would I purposefully incur that kind of wrath again by blabbing to the sheriff about it?"

An old feeling of anger started to kick around. Mack wasn't unused to it. He'd been living alongside that feeling since the day the warehouse burned down. The day that his knack for remembering faces put him in his own personal hell. The anger that was always there but kept in check by the unending patience he'd inherited from his father.

Ray, whose father was often found singing karaoke at the local bar despite it not having a karaoke machine, swore before he made his guess.

"I'd say Deputy McCoy spilled the beans," he added. "He's really been sticking with the sheriff lately. Anything he can do to prove he's useful, I'm sure he'd jump at it. He was on shift this morning, so I'm sure if the sheriff mentioned needing to identify a John Doe quick, he threw out your name. Though, let's be honest, almost everyone in town knows about your brainpower thing. He could have already found out."

Mack sucked on his teeth. He looked down at John Doe again.

"I wish you'd stop calling it a power," he told his friend. "Some people are just good at remembering things. I just happen to be good at remembering faces."

It was true—Mack had a thing about people, specifically remembering their faces. After seeing someone, his mind seemed to save them forever. He saw a face and it stuck in place.

It was one reason he was good at his current job.

Being able to do threat analysis for a client was a lot easier when you could bookmark all the people around them.

John Doe's face, however, wasn't familiar. It was an odd feeling for Mack, being in Willow Creek and seeing someone he didn't recognize. He had been born in town, lived in it with zeal until college and then, with a lot less enthusiasm, had come back to use his family's home as a base of operations. A place he came to when he needed a place to go, as his sister had disapprovingly said many times before.

If John Doe was a local, he'd managed to stay beneath the Mack Atwood radar all this time. An impressive but not impossible thing to accomplish.

Mack thought out loud now.

"Blond hair, dark from the dirt, nose with a crook in it from probably being broken once or twice, some stubble on his face, some freckles, too, and the upper body build of someone who took relative care of themselves by exercising and or a good diet..." Mack shook his head. "I've never seen him before. In person, print or online. I don't know who he is."

It wasn't the news Ray wanted to hear. It wasn't like Mack

enjoyed giving it. For Ray to call him to a crime scene had taken a lot for the man, but the new sheriff was known for his brashness and his charm and had no doubt used both to get the medical examiner to call in a civilian. It was probably called a favor, too. Sheriff Boyd seemed to like asking for those.

Being the favor himself, Mack had mixed feelings about not being able to come through.

"Sorry," he added, standing tall and wiping the dirt from the knees of his slacks. "Reelection optics for the sheriff aside, I know you're not a fan of homicide investigations. It would have been nice to make this part easier for you at least."

Ray waved him off.

"Don't apologize for something most people wouldn't even try. My phone is filled with contacts, and I don't think any of them would have beelined it to a crime scene after an early morning of flying. The detectives can deal with this. Me, too. I am a big boy, after all. You've seen my house, right? It's as intelligent and suave as me."

Mack snorted.

"Last I checked, your bedroom has a section of it dedicated to comic books. Comic books you've never opened."

Ray rolled his eyes.

"Hey, considering I deal with dead people all day, why don't you cut a man slack for having a hobby that brings him some joy? Plus, collecting is the new it thing. Everyone has something they want to preserve, but also, show off. I'm human like that, Mr. Brainpower."

Mack couldn't help but chuckle at that.

"I'll take your word for it, Dr. Dearborn."

A moment of silence bloomed between them as both took another regretful look at John Doe. The sound of car doors closing in the distance brought Ray back first. He nodded over his shoulder.

"That would be either our shining Detective Winters or the CSI crew," he said. "If you want to avoid them, I'd get going now."

Mack didn't need to be told twice.

"Good luck with this. Call me later."

Ray said he would, and Mack left the simple path and instead made a circle around to the parking lot with haste. Sure enough, a new cruiser was in the small lot. Detective Winters was nowhere to be seen.

It was a stroke of good luck that Mack wanted to capitalize on. He was in his truck and on the road within the minute. There he had been trying to avoid everything— Matthew Winters, memories of the warehouse fire and the dead—only to find all three as soon as he'd come back to Willow Creek. It made his next destination—the secluded Atwood home—all the more enticing.

The second he was through the front door, he decided, he wasn't going to come back out until his next contract. There were no if, ands or buts about it.

Yet, the closer he got to his childhood home, the more his mind went back to the park.

Mack protected the living as a bodyguard; Ray dealt with the dead.

And Willow Creek? It had a past of playing fast and loose with both.

Mack's chest started to grow cold.

That old anger in him wasn't just moving around, it was growing stronger. His grip on the steering wheel turning his knuckles white.

This was why he never stayed in town. No matter what he did, he couldn't escape the past.

Chapter Two

Downtown Willow Creek was divided into two parts. There was the business complex that housed everything law, everything financial and almost everything local politics. This complex, dubbed the Suit Hotel, had desk jockeys who worked in its many rented spaces and were always two things: uptight and dressed ready to kill.

Aiden Riggs took more than a small amount of pleasure walking into his office across the street wearing black joggers and a fitted tee beneath his jean jacket, his Converse high tops still a bit dirty and his hair purposefully styled to look carefree.

Riggs Consulting's lone office worker, Mrs. Cole, however, was less happy with his lack of professional flair. Two seconds through the door and she was already clicking her tongue in disapproval.

"I know I'm no fashionista, but I'm not sure wearing sweats to the office is the way to get more clients."

She pointed to the front display window, and Aiden knew she was motioning to the Suit Hotel. Still, he looked at the window and smiled. Only two of its eighteen tiny panels were transparent; the others were stained to look antique. A charming but failed attempt if you asked Aiden. Still, he'd fallen in love with the window first, the storefront second when he'd first visited the space six months prior. Sure, the office was small, but it was also unique.

It was also as far away from Bellwether Tech's ten-story corporate headquarters in Nashville as you could throw a business.

Right now Mrs. Cole was sitting at her desk in the main lobby; a few feet away was the door to Aiden's office. The two smaller, closet-size rooms next to it were a nook that counted as a break room and then the bathroom, the only two spaces not covered in the clutter that Aiden was so used to accumulating. Much to Mrs. Cole's objections.

Riggs Consulting was nothing like the monster Aiden had left behind.

Even now that thought put him in a good mood.

"Considering we're not hurting for clients, I'd say my clothes don't factor into their decision to hire us." Aiden motioned to his joggers. "In fact, maybe this should be the new professional standard. Are you sure you don't want me to buy you a pair? They're comfortable and, if you need to exercise in a hurry, efficient."

Mrs. Cole, a die-hard fan of pantsuits and floral brooches, narrowed her eyes. The first time Aiden had met her she'd had her hair up in curls and sprayed tight. Since then she'd become more relaxed. At least somewhat. In the words of her husband, she had forty-two years of being a proper Southern lady and a "youngin'" wasn't going to get her guard down that easy. Aiden, in his thirties and not exactly sure he should be considered as such, took the statement as a challenge.

One way or the other he was going to get Mrs. Cole out of her professional shell.

"You can pretend all you want that you don't love me," Aiden said. "But we both know you're my biggest fan."

He sidled up to her desk and put on his brightest smile. Mrs. Cole must have been caught off guard, because the corners of her lips twitched before she rolled her eyes.

"Now, don't you go sweet-talking me and try to make me forget why I'm fussing at you." She took a sticky note from her desktop and handed it over. "Instead go return this call."

Aiden took the paper and read the number in Mrs. Cole's pristine handwriting. He didn't recognize it. The name next to it, however, was an easy memory.

"Leighton called," he read, some surprise mixing in with fondness. "When?"

Mrs. Cole seemed to sense their banter was coming to an end and switched tones to the one she used when working. It wasn't fake, it was just focused.

"At seven thirty this morning," she answered. "I'd just unlocked the front door when the phone started ringing. Mr. Hughes said he might have a job for you but wanted to set up a meeting first."

That caught Aiden's attention even more.

"Did Leighton say if it was urgent?" Aiden checked his watch. It was almost ten in the morning. He'd come in later than usual after pulling an all-nighter for work the day before. You can't catch up on sleep once it's lost, but Aiden sure had tried.

Mrs. Cole shook her head but hesitated. She took her favorite pen in her hand and clicked it open and closed twice. Aiden had seen the same habit come up time and time again when the woman was trying to get her thoughts straight. After a few more clicks, she sighed.

"He said to give him a call at your earliest convenience…"

Aiden's eyebrow rose. She had stopped herself.

"But?"

"But he *sounded* like it was urgent. Like he was being

rushed." She clicked the pen again. "I know you need to finish up the last job's paperwork, but I'd go ahead and call him now just in case."

The touch of concern wasn't lost on Aiden. Mrs. Cole wasn't always one who emoted, especially not over a client. Definitely not over a former client who was also Aiden's ex.

"I'll call him as soon as I'm sitting down," Aiden assured her.

Mrs. Cole unclicked her pen top again. When she spoke, there was a maternal warning in her voice.

"And make sure to be on your best behavior when you call," she said. "That's not his personal number, so he might be at work."

Aiden put a gentle hand on her shoulder and squeezed.

"Yes, ma'am. Thanks for the message."

Mrs. Cole returned to the file pulled up on her computer screen, and Aiden took his leave to do just as he'd said.

The space in Riggs Consulting's only office was largely taken up by a wooden desk, an overly padded office chair and a long, narrow table along one wall that housed a bank of computer monitors, all waiting to be used. Aiden dropped his messenger bag on the worn love seat across from the table and went straight for the desk. The chair's wheels squeaked as he situated himself behind it. He couldn't help but compare it and the room around him to the IT department at Bellwether Tech.

If Leighton had called from there, the company's number would have been registered in the caller ID.

Aiden took his cell phone out of his pocket. No missed calls or texts.

If something was urgent, Leighton would have called his cell.

He nodded to himself, trying to dam up his growing sense

of worry. They might not have worked out romantically, but Leighton was a good man. Not to mention a client for little things he'd needed help with once or twice since.

Aiden dialed the number on the sticky note and forced himself to lean back in his chair. One thing he loved the most about working in code and on computers? They were a lot more straightforward than the humans who used them.

The line rang a total of six times before an automated voice mail recording picked up. It wasn't personalized. Aiden decided to be as vague.

"This is Aiden Riggs at Riggs Consulting. I'm returning a call from earlier this morning. Feel free to call back anytime." Aiden left his phone number but not Leighton's name. He ended the call.

Something felt off, but he couldn't place what.

"You're overreacting because you've been watching too many thrillers," he said to himself, aloud, after a few moments. "Pull yourself together, Riggs."

Aiden tried to do just that. He dived into the legal paperwork he needed to sign, checked his emails and found a few more tasks that were mind-numbingly boring to pass the time.

But Leighton didn't call back, and by lunch, Aiden couldn't deny he was feeling anxious about it. By noon he was calling Leighton's personal cell phone number. Two hours later he caved and called the last number he'd thought he'd ever dial again.

"Bellwether Technologies, this is the IT department, how may I direct your call?" Aiden felt momentary relief at a somewhat familiar voice.

"Hey, Jenna, it's Aiden. Aiden Riggs."

Jenna Thompson had been the lead executive assistant of the IT department since Aiden had started working there.

For six years he'd said hi and bye to Jenna in the morning and afternoon. She'd always been friendly. Even on the day he'd walked out.

"Aiden!" she exclaimed. "Of course I'd know that voice. How are you?"

He shifted in his chair, trying to physically move away from the growing discomfort. Just because he was a social creature didn't mean he always liked being social. Still, it wasn't Jenna's fault that he'd left the company. Acting coldly to her didn't unring the bell of what had happened.

"Hey, I'm good," he responded with tired warmth. "Keeping busy, tanning when I can. Still not eating my vegetables. You know, the usual."

Jenna laughed. The woman definitely had a knack for being peppy.

"You need to get on those veggies, but I'm glad you're doing well otherwise. Though I can't complain too much about your eating habits. You actually just caught me coming back from lunch, and I definitely decided on the bowl of ice cream over the fruit cup."

Aiden joined in on the humor.

Jenna was the first one to drop it.

"What can I do for you?" she asked. "Did you call for me or need a transfer somewhere?"

Aiden could have lied or smooth-talked his way to an excuse that got him some answers without outright asking, but the clenching of his gut that had been tightening since Mrs. Cole gave him Leighton's number wasn't easing. He decided to be blunt, despite the possibility of creating gossip.

"I actually was wondering if Leighton is in the office today?" he decided to go with. "I'd call his extension directly, but I never got the new number."

Silence.

Brief but heavy.

That's when Aiden knew that something really had happened. That Leighton hadn't called just to call.

"Um, I'm not sure," Jenna finally said. "I mean, I don't have that information right now. Could I call you back when I do?"

Aiden sat up a bit straighter.

"You don't know if he's in office today or you don't know his extension?"

She let out a bite of laughter. Nothing about it was genuine.

"Both?" she answered. "It's been a bit chaotic here the last few weeks, and there's been a lot of moving pieces. Let me call you back when I know more. Is this number good?"

On reflex he said it was. Jenna wrapped up the call soon after. She didn't even say bye.

Aiden stared at his phone once it disconnected.

He was still looking at it a few minutes later when Mrs. Cole came in.

"I was finalizing this month's schedule through email when a new one came in just now," she said. "I don't know the sender, but it might be spam."

Aiden took a deep breath and decided to push his worry away. Leighton was an adult. He'd call when he could.

"All right. I'll take a look at it." He took his computer out of sleep mode and pulled up his email inbox. True enough, the latest email was unread.

Mrs. Cole started to leave but paused in the doorway.

"By the way, you're not going to wear that tonight for the party, are you?" She eyed his jacket again with disapproval. For a moment, Aiden had no idea what she was talking about. Then he remembered with a sigh.

"I wouldn't call a grand opening for a coffee shop—at night, mind you—a party."

Mrs. Cole rolled her eyes.

"I don't care what you consider it. All the downtown business owners are going to be there—we're going, too." She pointed at him with purpose. "So make sure you go home early and get some clothes that have buttons and zippers, not drawstrings. Understood?"

Some employers might have taken the command as offensive, but Aiden knew that Mrs. Cole cared about him. That was enough to make him agree.

"Yes, ma'am," he conceded. "Buttons, not strings."

Mrs. Cole gave him a quick nod of approval and shut the door behind her. Aiden's smile fell away in the time between. Then he was staring at the opened email on his computer screen.

The sender's email address was omitted.

The subject line was only one exclamation mark.

There was no signature line or any mention of the sender's name.

But, despite having no proof, Aiden couldn't help but believe that the text in the body of the email had been written by Leighton Hughes.

If I die, Bellwether Tech killed me.

Chapter Three

Mack was never one to indulge in napping, but after he returned to the Atwood homestead and unpacked, his entire body decided to drag him down against his will. He went from alert and thoughtful to belly up in his childhood bedroom, the air conditioner blowing white noise and cold around him while the rest of the house didn't make a peep. Maybe it was that silence that really did the trick. When he opened his eyes again, the sunlight through the curtain had changed positions.

The house had also collected a few new sounds.

Mack stared at the ceiling as he heard the footsteps echoing from the other side of the house.

Someone was in the kitchen. Making coffee? Making lunch?

He didn't bother looking at his phone to see how long he'd been asleep. When he was working a contract, he budgeted every minute of his time. When he was at home in between? He didn't mind getting lost in the seconds.

The noise in the kitchen continued, though, and Mack knew it didn't matter if he wanted to stay right where he was for the rest of the day and night. He might not be on a contract, but he'd have someone to answer to soon.

He sighed into the old room and got up slowly. The bandage beneath his shirt caught and pulled a little, but he ignored the annoyance. Like the over-the-top greeting he was sure to get in the near future, there wasn't anything he could do to make the ache he'd gotten in the past disappear. He'd done everything right and still gotten a knife for his trouble. There was no point complaining about it now.

Mack left the bedroom with another heavy sigh.

Sometimes he couldn't believe the same halls he'd walked as a kid, he was walking as an adult. After all these years, after everything that happened outside its walls, here he was rattling around the same two-story house he'd learned to walk in. Life sure was interesting sometimes.

The same familiar path from his bedroom at the back end of the first floor to the kitchen spanned almost the length of the house. With his long legs, Mack's stride had him at the kitchen sink and staring at Finn within a few blinks.

Running into his little brother first was the most ideal situation he could have hoped for after coming home.

Finn, twenty-six but still as bright-eyed and smiling as he'd been as a little kid, greeted Mack with an outstretched hand holding a mug.

"I figured you'd rise and shine the second I made my afternoon coffee," Finn said. "Sorry if I woke you up, though. You must be tired after your early flight."

Mack took the mug and shrugged off the apology.

"You know I've never been one to sleep that long," he said. "I'm surprised I got the shut-eye I did. What time is it, exactly?"

Finn went to grab another mug from the cabinet. He was grinning.

"Must have been a good nap if you have no idea how long you were asleep. It's almost one."

Mack nodded. Not bad for a nap.

He took a seat at the eat-in kitchen table and stretched his legs out long.

Finn wasn't as tall as him, but he'd always made up any physical gaps between them with a cleverness and quickness that had often surprised, and annoyed, Mack growing up. Whereas he had the muscles and power, Finn had the talking down pat. He was the charmer of the family, the one who could outtalk anyone if given the opportunity. It made him a dangerous salesperson, which was why he'd become the only in-house medical sales representative at the hospital two years prior.

Finick Atwood was the second most popular Atwood still living in Willow Creek.

The first?

Well, Mack hoped to avoid her a little longer.

Something that Finn must have picked up on.

"I'd say you have a few minutes to drink that coffee before hell on wheels comes in," Finn said, a light laugh ending his words.

Mack snorted.

"Is that your twin radar warning you?" he asked.

Finn made a so-so gesture with his hand.

"That and the fact she called a few minutes ago."

His little brother gave him a quick look, but it said enough for Mack. Word about the John Doe at the park had already gotten out. Word about him being there, too, if he had to guess.

Mack took a long pull of his coffee. When he was done, he decided one more long sigh would do. Finn leaned against the counter by the window. He was keeping watch, but he wasn't going to ask anything until the third of their trio made it in. Instead, Finn did what he did best.

He found something else to talk about.

"A new coffee shop opened up downtown since the last time you were here," he started. "They're having a grand opening party tonight, and we've all been invited."

Mack knew where this was going.

"I'm going to go ahead and decline that invite," he said, sure to show his conviction. "I'd rather stay here and drink this stuff." He shook his mug. Finn snorted.

"You can talk big and bad all you want, but there's no point in fooling ourselves." He glanced out the window. A smile, more mischievous than it should have been, pulled up the corners of his lips. "We both know Mother Hen isn't going to let you skip a big social event while you're in town. And, if you don't believe me, then let's wait about thirty seconds."

Mack heard the gravel crunching and, like he knew where the conversation would lead with his brother, he knew that their mother hen had finally returned to the hen house.

"All right," Mack said, standing tall. "Let's get this over with."

The Atwood homestead stretched wide and dipped here and there for a good few acres of land. There were trees around every corner, a creek that ran around one edge of the property and a freestanding but vacated barn on the back half, a building none of them could consider getting rid of since their great-granddaddy had built it. Between the Atwood siblings, each had their own little favorite spot of the land for their own reasons. Mack's just happened to be the easiest to see.

Across the drive that led from the main road up to the house was a field. There was nothing special about it, and it held no function. It was simply an expanse of grass with no trees or flowers or fences. An open space with nothing to offer the world except the promise that, if you stood in its middle, there wasn't a thing that would touch you.

And that's why Mack liked it so much.

Just looking across the drive, not looking too far off at the trees, you'd find a bunch of empty.

There was a beauty in that, and it was a beauty that he often thought about when he was away from home.

Even now, over the wild blond hair of the woman hurrying out of her beat-up Bronco in between Mack and the field, he felt his chest loosen. His breathing calmed. His shoulders relaxed.

The empty comforted him.

Which was a good thing considering his sister was about to fill him up with her own worries.

"I told you to go straight home when you flew in and instead you go to a dang *murder* scene?"

Marigold Atwood was the youngest Atwood by mere minutes, but out of the three of them, she reigned queen. Since even before their father passed and their mother left, Goldie had been the one behind the scenes trying to make the best of their lives. From school to career to friendships and romance, she had her hands in all the Atwood pies. It had driven her twin, Finn, up the wall when they were teens, but now, in their late twenties, he'd accepted the fact that their sister had taken over the role of matriarch. It was easier to listen to what she had to say rather than avoid it. Mack being older than her had no bearing on that fact.

He tucked his chin a little and smiled a little more.

"Hey there, Goldie," he said. "I missed you, too."

Goldie wasn't as enthused. All five-nine of her stopped at the bottom step of the front porch and glared up at him.

"Give me one reason why I shouldn't smack some kind

of sense into you, Malcolm Gene Atwood," she said, ignoring his greeting.

Finn moved to Mack's side and sucked on his teeth.

"Oh, man, she three-named you," he whispered. "Rest in pieces there, brother."

Mack dropped his smile and held up his hands in defense.

"It was a quick detour and didn't require any heavy lifting," he explained. "All I did was go and look at something and then got my tail here and in bed for some rest. No harm, no foul."

Finn nodded.

"That's the truth right there," he confirmed. "I'm witness to the fact that he just got up from a nap."

Mama Goldie wasn't in the mood for their tag teaming. Her hands went to her hips and that glare became near slits.

"From what I heard you didn't just go and look at nothing. You went and looked at a dead body. Heavy lifting or not, your mind needs just as much rest as your body after a long contract." Goldie glanced down at his chest. "Especially after a job you bled for."

Her glare softened.

Any annoyance Mack had for his sister fizzled out, too.

Ray had said it once before.

"I've never met someone so loud at loving."

That was Goldie, all right. She didn't filter her worries or anger or happiness when it came to her loved ones. She said what was on her mind, and she said it with absolute devotion.

That's why Mack held back the urge to defend himself, his injury and his choice to go see Ray and John Doe.

Goldie was just caring loudly at him. It would be rude to try and make her feel bad about that.

Mack lowered his head until his chin was almost touching his chest. He kept eye contact but hoped he looked apologetic enough.

"I'm sorry," he said. "I should have been more thoughtful to myself. I also should have called. Sorry, sis."

A silence squeezed its way between his apology and her frustration. Finn was the first person to take advantage of it with his powers of persuasion.

"Make him show how sorry he is by getting him to come with us tonight to the grand-opening hoopla," he said. "He already thinks he isn't going to go."

Mack went from apologetic to trying to play wounded real quick.

"She just said I need to mind my health by resting. I don't think partying is what the doctor would order."

Both brothers turned back to Goldie. Mack should have known he was going to lose by the way Finn was already smiling. He for sure knew he was done when Goldie mimicked her twin's expression.

"I've never met a man who would take a knife to his body without blinking but will come up with excuses to avoid being social." She reached up and patted his shoulder. "If you can stand and brood at a crime scene, you can stand and brood in a coffee shop."

Mack opened his mouth to argue, but Goldie was already walking past him. The words she threw over her shoulder sealed his fate.

"And you're going to wear a suit while doing it, too."

Finn laughed, Mack sighed and Goldie could be heard chuckling as she went inside the house.

He didn't miss much about Willow Creek, not since the fire. Not since everyone forgot about his father. Mack, though, felt like he was slipping as close into comfort as he could when he was with the twins.

It was a feeling that stayed for a while as he kept his spot on the front porch. He stared out at the empty field and let his thoughts crowd it a little. Finn wasn't surprised at the fact that he'd been at a homicide that morning. Goldie hadn't asked a single question about it or John Doe. She also hadn't asked to see his wound, just as Finn hadn't, either.

"They're giving me space," Mack whispered to himself. He kept staring at the field. He knew it was the last empty he'd be getting for a while, especially if he was being forced to attend a party downtown. Mack had never been Mr. Popular in school, but his job certainly earned him a lot of questions whenever he was out and about in town. Goldie and Finn's natural charisma wasn't going to help matters, either. He could already picture both being pulled away to chat about something while he was left standing in the corner with his drink, watching the clock.

Mack gave the field another long look and slipped past his family to go back to his room. He scooped up his cell phone and clicked on Ray's number.

The call rang several times before his friend answered.

"Hello?"

Mack bypassed a normal greeting. He went straight for the bottom line.

"You owe me, so pay me back by standing with me at a party tonight. I can't take no for an answer, so don't try and come up with an excuse."

What was better than being forced to withstand a social event you didn't want to go to? Forcing someone to attend it with you.

However, to his surprise, Ray didn't come back with the sarcastic retort Mack would have expected.

"Let me call you back," he said instead. "I have someone here."

Mack tilted his head to the side. He couldn't help but be curious.

"Does that mean someone identified John Doe?"

Ray didn't answer for a moment. When he did his voice had lowered.

"It's gotten complicated," he said. "Let me call you later."

The line went dead before Mack could respond.

Complicated.

Mack's hands balled into fists. The memory of smoke filling his nostrils and pain filling his heart burned through him. The last time Mack had heard that word in Willow Creek his entire life had changed.

He refused to give Willow Creek that power again.

Chapter Four

Aiden walked into the party, and all he saw were lines of code. Thirty or so, with tags that read dressed-up in nice suits and dresses, shiny shoes and carefully styled hair, and each with one fundamental task to execute.

Mingle.

"I know you've had a day and a half, but try to enjoy yourself," Mrs. Cole said at his side. She brought him a drink from the coffee bar that was currently housing an assortment of bottles, cans, cups and finger foods. He could smell a little alcohol in it. This was the first time Mrs. Cole had offered such a drink to him. Aiden thought he might should mark the day. There was no need, though. Mrs. Cole had been hovering since they'd gone to the hospital together a few hours earlier.

Gossip had broken the sound barrier in Willow Creek and brought the terrifying news that a man had been found murdered in the park. After that, he'd gone to the morgue with Mrs. Cole knowing in his heart of hearts that Leighton Hughes had in fact met his end.

Yet, the medical examiner hadn't even let Aiden through the door.

"You said your friend has dark hair, dark skin and a

scar along his forearm. Our John Doe doesn't have any of the three."

The fist of relief that had punched into Aiden's chest had been one heck of a wallop.

That feeling didn't wholly stay.

Partially thanks to a man Aiden had instantly disliked walking up into their conversation with a particularly judgmental air about him.

"Word gets out about a homicide and you're the first to bust tail to get here to see if your buddy is the one we're trying to identify," he'd said. "Not many people's gut tells them to go check the morgue when someone is missing less than a day."

The man had shown his badge then.

Detective Winters, the sheriff department's ace.

A self-imposed description that had gotten an almost eye roll out of the medical examiner still standing at their sides. Aiden had watched the two stare at one another with what he could only interpret as genuine dislike until the detective had suggested they go to the department to talk. Mrs. Cole was the only reason he readily agreed. That and, well, he couldn't get it out of his head that even though John Doe wasn't Leighton, his friend was still in trouble.

A feeling that had pricked up an even older, familiar feeling he'd promised himself he'd never indulge again.

Mrs. Cole, who still didn't know the extent of how different he'd been before coming to Willow Creek, did a good job of helping him avoid falling back into that pit. Even without realizing it.

"You need to get out and socialize," she'd said. "If eating good food with good people isn't enough of a reason to get your mind clear for a while, then look at it as an opportunity to soak in the gossip. Who knows, you might find something interesting floating among the loose-lipped."

And that's what had gotten Aiden to the main room of Sue and Mae's Café.

He was looking at something he fully understood.

Lines of code, entry points for potential information.

Scripts being written, waiting for him to get the digital download.

If there was a link between Leighton and John Doe, maybe he'd find it here.

It was a long shot, but he'd take it.

He accepted the drink from Mrs. Cole and lowered his voice.

"Who has the loosest but most reliable lips here?"

On any other day, Mrs. Cole might have ignored the question, but she'd been overly warm to him since John Doe had entered their picture. It was touching. It was also useful. She scanned the guests in the main dining room and then nodded toward the wall opposite them.

"Patty Truit, the woman with the hair sprayed high over there, usually knows what people are doing in this town before those people even know they're doing it," she said.

Patty looked familiar. Mrs. Cole picked up on the realization.

"She brought in a fruit basket the first week after you opened. You don't come into town without an official in-person meet and greet from Patty."

"Then she's the one I need to talk to," Aiden decided.

"If you're looking for stray news, then she's definitely the one to hover around," she agreed. Aiden nodded and was about to set out to see exactly how useful that line of code was, but Mrs. Cole caught him by the elbow.

"But, first, we're going to be polite and say hello to our

hosts. Nice smile, Mr. Riggs. Make those buttons you're wearing shine."

Sue and Mae's Café was cute and surprisingly spacious. Housed in a stand-alone building across the street from Riggs Consulting, its perfectly square shape allowed for a large dining room with a long coffee bar and display case, walls covered in rustic decorations and enough floor space to fit the thirty or so guests comfortably.

Aiden followed Mrs. Cole into the thick of well-dressed people and right to the owners and said their greetings. Mae, the mother of the mother-daughter duo, was nice. Aiden had met her in passing before, and together they said all the polite, proper things. Sue, he guessed in her early twenties, wasn't as reserved. When Mrs. Cole and Mae were swept into another conversation deeper in the heart of the dining room, Sue's eyes became alight with enthusiasm.

"You used to live in Nashville, right?"

Aiden couldn't help but reflect the smile.

"I did," he confirmed. "For almost ten years."

Sue did a little dance with her feet.

"I love Nashville, like, truly love it," she said. "I went for a competition there a few years ago and had an absolute blast. We stayed at this hotel-resort thing that had like a city inside it. It was so cool and pretty."

"Ah." Aiden knew what she was talking about. He laughed. "That would be the Opryland Resort. It's very popular. I've gone there before, but it was for a conference. I've never had a chance to stay in one of their rooms, though."

That only made Sue all the more bouncy.

"Oh, it was a blast! Me and a few other competitors got lost *inside* on the first night. I've never almost gotten lost in a hotel before."

Aiden raised an eyebrow at the "competitors" part.

"What kind of competition was it? I know they hold all kinds."

Aiden had never met Sue before, but at that he could tell she realized she'd said too much. Her cheeks tinted red, and her smile wavered. She still answered, but there was a nervous trill of laughter attached to it.

"It was a computer thing. Not a big deal."

"Computer things are my bread and butter!" He waved her modesty off. "And usually competitions involving computers are no joke. Was it a coding thing? Software or hardware?"

She seemed worried that he might not like her answer.

Aiden decided then to change topics. However, a newcomer slid into their conversation with his own answers.

"Don't let Sue here sell herself short," he started. "You're looking at Willow Creek's very own video game queen right here. She placed in the top ten of the country, bringing honor and bragging rights to us all."

He was a good-looking man in a suit, closer to Sue's age and smiling as brightly as she had been a minute before. Aiden watched as the two seemed to be trying to have a conversation between their gazes and Sue's cheeks went to a shade almost as red as a stop sign.

Aiden didn't understand the embarrassment.

"What?" he said. "That's amazing. Video game competitions are fierce, not to mention the skill and focus it takes to actually place in them. If I were you, I'd wear that around on my shirt every day."

"Right?" the man exclaimed at his side. "See, Sue! I told you. You should be proud."

Sue didn't seem convinced. She smiled into a sigh then forced a laugh.

"It's in the past now." She motioned to the room around them. "This is my new focus with Mom."

The man shook his head. He gave Aiden a look that said they'd had a conversation like this before.

"I told her she should do both. Maybe even carve out a gaming, internet café-type corner in here." This time he sighed, but there was no real weight to it. "But who am I to force Sue Walding to do anything? Greatness should be able to make its own decisions, after all."

Aiden watched the man's words pull Sue's earlier smile back out to bloom again. He wondered what kind of relationship the two had.

"Speaking of greatness." Sue stretched out her hand and moved it between the two of them. "I don't know if you've met yet, Aiden, but, this is one of Willow Creek's favorite people, Finn Atwood. Finn, this is Aiden Riggs."

Finn shook Aiden's hand with vigor and laughed at the introduction.

"We all know there's only one true favorite Atwood here in town, but it's good to know Sue Walding thinks so highly of me." Finn looked to Aiden. "So you're Riggs of Riggs Consulting, right?"

Aiden nodded.

"That's me."

"I bet you're getting some good business here," Finn said. "I'm not putting down our town but I know a lot of our residents aren't that tech or internet savvy. My brother alone could keep you in business year-round."

Aiden opened his mouth to respond, but Sue popped up again like a flower angling for the sun.

"Speaking of your brother, I heard he came back to town this morning." She lowered her voice. "And got caught up in the trouble at the park."

Aiden's ears perked at that.

While he didn't know who John Doe was, Aiden did know he'd been found at the park. Was Finn's brother law enforcement?

His smile became tight, but he didn't seem offended by the question. Instead he lowered his voice to match Sue's volume.

"He was asked for a favor, but he didn't stay long."

Sue did something weird. She motioned to her face but didn't say anything.

Yet Finn nodded like she'd asked a question.

"He's here tonight, so if you want to know more you should talk to him. But, well, you know him. He'll find a way to escape soon, so I suggest you do it sooner rather than later." Finn turned to survey the room. He stopped and nodded toward a group by the front door. "There he is, already making eyes at the back door."

Aiden followed his line of sight out of curiosity.

He knew of the Atwoods only in passing. They lived on the largest piece of residential land in the county but weren't exactly rich. When people spoke of them, it had been pleasant enough. If any gossip had circulated about them, Aiden had missed it. He hadn't even known who made up the family behind the name, let alone that the Atwoods were popular enough to earn the title of town favorites.

But, when Aiden's eyes stopped on the spot where Finn was looking, he understood the Atwood allure.

Standing just inside the front doorway was a man who might as well have been a neon light in a dark, empty room. He was tall, a tree that reached for the sky with shoulders broad enough to hold it. His hair was neat and dark and made his tan seem more golden than not. His facial features were sharp, there was no stubble or five o'clock anything to detract from the near crispness, and from across the room Aiden could see that even his eyes had an awe to them. They matched his brother's blue. However, unlike Finn's brand of nice looks, his brother wrapped in a suit felt different.

You noticed him, though. The way he stood gave Aiden the impression that he might not be a man who wanted to be noticed.

It was a powerful look.

One that intrigued Aiden to no end, especially when that brother caught their collective gaze on him.

Finn said, "Busted."

Sue laughed a little.

Aiden didn't move a muscle.

The man's attention went wholly to him.

If Aiden's phone hadn't vibrated deep in his pocket, he might have just stood there and kept staring. Gotten a little lost. Instead he broke eye contact and pulled his phone out.

It was an unknown caller.

Maybe it was Leighton?

"Excuse me, I need to take this."

Aiden's mind left the man at the door altogether.

He didn't have time to wonder why the man was still staring at him as he walked by.

ALL MACK SAW when he walked into the party were faces. Ones that were, and had been, in his memory database for years. Locals, schoolmates, friends of the twins. The people who'd made up Willow Creek since he was a kid. Sure, he knew he hadn't seen some of them in a long while, but regardless, their faces would be in his memory, ready for him.

But then something happened.

Mack saw a face he didn't recognize.

The man wasn't nearly as tall as him, but somehow he

managed to stand out among the guests. Maybe it was because his appearance itself wasn't what Mack was used
to in Willow Creek. He was wearing all black, yet it was
like he'd been highlighted among the sea of outfits around
him. His hair was light and slicked back, showing a pierc-
ing at the top of one ear, and there was a relaxed sway to
his stance despite the fact that he wasn't moving. Compared
to the many faces that Mack had floating in his memory,
this man had no odd or special attributes to him. No mass
of freckles, no scars, no moles or birthmarks. Angled and
sharp features, sure, but nothing that should have set him
apart from others.

Yet Mack couldn't look away from the green eyes that
had locked with his.

Not even as the man walked out of the party.

Then, to confuse himself even further, Mack joined his
brother with a question instead of a greeting.

"Who was that?"

Finn smirked.

"Ah, I'm guessing it's weird for you to see someone for
the first time." He pointed to the front display windows.
"You know the consulting business I told you about across
the street? The one that deals with IT-y things? He's the
owner."

"Aiden Riggs," Sue supplied politely.

Mack nodded to her, since he'd glossed over a hello.
Among Finn's friends, he liked Sue the most. She'd never
peppered him with questions.

"He's been here about six months," she added.

Finn clapped Mack on the shoulder.

"And, like you, he seems to be a bit antisocial," he said.
"This is the first time I've seen him."

Mack glanced out the display windows. He couldn't see the man anymore.

Not that it should matter.

His interest was just the novelty of seeing someone new, he decided.

And that's the thought he kept with him as the minutes went by and Aiden Riggs didn't return. Mack continued to dismiss his attention on the man's absence as those minutes rolled into a half hour. Fifteen minutes after that, Mack decided he just needed to get his curiosity out.

So he googled the man's name.

Aiden Riggs had several search results.

His business was the first, his social media was the second and the third was a pinned review from a happy client.

The fourth, however, pulled Mack in.

It was an article with a picture preview. A tech company had won a bid, and among those who worked there was a group celebrating while wearing party hats and smiling wide at the camera.

Mack's eye was drawn to Aiden first.

Then his gaze swept over to someone else in the picture. Someone he recognized.

Mack froze in place.

Standing behind Aiden in the picture was a man with freckles all over his face.

A man Mack had seen that morning.

John Doe.

Chapter Five

The party across the street must have been wrapping up. When Aiden locked Riggs Consulting's front door, the night was oddly quiet. It probably didn't help that he'd spent over an hour in his office getting lost in his own little world. Not even Mrs. Cole's call of disapproval had brought him back to the festivities.

Aiden had had tunnel vision, and exiting said tunnel had become surprisingly difficult.

The unknown number that had called him at the party had stayed unknown.

No one had been on the other end of the line when he'd answered the phone, just some static and an eventual dial tone when the call ended. It had driven Aiden up the wall, especially after he'd called back and gotten a standard voice mail recording.

He'd stared at his phone for a bit after that, wondering if his anxiety was mounting for nothing. Maybe he was bored and Leighton, John Doe and the email about Bellwether Tech were just excuses for him to feel some kind of excitement. Maybe he was lonely. His only companions in Willow Creek were Mrs. Cole and her husband. Even then, it wasn't like he spent many after-work hours with them.

Maybe he was borrowing trouble just to feel *more*.

Aiden had shaken that idea off as soon as it had slid in. Still, though, he remained behind his desk. After that his attention had wandered back to the email about Bellwether Tech.

If I die, Bellwether Tech killed me.

Aiden didn't understand why the message hadn't had a name attached. If you wanted to report on your potential murder, then wouldn't you want to say who you were?

It made no sense.

None of it made sense.

That's when Aiden had finally had enough.

Just because there wasn't a name in the email signature didn't mean he couldn't find out who had sent it. Or, rather, where it was sent from.

"If you start peeking behind the curtain, you might not stop," Aiden had told himself before fully committing to his new idea. "This whole thing probably isn't a big deal. You're just nosy."

He'd stared at his computer for a while longer.

The last time he'd used a computer to snoop, he'd inadvertently changed the course of his future. All it had taken were a few keystrokes and clicks.

Did he want to do that again just to figure out where the email came from?

Was it that big of a deal?

What if the email was a joke? A bad one but a joke all the same?

Was it worth toeing the line between what he should do in his professional life and what he shouldn't do in his personal life?

Aiden had wasted most of his time in the office debating this question.

Then he'd caved.

While he was skilled in the IT field and did well enough on the hardware side of it, Aiden absolutely thrived at one specific thing.

He was an excellent hacker.

His fingers had flown across the keyboard like a warm knife slicing through butter. The mouse had felt like it was an extension of his hand, his fingers moving to a rhythm that didn't skip a beat. He found the anonymous email sender's location in under two minutes. During that time he'd even double-checked the name.

The urge to go further had nearly done him in.

Instead he'd pushed himself out of Riggs Consulting and now was deep within the night air.

"The email was sent from Willow Creek," he told the door, talking to himself to process the information. When he put the office key in his pocket, he exchanged it for the sticky note he'd written the sender's address on. "It has to be from Leighton, right?"

Why else would Bellwether find its way to him *from* a local address?

There was only one way to find out.

Aiden nodded to himself and thrust his hand and the note back into his blazer's pocket. He followed the sidewalk around the building to the parking lot that stretched behind Riggs Consulting. It only had two narrow rows of spaces and one lone streetlamp positioned between the asphalt and the wooded area enclosing the lot. Some parking spots were in rough condition and no one dared park in them. Others were for employees of neighboring buildings. After work hours, it wasn't unusual for Aiden's silver hatchback to be sitting solo in the lot.

That's why he had no thought to check that he was, in fact, alone.

He got into the front seat of his car and shut the door behind him. His laptop bag went on the passenger's seat; his phone went into one of the cupholders. As he'd done countless times before, he slid the key into the ignition with one hand and put his seat belt on with the other.

It was by pure chance that he saw the reflection of the man in the back seat in the rearview mirror.

Aiden didn't even have time to yell before an arm snaked around his headrest. The move pinned his neck against the seat with a viselike grip that was as strong as it was terrifying. His breath went out; his adrenaline soared. His hands went up next, trying to pry himself free.

It didn't work.

Aiden's fingers wrapped under the man's arm, but the grip remained tight. He tried to beat the arm next but none of his movements seemed to have an effect on his attacker.

That's when he tried to outthink his panic.

Wasn't there an easy way to get out of a hold like this?

He'd seen a viral instructional video about it before, but what was he supposed to do now?

Aiden swiped back behind him, hoping to land a hit. Instead he touched fabric, and even that he couldn't get a hold on. It was like the man had managed to find the one position that had utterly and completely made him defenseless.

So Aiden decided to make some noise.

He laid on the steering wheel, and the horn started to blare.

The grip around his neck tightened. Aiden swiped back again with one hand and tried to pry him off with the other.

His head was starting to pound; his lungs were burning. His vision was starting to be affected. Something was moving out of the corner of his eye with startling speed. He wondered if he was about to lose consciousness.

Then he thought he had.

Night air rushed into the car.

But not next to him.

A loud grunt sounded as the grip around Aiden's neck loosened.

A second later it disappeared altogether.

Aiden leaned forward, coughing and sputtering and trying to get the oxygen he'd been deprived of. He only managed to see what was happening because the action had changed locations.

Instead of the man choking him from behind, he was no longer in the car at all.

He was standing next to it, the back door wide-open.

And he wasn't alone.

THE MAN WAS BIG, but Mack was bigger.

When he grabbed him and yanked him out of the car, the man came out in one fluid movement. That might have been partially due to the surprise of Mack's sudden intervention, though. Mack followed the arc of his momentum and slung the guy farther away from the car. There wasn't even a peep out of him. Never mind a fight-or-flight response to the new danger.

That wouldn't last long.

Mack watched as the man caught himself before hitting the ground. He stumbled but he recovered quickly.

He was athletic, Mack figured.

He was also covered head to toe.

A dark blue hoodie was pulled tight over his head, covering his hair. He had on dark jeans and black tennis shoes, while his hands were wrapped in gloves and, from his nose down, his face was covered in a black gaiter. Mack could only see a sliver of a pale face and dark brown eyes.

Eyes that seemed to size him up with speed.

And make a decision even quicker.

Mack shifted his right foot back a little and tightened his stance just as the man lunged toward him. Instead of throwing a punch, the man swiped at Mack's blazer.

He was a grabber, Mack's least favorite type of fighter. A clinger whose whole strategy was to push or pull their opponent off balance to try and get the advantage.

Mack had met many a grabber before. He'd lost to one on his first-ever private security job. He'd been slung to the ground and then kicked over and over again before getting back the upper hand. Since then he had never lost to a grabber.

So he wasn't going to start now.

Mack caught the man's outstretched wrist with his left hand and then threw a punch straight to his nose with his right. Since he had the man in his grasp, he couldn't escape the hit.

The man recoiled with a yell. Mack had either busted his nose or broken it. If it wasn't for the mask, he was sure he'd see blood.

"Stop fighting," Mack warned his opponent. He'd lost his grip after the punch, but the man was holding his face and hunched over no more than a few steps away now. Mack could have kept volleying, but there was no point in forcing the man down when he was already going there himself. Just in case he wasn't aware of his odds, Mack spelled it out for him. "You can either talk with me or have me come at you again. Your choice."

Mack heard the car door open behind him. Shoes crunched the asphalt as Aiden must have stepped out.

Which meant he was okay.

A feeling of relief washed over Mack.

He pushed it away to focus on the hooded figure.

His eyes cut over Mack's shoulder. They narrowed.

Then the man turned tail and ran.

Mack wasn't going to let that one go.

"Call the cops," he yelled over his shoulder. Then he was boots to the asphalt.

The man might not have been an ace fighter, but when it came to running he was a rabbit after a carrot. He streaked across the parking lot before cutting left into the wooded area at its back. Mack knew Willow Creek inside and out. Just like he knew they would be forced to slow down to navigate the dense trees, he knew that on the other side of them was the back of Dillard's Grocery Store, followed by Second Street. If the sheriff's department dispatched from their headquarters over near the county line, then they would drive in on the other side of downtown. Which meant if Mack didn't catch the man soon, he stood a good chance of using Second Street to get away before backup came.

That possibility didn't sit right with him.

Mack leaned into his run and split between the trees. This patch of trees in Willow Creek was one of several wooded areas downtown. It didn't stretch as wide as some of the others, but it was enough to slow both Mack and the man down. A branch he couldn't see clipped Mack's shoulder a yard or so in. Then he heard the man ahead of him yell out as he must have also hit something. It didn't help that visibility was almost nonexistent. The possibility that he might actually lose him started to rise until a light in the distance became a beacon. The man was heading toward it, too. Mack watched his outline hustle in the direction before disappearing.

Mack burst out of the trees and skidded across the back alley of the grocery store. His legs were burning and his side had some sting to it, but his focus was narrowing back. He tilted his head to the side and listened.

Footsteps echoed to his right.

He took off again.

Sirens sounded in the distance. Maybe there was a cruiser that was closer than he thought.

Mack ran the length of the grocery store's building and rounded the corner.

He skidded to a halt.

The knife sliced through the night air and narrowly missed his arm.

He windmilled backward. It made him lose his footing in the process. Pain lit up his side as Mack connected with the paved path.

The man didn't waste the opening.

He followed Mack to the ground, arcing the knife downward.

There was no space or time to fully dodge or fully attack, so Mack did a little of both. He threw his arm up to cover the space above his head and kicked out. The man let out a yell as Mack's foot connected with his ankle.

But he didn't fall.

Instead he brought his knife back in an arc, this time with more power behind it.

Mack was going to have to take it. There was nothing else he could do. He just hoped to take it in the hand or arm, not the side or face. If the damage wasn't too severe, he could deal with the pain after he got the weapon away.

It was his only option.

The man was surprisingly fast.

Mack saw the blade of the knife coming down. He braced himself.

Then watched in confusion as the man went from standing to on the ground next to him, limp. The knife clattered to the pavement. Mack blinked several times.

That's when he realized a third person had entered their fight.

Standing behind where the man had been was none other than Aiden Riggs.

He had a wooden baseball bat in his hands.

He went from looking at the now-unconscious man to Mack. His eyes were wide, but his voice was steady. His first words to Mack were as out of pocket as his sudden appearance and save.

"Is it bad I want to call my Little League coach right now?"

Mack stared.

"What?"

Aiden shook the bat.

"He told me I couldn't hit the broad side of a barn even if I was standing next to it. Looks like my aim got way better, huh?"

Mack heard the nerves in Aiden's voice, the adrenaline no doubt still surging, and knew it was no small thing to hurt a person even in the defense of others.

Yet, in that moment, he did something that surprised him.

He laughed.

Chapter Six

The La Forge County Sheriff's Department was an uneven building resting across a raised hill and a flat piece of land. No one quite understood why they hadn't built the structure solely on the latter, since they'd had to accommodate for the weirdness by splitting their building in two. On the right, hill side of the building were the lobby and offices. On the left, flat side sat the cells and interrogation rooms meant for the detained.

Aiden was in a meeting room on the right side, glad he wasn't having to visit the other. He wasn't one to shy away from the ill-intentioned but he didn't think being in close proximity to the man he had beaten down with his Little League baseball bat was the best idea. A sentiment his Atwood friend had seemed to share. Once some deputies had found them behind the grocery store and asked them to come to the department and provide statements, he'd been loud in requesting they wait somewhere near the lobby but out of sight. So that's where they were, tucked away in a meeting room near the lobby, just the two of them.

And that's where Aiden had been trying his best not to let his mouth run off while staring at his temporary partner in crime.

Mack. Atwood.

Tall, dark, handsome and apparently not very talkative.

It had been making Aiden restless since they had settled into their chairs. One of them was fine with the silence. The other? Not so much.

Finally, as that other, Aiden broke.

"I know I already said it, but thank you again for helping me out." He rolled his chair up to the table a little more, hoping if he got closer to the man, he would be more inclined to be chatty.

Mack, however, wasn't fazed by the move. Sitting opposite Aiden like he was going to lead some kind of interview, he kept looking at his phone.

Aiden cleared his throat.

"I used to think people who check the back seats of their cars were being paranoid," he continued. "But now I don't think I'll ever not do that when getting into one. I still can't believe he was there. I also can't believe you showed up."

That part got a reaction, though not Mack's gaze.

"I was leaving Sue and Mae's party and heard you blowing the horn," he said matter-of-factly. "After that I just tried to help like anyone else would have."

Aiden was slightly suspicious now, as he had been earlier when he had tried to run the math in his head. It felt like Mack had shown up way too fast after Aiden had hit the horn, especially if he had been leaving the café across the street. Maybe that was another Mack Atwood power, super speed.

Then again, Aiden hadn't exactly been in the right mind to keep an accurate time count going.

His throat still hurt now as he spoke.

He pretended it didn't.

"Either way, I'm lucky you did," he said. "I guess I'm also lucky that I bring that bat everywhere with me. I've never had to handle someone wielding a knife like they were in some kind of action movie before."

Mack's eyes went up at that.

This was the closest Aiden had been to the man where he could see him in clear lighting. His eyes weren't just blue. They were the sea.

"You shouldn't have had to test your luck at all. I don't know what you were doing before you came to Willow Creek, but it's not a smart move to run after someone who nearly killed you."

Mack's words had a bite to them. Aiden didn't appreciate them or it.

"You saved me, and then I tried to save you," he returned. "I don't know how that's a bad thing. Especially since you were the only one without a weapon. If anything, *you* shouldn't have run after him."

The big guy wasn't a fan of that response.

He dropped his phone and crossed his arms over his chest.

"I was handling myself just fine, thanks."

Aiden mirrored his posture.

"The way I saw it, you were about to take a knife to the arm had I not stepped in."

The man snorted.

"Just because it looked that way doesn't mean I didn't have it handled," Mack grumbled. "I encounter things like this all the time in my profession."

"Almost getting stabbed?" Aiden leaned forward. "Or thumbing your nose at people who obviously helped you?"

Mack looked like he was ready to say something even more biting but stopped himself as the door to the room opened. Aiden's mood had already fallen, yet it managed to drop a few more notches as he recognized the new addition.

Detective Winters was dressed down in a collared shirt and jeans. He still had his badge on display, hanging around his neck. He adjusted it as he addressed Mack first.

"Well, if it isn't the prodigal son returned to town."

The tone was friendly, but the smirk that followed didn't match.

Aiden looked between the two men. The annoyance that had been there a few seconds ago had hardened into something a lot more meaningful. Aiden might not have known the Atwood man, but with one glance at how he was staring at the detective, there was no doubt that Mack didn't like him.

Not at all.

His jaw was clenched, his shoulders were tight and his voice had dropped into a smooth detachment.

"I'm not here long," was all he said.

The detective seemed bemused by the answer. He took a seat at the head of the table and leaned back in his chair.

"Well, it's good to hear business is booming. With the way that brother of yours talks about you, you'd think you were out there being a superhero."

It could be taken as a compliment, but the undertone was as lovable as his smirk.

Aiden couldn't help but respond.

"Considering he saved my life, I think a superhero is an apt comparison."

Aiden heard his own condescending tone loud and clear. Both men turned to him. The detective dropped his smirk. He sat up straight and fixed him with a stare that didn't waver.

"Mr. Riggs. We meet two times in one day. Once at the morgue, and now you're here at the department." He shook his head. "Is it boredom?"

Aiden felt his eyebrow go sky-high.

"Excuse me?"

"All I'm saying is that boredom in a small town can be a powerful motivator to do some questionable things."

Aiden tilted his head to the side. He narrowed his gaze.

"Are you asking me if I planned to have a random guy attack me because I was bored? Or are you asking if I went to the morgue today looking for my friend because I was bored? Because surely as a detective you have better questions than that to ask."

Out of his periphery, Aiden saw Mack cover his mouth by running his hand along his jaw. He could have sworn it was to hide a smile, but his attention was sticking closer to Detective Winters. There was no trace of humor left in the man.

Good.

Aiden had offended him.

You offended me first, buddy.

"The timing is a bit weird, is all," Winters answered.

Aiden tamped down the urge to throw his hands wide and point out that the timing wasn't convenient to him, either, but Mack took the conversational reins before he could find an actual appropriate response.

"I already told Deputy McCoy what happened," he said to Winters. "And the only reason we were able to give you the suspect at all was because Mr. Riggs here was quick with his bat. I don't think boredom factored into anything at all."

Aiden sat up straighter. He nodded.

Detective Winters kept his unflattering expression.

He, at least, didn't try to be insulting again.

"That hit is now giving us a headache," he said. "Jonathan was bellyaching so much that he's at the hospital for a CT scan. Though I think he's just stalling for time so his cousin lawyer can get in from Knoxville."

Aiden already knew that Jonathan Smith had been the man beneath the hoodie. The first thing Mack had done after Aiden had wielded the bat was take his mask off. He'd identified him quickly and with a lot of disbelief. Aiden had never seen him before and didn't recognize the name.

"Deputy McCoy said Jonathan tried mugging someone last summer," Mack said. "Last I heard, he was working with his dad before that."

Detective Winters shook his head.

"His dad moved out of state to live with his sister. After that Jonathan fell in with the wrong crowd. Debt up to his eyeballs. He's been popping up on our radar ever since. Though what he did tonight has been the most extreme thing we've seen."

The two of them shared another knowing look.

Locals.

Aiden was most decidedly not on the same level as them.

"Then what happens now?" he asked. "We've already given statements."

Detective Winters sighed. He was over whatever glee he'd had when he had entered the room. Now he seemed tired.

"We'll call if we need you." He pointed to Aiden. "Until then, I don't want to run into you again, okay? Not here, the morgue or tying up any more of our resources. Got it?"

Aiden saw red again.

Why did he feel like he was being blamed for what happened?

His hands fisted and, despite the warning, he was about to see how much he could really offend the detective.

Mack, however, stood and spoke before Aiden could.

"We'll head out now. You have our numbers." Mack turned to Aiden. "Let's go."

For a second, Aiden wasn't sure he would, but then his brain betrayed him. He found himself standing and then followed Mack out of the room and right out to the parking lot. All without giving the detective another piece of his mind.

A regret he vented as soon as they were in the night air.

"I don't know what your relationship is with that guy, but he's the worst. He acts like me getting attacked is not only inconvenient to him but also something I enjoyed." Aiden felt his face twist in anger. "I'm already having a bad day. I don't need him to add to it."

Because there was nothing else he could physically do, Aiden shook his shoulders out with some vigor.

Mack didn't react at all.

Aiden glanced over. The taller man looked as displeased with their experience as he was.

Maybe even more so.

Aiden guessed he really didn't like the detective at all.

He took a long breath in and tried to redirect his anger back to appreciation.

"Well, once again, thanks for the save," he said. "Whether it was my bad luck or not, I appreciate it."

Mack nodded.

Then he walked away.

Aiden paused on the way to his car. After the deputies had shown up, Aiden had driven his hatchback to the department. Mack had ridden with him but had stayed silent other than giving directions. Now Aiden wondered how he would get back to his vehicle, wherever it was.

He opened his mouth to shout out to Mack's retreating back when Aiden realized he was walking toward a truck idling in a spot on the other side of the lot.

He shouldn't have been surprised.

Of course Mack Atwood had someone waiting on him.

Aiden watched as his savior walked around to the passenger's side of the truck. He sighed and turned to his empty hatchback.

He bet it would be a long time before he ever saw the oldest Atwood brother again.

THE SUN WAS out and shining the next morning when three things happened to disrupt Mack's attempt at peace. The first was his sister at his door just as dawn hit. Goldie was a sight to see as she fretted around his room, trying to get a more detailed story of what had happened the night before.

"That's awful," she'd exclaimed once Mack had been done with his retelling of the events. "I never thought Jonathan would do something like that."

She had gone off on a tangent about how they'd known Jonathan Smith since middle school before she'd revealed her original reason for coming in to see him so early.

"That poor Mr. Riggs," she'd said. "He hasn't even been in Willow Creek that long and he's already dealing with death and danger."

And Detective Winters, Mack had wanted to add.

"I heard that other than Mrs. Cole and her husband, he isn't social with anyone else," she'd continued, all mothering voice. "I think I'll invite him to eat with us today so he can see some Willow Creek kindness."

Mack had quickly been against the idea.

"I don't think that's necessary. He might just want to rest today."

But Goldie was already set on the idea.

"Not only has he been through an ordeal, from what you have said, it seems that he's a big reason why you didn't take another knife. That at the very least should get that man a meal as a thank-you. Plus, knowing you, you probably didn't even say the words *thank you* to him. Instead you just grumbled and maybe nodded once or twice."

Mack couldn't deny that. They both knew she was right.

And according to Aiden himself, he'd thumbed his nose at the help instead of being gracious.

Still, it didn't mean he was happy about the invite.

He was even less so when the second of three things happened.

Aiden actually accepted.

His little silver SUV came bouncing down the drive at eleven on the dot.

Mack stayed on the front porch and watched the procession. He didn't know what he expected of Aiden in the daylight, but all his attention wrapped around the man the second he was outside.

Particularly the bruises.

They stretched around Aiden's neck in an ugly contrast to his tanned skin. They weren't as angry as they could have been, but they were undeniably there.

Mack tried to ignore them.

He'd already done enough as it was. He had helped Aiden after all.

Yet, the closer Aiden got, the less Mack could pretend they weren't there.

He also couldn't ignore the rising anger in him.

Suddenly he was back in that parking lot the night before.

He should have been faster.

What he hadn't told Aiden or anyone else after was that he had been following the man already. By chance he had seen Aiden leaving his office across the street. It had felt like a fated event. Mack had questions and Aiden had his answers, but before he could leave to ask them, he had been delayed by a few goodbyes from partygoers.

By the time he made it across the street, Aiden had already turned the corner.

Mack had debated whether or not to follow him.

Then he'd thought better of it.

Was it his place to find out the identity of John Doe?

Did he need to learn more about Aiden Riggs?

No, on both parts.

He could alert the sheriff's department to the article with John Doe's picture and, as for Aiden, he could simply never see him again and be okay.

It wasn't like he was going to be in town for long anyways.

Then the car horn had gone off.

After he'd followed the sound and seen Aiden in danger, all of Mack's decisions came fast. He had been all instinct.

Once the danger had been over, he had tried his best to revert back to his self-isolation.

He'd even forgotten to ask about the picture or John Doe in the hustle that had followed. The thought hadn't even crossed his mind until he was sitting in Ray's truck outside the sheriff's department after leaving Detective Winters. He had watched Aiden's taillights disappear, then he had given the Bellwether Tech article to Ray and decided his involvement with Aiden Riggs was done.

That was that.

No more getting involved.

But, now, it felt like fate again.

Aiden Riggs was standing in front of him, smiling.

And all Mack could see were the bruises around his neck.

Staying out of Willow Creek's problems might be hard, but it was something Mack knew was doable.

Yet, at that moment, he realized something truly startling.
Avoiding Aiden Riggs's troubles?
That might not be something he could do.

Chapter Seven

Aiden had somehow found himself sitting opposite Mack Atwood again. This time, though, there were more Atwoods to go around.

"You can call me Goldie, by the way," Marigold said to him, settling into the seat to his right. "It's a nickname I wear more proudly than my real name. Plus, it sure sounds cute when these two here have to say it when they're being serious."

She pointed to Aiden's left at the last of the three Atwoods surrounding him. Finn was dressed casually, but he still seemed stylish. He smiled wide and chuckled. Aiden understood again why he was touted as charming.

"Don't let this nice talk fool you, Aiden," he said. "If anyone is scolding anyone in this family, it's Goldzilla here. I'm the mouth of the operation, Mack's the brawn and Goldie is the brains. She has a running list of those who offend her and all the ways she can dress them down later. May ye never get on that list."

Aiden heard the woman in question scoff, but his attention was on the oldest Atwood.

Mack was also dressed down to comfort. He wore a long-sleeved beige shirt and blue jeans that ran somewhere in the middle of the denim-colored spectrum. They looked good on him, as did his dark boots. The only thing that seemed a bit off was his eyes. Ever since Aiden had said hello on the front porch, Mack had been staring at him more but saying a whole lot less.

Aiden would have been self-conscious about it, but he was starting to think that all the extroverted genes in the family had been pulled out and stored in the Atwood twins. The mouth and the brains. The brawn had gotten the strength and silence of the wind.

"Oh, yeah, this one here is definitely the talker." Goldie passed Aiden a glass of sweet tea and pointed the spoon she had used to stir the sugar in at her twin. "He can sell water to a whale or drive you to sleep in total boredom if he wanted. It's why we only let him use his powers at work. He's too dangerous otherwise."

Finn waved the comment off.

"Everyone has a skill they lean on. I bet Aiden here has some serious technical know-how to be running his own business."

It wasn't a question but Aiden saw it as his intro into the conversation. They all started to eat lunch as he joined in.

"I won't lie, I do know my way around a computer," he said. "Some kids played outside—I was stuck to a computer screen. My grandma hated that…until I fixed her bridge club president's computer after she'd gotten a nasty virus. After that it was amazing how quickly she encouraged me."

Aiden laughed, and Finn and Goldie followed.

"I bet you scored her some serious cool points in the club," Finn said.

Aiden nodded.

"She became the president's go-to lady after that, and I, apparently, became their sect's IT guy. I even left a party once in college to walk a member through hooking up a printer on the phone." The smile was already there, but Aiden felt it widen at the memory. "My date at the time thought I was lying about who I was talking to. He didn't believe me until I had her on speakerphone. He didn't invite me out again after that."

Aiden expected a hesitation. It wasn't unusual to get one. So he averted his gaze to his food to give the moment some space in anticipation.

But there was none.

"His loss," Goldie said without missing a beat.

"And the bridge club's gain," Finn said. "I also feel like that would look really good on a résumé. 'Bridge club savior.' Probably a better extracurricular than most college kids can put down anyways."

A weight settled against Aiden's chest. Goldie and Finn seemed totally relaxed.

Aiden had met good people before, and he had met people he wished he hadn't. He had been ignored, overlooked and praised. He had been abandoned, and he had been loved.

Willow Creek wasn't different.

Someone had hurt him.

Yet someone had also saved him.

Aiden didn't look up at the man opposite him but he decided then that all three Atwoods were the kind of people who made things warm. He'd been nervous about accepting Goldie's invite, but now he was glad he had. The heaviness on his chest was the good kind of heavy.

Aiden felt his shoulders relax a little.

Mack, however, tested that relaxation quickly.

"Were you in the technology field before coming to Willow Creek?"

Mack was leveling him with a stare that was as steady

as it was strong. Instead of a calming effect, those ocean-blue eyes made him anxious.

Mostly because he didn't like going anywhere near talk of Bellwether Tech.

So, he didn't.

"I was recruited to a big tech company in Nashville and worked there for a while," he skirted. "I'm sure a lot of people like the corporate feel, but I realized suits and corner offices didn't really hit the spot for me. That's why I came to Willow Creek to open Riggs Consulting. It seemed as far away from my last job as I could get."

Aiden hadn't meant to say the last part. He tried to amend it.

"You know, to get a better work-life balance."

Mack still didn't break eye contact.

"Why did you choose Willow Creek?" he asked. "It's not exactly a hot spot for entrepreneurs."

Aiden oddly felt like he was being accused of something. He tightened his smile.

"A coworker used to visit here a lot when he was younger. He talked it up so much that I decided to check it out myself after leaving the company. I guess you can tell that I was a fan." Aiden added a laugh. "It also helped that the rent for the office and my house here combined was still lower than my apartment in Nashville."

Finn nodded deep to that.

"Sue went looking at places to live there after competition and, well, she came back," he said.

"That might have been more of her mama's doing than price," Goldie responded, looking thoughtful. She clapped her hands on the next breath, beaming. "Well, I'm sure glad you ended up picking our little town, Aiden. If not this guy here would have probably found himself in more trouble."

She motioned to Mack.

The man was still all eyes on Aiden.

It was really starting to grate.

He sidestepped Goldie's compliment and went straight at the man with no manners.

"You know, I realize now that I don't actually know what you do for your job. It must involve travel, since you said you're leaving again soon."

This time Mack had a reaction. It was subtle but there. Aiden couldn't tell if it was a flash of anger, annoyance or a grimace. Considering how Goldie swooped in, he guessed he had definitely said something he shouldn't have.

"He *just* got back. And I'm sure his boss won't let him take another contract until he's had time to decompress from the last job."

Mack switched his gaze finally.

"I'm the one who accepts the contracts. It's my boss's job to hand them to me when they come in. Not baby me."

Goldie wasn't amused.

For the first time since they had sat down to eat, she lost her smile completely.

Then it was a staring contest.

Maybe that was just how the Atwoods emoted. Intense staring surrounded by silence.

Finn was still cheery, at least.

"I'm a medical sales rep at the hospital. I stay local mostly, so it's not as exciting as Mack here. He's in the private security business and travels to wherever the clients are. He just got back from a job yesterday."

Mack swung his glare to his other sibling, but the damage was already done. Now Aiden understood Detective Winters's superhero comment.

"Oh, really?" Aiden said. "Private security. Is that kind of like the Secret Service for the president?"

Mack snorted.

Finn continued with the save.

"He's a bodyguard," he explained. "High-end. Top of the tier. You want him on your side for sure."

Aiden was impressed.

"Oh, how Hollywood-sounding of you."

Mack was *not* impressed.

He looked like a man ready to scold, mouth opening alongside a frown, but he stopped without a word coming out. Aiden heard the sound of crunching gravel a few beats after the rest of the table. His head was the last to turn toward the front of the house.

"You two expecting anyone?" Mack asked as he pushed his chair back.

Goldie and Finn shook their heads.

"I wouldn't be surprised if it was Ray," Finn said. "He's like a moth to a flame when you're in town."

It was a statement that sounded intimate, but Mack shook his head. He spoke as he went to the kitchen window over the sink.

"Ray had to go into work early today."

Aiden was wondering who exactly this Ray was when Mack cursed low. It was like he pushed a button that activated tension in the room. Even Aiden tightened in his seat.

"What?" Goldie and Finn asked in sync.

Mack gave another cuss.

"It's the sheriff."

"What?" The twins spoke in sync again, but Goldie was the first to hustle to the window.

"Why is he here?" She angled her chin up at Mack. "Does he want something else from you?"

Aiden felt his eyebrow rise. He had only met the sheriff once since setting up Riggs Consulting. He'd come with a few other business owners and made polite conversation while dropping a few mentions about his reelection campaign coming up. Past that Aiden hadn't had a reason or chance to talk to the man.

Apparently Mack had.

Even from where Aiden was sitting, he could see Mack's jaw clench.

A moment of quiet wove through the four of them.

Then Mack was quick.

He turned to Finn.

"See what he wants," he said. "Call me if it's something I need to come out for. If not, don't tell him we're here."

Finn stood at attention and nodded like it was a normal thing to say when the sheriff visited. And maybe it was for the Atwoods. For Aiden, though, he was more than confused by the procedure.

"Is there something wrong with the sheriff?"

Mack moved across the room to him in less than two steps, took both of their plates and then set them on the countertop out of sight from the rest of the room. The sound of a car door shutting from the direction of the front of the house got Finn to the window for a peek.

"He's always a candidate for election first, a sheriff second," Mack grumbled.

Goldie was smoothing down her hair.

"That's Mack-speak for he talks too much and smiles even more," she explained.

"He also has a habit of asking for favors," Mack added. "And since I've already done a big one for him since being back, I'm not going to set myself up for another."

The doorbell chime sounded through the house. All the

Atwoods paused, like they were computer programs going through a temporary restart. Aiden used the momentary silence to question the trio.

"So, what am *I* supposed to do?"

Goldie and Finn might have been on the same page with their brother before, but at that question they looked to Mack for an answer, too.

Aiden had to give it to the bodyguard—for a big, muscled man, he was quick.

"You're coming with me."

THE SHERIFF CAME in through the front door as Mack led Aiden out the back. If the twins did their job right, they would keep him in the living room for the duration of his stay and he would never have the chance to walk past the few windows that showed them sneaking off. Then again, Sheriff Boyd had a knack for being sneaky when he wanted to.

That's why Mack's pace was quick as they headed across the yard, through the fence and out into the line of trees that separated the main house from most of the workable acreage. It wasn't until they were carving a path between oaks that he slowed. A beat after that, Aiden laughed.

"You must be a pretty good bodyguard," he said. "The way I just automatically followed you running *away* from the sheriff and then into some woods was effortless. You must have a good 'I protect people for a living' aura coming off you."

Aiden brushed his arm as he made room for himself at Mack's side.

Mack rolled his shoulder back and snorted.

"I'm not running away from anyone," he corrected.

"Ah, yes. Excuse me. You just happen to be giving me an

Atwood estate tour at a very convenient time." Aiden motioned to the trees around them. "Starting with this charming, secluded wooded area."

Mack didn't like being misunderstood. He cleared his throat and picked up the pace again.

"This is the only path that all three of us take to get to the barn," he said. "You'll be thankful for the shade when it gets really hot out in the peak of summer."

"Oh, so you're saying there's going to be a next time for us in these here woods?"

It was an off-the-cuff comment, a little joke that seemed to be part of Aiden Riggs's style, but Mack almost lost his footing at how comfortably it came out. In fact, he'd already been taken aback by Aiden's level of ease at the kitchen table. Mack would never be one to boast about the Atwood status around town, but he knew there was a certain nervousness that usually followed anyone who came to the house for a social visit. If not for the twins' popularity around town, that anxiousness came because of Mack and what had happened after the warehouse fire.

Yet, Aiden had settled among them all and answered every question, kept up with the conversation and even shared personal details they hadn't asked for. He also hadn't backed down at Mack's stare.

The man wasn't afraid.

That could be an indication of innocence.

That could also be an indication of guilt.

Confidence went both ways, after all.

Mack shook his head a little and tried to ignore Aiden's playfulness.

He stopped in his tracks.

Aiden took a few steps longer before he followed suit. He turned around and gave Mack a questioning look.

Even without his stylish party clothes, he stood out to Mack. Like someone had a spotlight tracking him.

It was unnerving.

It was also annoying.

Mack needed answers to get rid of both encroaching feelings.

He decided to dive right in.

"Did you used to work with Bryce Anderson?"

Aiden's eyebrow rose higher, but he didn't hesitate.

"Yeah, briefly," he said with a nod. "Why?"

"Were you close?"

This time his brows drew together, his nose scrunching between his eyes.

"I wouldn't say so. I saw him a few times in the office and even less times than that outside it. We haven't even talked since I quit the company." Aiden's hair shifted as he tilted his head to the side a little. "Why? How do you know Bryce Anderson?"

Mack could have lied. He could have avoided the question altogether. He could have kept asking his own as a distraction. Yet, he saw something in Aiden's answer that made him decide to not back away from the truth.

Sincerity.

In that moment Mack believed Aiden had had nothing to do with whatever had happened at the park.

So he told the truth.

"The John Doe you tried to identify yesterday was Bryce Anderson," he said, ripping the Band-Aid off. "I was able to identify him through a Bellwether Technologies company photo at the party last night. That's why I got to you so fast when you were attacked. I was coming to talk to you about it."

Aiden's expression turned to shock and stayed that way after Mack finished.

Then something peculiar happened.

Aiden didn't say a word.

For a moment, Mack respected the silence. It was a lot to process, even if they hadn't been close, but then that silence kept going.

And then Mack realized it wasn't silence at all.

It was Aiden Riggs making a plan.

One that apparently included him now.

Aiden reached out and grabbed Mack's elbow.

"I know you're a bodyguard, but can I hire you to help me find someone instead?"

Chapter Eight

There was an old Ford truck at the barn, rusted along the bumper and what must have been slick red paint when it was new now chipped here and there across the body. The tires were maintained, as was the interior. Though Aiden smelled a faint scent of smoke from the passenger seat cushion as he settled in.

Mack didn't explain the vehicle and started the engine with confidence. A confidence that didn't extend to him.

"I don't take personal contracts," he said for the second time. It had been only five minutes since Aiden had made the request, but it really seemed to have grated. Mack had huffed and puffed before turning him down the first time. "Even though I work for someone, I'm still considered a freelancer," he continued. "I only take what they assign me and then of those only what I'm comfortable with. Finding someone isn't on the list of skills I offer."

Aiden tamped down the urge to smile. The bodyguard was being so serious with his words yet failing in his actions.

"Then where are we going?"

Together they glanced at the sticky note in Mack's right hand. It was the address the anonymous email sent to Riggs

Consulting had come from. The location Aiden had planned to visit after lunch.

Until Mack had found another connection to Bellwether Tech.

Bryce Anderson.

Dead.

Murdered.

The moment Aiden had heard that, his brain had crunched the numbers on several scenarios. It just so happened that the man who had been towering over him in the woods had been his best chance at finding the truth. Or, at least, finding a direction to turn.

What Aiden *hadn't* planned on when asking for help was Mack actually agreeing to take him to the address while skirting the sheriff.

All while grumbling that he wouldn't help.

Mack took the note and tossed it over to Aiden now. There was still some grumbling in his words.

"I'm not helping look for anyone," he said. "I just happen to know where that place is and how much of a pain in the backside it is for nonlocals to get there. This isn't helping. It's courtesy."

Once again Aiden had to keep his smile under wraps.

"Ah," he said. "So it's all about good manners, then."

Mack pulled his phone from his pocket and nodded.

"Us Atwoods have a reputation to uphold in this town, after all."

He sent a quick text to someone before they started driving down a gravel path from the barn. It curved away from the direction of the house, too, until there was nothing but trees on either side for scenery.

"Will the sheriff come after you if he sees you leaving?"

Aiden pictured the sheriff pursuing them in a high-speed

chase while Mack just kept yelling out the window about not wanting to help anyone.

"We're taking the scenic route to the entrance. I texted Finn and told him we were leaving this way. He'll cover for us." There was that confidence again. Mack was a man unbothered while being a man who had become extremely bothered by Aiden's request.

He was a walking contrast.

One that surely had Aiden's attention.

"I can't believe I've been in Willow Creek for six months and not run into him and Goldie before. They seem like great allies to have in your corner."

Mack snorted.

Aiden thought he'd retort with something sarcastic. Instead there was a notable change in his tone. It was deeper. More serious.

"It is surprising you haven't seen them before. You must work a lot to almost completely miss the Willow Creek social scene."

He wasn't asking a question but there was definite space for an answer.

Aiden had expected as much. He'd also be asking his fair share had their situations been reversed.

"Yeah, I tend to get lost a lot," Aiden admitted. "In my work, I mean. Especially after hours. There's just something about the light of a computer screen in the dead of night. Sometimes Mrs. Cole has come in for work in the morning and I've still been up clicking away. It's not the best schedule for being social."

"I guess you couldn't do the same thing at your last job."

There it was. Mack's link to the topic of Bellwether Tech. Aiden shifted in his seat slightly. The trees around them started to thin as the gravel road curved slightly.

"It was an eight-to-five job with some overtime depending on the project. It's definitely different from my hours now."

What he wasn't saying filled Aiden's mind. He didn't dare let it spill out of his mouth. While he had asked Mack for help, he wasn't going to tell him everything that had gone wrong in his life.

Mack didn't need to know the real reason Aiden had left the company.

Mack turned his head, but Aiden wasn't sure if he was looking to the drive that branched off and went to the main house or checking his expression. Either way, Aiden put all his effort into a nonchalant smile.

One that said everything was fine and normal and not worthy of deeper conversation.

Although there was still Leighton to consider. Mack was quick to bounce over to him.

"And this guy that you think sent the email still works there? At Bellwether?"

"As far as I know. I haven't talked to him in a while, but he would have told me if he had quit."

Of that Aiden was sure. If only because of how Leighton and he had ended things.

"So you two are close."

It was another statement that required an answer.

Aiden nodded.

"We used to be."

If the sheriff saw them leaving through the main gate, he didn't come racing down the drive to follow them. Mack took the turn onto the main street and got them going toward town. Aiden almost thought the conversation was over until Mack continued.

"What happened between you two? You and this guy?"

That caught Aiden off guard.

"That's mighty personal there."

Mack wasn't budging.

"If he really is in danger and was the one who sent the email, then he's asking you for help or at the very least confiding in you," he started. "And you, someone who just said he isn't as close as he used to be with him, are investigating despite a potentially-connected current homicide and an unrelated violent attack. Both of which took place only yesterday. I just can't help but be curious as to what happened between you two that made your closeness cool. And how, even despite that fact, you two are trusting a whole lot in one another."

It was the most Aiden had heard Mack Atwood say in one go.

It also made his question reasonable.

That didn't mean it had an easy answer.

Aiden opened his mouth to respond, but what was he going to say? His mind went blank, then into overdrive looking for a vague answer that would stop any more questions.

Luckily, he didn't have to make a choice.

Mack slowed significantly. At first Aiden assumed it was because of the road. The route to the Atwood estate was no joke. It had taken almost twenty minutes to go three miles and, of those twenty minutes, Aiden had white-knuckled the steering wheel the entire time. The road had wound its way up the mountainous terrain where at any given moment there was a drop covered by trees on one side of the vehicle and a wall of rock on the other. Aiden had already thought with conviction that there was no way he would have ever driven the path at night or while it rained.

However, now Mack was slowing down and saying something beneath his breath.

Aiden focused past his internal self-conflict and realized the reason for the decrease in speed wasn't caution. It was because they were being forced to stop.

A shiny black truck was parked in the left lane with flashers on. Orange cones were set up behind it and in the right lane. There was a man leaning against the hood wearing a hazard vest over jeans and boots. When he saw them, he pushed off and made a stop motion with his hand.

"Roadwork?" Aiden guessed.

They were at a portion of the road that was more straight than curvy. The truck was parked next to a guardrail that separated it from a drop and the woods that stretched between them and the main part of town.

Mack came to a stop but not too close to the man.

"It sure is a fancy truck for work," he said, putting them into Park.

The man in the vest gave a thumbs-up before motioning to Mack to come to him.

"Stay in the car," Mack ordered. "I'll handle this."

Aiden was surprised he listened so quickly, but, then again, Mack probably knew whoever it was. He watched as the two greeted each other, friendly enough. The worker pointed to the trees and then the road. Aiden couldn't see Mack's face but saw his shoulders shake in laughter—something Aiden realized he would have liked to see up close—before the two directed their attention back at him.

His face heated at the sudden interest. Then he noticed a car had driven up behind them and stopped, also waiting.

The worker nodded to Mack, said something else that got a smile from the man and then he was walking back to the truck.

However, he didn't go to the driver's side. Instead he walked around the hood and opened the passenger's door.

He was still smiling.

It didn't match the complete ice in his tone.

"I want you to stay calm but listen to everything I'm about to say. Okay?"

Mack made a show of pointing past him to the trees and then the road, just as the worker had.

"Put your hand on the gearshift but keep looking where I'm pointing."

As if Mack's orders were king, Aiden's body went on autopilot. He slid his hand over and grasped the gearshift knob. In tandem Mack draped himself between the body of the truck and the open door.

In any other circumstance, Aiden would have believed him to be relaxed.

"Unbuckle your seat belt. Don't worry about being obvious with it. They want us out of the truck."

With his right hand, Aiden complied again. This time, though, he had to question it.

"The worker said he wants us to leave the truck? Why?"

Mack surprised him with an exaggerated laugh.

His voice dropped so low that Aiden's adrenaline spiked before Mack gave him the bottom line.

"This is a trap, and I'm pretty sure him and the car behind us are about to try and take you, so I'm going to take you first." The statement was so fast and so blunt that Aiden couldn't form the words to question it. Not that Mack gave him the room. He had another order waiting, and it made the spike of adrenaline in Aiden turn into a surge.

"On the count of three, you're going to put the truck in Neutral—that's two clicks backward on the shifter—and then I need you to jump out and run into the trees behind us. No stopping, just running. Got it?"

Movement caught Aiden's eye. This time in the rearview mirror. The driver of the car behind them had opened their door.

All of Mack tensed.

Aiden knew their time had already run out. So did Mack. *"Three."*

One word and absolute chaos.

Aiden downshifted the gear two clicks while Mack threw open the door as wide as it would go. The second the truck went into Neutral it started to roll. Fear that he wouldn't be able to exit the vehicle without falling or getting tangled up wrapped around Aiden. Just as Mack's hand wrapped around his arm.

The force was startling, but Mack pulled him out in one fluid move.

Then the yelling started.

Followed closely by the running.

Aiden went to the edge of the road, fully ready to go into the trees, but he stopped short.

The trees were there, but so was a drop.

It wasn't total, but the slope was significant enough that Aiden forgot Mack's instruction completely.

There was no way he could run down it; even if he could have seen where the slope led, the journey to get there wouldn't be a fun ride.

There had to be another way.

There had to be another path.

There—

A hand, warm and strong, wrapped around Aiden's.

Then Mack was off the edge of the road in a flash.

Hand in hand, they ran as fast as they could and made their escape.

Chapter Nine

If they had been a hundred yards farther up the road, Lover's Ledge would have saved them. It had a cliff overhang but that only stood over a drop that totaled four feet before hitting a stretch of even terrain. *That* would have been okay to run, jump and fall off, no problem.

But, no.

Mack had fallen into a trap that butted up against one hell of a hill covered in trees.

Keeping his footing was hard enough.

Keeping his footing while attached to another man was impossible.

They made it past the first oak, and then Aiden was a goner. His hand ripped out of Mack's as he fell. The imbalance made an already bad situation worse. Mack went down hard.

If they were at Lover's Ledge? The fall would have been quick and final.

They would have stuck in place.

But this wasn't Lover's Ledge.

Mack's fall became a roll, a violent tangle of limbs and speed. He tried to grab onto something—anything—to stop, but the world continued to be a painful blur.

Then the ground disappeared altogether.

Mack didn't have time to think, react or brace as he dropped over what must have been another ledge.

The ground met him again soon after.

A few seconds later, he met something else.

Mack hit the side of a raised clump of dirt and tree roots that stopped his momentum instantly. Air left his lungs. Pain filled him.

There wasn't time to think about either.

He could see the incline he had just come down. Aiden was still falling and coming down fast.

Mack didn't have a thought in his head after seeing that.

He moved faster than he ever had before and got into the path of Aiden's descent.

He readied to catch the man. There was no time to brace himself.

All Mack could do was take as much of the impact between the tree and Aiden.

And that's what he did.

Aiden slammed into Mack.

Mack didn't register the pain. He fastened his arms around the man as best he could.

The tree behind him came next.

Then that was it.

No sooner did he have Aiden in his arms, the world Mack knew went absolutely dark.

THE WORLD WAS FLOATING. It was trees and leaves and dirt and pain all just floating around him. It was also warm. Aiden sucked in breath after breath. His ribs ached. His ankle throbbed. Something was wrong with his face. It was cut or bruised or some combination of the two. It hurt. It all hurt.

There was also that warmth. It ran along his back, but it

was the only thing that wasn't pulsing with pain. With great effort he caught his breath and craned his head around the best he could to see what he was sitting up against.

Then the world finally settled.

Dark hair, slack face.

"Mack!"

Aiden couldn't maneuver correctly after that. He tried to scramble off the man while also turning to face him, but his body was all awkward movements. Disjointed. He tipped over and his shoulder connected with the leaves beneath them. He yelled out as the pain in his ribs radiated from it. But Aiden wasn't slowing. He had a new urgency in him. It ratcheted higher every second that Mack wasn't saying something.

Finally, Aiden managed to roll over and sit himself up.

His stomach fell the second he was able to get a good look at Mack.

Where Aiden suspected that his face had met an angry fate on their fall, there was absolutely no denying that Mack's had taken a definite beating. His lip was busted, his right eyebrow, too, and a nasty bruise would take over one eye in the near future. His body hadn't fared much better. At least, not his clothes. His shirt was ripped long across the middle, his jeans torn in patches at the thigh. On first glance, there were no obvious broken bones or injuries that needed immediate attention, but that was to say nothing about the blood above Mack's hairline.

That and the fact that the man wasn't moving at all.

"Mack?" This time Aiden lowered his voice.

Mack didn't move an inch.

Aiden took a deep breath and held his index finger beneath Mack's nose. He was frozen as he waited.

"Come on," Aiden whispered again. "Be okay."

Dangerous Recall

Like the command willed it, air pressed against his finger.

Mack was breathing.

Mack was alive.

Aiden could have cried.

"Thank you," he told the big man.

He rolled back and sank to the ground. The adrenaline he'd been carrying was crashing. He needed to pause for a second and get his bearings. He needed to—

A man shouted somewhere far off. Aiden couldn't make out exactly what was said but it was enough to remind him why it was they were in this predicament in the first place. He turned toward the path that they had fallen down. Aiden didn't know the landscape enough to make the best guess at how far down they were from the road. Maybe one hundred yards? Two hundred? More? All he could see was the small ledge above them in the distance.

Even if the men from the road wanted to follow them, they'd have to take their time to avoid the leaf-covered ski slope and mini cliff.

That would give Aiden some time to try and get help.

He got to his feet with greater effort than before and went for his cell phone in his front pocket.

It wasn't there.

Aiden patted the rest of his pockets. It was nowhere.

"No." He whirled around in their immediate area, eyes scanning the ground.

Nothing.

Aiden followed the path he had taken down after the ledge.

No luck. The phone must have come out somewhere in the fall.

He cussed to the trees.

Getting into Mack's jean pockets next wasn't easy, and

it certainly wasn't fruitful. If he'd had his phone on him, it was long gone.

Another shout sounded again. Aiden couldn't tell if it was closer or not.

Would they really come this far down to get them?

And who were the men to begin with? Were they really after Aiden? If so, why?

Aiden's eyes traced Mack's face. He lingered there for a moment.

He shouldn't be surprised by now, but there it was, the feeling of something new and unexpected.

Aiden didn't know what was going on, but he knew the second Mack had come back to the truck that he had been working on pure instinct. An instinct that had told him that Aiden was in trouble. An instinct that had sent them over the side of a mountain without hesitation.

An instinct that Aiden trusted.

He didn't know why the men were after him, but Aiden was sure of one thing.

Mack had put his life on the line to protect him.

Now it was Aiden's turn.

Chapter Ten

There was a thumping.

Mack blinked against his confusion, then his pain. He went to touch the part of him that hurt the most but hit something on the way to his head.

"Hey!"

It was the perfect example of a loud whisper, and it came from behind him.

Against him.

"Don't say anything," the voice continued. Mack felt the vibration through his back. He blinked several more times, trying to figure out why until the thing he'd hit moved.

It was an arm, and it was wrapped around his chest.

It was Aiden's arm around him.

"Are you *holding* me?" Mack's voice came out broken. It hurt his head to talk. He knew without touching it that there was definitely blood somewhere above his forehead.

He tried to move, but Aiden tightened his hold.

He shifted until he was speaking at Mack's ear.

"I've just burned a billion calories dragging you *away* from danger," he whispered. "And I have no idea where I am and I can't tell if those guys are close to us anymore, so instead of getting your pride in a tizzy, can you help me listen?"

The scenery made more sense now.

Mack looked up and saw trees, not the ledge they had rolled off. The sunlight was also coming from a different direction. They had indeed moved. He could see the trail in the leaves and dirt that Aiden must have made while moving him.

The thumping also made sense now, too.

It was Aiden's heartbeat coming through Mack's back. It was racing.

Mack cleared his throat and nodded. He closed his eyes again and listened. For a moment all he heard was Aiden's breathing, then a few birds. Leaves shifting in a breeze that went over the treetops.

Aiden breathing again.

Mack opened his eyes.

"I don't hear anything."

Mack felt Aiden's relief in an exhale. The hold around his chest loosened.

"I heard them yelling earlier and didn't like how out in the open we were," Aiden said. He wasn't whispering, but he was notably more quiet. "I got us maybe five minutes away from where we were before I gave out. I don't know if you know this, but you're a big guy. If anyone tries to kidnap you, just play dead and I bet they'd leave you alone."

Standing up was a chore all its own, but untangling from Aiden while doing it was a pain. Not being sarcastic back to him was also a struggle. Mack tamped the urge down as he righted. Last time he had seen Aiden, he'd been trying to absorb his impact from a tree; now it was Aiden who had been between him and one. He held his hand out to Mack for assistance.

Before he agreed to it, Mack looked the man up and down.

Aiden had been lucky, at least on the outside. His clothes

were torn in a few places and there were some scratches along his exposed skin, but none seemed too deep. There was dirt on his face and a bruise was no doubt forming along his jaw but, all in all, the man looked in good shape.

But the wince that contorted his face when Mack pulled him to stand definitely wasn't great.

"What hurts?" Mack asked, taking a step back to survey him again.

Aiden cradled his left side but gave a wry smile.

"Everything, but my ribs are really giving the rest of me a run for my money," he said. "I'm not a medical expert, but I'm guessing they're either bruised or broken. And, since I'm breathing okay and not unconscious, if they broke, then they didn't puncture anything." Aiden's gaze went somewhere above Mack's forehead. "What about you? You definitely were knocked out."

Mack snorted and motioned to his head.

"I've had worse."

Mack waited for a long-winded retort, but Aiden simply nodded.

"Good. Because I need you to tell me in a completely confident way that you know where we are and how to get us out of here without running into more trouble. Or, worse, another mountainous slip and slide."

It was a reasonable request, yet the way Aiden said it shifted something in Mack. Aiden needed his help, and it made sense that he would. Mack was a local, and he did know the area they were in.

Yet, that wasn't all.

Mack didn't just want to keep Aiden safe, he truly wanted to comfort him. He wanted him to believe in him.

"I do know how to get us out of here," he said, making

sure his voice was even and strong. He motioned to his right. "The road is back up that way."

Aiden nodded.

"I didn't want to jostle you too much, so I dragged you as much in a straight line as I could from where we fell."

Mack turned to the opposite direction. He used to know the woods better than most locals, especially as a teen, but it had been a while since he had explored them with Ray or the twins. He imagined an aerial view of the mountainside. He knew where Lover's Ledge was. At least roughly. Which meant he knew with about the same certainty what was behind them. From there he could guess what direction led them to something useful. If he was right about where they currently were, then if they kept straight and went down the mountain they would either hit the no-outlet Cayman's Loop or...

A part of Mack hoped he had no idea where they were.

Out of every inch of Willow Creek, it would be simply cruel to be forced to see that place again.

Mack shook the possibility off.

The more he thought about it, he imagined them slightly more to the east.

"We need to walk down the mountain before we can get to anything. We're on the opposite side of where the road leads, but if we keep going this way, we should come to Cayman's Loop. It leads to a street that branches off from the main one that leads into downtown."

Aiden's eyebrow rose.

"Cayman's Loop? That sounds like a nightclub."

"It's an outlet with some houses along it. They took some storm damage years ago and never got repaired, so they're empty, but the road will be good enough for us to follow." A thought occurred to him. "Do you have your cell phone?"

Aiden sighed.

"I did before I turned into a rolling stone," he said. "I'm assuming you lost yours in the fall, too."

Mack didn't have to check.

"I put mine in the truck's cupholder before we ever stopped." He cussed low. "Unless those guys left it and the truck on the road, it'll be a bit before the twins realize we're missing. Let's get going so we're not out here at night. We have a decent walk if we don't want to fall again." Mack's head throbbed as if to agree with him that he didn't need any more fall damage, but he pushed through the discomfort to start their trek. Aiden fell into step without a word. His gait sounded off, though he moved well enough along the leaves.

That silence didn't last long, though. No more than ten feet from their starting point, Aiden became chatty.

"I have a lot of questions but I want to ask about the truck thing first."

Mack already knew what was coming.

"You mean why did I get you to put it in Neutral?"

Aiden snapped his fingers.

"Bingo."

It was Mack's turn to let out an exhale that dragged.

"They took the time to set a trap, to get a vest and cones and set it all up on the road. The guy even made up some weak excuse about needing to take down some branches. He even small-talked me about the weather. So I figured they were trying to be more stealth than open aggression."

"So you sent a truck their way hoping they'd deal with it first before coming for us."

It was a good guess and the truth.

Mack nodded.

"You gambled," Aiden added. He laughed. "I guess it's always the quiet ones who do the unexpected."

Mack glanced over at the man. He was still holding his side but held on to his smile for a moment. Most people in their situation would be a mess. Aiden Riggs was somehow finding humor.

"I thought our chances were better than if I'd tried to drive away," he admitted. "I think there were more people in the truck, plus there was the guy in the car."

They had been outnumbered, and Mack hadn't known by how much. That was enough to get him worried. The gun he'd caught a glimpse of on the man wearing the vest? If he had one, who was to say the others didn't? Could they have driven away without finding out?

Mack hadn't been sure. So he had gone to a different extreme.

He had forced them to juggle while basically jumping off a cliff.

When Goldie found out about this, she would surely kill them.

Mack's mood plummeted. He hoped the men didn't think about going to the house. There would be hell to pay if so. He sidestepped over a large outcropping of tree roots. He slowed until he heard Aiden clear them, too, then returned to his faster clip.

"I guess it would be silly to think they were after you for some kind of vengeance," Aiden said. "Like someone you ticked off on a bodyguard job or a romantic betrayal that led some powerful group of unknowns to come after you? You know, all movie-like."

Mack had to snort at that.

"Negative. I'm going to say this is about you and not me."

Aiden was quiet a moment. When he spoke again, he seemed to have sobered.

"Bryce was killed, Leighton is missing and I was sent an email pinning blame on Bellwether Tech," he summarized. "You're right. All signs point back to me."

The ground started to slope more. Mack slowed again. He was hyperaware of where Aiden was in proximity to him. He wasn't about to let the man fall again. It was already a miracle both of them could even walk at the moment.

"And you were attacked last night, too," Mack pointed out.

"Do you think that's related? Don't you know that guy, though? Wait, did you recognize the worker guy just now, too?"

Mack usually disliked when people kept asking him if he recognized someone. Right now he was angry at himself that he hadn't.

"I've never seen the men at the road before, but we can't rule out Jonathan's involvement. It's too coincidental." And Mack had every intention of asking Jonathan his own set of questions the second he could. Until then he had to make do with the man of the hour. Though he felt himself hesitate a little. Being too blunt didn't feel right at the moment, so Mack tried repeating Aiden's earlier humorous attempt.

"Did something happen at Bellwether Tech to make someone vengeful against you? Did *you* tick someone off or pull off a romantic betrayal that got a target put on your back?"

There Mack was again, waiting for some sarcastic back-and-forth. Yet, all he got was silence.

It stretched.

When Aiden finally responded, it wasn't sarcastic at all. It was cold.

"I was the one betrayed."

Mack stopped in his tracks.

"What?"

Aiden didn't meet his eye as he faced him. His arm was still around his side, but the other hand was balled into a fist held low. His jaw was clenched.

It was such a contrast to the man before. Mack didn't know how to feel about it, either. Was he talking about his ex? His former job? Someone else? How big was the picture around Aiden Riggs that Mack still needed to step back farther to be able to see?

"What do you mean?" he repeated.

Green eyes found their way to his, a slow slide up.

Mack couldn't help himself. He took a step closer, the urge to reach out nearly overwhelming. Touching the man wouldn't give him answers, but he wanted to regardless.

Aiden's jaw unclenched. The tension that had built a cage around him stayed.

"I know I owe you of all people an explanation, but I can't give that," he said. "Not until we know for sure that I'm really in the middle of this."

Mack glanced down to see his other hand ball into a fist.

"Waiting to tell me what's going on could put you in more danger." Mack leveled his gaze with the man again. Those green eyes were trees that made up a forest.

Trees that stayed absolutely rooted with conviction.

Aiden's voice was clear and even when he spoke again.

"Waiting to tell you might put me in danger, but telling you? That's a guarantee that you'll be stuck right in there with me." Aiden motioned behind Mack. "Help me get to town and then I can do the rest."

He took a step around Mack and started back down the mountain.

Mack watched him for a moment.

Aiden had just let him off the hook, cleared him of the obligation to help. Mack should have felt relieved. He should have been more than glad that for once someone hadn't pushed him to help with their problems. That he had been given the okay to leave when his next task was done.

So why did he feel more hooked than ever?

Chapter Eleven

Aiden was staring out from the tree line and trying not to let the growing darkness above make him anxious. They'd finally made it to the bottom of the mountain. That was a win, no matter how tiring, painful or awkward it had been.

And it had been all three.

Mostly because the two of them hadn't said more than a few words during their trek downward. Aiden refusing to tell Mack anything about his past had done in their conversational relationship. The only talking they had managed in the last few hours was related to what they were doing in the moment.

Watch out for this hole.

Make sure to hold on to this tree while going around it.

Lean back while walking down this slope to keep from falling.

I hope we can beat the rain.

The sky overhead was still a threat, but the rain had held off so far. Aiden hoped their luck on that front kept going. Their luck on the other pressing matter? He wasn't so sure.

"Do you think we'll run into them?" Aiden asked Mack. The bodyguard had been scanning the field past their hiding place for a minute or two without a word. "The men from the road."

Aiden could take the silence during their journey to flat land—mainly because it was his fault—but now he wanted to hear Mack. He needed to hear him to keep his nerves in check.

Mack obliged, but only after heaving a big sigh.

"I grew up in Willow Creek and have lived on this mountain for almost my entire life, and I still don't know exactly where I am. If they manage to find us now, then hats off to them." He pointed ahead. "I'm thinking that Cayman's Loop is past that outcropping of trees, though. We won't have cover as we go to it, so let's be fast just in case."

"And what's the plan again when we get to Cayman's Loop?"

Mack turned his face up toward the sky.

"We follow the road to downtown, keeping to the shoulder, which should have some more trees for cover. Even if it doesn't, we should be able to hear someone driving up for most of the road."

"And if it's not Cayman's Loop?"

Aiden thought it was a valid question.

Mack ignored it.

"Are you ready?" he asked instead. "We need to go."

There was no time to answer. Mack was out in the open and moving quickly. Aiden followed. He wasn't the only one. The time it took them to make it to the next group of trees timed perfectly with a crackling sound that sent chills down Aiden's spine.

Thunder.

It even made Mack pause.

"We might need to use one of the houses as a shelter so we don't get caught in the rain," he said over his shoulder as they moved through the trees. "Trying to make it on foot to town while it's pouring is borrowing trouble we don't need."

Aiden had started watching the ground between him and Mack, trying to be careful not to trip. While he believed his injuries were all minor, he didn't want to collect more.

However, he ran smack-dab into a wall of muscle and silence before he realized that Mack hadn't just stopped talking, he had stopped moving, too.

"What?" Aiden asked after bouncing back and pawing at his forehead. When Mack didn't react to the hit, Aiden dropped his voice into a panicked whisper. "What is it? What's happening?"

Aiden peeked around Mack's shoulder.

The trees had thinned. In the distance was a building. It wasn't a house, and it stood alone. Half of the structure had crumbled, but the other half seemed sturdy enough to protect them if the rain set in. Relief started to pool in Aiden's chest. He was also just glad to see something other than trees.

A sentiment Mack didn't share.

"Cruel."

It was one word, and Aiden wasn't even sure he'd heard the other man right.

"Cruel?"

Mack didn't move.

"Cruel," he repeated.

Aiden stepped closer and tried to figure out what Mack meant. What was cruel? That they weren't at Cayman's Loop? There were no other buildings that Aiden could see? Maybe that was what Mack was taking so hard.

Yet, the second Aiden took in the bodyguard's expression, he had no idea what was going on.

Mack was a quiet man. That had been obvious since the moment they met. Sure, he chatted when he needed to, but he very much seemed a man who thought more than he ever spoke. A quality that, if Aiden was being honest, he wished he himself could master. That quiet, however, had a rhythm to it. Others ebbed, Mack Atwood flowed.

Now, that quiet man seemed absolutely hollow.

Not quiet by choice. Quiet by circumstance.

By anger? Pain? Something else that Aiden couldn't understand since he had only known the man two days?

Standing there, staring up at Mack's new quiet, Aiden believed he was right.

Whatever had happened, whatever had caused it, something in Mack had broken the moment he had seen the building.

And when the rain started, Mack's broken stayed just as broken.

Aiden put his hands over his head.

"We need to get some cover," he said. "Let's go."

The rain went from light to pouring within the space of his words, and still Mack's refused to move.

"I'll walk to town," he said. His voice was stone. "You can go stay in there."

His hands were useless as cover. Aiden shook his head.

"If you're going to town, I'm going with you."

"It's too dangerous. Just stay there."

Mack started to walk. Aiden panicked and grabbed his elbow. He raised his voice to make sure he could be heard over the rain.

"We either go in there," he said, pointing to the building, "or we walk to town *together*. Those are the only two options."

Lightning flashed, and thunder boomed right after. It was so loud that it reverberated in his chest. Aiden tightened his grip on Mack's arm.

He couldn't be sure, but he thought Mack said "Cruel" again.

What he did know was the man made a decision.

And he wasn't a fan of it.

"Fine."

They walked toward the structure, and Aiden could see it was a warehouse. Or used to be. It was also a lost cause. Water and fire damage, missing walls and half of the roof crumbled, broken and boarded windows. Even the side door wasn't closed all the way.

Aiden was about to see if the inside was as severe, but Mack grabbed his hand before he could open the door fully.

"We can wait out here," he said, motioning to the overhang above them. Like the building, it had seen better days, but the part over the door, and what must have once been a loading dock, was still intact. Still, Aiden wasn't sure it was smart to stay outside. He said as much.

"It would be a shame to survive our exciting romp down the mountain only to be done in by lightning." Aiden tried to go for the door again. Mack didn't let go of his grip. Instead he pulled against it.

"This place has been abandoned for almost twenty years. It's not safe." Mack pulled Aiden away from the door, then he dropped down to sit on the concrete near it. "Let's stay out here."

Aiden's hand was still wrapped in Mack's grip. Aiden looked down his arm at the man. He seemed smaller. It pulled at Aiden. He sighed but nodded.

"I basically followed you off a cliff earlier, so why would I go against your instincts now?" Aiden lowered himself to the ground. Mack let go of his hand after he settled. He was staring ahead of them, out at the rain. From where he sat, Aiden could see a sliver of a parking lot to his right. There was a whole bunch of nothing in front of them and to the left. Aiden wasn't used to running into so much open space and trees. Where he had lived in Nashville had been blocks of tight living spaces and offices.

It was nice to have an open place to breathe.

It would have been nicer had people not been chasing them to get here.

"Do you think anyone knows something's up with us?" Aiden asked. "I mean, that we're missing and not that just out and about. Though, are we considered missing if we know where we are?"

Mack only moved his lips when he answered. The rest of him seemed to have hardened along with his mood.

"It depends on the truck and the sheriff. If the truck was found empty and the twins found out about it, they would have started the search. If the sheriff kept talking with them for a while or asked for a favor that got them away from the house, then they might not have had the time to reach out or realize I'm not with my phone."

It was clear he'd been thinking about this for some time. Aiden's mind while coming down the mountain had been filled, too, but mostly with Bellwether Tech and Leighton. He hadn't been as practical as the bodyguard, apparently.

"Then there's the possibility that those guys made the truck disappear, so even if the twins realize we're missing, they probably have no idea where to look," he added. "I wouldn't think to look off the side of the mountain first. I definitely wouldn't think to look here."

He put emphasis on the word *here*. So much so that Aiden focused on it rather than their predicament.

"You said this place has been abandoned for almost twenty years. I'm surprised it hasn't been demolished and the land used for something else. When I first was looking at places to live in Willow Creek, the Realtor showed me some plots of land that were wildly expensive. I bet this one would go for a ton of money."

Mack didn't skip a beat.

"The owner won't sell."

It was a steel gate slamming down on the conversation. Aiden tried to respect it. He had, after all, been the one to shut Mack down about his past in the woods. Demanding small talk now would make him a hypocrite.

So Aiden tried to focus on other things.

The rain was heavy and steady. It wasn't getting better, but it wasn't getting worse. He was starting to get cold from his wet clothes, but his side and chest bothered him the most. Aiden went back to cradling his ribs again, though it didn't do much to help the pain. He sucked in a breath as he readjusted and was glad that Mack couldn't see him wince. The glow from the sun had long since gone. Aiden could barely see the man next to him.

Which was good, because Aiden couldn't stand this new silence between them.

"So, other than the twins, would anyone else notice that you've gone missing?" he asked. "You grew up in Willow Creek? I heard you Atwoods are pretty popular."

"Other than my friend Ray, no." Mack sounded strained. Aiden worried that he'd hit a nerve. He tried to make up for it.

"No other family or friends in town? Former classmates? A girlfriend?"

Aiden stopped himself when he realized he was fishing for information and not just making casual conversation.

But he also wanted to know the answer.

Mack Atwood was an interesting kind of mysterious. A reclusive bodyguard? Surely there was more to him than that.

So, Aiden waited.

And waited.

Finally, he turned to face Mack, ready to tell him that he could simply say he didn't want to answer instead of ignoring him. However, Aiden realized then that he'd been so focused on the wrong details that he had managed to glaze over some of the most pressing ones.

Mack was hurt.

He wasn't struggling for conversation. He was struggling to stay conscious.

Aiden watched as his silhouette slumped. Mack's head started to fall forward. It was a miracle Aiden was fast enough to catch him.

"Mack!"

The yell was useless.

The bodyguard was out.

Still, Aiden tried again.

"Mack?"

But there was no response.

THE FLOOR WAS tile and not at all cheap. Porcelain with several intricate designs placed every few feet. No design repeated. Several were multicolored, small squares that were rich in shades and hues that only the wealthy seemed to be able to afford, and some praised a single color only.

Every part of the floor shined.

The woman standing at the end of the foyer was no exception.

From her makeup and nails to shoes that cost more than most people's rent for an entire year, anyone looking her way would know that she was no mere mortal. She was money. She was power.

She could destroy him with a wave of her hand.

The downturn of her lips at the sight of him showed that she in fact was considering it.

He stopped on a circular design just out of her reach. The tiles were all blue. It reminded him of the angry clouds right before a storm. Maybe that's why she liked talking there. It set the tone. A subtle warning hidden in tile and grout.

He had to make sure it wasn't the last thing he saw.

He cleared his throat.

"Taking responsibility for what happened won't change that it happened," he started. "But I am fixing the problem I helped create. It will be resolved soon."

Her lipstick matched her shoes. It was hard to keep his eyes off both as she shifted her weight and spoke.

"I'm glad you've paid attention enough to know that people making excuses give me a migraine. But." Her voice had gone low. It was more intimidating that way. Sometimes he would have preferred it had she yelled. "People telling me they'll solve a problem instead of telling me they already have?" She tsked. "Well, it's less like a migraine and more like a sinus headache. One of those that builds and lets me know that in the near future I'm going to be downing ibuprofen and looking for a dark room."

Those perfectly manicured nails went to his collar in a flash. They wrapped the cloth into her fist and tightened his shirt around his neck.

"Money. Money can fix almost every problem in this world." Her voice was still hauntingly low. He kept eye contact, afraid if he looked away the attack would be more ferocious.

"*My* money?" she continued. "My money should have already taken Aiden out of his world and put him right here in ours."

She tightened her grip. He couldn't help but cough as it cut into his air supply for a moment.

She waited for him to get his composure back.

Then she let him go and straightened herself.

Her smile came back, but it was a twisted thing. There was no hidden threat there. It might as well have said in blinking neon lights that what she said next was her bottom line. And if he messed up, then he wouldn't be long for any of their worlds, money or not.

"I want Aiden," she started. "It's as simple as that. However, I don't need him. If he keeps making a fuss like he is, then I still want him, I just don't need the alive part. Understand?"

He knew he should just nod, but he had to vent his frustration.

"It's not Aiden that's the problem. It's that damn Atwood guy. Every chance we've taken, he's blocked it. If we could change the plan a little, we could get Aiden without anyone even—"

The slap was so fast that he never had a chance to react.

One second he was looking at her and the next he was facing to the right, his gaze fallen to another intricate tile design on the floor.

This one had shades of violet.

"There is a reason I do what I do," she said. "If you want to make sure your friend keeps on living, then I suggest you think about getting rid of the Atwood problem. Not my plan. Or else I'll throw everything away and destroy you, Aiden and anyone else you've involved. Understood?"

He nodded.

"Understood."

He heard her heels click against the tile as she left the room.

Leighton didn't follow right away, because he knew as

soon as he left the beautiful room that he would have to do something awful. It didn't feel right.

So, he stared at the tile a little longer.

Mack Atwood.

He wondered how hard it would be to kill him.

Chapter Twelve

He smelled smoke. Then he smelled rain. After that, he smelled oranges.

Mack opened his eyes and squinted against the light. It wasn't bright, but it was a shock all the same. Maybe not as much as what he saw when he adjusted to it.

He was no longer outside. No trees or mountain or a haunting memory standing sentry in the rain. He was in a room, a noisy one at that. Something was beeping, someone was whispering and farther away he could hear the sound of movement. The room was also warm. So was he. There was a blanket over him, tucked beneath his elbows. There was also a second, flannel one across the foot of the bed.

The bed.

It had rails, and he was propped up on two pillows.

It also had a tube. One that ran from his hand to the machines to his left.

The hospital.

He was in the hospital.

The whispering near him stopped.

Mack saw the two sitting on the couch under the window first, but the moment Ray saw him, he was up and moving. Goldie somehow managed to be faster. She was holding Mack's hand before Ray could reach the bed.

"I swear I'll go gray before I'm thirty with how much you make me stress, Malcolm Atwood." She shook her head. "I don't know what we should do with you."

She squeezed his hand. Her eyes were rimmed red. She had been crying.

Ray hadn't been, but he nodded with emphasis.

"It would be nice if you could live a less exciting life," he commented. "One that doesn't involve going to the hospital. I already work here. I don't like to visit here, too."

Mack wasn't sure how he had gotten there or what he had done to make them worry so much. In that moment, he only wanted to know one thing and one thing only.

"Where is he?" he rasped. "Where's Aiden?"

The last thing Mack remembered was sitting outside the warehouse. That was it.

Goldie shared a look with Ray. Ray smiled.

"He's in the room across the hall."

Mack tried to sit up more. He immediately regretted the decision. Pain bit at several parts of his body. His head also throbbed at the movement.

"Is he okay?"

Goldie and Ray both reached out to keep him from moving.

"Calm down there, cowboy," Ray said. "Don't worry, he's fine. Roughed up a bit, but he'll be good once he's had time to rest."

Relief temporarily pushed out Mack's pain.

"Not that you asked, but you *also* are okay," Ray added. The corner of his lips turned up. He pointed to Mack's head. "You have a concussion." He pointed at his own back. "Several gnarly bruises along your back, one that I'm guessing came from slamming into a tree, and—" Ray hovered both hands over his torso "—some superficial cuts along here. But the majority of your blood loss came from here."

Ray tapped the area around his chest.

Mack was confused.

"Blood loss?" He didn't remember that being an issue before he passed out. Twice.

Goldie was quick to answer. Mama Atwood couldn't hide the anger in it.

"You popped the stitches on your knife wound from your last job. I don't know how long you bled for, but Doc Ernest thinks it's one of the reasons you passed out when you did. By the time Ray and Aiden got back to you, your shirt was almost completely soaked in it."

Mack felt his eyebrows scrunch of their own accord. He was more interested in the Ray and Aiden of it than the fact that he had been slowly losing blood without realizing it.

"When you two got back?" he asked his friend. "What happened? How did you find us?"

Goldie and Ray shared another look. No words, but it was enough to come to a silent agreement. Goldie's eyes narrowed, and Ray nodded. He crossed his arms over his chest.

"It was complete luck, to be honest," he started. "I was heading to your place but going slow because of the rain. I don't think I would have seen him otherwise."

"Who?"

"Aiden," Goldie answered.

Ray nodded.

"He was running down the side of the road," he continued. "I recognized him from when he came to the morgue. I also knew he was supposed to be eating lunch with y'all. So when he started waving me down like a madman, I pulled over."

Mack grumbled.

"That was dangerous. He shouldn't have done that. It could have been someone else."

"He was trying to get you help," Goldie interjected. Mama Atwood's anger was coming back. "If he hadn't, who knows how long it would have been until you were found."

Mack decided it was smart not to respond.

"Anyway, as soon as I got him in the truck, we tore out there to get you and brought you in ourselves." Ray nodded to Goldie. "You've been out for about three hours."

Mack couldn't believe he'd passed out twice in one day. Or that he had lost three hours.

"What about the guys on the road?"

This time Ray's anger came out.

"Aiden gave as many details as he could remember about what happened, but we have no idea where your truck is or where they went after you two went down the mountain. The cowards seem to be good at hiding." His eyes widened. "Did you recognize them?"

Mack shook his head.

"I didn't get a great look at the driver of the car, but the man in the vest I'd never seen before."

"And you're sure they were after Aiden?" Goldie asked.

"Yeah. The second I had him out of the truck, they were running toward us." He could have explained more of the situation—Leighton, Bryce and Bellwether Tech—but Mack had more pressing matters.

"Has Detective Winters come yet?"

At this, Goldie bristled.

"He did. So did the sheriff."

"Aiden and I spoke to Winters," Ray said. "Goldie here handled the sheriff. Both lit off to try and find the guys. Now we're all in a holding pattern. Speaking of, why don't you let Finn know Sleeping Beauty here is awake?"

"Finn's here, too?"

Goldie leveled a glare at him.

"Of course he is. You get yourself a ticket to the hospital and us three will always be in the audience. Those are the rules. Now, don't move too much. I'll be back in a bit. I'm also going to grab Doc Ernest and let her know you're up. No moving, okay?"

Mack thought better about saluting.

"Yes, ma'am, Mama Atwood. No moving for me."

Goldie snorted but seemed pleased with his response. She squeezed his hand one more time and left the room right after. Ray didn't budge from his spot. He lowered his voice.

"Really, though, how are you? I'm not going to lie, you looked pretty rough when we got to you."

"I'm fine." It was an automated response. He didn't like when others worried about him, and apparently that's all they had been doing for the last few hours.

Ray sighed. He rubbed a hand along the back of his neck.

"Goldie had no idea you were in trouble. Like, absolutely no idea. She thought you two had gone to Aiden's place or somewhere to lie low away from Sheriff Boyd and his favors. If Aiden hadn't left to try and get help, y'all would probably still be out there in this rain."

He glanced at the window. Mack did, too. The blinds were opened enough to see that the world outside was still dark and angry. When Ray's gaze slid back to Mack's, he seemed to be searching for the right words.

Mack waited until he had them.

"I don't know exactly what's going on or if Aiden is someone to be trusted but, I will say this—he genuinely was worried about you," he finally said. "When he saw just how much you'd been bleeding, he seemed more upset than even me. He also refused to get seen in the ER until you were in a room. He actually got scolded by Scott, the doctor on call, for being stubborn." Ray grinned, but it fell just as fast. "I also heard them ask if he wanted to call anyone to stay with him, but he said there was no one. Not even his emergency contact would come if he asked. I don't know if he meant that to get sympathy or not, but it sure tugged at all of us. Finn and I have been taking turns hanging out with him since then."

That surprised Mack. Aiden seemed too social to have no one in his life.

"All his people must still be in Nashville," Mack reasoned. "Did he say who his emergency contact was?"

Ray's eyebrow popped up, but he didn't question it.

He shook his head instead.

"Whoever it is, I heard him say he needed to change it."

Mack wondered if it was his ex, Leighton.

"I was the one who was betrayed."

Aiden's confession in the woods only added to Mack's dislike for Leighton. He seemed to be nothing but a source of trouble. Then and now.

Mack motioned to himself.

"When can I leave?" he asked. It timed poorly with the door opening. Finn came in with a look that said that Mack definitely wasn't leaving any time soon.

"You can leave after rest and observation," Finn answered. "Neither of which you've cleared yet. So, hate to say it buddy, but you're here for a bit."

Mack grumbled.

Finn and Ray started to talk about how Mack was as fussy as a little kid at day care, wanting nothing more than to go home.

He didn't have the energy to tell them they were wrong.

He didn't want to go home.

He wanted to see Aiden.

THE HARPER FAITH HOSPITAL was small but, according to Finn, it was mighty. He chose to work there, in part, because of the great service and pristine conditions.

Aiden couldn't say he was wrong. So far he had been met with star treatment. Though, as the day stretched into late night, he started to suspect that was more because of the Atwoods than anything else. Goldie and Finn had revolved in and out of his room like clockwork until Aiden had finally convinced them, and Ray, that he was okay and wanted to be alone. They had all made sure that the doctor and nurses were aware that Aiden was someone they knew and they wanted him taken care of.

It had been touching and uncomfortable. Aiden wasn't used to that kind of attention.

Now, it was the middle of the night, and he found himself a little lonely. Maybe because he couldn't sleep. The wrap around his ribs was tight, and his ankle was in a temporary splint. Getting comfortable had been as much a battle as racing down the mountain. He was readjusting his pillows for the umpteenth time when a knock sounded on the door.

It was quiet.

Aiden looked at the clock on the wall. It was almost two in the morning.

"Come in?"

The door opened slowly. Mack walked in even slower. He was in a hospital gown and still hooked up to an IV pole.

"What are you doing up?" Aiden heard the scolding tone the same time as Mack.

He rolled his eyes.

"I just got Goldie off my back—I don't need you nagging me, too," he said. "This room is the same as mine, so who cares if I'm here or there? I'm a big boy."

He grumbled his way across the space and settled in the

chair that Finn had been using. It was pushed up near the bed and put him close enough that Aiden helped hold the IV pole while Mack sat down. When he was settled, Mack swatted that hand away.

"Everyone keeps acting like I'm made of glass. I don't need any special handling. I'm fine."

Aiden narrowed his eyes.

"As someone who saw you being cut out of your clothes earlier in the ER, excuse me for still being a little concerned."

Mack seemed to consider that. A look of acute discomfort washed over him. He grumbled again, but there was no real weight to it.

"I don't like owing people, but I wanted to say thanks. You know, for getting me help and everything." Mack didn't look back to normal, but he definitely looked better than he had when they had rushed into the hospital lobby. Aiden was glad to see that his annoyance had resurfaced. "I'm not happy with how you went about it, but I can't complain about the results." Mack eyed his chest. "I guess we both needed some medical attention."

Aiden felt a flare of self-consciousness. He hadn't seen a mirror since he had been settled in his room but could only guess how awful he must look. Him being wrapped up like a mummy wasn't helping.

"If it wasn't for me, then you wouldn't have been in that situation," he pointed out. "It was the least I could do."

Mack looked like he wanted to say something but ended up nodding. Aiden's self-consciousness turned to guilt. In the past few days he'd gone from not knowing Mack Atwood to sharing a hospital room with him in the early hours of the morning.

To knowing his trauma.

Aiden's guilt was tenfold, and it was all thanks to Ray.

"It had to be here," Ray had said, staring through the windshield at the warehouse. The three of them had just gotten back to the truck. Aiden had been in the back seat holding the unconscious Mack, blood and rain mixing into their clothes.

Aiden could tell how upset Ray was for his friend but, in that moment, he had become distracted by what he was saying.

By the warehouse.

"Out of all the places in this town, he had to find here."

The comment sat for a few seconds before Ray went back to the task at hand and floored it to the hospital. It hadn't been until hours later when Ray had come in to say good night to Aiden that he had picked back up on the thought.

"Did Mack know y'all were heading to the warehouse when you were still on the mountain?" Ray had been sheepish.

Aiden had shaken his head.

"No. He thought we were going to Cayman's Loop."

Ray had looked pained at that.

"What did Mack say when he saw it was the warehouse?"

Originally, Aiden had wondered what the relationship was between Ray and Mack. It was obvious they were close. Ray made no issue about showing that fact, either, and, as far as Aiden could tell, Mack reciprocated that love.

If Aiden was being honest with himself, it had made him a little jealous. Ray talked a lot, just like Aiden, yet he doubted Ray got the look of annoyance as much as he did.

But, with Ray standing in his hospital room, almost sheepish, Aiden felt that the love for Mack was different. It felt more like Goldie and Finn's affection. Brotherly.

Aiden had answered truthfully to respect that bond.

"Cruel. He just said, 'Cruel.'"

Ray's face had fallen. He had opened his mouth, then closed it. Then opened it again.

"It's not my story to tell, but I'm not sure Mack can ever tell it. And I think you need to know why it is he can't let go of some things, even when they're dangerous."

Then Ray had come close to the hospital bed and told the story of why Mack Atwood hated the warehouse at the bottom of Willow Creek's only mountain.

"It used to be a storage-for-rent space for spillover product and equipment used mostly by companies out of Nashville for a cheap price. Nothing too fancy but popular enough that the contracts kept coming in. There was one client, though, who was a real pain. Always angry, rarely following the rules and eventually going as far as attacking the manager one day. No one really knows why the fight started, but when the sheriff's deputies showed, the client was told to leave. He wasn't happy about it and took his business elsewhere, though it suffered losses thanks to the bad attention. Then the fire broke out in the warehouse." He had paused there. It was like he'd aged twofold within the span of him talking. Just as Mack had aged after seeing the warehouse for the first time.

"The sprinkler system didn't go off, and the fire ate away at the office. There was so much smoke that most of downtown came when they saw it. A few of us even beat the fire trucks." He had sighed. "Mack was with me and we tried to help, but by the time we realized the manager was still trapped, it was too late. He didn't make it."

Aiden felt like he knew where the story was going. Still, he had to make sure.

"Who was the manager to Mack?"

Ray's frown had sunken in deep.

"His dad. It was his dad."

Cruel.

The comment had made sense then.

But that wasn't all.

"Mack has this thing with faces," Ray had continued. "He can meet someone only once and that's enough. From then on that face is stuck in his memory—even if someone ages or changes up their look, he can still almost always recognize them. That's why I believe him when he says he saw the client who caused trouble running from the warehouse the day of the fire, even though no one else does."

"What do you mean, no one believes him?"

Anger had taken over Ray's expression.

"The detective at the time chalked it up to grief. That Mack needed someone to blame, especially after the investigation was closed and the fire ruled an accident. But the rumor was that the client was let off because of a sob story about him being a dad with a kid who needed him and he really played up the story well. Regardless of what happened, Mack stuck to his guns and didn't let it go. Even when everyone else did."

Ray had met Aiden's eye then.

"He's quiet, our Mack. He was before the fire and became quiet again after. But, when he was trying to get justice for his father, he became loud. Angry. Someone who didn't give up and never gave in. If it wasn't for the twins begging him to try and move on and live his life, I'm not sure where Mack would be now. But one thing I *do* know is whatever is going on with you, with those guys, he's angry about it. And, quiet or not, he's going to see it through. If not for you, for the mere fact that they did the one thing everyone in this town knows not to do when it comes to Mack Atwood." He hadn't paused for dramatic effect, but Aiden had felt goose bumps crawl along his arms at Ray's next words. "They reminded Mack what it felt like to be loud."

Now, that man was sitting next to him, simply trying to get comfortable in a chair.

Aiden made a decision.

It was time to tell a story.

Aiden cleared his throat.

"I found out a secret about Bellwether Tech, and I think it's worth killing for."

Chapter Thirteen

"Bellwether Tech isn't original. They didn't break the mold with their security system or their programming. All they did was promote it differently than what was on the market at the time."

Mack watched Aiden squirm a little. He wasn't sure if it was because of the topic at hand or if his injuries were still bothering him. Without a gown covering Aiden's top half Mack could see that most of the man's torso and chest were wrapped up. He knew from experience how uncomfortable that could be.

If he wasn't invested in what Aiden was saying, he would have let his anger roll around some more unchecked.

Instead he leaned in when Aiden asked him a question.

"Do you know what Bellwether does? I mean, what their main product is."

Mack hadn't known before meeting Aiden, but afterward he'd done some light research.

"The Sitter. It's a home security system with cameras and alarms."

Aiden nodded.

"Instead of competing with other home security systems for people at home, it was marketed as a system that worked as a house sitter for those who were away from the home.

Specifically for people who traveled a lot or were deployed. Not really revolutionary, but then the system went viral after a service member who was deployed in Germany was able to see that his home was being broken into. From there he was able to coordinate in real time with the local authorities to catch the guys, who were trying to make off with his late wife's jewelry collection. Something that obviously meant a lot to the man."

"I actually remember that story," Mack said. "It was on the news with the guy tearing up about almost losing what he had left to remember her by. I didn't realize that was connected to Bellwether."

"That story is what really made the company go boom and also made it a fan favorite of veterans and service members. Last I checked, nearly 75 percent of users were deployed. The company also took advantage of the popularity and offered discounts specific to those in the military, too."

Aiden took a deep breath. When he let it out, his body dragged down a little with it.

"When I joined the company, it was at the height of their popularity. It was a low-level job that I was overqualified for. They'd just gone through several rounds of hiring to meet their new demands and I'd missed out. Still, I liked Nashville and wanted to work for them, so I didn't mind doing grunt work for a while. That's when I met Leighton Hughes."

Mack wanted to grumble at the name. He didn't. Aiden kept on.

"He was big in the IT department and well respected by the higher-ups, especially the owner. We became friends after meeting in the company cafeteria and started eating lunch together every day. We talked about work at first, and then one day we were talking about each other. Somehow after that we were dating." A brief smile passed over Aiden's lips. Mack shifted his weight in his chair. "We were together when an upgrade to the Sitter went live. And broke everything in our system. I mean, catastrophically broke. Everyone was rushing into the office at three in the morning in their pajamas trying to fix it. It was chaos. I was driving Leighton in while he had his laptop up in the passenger's seat and his phone *and* my phone both on speaker. By the time we got to the office, no one had a workable solution."

The way he said *no one* gave Mack the impression that there was, in fact, one person who had.

"No one except you, I'm guessing," he said.

"I got lucky," Aiden admitted. "I found the problem and had it fixed within five minutes. But, after that, I was promoted to the lead IT team." Aiden's smile was quick again. There was pride in it. Strangely, Mack felt it, too. "Alongside Leighton, I was invited into the inner circle of the higher-ups with the new job. Wining and dining, fancy events—you name it and I had a pass to be there. I was trusted."

There was no more pride. No more smiles. Aiden seemed to fold in on himself.

"So I didn't question it when I was called in to the office late one night. We'd just done a minor update, so I thought I was there to fix something with that. Instead they presented me with a special project, one that they didn't want getting out. At first, I didn't question that, either. I think some of that was my ego getting the best of me. After working my butt off in college and through part-time jobs, I finally was being acknowledged and praised for my skills." He sighed. "Then I saw what they wanted me to do."

Aiden stopped. Like he'd run into a verbal brick wall. When he didn't start again, Mack reached out. It was as easy as breathing. He placed his hand on top of Aiden's. The new weight seemed to focus the man again.

Then there were trees in the room between them. Green eyes searching Mack's.

"I don't have to tell you," Aiden said. It wasn't a statement of defiance but an offering. Mack patted Aiden's hand.

"I want to know."

"Are you sure?"

Mack was. He nodded.

"Tell me."

Aiden held his gaze a little longer. Then he shared his secret.

"They wanted me to hack into a specific home's live feed, cut it off and loop it with preexisting footage. And they needed me to do it in under one minute." His defeat turned to anger. "I was told that it was a test. A way to see if hackers could infiltrate the system and manipulate the program. I should have asked more questions, but I was so excited to have a new challenge, so I did it. Fifty-four seconds. That's all it took."

Aiden's fist balled beneath Mack's hand.

"But then Leighton started acting weird, and I couldn't let the feeling go that I'd done something wrong," he continued. "So, I went a little overboard. I hacked into our secure server...and then the personal computers of the vice president and CEO."

Mack felt his eyes widen.

Aiden nodded.

"I know, I know. I went from one extreme to the other, but when I was in Bellwether's security logs I kept finding the vice president's digital prints everywhere. Then when I went into his computer, I found a digital calendar with customer names pinned at odd times. I couldn't figure out why, and so I went to the CEO's personal network after finding a message chain between them about a video file the CEO wanted destroyed." His words had sped up and were almost crashing into each other now. "From there I found two videos in the trash that hadn't actually been completely deleted, restored them and realized I was looking at previous live footage from a customer's home. In the video the man was meeting up with a woman—a woman who was not his wife. I then went back to Bellwether Tech's storage and realized that every trace of the video had been deleted and in its place, with a fabricated time stamp, was a looped video from a previous recording."

Aiden had to stop to catch his breath.

Once done, he was full speed again.

"Then I looked into the CEO's personal finances and found a transaction for $50,000 that had been transferred the day before the footage had been changed and deleted. That got me curious about who paid it, and I realized it was the customer from the video. From there I was able to find security footage that showed the vice president and the customer meeting in the parking garage, the customer looking absolutely furious. I kind of figured out what happened from there."

"Your company used a home's footage from the Sitter to blackmail a customer," Mack laid out.

Aiden was defeated.

"And I had helped them get into another home's live footage and loop it after that."

"What did they do with that customer? Did you figure it out?"

Aiden shook his head.

"Instead of investigating by hacking absolutely everyone,

I decided to confide in someone I trusted in the company to hopefully get some help. That was a mistake."

"I was the one betrayed."

Mack recalled Aiden's earlier confession in the woods.

This was where Leighton Hughes came in.

"I told Leighton everything I knew and asked him to come to the police with me." Mack felt Aiden's fist tighten beneath his hand again. "But Leighton convinced me to let him figure out what was really going on first. And I, well, I believed in Leighton's judgment. I believed in him."

There was that wall again. Aiden skidded into it and stopped talking altogether.

This time Mack waited for him to find his words on his own.

After a few moments, he did.

"A couple of days later Leighton told me he'd handled it and nothing like that would ever happen again. I expected a resignation or a change in management, but nothing happened. When I confronted Leighton about it, he told me that the CEO and vice president had apologized profusely and given the money back. I wanted to check if that was true, but Leighton…he lost it. He told me if I ever loved him that I'd drop it, leave well enough alone. And so I did. I quit the next day and never went back. Leighton and I tried to stay together, treating what happened like it was some kind of professional experience only, but I couldn't get over the fact that he was okay with everything. That he still was working there, still attending the parties, still rubbing all the elbows. So, I ended things there, too. Six months later, here I am."

Mack could tell the story was through by his body language alone. He looked relieved and tired all at once. Mack felt for him. Maybe too much. He pulled his hand away and straightened his back.

"Did anyone else know about what happened? Did Bryce Anderson?"

Aiden shook his head.

"I didn't tell anyone. Only Leighton. I wasn't even there when he confronted the vice president and CEO. When I resigned, Leighton handled that himself. I told everyone else I was leaving for personal reasons. No one asked past that. That's why I want to find Leighton so badly, too. He's the only one who can answer at least half of my questions."

"But he hasn't gotten back in touch with you since the message he left with Mrs. Cole," Mack finished.

"Yeah. And I really do think the email came from him, too."

Aiden's eyes widened.

"The email that was sent from an address here in Willow Creek. The same one I still haven't been able to check. Every time I'm headed that way, someone tries to grab me."

He said it in a mocking way, as if it was a small inconvenience, but Mack saw some discomfort at the memories. It didn't help that they were in the hospital after the most recent attack.

Aiden hung his head low. One of the bruises along his jaw was a sickening purple.

"I know I could go to the police about what happened at Bellwether Tech, but now I'm afraid if I do that it might somehow put Leighton's life in danger. I also know he's my ex and I shouldn't be worried like this but, he was a good guy once. Until I know he's not now, it's hard to ignore that fear."

Aiden kept his head down. His hand, however, reached out. It wrapped around Mack's.

"If you were me, what would you do?"

The touch, the question, the way Aiden's voice wavered

during both, made Mack tense. Adrenaline surged, his breath quickened in response. Suddenly the fluorescent lights overhead became louder. The machines beeping, gunshots. Mack's heartbeat, fireworks in a calm night sky. His mind raced along with the changes.

His mouth formed the words before he realized what he was saying.

"You're smart. You don't need to know what I would do. Trust yourself." Aiden's hand was smaller than his, but it warmed his easily. *"But—"*

Aiden raised his chin.

"But?" he repeated.

The trees were back. Mack stared into them.

"But, whatever you decide, I'll be right there with you."

Aiden's eyebrow rose sky-high.

"You've already done enough," he tried.

"As a friend, maybe. But not as a part of my job."

"Your job?" Aiden repeated.

Mack smirked.

"Congratulations, Mr. Riggs, I'm officially your new bodyguard."

HARPER FAITH HOSPITAL was nice and all, but Aiden preferred seeing it in the rearview mirror.

"I know we were in there for only two days, but I'm very, very happy we're going in the opposite direction."

His back seat buddy, Mack the Bodyguard, snorted. Their driver, Finn, laughed.

"I don't know who complained more about his stay," he said. "You or big bro there. I thought Goldie was going to lose it on you two when you tried sneaking out after day one."

Aiden and Mack shared a look. Mack played it cool; Aiden's cheeks heated a little. True enough, the morning after they had talked in his room, they had tried to get discharged early. Goldie had appeared like magic before either could go through the process. Aiden thought if anyone could get around her, it would be Mack, but after she had pulled him into another room and given him a thorough talking-to, he'd come back like a dog with his tail tucked between his legs.

"Let's just wait until the doc says we can go," he had said, like it was his idea first.

Aiden had listened, though that had less to do with being reasonable as Goldie had said and more to do with what Mack had agreed to do.

He was now Aiden's bodyguard.

Aiden would have been less surprised if Mack had admitted to being close personal friends with Dolly Parton.

When he had told Mack his story, he hadn't been fishing for sympathy or pity. He had wanted to give Mack context for what he'd gone through. Though Aiden also knew sharing the secret wasn't entirely selfless.

It had felt good—more than good—to share his regret. His worry. His shame. Not only in him walking away from a problem he knew existed but for how he had found that problem out in the first place.

He'd broken several laws and done the one thing he had told himself he wouldn't do again once he was an adult.

No more hacking.

No more peeking behind the curtain.

But, once he'd looked, he hadn't been able to stop himself. It was like an addiction.

An addiction that he'd admitted to one person and one person only.

Aiden could feel Mack's body heat against his leg. Finn's car was on the small side, and the front and back seats were filled with work materials. Aiden had thought Mack would make a fuss at having to scrunch into the back seat, but he hadn't. Instead he had asked Aiden several times if he was sure he wasn't in any pain once they were seated.

He was, just a bit, but moving to the front passenger seat wasn't going to change that.

Willow Creek always had some housing turnover, according to Aiden's Realtor, simply because of time. People grew older, left homes, got new jobs, fell in love and passed away. All those reasons were why he had been able to buy 142 Lockley Way. One story, wrapped in whitewashed brick and absolutely spacious compared to his last apartment, the house was an oasis spaced between elderly neighbors and a new family with two babies. None of these neighbors were outside as Finn parked at the curb.

Aiden was surprised to see a truck in the driveway.

"It's mine," Mack said, answering his unasked question. "Your car is still at my place. We can get it later."

Aiden felt a little heat crawl up into his cheeks again. He had gotten into the habit of feeling out of the loop when he was with Atwood and Company. Even though apparently he was in the center of their attention the last few days.

"You know, you really don't have to do this." It wasn't the first time he had said it.

It also wasn't the first time Mack had waved him off.

"There's no going back now. I'm already on the clock." He opened the car door but paused to talk over the seat to Finn. "I'll keep you updated. Let me know when you get home."

Finn saluted over his shoulder.

"Yes, sir. You have all our numbers in your new phone, right?"

"Sure do, Wonder Twin. Thanks for the ride."

Mack was quick for a man with two sets of stitches and

a patch quilt of bruises. He was out of the vehicle before Aiden could finish unbuckling. He disappeared behind the car and opened the trunk.

Finn redirected his attention to Aiden.

"Since they found your phone on the mountain and you have our numbers, we expect you to call or text if you need anything. That's me, Goldie and Ray. Anytime, any day."

Aiden smiled. He was as touched as he had been when the three of them had taken his phone from Deputy Mc-Coy's hand at the hospital and passed it around to put their numbers in.

"I will," he promised.

Finn nodded. Then his eyes softened.

"I know Mack is strong, but sometimes it's the strong ones who need the most from the rest of us," he said, voice lowered. "Watch his back while he watches yours. Okay?"

Aiden didn't have time to answer, but maybe it wasn't needed. Finn's attention went back to the front of the car as Mack appeared at the opened door. He held his hand out and down. Aiden took it and was guided outside with obvious care.

"You know, I'm also not made of glass," he deadpanned to Mack. "The doctor even said he was surprised at how resilient my body is to pain."

Mack snorted.

"I'm not sure that's something you should brag about." He thumped the roof of the car. Finn took it as his sign to leave. He was no sooner out of the driveway than Aiden realized what Mack had taken from the trunk.

"What's in the duffel?" Aiden asked. It was different from the one he'd had at the hospital the last two days.

"It's my go bag. Clothes, toiletries, a few tools of the trade."

Aiden cocked his head.

"And why do you need a go bag?" He laughed. "Are you an undercover spy who's just been found out by some kind of tyrannical mob boss? Please tell me your passport isn't in there."

Mack rolled his eyes.

"I definitely can tell you feel better based on how much you've been talking today. You could almost give Finn a run for his money."

He said it like he was annoyed, but Aiden didn't feel it like he had when they had first met. He wondered if that's how Mack operated as a bodyguard. Instead of lurking in the shadows, ready for anything, like Aiden had pictured, maybe the oldest Atwood was more hands-on.

The thought stirred something in Aiden, but he focused on the conversation at hand.

"Seriously, though, why the bag?" he asked. "Aren't you just here to take a look at my house and then bring me back to my car at yours?"

Mack snorted this time. He grabbed the sleeve of Aiden's shirt and pulled it and Aiden along with him toward the front porch.

"I hate to break it to you but, until we get to the bottom of this, I'm not leaving your side."

Aiden's heartbeat picked up a little at that.

"What about tonight?" They hadn't explicitly laid out any plan, let alone sleeping arrangements.

Mack answered like it was no big deal.

"Day or night, wherever you are, I'm going to be right there next to you."

Chapter Fourteen

What Aiden didn't know was that Mack had already scouted his house before they had even left the hospital. It wasn't that he was trying to keep secrets from the man, it had just been a matter of efficiency.

"You guessed right," Ray had said once the task had been done. "Aiden's one of those trusting types who hides his spare key in the flower bed. I found it under a fake rock."

At the time of the call, Mack had been in the hallway outside said man's hospital room. He'd had the urge to go inside to scold him about having better safety measures. Instead they had used the breach in security to send Ray and Finn inside to make sure there was nothing or no one lying in wait.

It was usually a task that Mack would have carried out, but leaving Aiden alone wasn't an option anymore. So, he'd listened as his best friend and brother more or less broke into Aiden's house, all in the name of safety.

Thankfully, there was nothing too alarming.

"Other than the most tricked-out home office I've ever seen, I don't think anyone has been inside here doing anything bad," Ray had concluded once they had finishing sweeping the place. "I think it's fine to bring him here for now. Though, if he's being targeted, location might not matter if they're eager."

Mack knew this, just as he knew the house had been fine an hour earlier. It's why he put himself between Aiden and every room after they went inside. It's also why he had his Taser and baton in the bag across his shoulder. He wasn't a fan of guns, but he had no qualms about using anything else to defend his client.

Client.

Mack watched as Aiden peeked around the door into his office.

"I'm glad Mrs. Cole conditioned me to clean up after pulling all-nighters or else this room would look like a frat house after-party. Empty cans, food wrappers and random underwear hanging off the ceiling fan." Aiden made himself laugh. Some of his hair fell at the movement, brushing into his eyes.

Normally this would be when Mack repeated the word *client*. Reminding himself that he was there to keep someone safe, not joke around. Not chat. Not look at simply for the sight.

Yet, the word that came to mind wasn't *client*. It had nothing to do with a job.

Handsome.

Aiden Riggs was handsome.

There wasn't a specific thing about him that Mack liked. It wasn't his high cheekbones, his full lips, the mole near his green eyes or the dimples that came out when he smiled. It wasn't his earring or his clothes that always seemed to have some kind of stylish black piece. It wasn't his lean frame or the fact that they had an intriguing height difference between them.

It wasn't just any one thing, he realized.

Mack liked all of it.

But the thing he liked the most had nothing to do with the man's looks.

Aiden just kept going.

Talking, laughing, smiling, worrying, caring, joking. He just kept on no matter what had happened. No matter that his body was broken and bruised, no matter that he was scared and angry and confused.

At first Mack had preferred being alone. Then he hadn't disliked being around Aiden. Now he was standing in his house and wanting to know more about him.

Also wanting to tuck his hair behind his ear.

Mack flexed his hand. He cleared his throat and instead nodded to the computer setup that Ray had already commented on.

"I doubt a frat party would have something like this going on. I know I'm more of an analog guy, but surely this isn't normal."

The room was on the small size, but Aiden had utilized all the space well. A long desk stretched along the back wall and had two tiers of shelving at the top. Then there were three monitors, all mounted on the wall with what looked like adjustable rods. Mack spied at least four keyboards, two of which had multicolored LED lights along them, and there were several gadgets and cute trinkets holding pens, pencils and sticky notes. Mack eyed a pair of headphones displayed near the center monitor.

"That definitely isn't something I think I'd see at a frat party," he added.

Aiden scoffed and brushed past him. He picked up the headphones and slipped them on. They were silver and white. They also were shaped like cat ears.

"I'll have you know that these are trendy, thank you very

much. And look, you can do this, too." He reached up and clicked a button. The cat ears lit up. Aiden smiled wide. "Let me guess, you have some no-nonsense things at home. I bet they're earbuds. And you only wear them when you're mowing the lawn or something."

Mack pulled out his cell phone.

Aiden was still waiting for an answer to his teasing.

Mack took a picture instead.

"Hey, now." Aiden reached out for the phone. Mack took an easy step away from his grasp.

"As your bodyguard, I need a current photo of you just in case," Mack explained.

"Not of me in cat ears!" Aiden took the headphones off, but the damage was done.

"I'll make that call. I'm the professional here, after all."

Aiden kept fussing. Mack expected him to keep going longer, maybe even trying to swipe at him a few more times, but the man's expression changed. It was like he put on a mask. His smile melted. What was left was a seriousness that made Mack straighten.

"Will you really follow me anywhere?" he asked. "As my bodyguard?"

Mack nodded. "Within reason," he amended. "I won't let you put yourself in danger willingly, if that's what you're asking."

"What if I'm not entirely sure if a place is safe or not?"

Mack's eyebrow rose in question.

Aiden reached into his pocket. He pulled out a sticky note and handed it over. It was an address. The same one they had been on the way to visit before they had been stopped by the men on the road.

"I know the sheriff's department is looking into Leighton being missing, where your truck is, who those guys were and where they went, plus who killed Bryce, but I never told Detective Winters about this." Aiden shrugged to himself. "I don't know why I didn't but, well, I didn't. Now, I want to still keep it from him because *I* want to see what's there first. And I want you to be there with me. What do you say?"

Mack should have said no—he should have said let law enforcement know they might have a lead—but he didn't.

"Are you sure you're up for it?"

Aiden didn't miss a beat.

"With you by my side, why wouldn't I be?"

THE WEATHER WAS NICE. The sun was out, a breeze kept coming and going and there was something blooming nearby that smelled like heaven. Willow Creek wasn't all bad. Minus the murder, road traps and mountains soaked in rain, Aiden was reminded why he'd picked the scenic little town to settle down in.

It had a charm to it. A cinematic filter that made the buildings, fields and good number of trees charming and warm.

He nodded to himself, still happy with his decision to open Riggs Consulting. Nashville wasn't bad, but Willow Creek felt more like his speed.

Again, minus the murder and mayhem.

"How many pain meds did you take?"

Aiden turned his head from the window and looked long at his driver.

Mack had one hand slung on the steering wheel and the other resting on the gearshift. It was automatic, not manual, and not needed, but the stance screamed smooth. So did the jeans, the black tee and the flannel button-up left open wide. Never mind the man's obvious good looks. He bet if he told Mack how attractive he was, Mack would snort and say he was talking too much. Then, since Aiden had grown fond of annoying the man, he would have come back and said something about how anyone talked more than the wall that was him.

But, since Aiden was genuinely curious about what Mack had asked, he delayed that urge.

"Excuse me?"

Mack smirked.

"I'm wondering if you snuck some extra pain meds before we left the house. You're humming."

"I was humming?"

"Mmm-hmm."

Aiden was taken slightly aback by that.

"I guess I was in the zone."

He motioned toward the scenery they were currently passing. It was a small field on the far side of town, in the opposite direction of downtown and in one of the few areas of town that Aiden hadn't actually visited before. Mack said he knew where the address was located but also hadn't visited the area. At least not in the last ten years or so.

"I usually don't get out to enjoy nice weather like this," Aiden added. "Forgetting to go outside can be a hazard of the job sometimes. It wasn't until Mrs. Cole got friendly that she and her husband started forcing me outside on occasion. She sometimes calls me her potted plant. She's afraid that if she forgets to give me sunlight, I'll wither."

"You have a Mrs. Cole, I have a Goldie," Mack mused. "Though I'm not a vampire like you. She worries that I don't eat enough." His big hand made a thud against his stomach for emphasis. "I don't know why. I think I'm pretty sturdy as it is."

Aiden's gaze betrayed him and cut down to Mack's torso.

Then it had the audacity to slide slowly up his chest. That black tee sure did fit nice.

"My eyes are up here, Potted Plant."

If Aiden had been the one driving, he would have wrecked them out at that. Mack's easy blues met his stare with a knowing look. Aiden's cheeks felt like fire.

"You're the one who slapped yourself and got my attention," he defended. "I'm not a potted plant *or* a vampire. I'm just a genius hacker who has a problem with hyperfocus and sleep schedules. I think that's pretty typical in my line of work."

Mack's eyes went back to the road ahead. He put his blinker on as they got closer to a small intersection. It had seen better days. No one was around in any direction, either.

"I don't think you're typical," Mack said after a moment. "I don't know about genius, though. Aren't they usually not so self-aware to claim that about themselves?"

Aiden rolled his eyes.

"Tell me your favorite color, the first job you ever had and your childhood best friend's name and I can have your Social Security number within ten minutes. Ten minutes after that and I'll know everything about Malcolm Atwood. A few minutes more and I could destroy you if I wanted, easy. If that's not genius, then give it another name."

Mack was quick.

"Stalker."

Aiden mocked offense. Too well. He slapped his hand against his chest to be dramatic. But he forgot he was actually hurt. Pain radiated from the hit. He winced. The truck slowed; Mack's concern did not.

"Are you okay?" He reached over like a mom trying to use her arm as a seat belt after having to slam on the brakes. Aiden sucked in a breath and nodded into an embarrassed laugh.

"I forgot that I fell down a mountain." He patted Mack's arm. "I'm good. Sorry for the scare."

Mack shook his head.

"This is why you need a bodyguard. I can't trust you by yourself."

There Aiden went again with his blush.

"You sure know how to make a client feel special." He swatted Mack's hand that was still hovering away. "I bet your girlfriend sure likes that sweet-talking."

It was another casual girlfriend comment, a way to try and annoy Mack. Yet Aiden would be lying if he said he didn't hold his breath a little waiting for a response.

And he sure got one.

Just not one he wanted.

"That's the address up ahead."

Aiden whipped his attention back to the windshield. They were driving along a narrow street, trees back on each side. Ahead of them was a two-story house. It had blue shutters, a tin roof and a hand-painted sign that hung from the mailbox. Aiden couldn't read it until they were parking at the curb next to it.

"'Bluebird Breeze,'" he read aloud. "This also sounds like a really bad name for a club."

Mack peered out past the sign to the house.

"I think it's a vacation rental." He pointed to the side of the house. "There are Realtor locks on the garage and front door. No cars in the driveway, either."

"I didn't know there were rental properties here in Willow Creek."

Mack nodded.

"Goldie said they've gotten more popular. There's a few

in the new neighborhoods. I didn't think there would be one out here. Last time I was out this way, the De Lucas lived here. There's no way that Mr. De Luca would let anyone name his home, former or current, after a bird, though."

"If this is a rental then maybe Leighton is staying here. Or was." Aiden didn't understand why Leighton would be at a rental in town without letting him know ahead of time. At least not why he would be there only to send an email and not come see Aiden in person. Riggs Consulting was downtown, but it wasn't that far. "Let's go," Aiden added.

He had no idea what they would find, but he was ready to look.

Mack must have been on the same wavelength.

"Let's go, then." He unbuckled his seat belt and then surprised Aiden by reaching across him for his buckle. Aiden froze as it came undone.

That cold thawed in an instant when Mack sat back in his seat.

"And, by the way, I don't have a girlfriend."

Then that bodyguard went and exited the car like he hadn't just set Aiden on fire.

Chapter Fifteen

No one was home. All the doors were locked, no sound or movement came from inside, and the number on the Bluebird Breeze sign went to an automated voice mail recording.

"I don't know what I expected, but this is disappointing." Aiden was peering through a window over the front porch. Mack could hear that disappointment with ease. Even though he didn't want to deal with Aiden's ex, he was also put off by their lead not going anywhere.

"We'll just have to get in touch with the owner and see if they can tell us who booked this place," Mack reasoned. He left off the fact that he preferred this safer option over potentially running into more trouble.

Aiden sighed.

"This won't do." Aiden walked past Mack and to the truck with purpose. He opened the back door and set up his bag on the seat. "We tried the usual way to get our information. Now we're going to try the impatient way."

Mack looked over the man's shoulder as he pulled out his laptop and powered it on. It didn't look as high-tech as the computers in Aiden's home office, but the thing responded to his touch faster than Mack's phone had ever worked for him.

"What are you doing?"

Aiden's fingers were lightning across the keys, and not for one second did his gaze seem to track their movements. Working with computers really was second nature for him. All Mack could do was watch as different windows popped up on the screen and were filled with words and code he didn't understand.

"Bluebird Breeze is listed on a rental website," Aiden said after a moment. "It's not a big-name website, though. It looks like it might be local to a realty place in Knoxville, not Nashville. Not that that means much, but I always feel more comfortable digging in someone else's sandbox when said sandbox is at least an hour or two away from me."

His clicking and typing accelerated. Mack became worried.

"Wait. What do you mean, digging in someone else's sandbox? What exactly are you doing?"

Aiden didn't break his stride.

"I can tell you now or when I'm done. I'll let you decide which is better for your grumpiness levels."

Mack rubbed along his jaw.

"What's the difference in you telling me now or when you're done if you still tell me?"

Aiden stopped for a moment to read something on the screen. Mack couldn't have deciphered it had you begged him.

"If I tell you now, you might feel inclined to stop me, and I'm not in the mood to do that," Aiden explained. "This will only make me sarcastic and want to fight you. Then you'll undoubtedly get grumpy, which will only make *me* grumpy and suddenly we're back in the truck not talking while a murder mystery and an unknown group of guys makes our lives miserable. *But*, if you wait until I'm done, all you can do is scold me with some kind of life lesson. And I won't fault you for that, because I'm sure I can use more of those."

He delivered the whole speech almost within one breath. Mack would have been impressed if he hadn't had to make a choice.

"You'd lose in a fight against me," he pointed out. "So just tell me when you're done."

He expected Aiden to say something snappy, but the computer whiz was all in on the task at hand. Since Mack didn't understand what was happening on the screen, he lowered his chin and stared down at the man typing.

Aiden was a man possessed. The focus was unlike any Mack had seen from him. His jaw was clenched, his eyes narrowed yet constantly shifting. There was a crease between his brows. One that, even in profile, was severe. The corners of his lips downturned and deepened. He could have been searching Google for a pound cake recipe, stealing nuclear launch codes or erasing every trace of Mack's life online...and Mack would have kept on staring.

Aiden Riggs was back in his element and, for the life of him, Mack couldn't look away.

For years Mack had spent his career protecting people. Business tycoons, children of important people, the wealthy, the unfortunate, the paranoid. He had spent countless hours standing in rooms, in hallways, sitting in cars, walking in darkness, scanning faces and watching shadows. He had met people so completely opposite him, so eerily similar and all temperaments in between. People who had achieved greatness, people who were aiming higher. People who wanted to be just like everyone else. People who never could be.

Mack had felt like he had met every kind of person, seen every kind of marvel on the job. However, watching Aiden use a laptop in the back seat of his truck, not understanding a thing he was doing, had Mack transfixed.

I like this, he realized.

Then, within another breath, he realized something else. *I like him.*

That was it. Aiden wasn't a rich socialite with a secret. He wasn't the son of a CEO at war with his rivals. He hadn't created a new drug that would revolutionize the world. He probably wouldn't ever change even part of the world.

Yet, with almost no effort, he had gone and changed Mack's.

It didn't make sense. There was no logic to it. He was just a man who had spent a week meeting bad luck at Mack's side.

But there it was.

Mack liked Aiden. He liked that he talked too much. He liked that he was annoying. He liked his clothes and his earring. He liked how he was short and had eyes that reminded him of trees. He liked that his family and Ray had fallen into step alongside him. He liked that he was obviously smart but didn't really push it home. He liked that he'd chased down a guy who had just attacked him, trying to help Mack. He liked that, even though Mack had been rude to him, that he'd still stood up for him against Detective Winters's snide comments.

He liked that Aiden had asked if he had a girlfriend.

And maybe the most telling thing was that Mack had liked telling him that he didn't.

Mack liking men wasn't the part that had him surprised—he had always liked men. It was the actually wanting to date someone, to be with someone, feeling that had been absent. Now, though, was the strange part. In the most opposite of romantic settings, he was having such an epiphany about himself. He wanted more, finally, and Mack wasn't mad about it.

"I married your mom despite her entire family being against it. The hassle of us dating was enough to make any hero in a romance movie run for the hills. But, you know what, son? I have a rule about the heart. If people say your love doesn't have a place in this world, the most fun thing you can do is prove them wrong by carving out your own little island for it. What's more fun than waving at angry people on shore from your own slice of paradise?"

His father's words had been imprinted in his memory like every face Mack had ever seen. It helped that he and the twins had grown up hearing the ill-fated love story between their parents every time one of them got wistful. Even though eventually their grandparents had softened and accepted their father.

Goldie had particularly liked the image of sunbathing on a beach, hand in hand with the love of your life while smiling slyly at a bunch of people miserable behind their binoculars on a dirt-covered shore.

That was too flowery for Mack, but he took the lesson to heart.

Like who you like. Love who you love. Don't fight it. Live better than those who want to try.

The sound of clicking keys penetrated Mack's trip down memory lane and brought him back to the present.

He liked Aiden, and he accepted that. But it didn't mean he was going to act on it.

They weren't on an island. They were in Willow Creek, and someone in town wanted Aiden. Until they could figure out who and why, Mack couldn't let himself be distracted.

The knife wound on his side seemed to wake up long enough to agree. He had been distracted by something trivial on his last job and had wound up in the hospital. If he gave in to something like his feelings?

Well, Mack didn't want another trip to the hospital, or worse, for Aiden.

So, he decided to stay quiet. To push everything down and focus on the task at hand.

A task that Aiden had finished. He pointed at the laptop screen with enthusiasm.

"And that's why I'm amazing," he exclaimed.

Mack cleared his throat.

"Does that mean it's time for you to explain it to me?"

Aiden laughed and nodded.

Then he became serious.

"So most of these smaller businesses have a habit of being a little lazy with their reservation systems. I found the last three guests who rented this place. The last one made a reservation a month ago, and it showed her checking in last week. See? Right here." He highlighted a line of text. "It was made under the name Taliyah Smith."

He turned to face Mack, eyebrow raised.

"I thought it would be Leighton. I don't know a Taliyah Smith."

Mack gritted his teeth.

"But I do." Aiden's eyebrow rose higher. Mack wasn't sure his answer was going to make that confusion go away. "Taliyah Smith is Jonathan Smith's sister."

Aiden's eyes widened.

"Jonathan Smith, as in—"

"—as in the man who attacked you in your car the night we met."

AIDEN WAS RIDING a new adrenaline surge.

It made watching Mack pace next to the truck while on

the phone that much more frustrating. He wanted some action. He wanted some progress. Instead all he could do was tap his foot and wait.

Not that that did him any good. Mack ended his call and sighed his way over.

"Jonathan is in the county jail but, before that, he'd been staying with his ex-girlfriend over on Mockingbird Drive. That's on the other side of town. The sheriff's department confirmed the story. At least, that's what Goldie found out."

Aiden crossed his hands over his chest. It hurt a little, but his confusion outweighed it.

"What about his sister, Taliyah?"

Mack shook his head.

"The reservation might be under her name, but she's with their dad out of the country. Has been for almost two weeks."

Aiden swung around and gave the Bluebird Breeze a deadly stare.

"So there's no reason for Taliyah to reserve this place, and there was no reason for her brother to stay here." He grumbled out sounds of frustration. He felt Mack's presence as the bodyguard stopped at his side. Normally the one to grumble, he was more graceful with his.

"Is there any connection between Leighton and Jonathan?"

The thought had already crossed his mind. Aiden had to shrug.

"As far as I know, I don't think so. Then again, other than a few phone calls and messages, I haven't exactly kept close tabs on Leighton since we broke up."

"Maybe Leighton was never here."

It was such a startlingly simple statement that Aiden

caught himself gaping at the man. Mack met his look with an even one.

"You might not know where Leighton is, but the fact is, you've never known where he was." Mack nodded to the house. "Just because we know Bryce Anderson couldn't have sent the email about Bellwether Tech to you from here doesn't mean Leighton was the one who for sure did. Bellwether Tech is a large company with many employees. Then there's the people who don't work there who might be holding a grudge or fear that place."

"Then what about Leighton's call to me?" Aiden postured. "The timing of that can't be coincidental, right? That's too much."

"But just because he called doesn't mean he was here. Or that the email came from him. Or that him not being able to be reached is for sure connected." He shrugged a little. "Coincidences are rare, but that doesn't mean they don't happen. Who knows, Leighton might have called you on the way to a vacation or some out-of-pocket trip with no service. He could be on a cruise."

"All right, you're reaching now, Mr. Bodyguard," Aiden said.

Mack held his hands out, palms raised in a giving-up gesture.

"I'm just saying, Mr. Potted Plant, that Leighton Hughes might be somewhere out there with no idea that you're looking for him."

Aiden opened his mouth. Then he closed it. Then he opened it again. He narrowed his eyes and locked in on the Bluebird Breeze. Was there a possibility that Leighton really had no connection to what was going on? That Bryce's murder, Bellwether Tech and the men who had tried to take him were their own circle in a graph while Leighton was the other with no overlapping in between?

Maybe Aiden was putting the two together. Maybe he was still touchy about what had happened. Maybe he still blamed Leighton, in some part, for his complicity. Maybe he still blamed himself for keeping quiet, and who better to shift that blame onto than the man who was beside him as he rose within the company?

"Ugh. This is too frustrating." Aiden balled his fists and shook them. "I'm going to try to get in," he decided. "This house might not be the smoking gun that leads us to Leighton, but its reservation is until the end of next week. So there might be something inside that makes this all make way more sense."

"We've already looked at all entrances," Mack reminded him, falling in step behind him as he charged to the front porch.

"Well, that was before we knew that this place had a weird connection to the chaos that's been our last week. That makes me more motivated to be detail oriented. Now, help me look again or be the silent, broody and attractive wall of bodyguarding prestige I know you can be and keep me covered."

Aiden peered through the windows as best he could now that he had a better reason to do a good job at looking. Before he'd been hesitant. Mainly for the fact that he'd worried he would be caught. Now he wanted to do the catching.

Mack did his job of being his cover and quietly followed Aiden around the house again. It's why he was able to hear Aiden's cry of excitement the second they both realized they had overlooked something on their first walk-around search.

"It's not actually locked!"

The Realtor lock on the back door was around the handle, but looking closer Aiden realized the latch wasn't all the way closed. Which meant at the moment it was just a complicated-looking door hanger.

Aiden reached out and tested the door itself. The knob turned, no issues.

Mack's hand wrapped around Aiden's wrist.

"And that's my cue." He pulled Aiden away from the door gently. "Stay here."

"The best you'll get is me standing behind you." Aiden hurried. His adrenaline was surging again. Whatever was inside would give them an answer they didn't already have. Whether that was being able to call this a dead end or that was them finding a lead that blew their amateur investigation right out of the water.

"You need to stay here," Mack tried again.

Aiden waved off the concern.

"You're supposed to guard my body, not tell my body to lounge on someone's back porch while yours goes inside. Now, let's hurry. I'm getting anxious over here."

Mack gave him one of his best sighs and then gave in. He let go of Aiden's wrist but only after angling in front of him.

Then he opened the back door, and the two of them went inside.

Bluebird Breeze was indeed empty. No one yelled at them in surprise, nothing jumped out at them as dangerous and there were no blatant clues that yelled out, "here's your answers" sitting around.

At least on the first floor.

Mack led Aiden up the stairs onto a small landing. It fed to three doors. The first was to a bedroom that looked untouched. The second was to a bathroom that seemed equally untouched.

The third was to the largest bedroom.

At first it seemed as uninteresting as the rest of the house, but there was more than the standard rental home furniture set.

On top of the desk situated along the wall when you walked in was a laptop. It was open and plugged in. There was a screen saver running, a spinning whirl of different-colored strands.

Mack stopped Aiden before his excitement could fully set in.

"The roadwork was a trap," he whispered. "This feels the same."

Aiden would have agreed, but something was already pulling him toward the laptop. A sticker was next to the trackpad. It was of the stars and moon.

Aiden knew it had cost almost ten dollars despite its small size.

He knew that because he'd been the one to buy it.

"You were wrong," Aiden said, stopping in front of the laptop, eyes still on the sticker. He felt Mack stop at his elbow.

"About what?"

Aiden woke up the machine by clicking the space bar.

The screen saver was replaced by the desktop. The background was a picture of two people enjoying a snowy landscape together, both bundled up and happily holding hands.

"This is Leighton's personal laptop," Aiden said, though he doubted he needed to explain that now. Standing next to Leighton in the picture was none other than Aiden.

"I guess he's connected after all."

Chapter Sixteen

The stars above him swirled electric blue and green. Mack watched as the LEDs scattered, faded and danced across the ceiling of the small room on a loop. The night was clear and probably had a much better view of actual stars, but Mack had been charmed by the fake ones inside Aiden's bedroom.

They made him feel like a little kid at an observatory. Sure, it wasn't the real thing, but there was a comforting magic to the show. It wasn't real, but that didn't mean it wasn't special.

Though he did suppress a chuckle when Aiden turned the night-light machine on without a second thought. Just as he had turned on the sound machine, handed Mack a vibrant floral quilt his grandmother had made him and put the llama-shaped pillow at the head of Mack's makeshift pallet on the floor.

These things were obviously part of Aiden's normal routine and, even though it was nowhere near what Mack was used to, Mack found some comfort in being included in it.

That comfort was an isolated event that didn't last as long as he would have liked. Less than an hour after the overhead lights had been switched off, Aiden let Mack know that sleeping wasn't going to happen for him.

"Are you awake?" he whispered, loud enough to hear over

the sound machine but soft enough that if Mack had been asleep he wouldn't have woken him. It was the most Aiden could have done to restrain himself if he had something on his mind. Which Mack had no doubt he did.

"Yeah. What's up?"

Mack was on the floor next to the bed and couldn't see Aiden from his point of view. Only the window and bedroom door. Still, he pictured Aiden rolling onto his side, a crinkle between his eyes, as he talked in his direction.

"I just can't get over a lot of things that happened this afternoon," he said. "I mean, it was too easy, right?"

Mack wasn't sure what Aiden had done to the laptop at Bluebird Breeze could be considered easy. Like he had done in the back seat of the truck, Aiden had used his computer skills to do several things Mack didn't understand. Instead of waiting until he was finished, though, Mack had insisted on a play-by-play.

That's how he had gotten a real-time rundown on Aiden's disbelief and pain.

"I just don't buy it," Aiden added on now. "Leighton is the bad guy? I mean, yeah, he wasn't the best boyfriend and he might have let a job confuse his principles, but a murderer?"

This wasn't a new train of thought from Aiden. He had said as much when they had first read the private messages between Leighton and Bryce Anderson. Messages that damned Leighton unconditionally.

"You read what he said yourself," Mack had to remind him. Though he made sure to keep his voice on the gentler side. "It was two pages of the two of them fighting about hiding the truth. Then Leighton told Bryce to meet him at the park. The same park he was killed at. Then Leighton went missing after that."

Aiden's face appeared over the side of the bed. His brow was indeed creased.

"But why? What was his motive?"

Mack propped his head up on the back of his arms.

"Bryce must have found out about the blackmail at Bellwether. Maybe instead of leaving like you did, Bryce wanted to make it public."

Aiden's face twisted. The shadows made his expression look even more severe.

"So Bryce was being a hero and, instead of me helping, I left opportunity for my ex to be the villain."

Aiden said it in his usual sarcastic way, but Mack knew there was hurt there.

"Your choice to trust Leighton doesn't mean any of this is your fault. In fact, if you had tried to go public first, who's to say you wouldn't have ended up with two bullets to the gut?"

Mack had meant to be comforting. Aiden disappeared from view with a loud, long sigh.

"I still can't believe Leighton did this," he tried again. "Not only did he have the conversation saved on a laptop, which he left at a rental, by the way, but his laptop was also left unlocked. No password. No PIN. Nothing."

Aiden's head appeared over the edge of the bed again.

"I know I've always been a lot more conscious of cyber-security than most since I kind of have a knack for hacking, but there's no way Leighton left his personal laptop that unprotected. It makes no logical, professional or tactical sense."

Mack couldn't argue with that. The best he could do was offer a possible reason why the error in judgment had been made.

"In stressful situations, some people don't make the best decisions. Maybe he was rushing."

"Rushing to what?" Aiden hurriedly tacked on. "There was nothing else in that cabin. Just his laptop. Did he run in, plug it in, steal the Wi-Fi, then leave to…"

The shadows of his hands waved through the air. He wanted Mack to fill in the blanks.

Mack already had a theory for that.

"He could have been busy trying to get you." Mack's dislike of Leighton Hughes had tripled in size in the last six hours. The more he thought about him, the larger it would grow.

"You really think that's why he called me? He wanted to lure me somewhere?"

"It would make sense."

"Then why not answer when I called him back? Did he decide to change tactics to stay off the grid? But, if he did that, then why send the email? He had to have known I'd track the location and show up at the rental house. If that's what he wanted me to do, then why include Jonathan Smith in the plan?"

Aiden was talking fast again. Barely a breath in between questions.

"Maybe he got impatient. You did go to a party before finding the location of the email."

Aiden didn't immediately respond. After a few moments, Mack almost sat up to check on the man, but then the sheets rustled and the sound of him shifting preceded to Aiden getting off the bed. He had his pillow under one arm and his blanket under the other.

Mack started to sit up, confused, but Aiden didn't react to it. Instead he threw his pillow down on the floor. He lay down right next to Mack.

"But hear me out," Aiden started, not at all addressing his change in location. "The only connection we have be-

tween Leighton and Jonathan Smith is that Leighton's laptop was found in the rental that Jonathan's sister reserved.
That in itself seems way too complicated to make sense
if they are indeed connected. Who made the reservation?
And why? If Leighton wanted to kill Bryce, isn't that too
many unnecessary hoops to jump through? And, a better
question, why the heck didn't Leighton kill Bryce in Nashville? Why travel to a small town where the body would
immediately be noticed? How in the double heck does *any*
of this make sense?"

Mack was still sitting up.

He only had one question currently.

"Why—why are you on the floor?"

Aiden didn't skip a beat.

"I was getting tired of talking to you without seeing you,
and I doubted you'd take my offer to come up and stay on
the bed," he explained. "Even though it's a king-size beast
that takes up more than half of this dang room. When you
said you'd be next to me until Leighton or those guys were
found, I believed you. When you insisted on lying on this
hard floor with only some sheets and a quilt, I thought you
might be bluffing."

Mack didn't know what to do for a moment. They were
simply talking about current events. Right? He cleared his
throat and leaned back onto his pillow. There wasn't a lot
of floor space before two grown men were sharing the area.
Now Mack could feel Aiden's side dangerously close to his.

"Usually my clients aren't as relaxed as you," Mack said,
shifting a little to create some more room. "They're not this
talkative, either."

Aiden snorted.

"Don't act like you don't enjoy me. I'm a delight."

Mack took back his own trademark snort.

"You're confident. I'll give you that."

The stars overhead started their loop over. Two grown men lying under a child's night-light. How had his week home turned into this?

"What are you going to do now?" Mack laced his hands over his chest. The stars disappeared from his mind and were replaced by thoughts of the next week.

After finding the conversations between Leighton and Bryce on the laptop, Mack had called the sheriff's department. He had been hoping to get a different detective but knew that Winters would be the lead.

And he had been.

Though he'd been uncharacteristically quiet, the detective had said that they would get to the bottom of everything. Mack had expected suspicion, a scolding, too. Instead Winters had asked very little and said that he would be in touch.

His uncle had been the same way. When a case became too complicated, it was easier to let it go than dig in and hold on.

It's why no Atwood child could stand a Winters.

"I feel like I'm being forced into a waiting game," Aiden finally answered. "The only way to win at one of those is to do the one thing you can—wait. But that thought makes my skin crawl."

Mack could feel the breath Aiden let out.

"If Leighton is the big bad wolf and he killed Bryce, I'd like to find out exactly what Bryce knew."

"You think that it might not be Bellwether Tech related?"

Aiden didn't say anything for a bit. Mack turned his head to check on the man. His eyes were closed. He kept them that way when he answered.

"I think that Bellwether Tech might have more than the

one skeleton in the closet. And maybe it's finally time that I do something about it."

Mack waited for a follow-up explanation. He didn't get one. The quiet sneaked back into the room and filled the spaces in between. Mack stayed just where he was as he watched Aiden lie still. It wasn't until sometime later that he realized the man had fallen asleep.

And, some time after that, Mack did, too.

AIDEN WOKE UP on the bed the next morning and had the time of his life trying to remember how he got there. He rubbed the sleep from his eyes, scoured every inch with his gaze after that, tried to recall the last thing he remembered and still came up with nothing.

One second he had been talking with Mack on the floor, and the next it was morning and he was snuggled up on his llama pillow.

"I didn't even drink," he breathed out to himself. He must have been more tired than he had realized to pass out that soundly.

Aiden peered over the side of the bed. His grandmother's quilt was folded neatly against the wall. Mack was nowhere to be found.

The smell of something delicious, however, was.

Aiden grabbed his cell phone off the charger and followed the scent down the hall.

What a sight he was met with.

Mack was wearing a dark blue tee, black pants and the llama-print apron Aiden had been gifted on his last birthday. He was standing at the stove, two skillets going at once. There was bacon in one and eggs in the other.

Aiden was immediately suspicious.

"Since when did I have food?"

Mack's professional bodyguard skills must have already been working. He didn't turn in surprise at Aiden's sudden appearance. Instead he shook his head.

"Unless you count junk food, you definitely didn't," he answered. "Lucky for us that Goldie was coming to town. She dropped these, and those, off."

He pointed around his arm to a box on the eat-in kitchen table.

"They're doughnuts from Sue and Mae's. She didn't know which you might like, so she got a spread."

Aiden's mouth was watering right alongside his chest filling with some warmth.

"No wonder you Atwoods are so popular in town. You're good hosts even when you're in other people's homes."

Mack grabbed a fork and went to flip a piece of bacon.

"Don't lump me in with the twins. This is the first time I've even cooked for someone other than them."

Aiden was glad that the bodyguard wasn't facing him. His face heated as if he was the one slaving over the stove.

Mack Atwood was cooking for him.

That was an achievement he had unlocked without realizing it was one he had wanted.

"Go wash up, and it should be ready when you're done," Mack added.

Domestic Mack Atwood.

It wasn't a bad look, that was for sure.

"Yes, sir."

Aiden washed his face, brushed his teeth and exchanged his pajama pants for joggers. He combed his hair, decided it needed some gel and went back to the bathroom to style it. Mack had gone through the trouble to cook; Aiden should at least go through the trouble of looking his best.

He nodded to himself, thinking that was a normal response to someone cooking for him, when his cell phone started vibrating in his pocket.

The caller ID stopped him in his tracks.

That's when he remembered something he didn't even realize he had forgotten.

He answered on the second ring.

"You thought I'd forgotten about you, didn't you?"

Jenna Thompson was as chipper as ever. In fact, the only thing that Aiden believed had changed about the woman since he had last seen her at Bellwether was her location. Instead of being in Nashville, she was settling onto the couch in Aiden's living room.

Aiden had been surprised by her call. Mack had gone quiet. He pulled a chair to a spot across the couch for Aiden to sit in. Then he stood next to it. He no longer had his apron on, but there was a spatula in his hand. If Aiden hadn't been so thrown by Jenna's call and then appearance, he would have teased the man.

Instead his focus zoomed in on the younger woman, who was all smiles.

"It was me who forgot," Aiden admitted. "So much has happened that my mind let it slip that I'd called you last week."

It was true. On both counts. Over the phone Jenna had told him she would call him back once she asked around about Leighton. She hadn't.

"But, even if you'd forgotten, you didn't have to come all this way," Aiden tacked on. "Another call would have been just fine."

At this Jenna's smile faltered. She glanced over at Mack, then back to Aiden.

"Oh, yeah, I'm sorry," he said. He held his hand out toward Jenna and did a late introduction. "Mack, this is Jenna Thompson. We worked together at Bellwether Tech. She's the lead assistant in the IT department. Basically one of the low-key superheroes of the department. I called her last week to see if she knew where Leighton was, since she usually knows everything there is to know in the department."

"It's the business," she commented.

"A business that I don't think many people would have done as well as you in."

Jenna waved through the compliment. Mack was still silent. His eyes were fastened to Jenna. Aiden continued the introduction.

"And Jenna, this is Mack Atwood. He's my—"

Aiden stopped middeclaration.

While he and Mack had used the term *bodyguard* several times, the fact of the matter was, Mack wasn't a true hired hand. They had no documents between them, no signatures or payments. Nothing other than verbal agreements that, if Aiden was being honest, he wasn't sure were completely sincere. It was something he had already thought about the night before when he couldn't fall asleep.

Mack was his bodyguard until they actually got down to the details. And if Mack didn't feel the obligation to be one? Would he leave? Would he end their partnership and head back into his quiet world at the Atwood estate before jetting off to a new job somewhere else?

Aiden didn't think Mack would simply abandon him, yet he hadn't been able to stop the wayward worry that it might happen if they really got down to what being his bodyguard really meant.

So, using the title out loud now to Jenna had him at a crossroad of crisis.

One that the man at the center of his worries pulled him out of with an absolutely bombshell of a redirect.

"I'm his boyfriend."

Chapter Seventeen

The words came out before Mack had realized he was going to say them. Once they were out there, though, Mack didn't take them back.

Aiden also didn't try to undo them.

Though Mack knew the man had been caught off guard. His cheeks were a dark shade of red. Even his ears were turning.

Jenna looked between them.

"Your boyfriend?" Her voice had gone a little flat.

Mack didn't like that.

He didn't like her, and he wasn't exactly sure why.

Maybe it had to do with the fact that she was from Bellwether and, like Aiden had said, instead of just calling she had shown up at his home in Willow Creek.

Regardless of the reason, Mack had wanted a different claim to Aiden. A way to show the woman that he was invested in Aiden. That he was on his side and not going anywhere.

Thankfully, Aiden played along despite him being flustered.

"He's my boyfriend," he repeated.

"You actually caught us about to have breakfast." Mack placed his hand on Aiden's shoulder. His thumb was resting on the back. Mack put a little pressure into it. He hoped Aiden understood that he wanted the woman to explain why she was there sooner rather than later.

Aiden must have gotten the hint. He placed his hand over Mack's and patted it once.

"What can we do you for, Jenna? Did you really come all the way to Willow Creek to see me?"

Jenna's resting smile went flat, too. She sighed.

"Actually, I came because of our CEO. Not because of you."

Mack felt Aiden tense beneath his hand.

"What?"

Jenna pulled a card out of the purse on her lap. She handed it to Aiden.

"He was contacted by this detective from the sheriff's department here about Bryce's homicide investigation. He's there right now with his wife. I came down separately with Leighton's work laptop, as they instructed. Once I dropped that off, I realized I had been rude and never gotten back to you, so I thought I'd reach out."

Mack spied the business card over Aiden's shoulder. It belonged to Detective Winters. So he was actually investigating.

"I was also asked about Leighton's latest work activities," she continued. "I don't think I was much help, though. Other than to apologize for not getting back to you faster, I wanted to tell you in person that I have no idea where Leighton is or what's going on. I wanted to be helpful. I'm sorry." She glanced once again at Mack. He didn't know the woman but could tell she wanted some privacy from him.

Tough cookies.

Mack wasn't going to leave.

"Mack, could you go grab Jenna here a cup of coffee?" Aiden patted his hand again. "Please?"

He wanted privacy because he knew that's what Jenna wanted.

Mack held in his grumble.

If they had been in a public place, he wouldn't have moved from his spot, but since the kitchen was only a few feet away, he relented.

"Sure thing." He didn't bother to hide the tightness in his tone. Jenna, at least, seemed to be grateful. She was smiling again when Mack excused himself.

As soon as Mack was in the kitchen, he heard Jenna start up. Whatever she wanted to say, she had a lot of that something. She also kept that something on the quiet side. Mack could hear her talking but not the words themselves. It frustrated him. He was unkind to the coffee maker as he smashed the On button.

Why were so many Bellwether Tech people showing up in Willow Creek? He understood the investigation, but there seemed to be too many key players from Aiden's past moving around them.

If Detective Winters had called in the CEO and his wife, did that mean he had found out about the Bellwether blackmail?

The coffee started to brew. Mack used the sound to cover his backpedaling to the kitchen doorway. From his vantage point, he could only see Aiden's face. That was enough for him to know that whatever Jenna was saying had captured 110 percent of his attention. He had that crinkle between his eyebrows and was leaning forward slightly.

Mack wondered how much Jenna knew. If she was the head assistant of the IT department, didn't that mean she would have dealt directly with Leighton, Bryce and Aiden when everything had happened with the blackmail? Could she really not have known?

He backtracked to his phone on the table. He wasn't some pro hacker, but he could google Jenna's name to see if anything popped up. So far he had only seen the group picture with Aiden and Bryce after they won a bid. Everything else about Bellwether Tech had been text articles. He was good with faces, but names had never been his forte. If Jenna's name had been in an article, Mack might have missed it.

The sound of the coffee dripping continued as Mack brought up his phone's search engine. It filled the cup and stopped by the time he hit Enter on "Jenna Thompson, Bellwether Technologies."

The smell of the freshly brewed drink filled his nose as he clicked on the first article in the results.

It was about the newly appointed head of the IT department before Aiden's time. Her name was among the list of other hires, Leighton and Bryce included. There were two pictures. The first at the top of the story was of the department sitting around at their cubicles. Mack recognized Leighton at one desk, Bryce, too, farther away from the camera. The second picture was buried in the middle of the article.

It was of an older man in a suit posing with the group.

It was a man he recognized.

Every sense Mack had stopped. Every thought evaporated into the blank nothingness that had exploded around him.

He couldn't see or speak or hear or smell or figure out if his thoughts had stopped or were just going so fast he couldn't see them.

It was how Aiden was able to get in front of him without alerting Mack at all.

"Mack? Are you okay?" His voice broke through the nothingness as he took Mack's face in his hands. "What's wrong?"

Mack looked down into Aiden's eyes.

The forest.

All at once his thoughts shifted.

"You've never said the CEO's name. I've never seen his picture."

Aiden's eyebrow rose. He dropped his hands.

"I guess I haven't, but why does that matter?"

Mack held up his phone and pointed to the picture.

"Because I've seen him before. He was younger, but it's definitely him."

"Who?"

Mack didn't have to look again. He was, after all, a man with his own superpower. Someone who, once he saw a face, remembered it forever. The man had aged, but he was the same.

"This is the man who I'm sure killed my dad."

"What?" Aiden's gaze dropped to the picture while his pitch went sky-high in disbelief. "This is the man you saw running away from the fire? The client your dad reported? How is that possible?"

Mack was about to ask how Aiden knew about the warehouse fire, but Jenna walked into the kitchen, face blank.

"You're Malcolm Atwood?"

He couldn't read her expression. Aiden took his hand.

"Do you know him?" he asked.

She didn't answer right away.

She didn't get a chance to do it at all.

Someone knocked on the front door.

All three of them turned to face it.

The knock came again.

Mack addressed Jenna first.

"Was anyone else supposed to come here with you?"

She shook her head, but she didn't say no. Her eyes narrowed on the door as another knock sounded. Aiden squeezed Mack's hand.

"It could be the twins? Or Ray?"

"They would have warned me. Stay—"

Someone was unlocking the front door. Aiden shared a look with Mack. It clearly said that no one should have had a key to his home.

Mack was in the hallway in a flash. The sunlight that streamed in through the open door met the hardwood in front of him. It took him too long to realize what he was seeing.

Who he was seeing.

"You," he breathed out.

Leighton didn't take his time.

He pulled his gun up and shot.

AIDEN WAS GLAD THAT, for once, he was slow. While Mack, and even Jenna, had hurried into the hallway from the kitchen, Aiden had lagged. Like he had bad internet, his actions had taken a few beats too long. His software was processing too much, and his hardware couldn't keep up.

That's why he had one foot in the hallway and one in the kitchen when Leighton raised his arm.

Whatever lag Aiden had just experienced resolved itself. His hands wrapped around Mack's arm, and he pulled him backward with everything he had.

It might have been enough.

Mack yelled out just as Jenna screamed. Aiden didn't know where she went, but he and Mack stumbled back into the kitchen, nearly falling to the tile in the process. Mack was quicker than that, though. He spun with their momentum, keeping them both on their feet while also pushing them back farther into the room.

He shook Aiden off him and was going right back to the hallway in one fluid motion.

"Mack!" Aiden yelled, but he had other things to do.

Leighton appeared in the doorway and crashed into the wall that was Mack Atwood.

Another shot sounded. Aiden shouted as one of the cabinets along the wall seemed to explode. He couldn't help but close his eyes and shrink in response.

When he opened them again, he saw Mack connect a fist against Leighton's side. The other man bowed at the power.

He didn't drop the gun.

Mack had one hand around his wrist, struggling to get control.

Then Jenna threw a lamp.

It was cheap and had been sitting on every living room side table Aiden had ever had, but it was made of glass and, apparently if thrown hard enough, it was mighty all its own. It hit Leighton's shoulder and shattered. The impact and aftermath threw off the tussling men's balances. Leighton went one way and Mack the other.

Jenna had wanted to help, but she had made an opening that only hurt.

Leighton hit the hallway wall; Mack hit the kitchen floor.

There was only a few feet of space between them, but Aiden knew the problem as soon as the others did, too.

Mack wouldn't be able to get to Leighton or cover before Leighton had the time to pull the trigger again.

That's when Aiden made a split-second decision.

He couldn't stop Leighton, but he could move enough to make a difference for Mack.

So, he did.

Every muscle in Aiden's body seemed to come alive. One second he was standing off to the side, terrified. In the next he was standing in front of Leighton and his gun, arms wide and sorry to no end that the last thing he would see wouldn't be the man on the floor behind him.

"No!" he heard Mack yell.

But it was too late.

The gunshot was so loud Aiden was sure the entire world could hear it.

His eyes closed on reflex. He braced for pain.

It didn't come.

At least it wasn't his.

Aiden opened his eyes. Leighton crumpled to the ground. The gun in his hand hit the floor and skidded in front of the refrigerator to their right.

Aiden didn't understand.

Why was Leighton on the ground? Why was there blood pooling from his side? Why wasn't it Aiden?

Two large hands wrapped around Aiden's arms. They spun him around.

It was Mack.

He was saying something, but Aiden couldn't make it out.

There was blood on Mack's arm.

"Are you hurt?" Aiden heard the absolute panic in his question. Mack seemed to be taken aback by it, too. His eyes widened.

"I'm fine," Mack said. "Are you? Aiden. Are you?"

Aiden nodded.

It must have been enough for the bodyguard. His expression softened.

"I want you to stand right here. Don't turn around, okay?"

Aiden nodded again.

"Jenna? Keep the gun on him for a second, okay?" Jenna yelled from the other room that she understood.

Was she the one who had shot Leighton? Aiden had a lot of questions. Instead of asking any of them, he decided to listen to Mack.

He stood still and he didn't turn around.

Chapter Eighteen

The deputies from the sheriff's department didn't arrive until half an hour after three people had been shot inside Aiden's home. The ambulance was slow, too. The twins were faster. Goldie screeched up in her small four-door first. She took Jenna and was off to Harper Faith like the mama she was. Finn came in right after. He had to slow down, because Leighton had needed all the help he could get, even while being moved to the truck.

Finn wasn't a doctor, but working in the medical field had taught him a thing or two, so he became their make-shift EMT in the back of Mack's truck. Aiden became his assistant, as much as Mack wished he didn't have to deal with any of it. They had run out of options, though. Mack refused to let Leighton die in Aiden's home. The memory of the fight alone was bad enough.

But Mack needed to drive like the true local he was and get everyone to the hospital as quickly and safely as possible, so Aiden sat in the back seat doing the best he could with triage using a roll of paper towels. Because, as he later told Mack in a quiet voice, he'd been worried about staining Mack's truck.

They all made it in good time. Ray had lit the beacon ahead of them, and ER nurses and staff had been waiting for their arrival. Leighton had gone to surgery, Jenna had been taken to a room and when Mack was getting his graze cleaned in one of the emergency room cubes, he found out why the response to his call had been so slow.

"Caleb Holloway and his wife were run off the road over on the Danberry Bridge," Ray explained.

Caleb Holloway. The CEO of Bellwether Tech. The man Mack had seen running away from the warehouse fire, despite no one believing him.

"Both were sent to Nashville in critical condition," he continued. "I think the wife is being airlifted somewhere else up north."

His face was drawn. Severe. Mack didn't understand why. Only Aiden and Jenna had heard his realization about the connection between the CEO and his father's death. He hadn't had time to tell anyone else yet.

"Who ran them off the road?" Mack asked. "Was it Leighton?"

Ray shook his head.

"Whoever did it wrecked the truck and took off before anyone could respond." His expression only soured further. "Mack. It was your truck. The one that you were driving when those guys stopped you and Aiden."

They let that sit for a few moments.

"I guess Detective Winters and I are going to have a lot to talk about when he gets here," he said.

Aiden came back with Finn then. They had gone to his office for some extra work shirts. Both had been covered in blood. None of it theirs. There were still some on their pants, but it would have to sit for a while. No sooner had they walked into the cube did deputies start coming in. Detective Winters wasn't far behind.

"I'll take you to Aiden's house," Mack had told the detective. When the man didn't like the directive, Mack made sure his bottom line was clear. "Aiden stays here with Marigold and Finn."

The detective must have been really stressed. He had thrown his hands up and said he didn't care. If Mack had been on better terms with him, he would have felt some sympathy. Instead the detective followed him to Aiden's, where Mack walked him through everything that had happened.

"Jenna had a small handgun in her purse. After she threw the lamp, she pulled it out and shot. I was able to grab Leighton's gun after that." Mack felt rage course through him. His hand fisted at his side. It took effort to unclench his jaw to speak again. "If it wasn't for her, this would have been a lot worse."

The detective rubbed the back of his neck.

"Looks to me like if the assistant of the year wasn't packing, Mr. Riggs sure wouldn't be walking around. I guess he decided to play bodyguard, huh?"

Mack had to double down on his effort to keep his rage from coming out.

The detective pulled his phone out and read a text.

He cussed low.

"This entire thing is a whole cluster, and I'm not even sure where that cluster starts." He opened another text. Mack could see the sheriff's contact name as the sender. "But I can only do so many things at once."

He looked down at the blood on the floor. He sighed.

"Come to the department tomorrow. Bring Bodyguard Riggs. I'll keep tabs on Ms. Thompson and Leighton Hughes. I can't help thinking that half of our problems are because your group keeps nosing into problems that aren't yours. Go home tonight and stay there. Don't give us any more headaches. Okay?"

Mack decided then to sit on the fact that Caleb Holloway was the same man Detective Winters's uncle had insisted was innocent all those years ago.

"We'll try our best to avoid all the bad guys you're having trouble catching," Mack snapped back. "Just try to do a better job, okay?"

Detective Winters looked like he was sizing Mack up.

Then he must have decided against doing anything more.

He left Aiden's house and took the last of the deputies with him.

Mack looked back at the blood on the hardwood.

That could have been Aiden's.

It was Mack's turn to cuss. He didn't do it low.

After that things became calm in comparison. Jenna, who had taken the first shot to her arm, was resting. Ray said he would keep an eye on her during his night shift and told the Atwood siblings and Aiden in no uncertain terms to go home. Mack was more inclined to listen to him over Detective Winters. The four made their way to the Atwood home as the sun set. Finn made sure they ate some food, Goldie prepared the guest bedroom and when Aiden insisted he didn't want to be a burden by staying, the twins refused to let him leave.

"We know what you did for us," Goldie said. Her eyes cut over to Mack. "You didn't have to be his shield, but you still did it. Even if it didn't come to that, you put yourself in harm's way to protect one of us. Which makes you one of us. So, you're staying here tonight. Finn will have some clothes that should fit you, and we have extra toothbrushes in the guest bathroom. Anything else, you ask."

Mack had waited for Aiden to fight that again, but he

relented with a quiet thank-you. The twins excused themselves to their rooms. Mack was supposed to guide Aiden to the guest bedroom, but he didn't. Instead he took him right to his room.

He shut the door behind them.

It was the first time they had been alone since that morning.

Mack was having a hard time speaking.

So, he didn't.

He closed the space between himself and Aiden in less than two steps. He closed the space between their lips even faster.

Mack hadn't meant for the kiss to be as hard as it was, but there was no denying its force. All the anger at Leighton, at himself, at Aiden for uselessly putting himself in danger came out. It pushed his lips against Aiden's with a sense of relief pulsing through.

He was angry that Aiden could have been hurt, or worse, because of him.

He was angry that Aiden had gone through so much in the last week.

He was angry that he hadn't done more for him. That he hadn't said more.

But Aiden was okay. He was here. Mack could see him, could feel him.

He softened the kiss and then broke it.

If Aiden reciprocated, he didn't know.

Mack was just glad he was there.

He rested his forehead against Aiden's and spoke in a whisper.

"My favorite color is green, my first job was a cashier at the dollar store and my childhood best friend's name is Raymond Dearborn."

Mack felt Aiden's brow crinkle beneath him.

"Huh?"

Mack took a moment before he stepped back from the man.

"Yesterday you said you could destroy me if you knew those things about me," he explained. "I'm here to tell you that you have my full permission to do that. You, Aiden Riggs, can destroy me but, please, promise me that you will never, ever do that again."

When Aiden didn't respond, Mack took his chin in his hand.

"Promise me," Mack repeated. "Please."

Aiden's voice was soft, but Mack still felt it in his chest.

"I promise."

THE SHOWER HAD no chance of waking Aiden up. Simply for the fact that Mack had already done a thorough job of it.

Aiden was wrapped in a towel and staring at the mirror. It was partially fogged up, but he could still see how overwhelmed he was written right there in his reflection. So much had happened within the span of a few hours. So much that he had begun to feel numb somewhere between rushing Leighton into the hospital to watching Mack leave the hospital with Detective Winters.

Aiden had just stopped feeling.

Whether it was because everything was too much or a defense mechanism, he wasn't sure. He had simply decided to go with the flow with as little resistance as possible. He figured maybe that way he could make it to the end of whatever was going on.

Then Mack had kissed him.

It was like their roles had reversed. Aiden felt Mack's emotion, heard it, too, and watched as the quiet man of muscle and brawn had sunk a bit. He hadn't commanded Aiden to stay safe. He had been begging. And Aiden had barely reacted. He had agreed, sure, but when Mack stepped away from him and directed him to the bathroom, Aiden had simply gone.

He'd even taken the bag that Mack had packed for him at his house without a word.

That bag was resting on the counter. Aiden let his hand drop and opened it to see exactly what Mack had thought to take.

Only seconds rummaging inside it and Aiden knew two things without a doubt.

One, Mack hadn't just thrown the first thing he saw into the bag. He had taken his time and been thoughtful about it. He had listened to Aiden when he had been rambling about his favorite sleep clothes, he had made sure to get the right toiletries, including his hair gel, and even his box of accessories had made it inside, his favorite ring on top. Mack had also packed his favorite joggers and several carefully folded shirts that had been hanging in his closet. But, the item that really got Aiden was the one he had been most self-conscious about when Mack had first come into his room.

He had packed Aiden's night-light that projected stars.

Aiden ran his finger along the power cord. It was wrapped carefully around the base.

That's when Aiden came across the second thing he knew without any doubt.

He kept the realization to himself as he changed and went back to the bedroom.

Mack had a comforter and pillow in his arms. He nodded to the bed.

"You sleep here, and I'll take the floor. I already found a place to set up the stars, and the sound machine can go—"

"I want you to stay with me." The words came out strong. True. Aiden went to the bed. "Here, I mean. Not on the floor."

He slid under the covers and closed his eyes. His heartbeat was racing, but he felt oddly calm despite it.

Mack didn't respond. At least not in words. A few minutes passed before Aiden felt the bed dip down a little next to him. The sheets and comforter rustled as he settled beneath them. A soft click sounded. Aiden opened his eyes just as the stars from his projector scattered across the ceiling.

He watched them for a moment.

Then Aiden rolled over to face Mack.

He wanted to say a lot, to shower the man in thank-yous and I'm sorrys. Tell him that he liked him, that he was glad he'd met him and wanted to see him a lot in the future. He wanted to ask him about his feelings, not for him but for everything. He wanted to know his favorite song and his most exciting stories from his job. He wanted to ask where the baby pictures were, if his college experience had been fun and what the Atwood patriarch had been like.

Aiden wanted more of Mack, and he had every urge to start right then and there to get it.

But, when he rolled onto his side, Mack was already there staring across his pillow at him.

All questions and conversation ended right there before they ever started.

Aiden didn't want to talk anymore.

He placed his hand on Mack's chest. He placed his lips on his next.

Unlike the kiss earlier, this one was soft. Calm.

Aiden hoped it soothed Mack of every one of his troubles.

And Mack took the kiss like Aiden had earlier. He was still until Aiden pulled away.

For a moment, he worried that he had misunderstood. That Mack hadn't wanted to be this close.

That worry didn't last long.

Mack wrapped his arms around Aiden and pulled him closer. This kiss went deep. After that there was no more one-sided anything.

Aiden responded to his lips with a ferocity that he felt in every part of his body. His hands slid up Mack's chest and grabbed onto his shoulders. One went farther up and wound into his hair. It acted as an anchor as Mack deepened their kiss even more. His tongue parted Aiden's lips, and together they started to explore each other's mouths.

Mack tasted like peppermint.

Aiden wanted more.

Apparently so did Mack.

When Aiden started to pull up the edge of Mack's shirt, Mack broke their kiss long enough to throw it off himself. It disappeared into the darkness of the rest of the room. Aiden's disappeared next.

With a new area to explore, Mack did just that.

He took Aiden's wrists, pinned them and him against the bed and rolled over on top. Mack straddling him was a sight to see. It was, however, a feeling that Aiden didn't think he would ever forget.

He took the small space of time where their lips weren't touching to do his own exploration.

Aiden trailed his hands across Mack's bare chest.

No doubt, Michelangelo would have sold his soul to sculpt such a man.

Aiden was about to say so when he came to the bandage on his side. It was small but blaringly there.

Mack must have sensed the mood had paused. He looked down as Aiden lightly touched the spot next to it.

"It doesn't hurt," Mack said. His voice was soft, a whisper. Aiden wasn't sure he trusted it. If Mack was in pain, would he really admit it?

Mack lowered himself. The kiss he gave Aiden next was brief. He ran his hand along his jaw, his thumb trailing across Aiden's lips next. Mack's gaze stayed there as he spoke again.

"But, if it did, would you distract me if I asked you to?"

Aiden was already 100 percent in, but the smirk that grew along Mack's face sealed every deal there ever was or would be.

He nodded.

"I'll see what I can—"

Mack cut him off with another kiss that spoke to every inch of Aiden's body.

There was no more talking after that.

Chapter Nineteen

Mack woke up warm.

The man lying against his chest was only partially the reason. Sunlight was pouring through the window over the bed. He'd slept through the night. Soundly, too.

Aiden shifted against him. Mack readjusted the arm he had around him. Aiden tensed but didn't say anything for a few minutes. Finally, Mack chuckled.

"Let me know when you're done pretending to be asleep and I can tell you good morning," he said.

Aiden pulled the covers up to cover the bottom half of his face. He spoke against Mack's chest.

"I wasn't pretending to be asleep," he defended. "I thought you might be and didn't want to wake you. It's called being considerate."

Mack smiled and ruffled Aiden's hair. The contact only seemed to make his new anxiety worse. He did a little shimmy away from Mack's hand and tried to put distance between them.

Mack didn't allow it. He let Aiden put his head on the other pillow but kept his hold around him.

"No need to be shy now," Mack pointed out. "So why don't we lie here for a little longer before we get the Atwood twin interrogation that's surely waiting outside that door?"

Aiden met his gaze with wide eyes.

"What do you mean, the Atwood twin interrogation?" He lowered his voice but the panic was clear. "You don't think they know about us—about what we—" His cheeks turned a fun shade of red as he motioned between them.

Mack struggled to keep a straight face.

"I think the fact that you didn't sleep in the guest room might make them suspect that something happened," he stated, matter-of-fact. "But Goldie peeking in here an hour ago to check on us and seeing you in my arms might have been the real tip-off."

Mack couldn't help it. He smiled as Aiden's shade of red deepened. He pulled the covers up and over his head.

"Oh, my God." Aiden did another little shimmy in place. "How embarrassing. I'm so sorry."

He could feel Aiden try to pull away again, so Mack did his own pulling. He moved the covers and threw them down the bed. After their shower the night before, Aiden had changed into the sleep clothes Mack had packed, but now you would have thought with the way he scurried for the sheets that he was as naked as a jaybird.

"Why are you apologizing? It's not like you tricked me into this. I think it was me who actually started it."

Aiden slapped his hands on his face to hide.

"But I'm the one who told you to stay with me in bed."

Mack really couldn't help it this time. He let out a boom of laughter. Aiden peeked through his fingers at him.

"If you want to get technical, I'm the one who brought you to my room first."

Aiden didn't say anything. Mack sighed.

"If I regretted last night, I would have already left. Even if this was my room."

Aiden lowered his hands.

"What about the twins? Aren't they going to give you a hard time?"

Mack nodded.

"If you mean are they going to tease me like I did when Goldie and I found Finn making out with Lisa Perry in the living room to a 'sexy' music playlist, or when we caught *John* Perry, Lisa's cousin, sneaking out of Goldie's bedroom window wearing nothing but his boxers, then yes. They are going to give *me* a hard time. You? The second we leave this room, you'll probably be offered the best food we have."

Aiden didn't look too sure about that, but on cue his stomach growled.

That seemed to sway him. He lowered his hands. Mack felt him relax.

"I wouldn't mind eating anything at the moment. I only had a few bites of food yesterday."

Mack saw it then. He was pulling in all the memories of the day before. Worry pressed down on his expression. Mack wished he could fix it. The best he could do was make sure he was fed.

"Come on, then. Let's go get some food."

Aiden agreed, and any self-consciousness he had about the time they had spent together went to the back burner. He excused himself to the bathroom to get ready, and Mack threw on a shirt to go deal with the wolves first.

The wolves greeted him with twin grins in the kitchen.

Goldie did it over her coffee, Finn with a fresh pancake on his plate.

Mama Atwood spoke first.

"I know we don't often have people over, but maybe we can set up some kind of system where we lock our doors? Or put a do not disturb *something* on the doorknob? Anything that would give us dear sweet siblings some privacy."

Mack rolled his eyes and pulled down two coffee cups from the cabinet.

"Or we could do this novel thing where we knock and don't just enter a bedroom unannounced."

Finn laughed.

"That's what I told her, but she insisted on checking on you since you never sleep in like that," he said. "I tried to stop her, honest."

Goldie swatted at her twin.

"You tried to stop me, my butt!" she exclaimed. "I'm the one who had to stop *you* from sneaking a peek once I told you those two were in bed."

Finn shrugged.

"Hey, you already ripped that Band-Aid off, so me looking didn't really do any more damage."

Mack got Aiden's cup of coffee brewing. He leaned against the counter as he waited.

"You two go ahead and get it all out," he said, crossing his arms over his chest. "Aiden's already worried."

Goldie looked like she was teeing up to explain there was no reason to be worried, but Finn had questions and knew he had to get them off quick.

"So what's up with you two? Are you guys together now? How long has this been going on? Who initiated it? Who was the big spoon? I feel like it would be you just because of the height difference, but also I've seen the way you look at Aiden when he isn't looking and I think you'd let yourself be a little spoon for him. Also, Goldie said there were stars in your room? What's up with that?"

For a second Mack was too stunned to respond. Goldie, however, nodded.

"I want all those answers, too," she said. "Also, how are

your wounds? Did you hurt them? How do you want us to act when he comes in?"

Mack knew that, based on his personality, he should have been annoyed at the barrage of questions. That his introverted self should have felt the need to slough off any chance of him answering like he was in some kind of postgame media interview.

Instead, he felt pure love for his siblings.

Not a day went by when they didn't love and support him.

And not a day would go by when Mack didn't do the same for them.

So, he decided to answer them out of familial trust, loyalty and love.

However, that didn't mean he was giving them all the details.

Mack took a deep breath then rattled off the answers he was willing to give.

"We haven't talked about any of this at length. I kissed him first. It's not your business who was the big spoon or little spoon. Aiden sleeps with a star projector that's actually pretty nice. My chest and side wounds are healing fine, so there's no issue there. As for how to act, be yourselves." He narrowed his eyes at Finn. "But all intimate questions I ask you to keep to yourselves or I'll sock you upside the head. Got it?"

The twins used their powers to sync up.

They both saluted at the same time.

"Accepted terms."

"Yes, sir."

Aiden's coffee was ready. Mack turned to make himself a cup and smiled once his back was to his siblings.

He wasn't a fan of returning to Willow Creek, but he

would never grow tired of being with Goldie and Finn. Along with Ray, they were his people.

By the time Mack's coffee finished, Aiden made his appearance in the kitchen. He had changed into the outfit Mack had packed, styled his hair and put on what Mack suspected was his favorite ring. He smiled sheepishly and said good morning.

Goldie was up in a flash.

"Good morning," she sang back. "Go ahead and sit down and I'll make you a plate. Do you like pancakes? If not we have some muffins I bought yesterday from the bakery. They're still absolutely delicious."

"Can confirm," Finn added. He held up a muffin wrapper. "I already demolished two of them as soon as I opened my eyes this morning."

Aiden said he was good with pancakes and settled opposite Mack's open seat at the table. Goldie made him a plate, Mack slid over the coffee and Finn pushed over the fruit plate he and Goldie had been snacking on. Aiden was a chorus of thank-yous, and when Mack sat down, he shared a quick look with him. His eyebrow seemed to raise in question. Mack smiled into his coffee.

And that was that.

The four of them ate their breakfast while enjoying small talk about nothing in particular. It was a skill to avoid all the things they could have been talking about. A skill that only extended until the dishes and food had been cleared away.

Mack wasn't happy to be the one to drag them back to the reality, but he didn't think he could put it off any longer. He opened his mouth to start in when Aiden surprised him. His leg reached out under the table and pressed against the side of Mack's. It wasn't a playful touch. Somehow Mack knew it was Aiden's way of letting him know he wanted to speak first.

"Only a handful of people know what I'm about to say, but I think it's only right for you to know." He was talking to the twins. "I'm not exactly sure how it plays into what's been happening, but I've made a decision and it needs some context."

Mack pressed his leg against Aiden's beneath the table as he listened to him explain why he had left Bellwether Tech. It was the same story he had already told Mack, but this retelling was stone-cold. Facts, no emotion. Maybe that made it easier. Maybe that made it harder. Either way, the twins listened with rapt attention.

"I've thought about it since the hospital yesterday, and the best I can guess is Leighton was trying to cover for the CEO," he said once the story had been told. "I'm not sure how Bryce figured into it, but maybe he also found out like I did. I—I never thought Leighton was the kind of man who could...who could kill, but I'm guessing I was on his list."

The twins had taken the story in stride.

Goldie's eyebrows drew together in thought.

"So we think Leighton went after Holloway? That's why he and his wife were run off the road."

Aiden shrugged.

"Maybe Holloway realized that Leighton was trying to cover things up and only making matters worse and tried to turn him in? Or betray him? I don't know. That's one of many questions I wish I could ask Leighton right now."

"Have y'all told Winters yet? Or the sheriff?" Finn asked.

In unison Mack and Aiden shook their heads.

"I've decided I want to tell them today at the department," Aiden said. He looked to Mack. "I should have come clean about this before ever coming to Willow Creek but, well,

I trusted the wrong person. Now I'm going stop putting it on other people and tell the truth myself. Holloway needs to be held accountable for what he's done, and if I can help, I'm going to do it, no matter what."

He gave Mack a significant look.

He had made an opening for him but hadn't forced the next issue.

Mack was thankful for it.

He took a deep breath in and let it out slowly.

"Which brings me to something I haven't had the chance to tell you two yet." Aiden pressed his leg back into Mack's. It was oddly reassuring. He dived in. "The client Dad reported to the sheriff's department after they attacked him. The guy I saw leaving the warehouse during the fire? I found out yesterday that he's Caleb Holloway. The CEO of Bellwether Tech."

This time the twins were a lot more vocal.

They, however, did not ask if he was sure.

"What?" they said together.

"But I thought he left Tennessee and never came back," Finn said.

"To be honest, I stopped looking into it when I started my career as a bodyguard." Mack glanced at Goldie, but he said the next part to Aiden since he was the only one who didn't know. "The boss who handles my contracts warned me that I was getting too obsessed with trying to figure out a way to prove that the fire wasn't an accident. I tried to find a way to connect it with the client, but I had a hard time finding anything. I might not have even remembered the name since I never imagined he would amount to anything like a CEO of a big tech company. His face, though— that I'll never forget."

Aiden nodded. He was crestfallen in the next second.

"I just hate that I've brought this to y'all," he said. "My ex-boyfriend hurt you, tried to do worse and then my ex-employer...did that to your dad." He let out a little laugh filled with sorrow. "If I had never come to Willow Creek—"

"Then no one would know Bellwether Tech needs to be taken down," Mack interrupted. "You didn't create these problems—you were just the unlucky one who realized they were there."

Finn agreed.

Goldie was hesitant, but not at that.

"Ray said that Caleb Holloway and his wife were taken to a hospital up north, a private one with a ton of specialists. It sounded like he might not make it."

They became silent at that.

Mack had thought about Holloway a lot the day before while cleaning Aiden's floors.

"Proving that he was at the warehouse the day of the fire, we know, is a hard ask, since all we have to go on is my memory. Proving after all these years that he started the fire? Probably impossible." Mack had also already made a decision. "As much as I hate it, I want us to only focus on what's happening now."

He counted each point out on his fingers.

"Aiden finds proof that the CEO used Bellwether Tech security footage to blackmail a user. Aiden loops in his boss, Leighton, and is told the situation has been handled. Aiden leaves when no harsher punishment is given and comes to Willow Creek. Over six months later, he gets a call from Leighton the morning after Bryce Anderson, who also worked at the company, is killed at the park, along with an anonymous email warning him about Bellwether Tech. Leighton goes missing, and Jonathan Smith attacks Aiden in his car." He took his five points and made a fist on the tabletop. He continued with the other hand.

"The next day, at least two men come to take Aiden, but instead all they get is my truck. Once me and Aiden are out of the hospital, we finally follow the address that the email was sent from to Bluebird Breeze, where we find Leighton's damning laptop. We loop in Detective Winters, and Leighton becomes suspect number one in Bryce's homicide case, which brings the Bellwether Tech top echelon to Willow Creek. The CEO and his wife are run off the road by someone in my missing truck, and Leighton comes to my house with a gun he definitely wasn't afraid to use." Mack had one finger left. He folded it and made another fist. "And that brings us to now."

They fell into another little silence. Aiden didn't look like he would be the one to break it. Finn did after a long drink of his coffee.

"If Holloway and his wife hadn't been run off of the road with your truck by those men, it would sound like Leighton was behind it all," he said. "But those men don't make sense in that scenario. Who are they and why did they seem to target the Holloways?"

"They could work for Leighton," Mack supplied. "Maybe something went sour between him and the CEO. Maybe the best way he thought to cover himself was to take out the only other person who knew about the blackmail."

"Assuming this is about blackmail at all." Aiden was quiet, but his words held an undeniable weight. He went on to explain without them needing to ask. "We think this is all about covering up the blackmail, but we haven't actually found any proof that it's connected. What if this isn't about the blackmail at all? What if we're focusing on the wrong thing?"

That stopped Mack.

Only because he was right.

Had they ever confirmed that any of this was connected to the blackmail?

Aiden followed up with a simple conclusion.

"We need to talk to Leighton," he said. "He's the only one who can give us answers at this point."

Mack didn't correct him, because he surely wasn't wrong. Aiden and those forest green eyes were all on him.

"Let's go to the hospital before we talk this all out with Detective Winters," he added. "I also want to check in on Jenna."

"We can bring her some food," Goldie suggested.

Finn nodded.

"Ray should be at the hospital finishing up, too," he said. "We should feed him, especially after what he did yesterday."

At the time, checking on Leighton's status, visiting Jenna and bringing some cheer to Ray after a long shift made sense.

So, Mack agreed to it.

That's how everyone Mack cared about ended up going to Harper Faith that morning.

And that's why, hours later, Mack would be fighting to save them all.

Chapter Twenty

Everyone split up.

Goldie took a bag of food to Ray's office in the basement of the hospital. Finn and Mack went to the postsurgery floor to get an update on Leighton's condition. Aiden went to the fourth floor of the main building to visit Jenna. He also had food for her but wasn't sure what she could and couldn't eat. She had been shot in the arm and had surgery, but everything had been a success.

Aiden knocked, worried he might disturb her, but found her sitting up with a magazine and smiling after he was told to come in.

Give it to Jenna Thompson—she was always chipper.

"Well, look who it is," she said in greeting. "What brings you here this early? Is everything okay?"

Aiden shook the bag in his hand.

"Food delivery and general inquiries about your health and happiness, madam."

Jenna took the food with a laugh.

"Well, isn't that the sweetest, sir." She placed it on the table positioned over her lap. Her phone vibrated, and she typed out a quick text, then motioned to one of the chairs next to the bed. "I thought after all the excitement yesterday you would still be in bed. At least, that's where I would be.

I just came in on the tail end of your adventure and can't believe all the things you guys have been through."

Aiden gave a pointed look at her bandaged arm. "I think you've been through more than I have," he said.

"Hey, now, that's a good thing. So don't you dare do that brow crinkle and feel bad. None of this is your fault. Okay?" Aiden smiled to be polite. The guilt in him didn't ease. He also wasn't sure what all Jenna knew. She made a show of looking back at the door. "Where's your boyfriend?"

Aiden felt some heat crawl up his neck a little. Waking up in Mack's arms had been a surprise, despite knowing that he had gone to sleep within them. The morning light had made what felt like a dream extremely real. And when things became real, they had a better chance of someone regretting them.

That's what Aiden had worried would happen with Mack. That he would wake up and regret everything. That the kiss had been impulsive and their night together was just two people thankful to be alive. But, even before Aiden had opened his eyes, he had known that for him there was no regret. That wanting to be close to Mack wasn't just because they had gone through danger and barely made it out alive.

Aiden cared about Mack. When the danger was there, when it wasn't, when they were with his family, when they were alone. Did Mack feel the same way or was he still just wrapped up in the mystery that had taken them all in?

Aiden wasn't sure.

But, for now, even the mention of Mack made him heat.

Jenna's eyebrow rose in question.

He had taken too long to answer.

He tried to play it off.

"Oh, uh, he's with his brother and sister in the basement." Aiden decided to lie simply because he didn't want to involve Jenna any more than she already was. She didn't need to know that Mack and Finn were seeing if they could talk with Leighton. Though he did realize his answer was confusing, too. "Ray—I mean, Dr. Dearborn—has an office there. They are all very close and brought him some food, too."

"Wow. Those Atwoods sure are nice. I get why people move to small towns if there are people like them around."

Aiden felt a flare of pride.

"They definitely make this place better, that's for sure."

Jenna was watching him intently. Aiden wondered if it was so obvious that his feelings were a lot more invested in the family than if they were just friends. He wanted to change the subject but wasn't sure the right way to go. So, he stuck with the theme of family.

"Are you expecting anyone from Nashville to come today? Or have you told anyone that you were hurt yet?" He imagined her on the phone telling her family and friends back home that she was A-okay and not to worry about her. That, like Mack, she had only gotten a flesh wound when in reality she had been shot.

Jenna laughed.

"Don't worry, my family knows I'm here." Her smile faltered. "They can't come right now, but I'm okay."

Aiden felt another flare of emotion. This one was sympathy.

"Well, I'm here if you need anything," he said. "After we go to the sheriff's department, I'll come back here and hang out with you, too. Tell me what you want for lunch, and I'll make it happen."

Her smile came back.

"Mack Atwood might be helpful, but I'll always be Team Riggs. You've always been so considerate."

Aiden snorted. He was about to make a joke about doing the bare minimum but, just like that, a memory resurfaced. With it, a question.

"By the way, how did you know about Mack before you met him?"

Jenna's brow creased. She tilted her head a little in question.

"What do you mean?"

Aiden didn't have to think on it too long. Even though a lot had happened after it, he still remembered her words verbatim.

"'*You're* Malcolm Atwood.' That's what you said in the kitchen before Leighton showed up," he said. "You seemed to have recognized him after he spoke about CEO Holloway."

A knock sounded on the door. Jenna's demeanor changed with it.

"Come in," she called. Her voice dipped lower. Aiden realized that she was wearing lipstick. It was red and neat.

A tall man with a buzz cut walked in. Jenna didn't say a greeting. She didn't say anything to him as he shut the door behind him.

Aiden looked expectantly at the woman to introduce them, but she remained quiet.

Her earlier smiles, all chipper and polite, twisted into a smirk. It felt like the Jenna before had gone and the Jenna that was there now had something to say.

"Since we're strolling down memory lane, I lied about something when I first came to your house," she said. "I might as well come clean now. Remember when I said I had forgotten about you?"

Aiden nodded on reflex.

The man at the door crossed his arms over his chest and leaned back against the door.

Aiden realized too late what was happening.

Jenna's smirk deepened.

"I never forgot about you, Aiden Riggs," she said. "I was just saving you for last."

LEIGHTON WASN'T AWAKE. His doctor didn't think he would be for a while. It was frustrating. Finn patted Mack on the back once they said their goodbyes to the doctor.

"We knew there was a good possibility that he wouldn't be able to talk when we came," Finn tried. "At least we know he's out of the woods."

Mack was grateful for that. As much as he didn't care for Leighton, he wanted his answers. Rather, he wanted Aiden to have those answers. It wouldn't make his pain go away, but it would help knowing the truth. At least, he hoped.

"I'm glad Aiden didn't come with us to see him, though," Finn added. "I know it's his ex and all—an ex who tried to kill him—but seeing him still has to be weird. They dated for a while and were friends afterward. No matter what happened, there's got to be some complicated feelings there."

"Why do you think I didn't fight Aiden on going to see Jenna instead?"

Finn put his arm around Mack's shoulder and swayed them both.

"Whoa, look here everyone. Mack got himself a boyfriend and is all in touch with other people's emotions. Love it. Love the energy. Keep up the good work, my dear sir."

Mack snorted and shook Finn off.

"Aiden isn't my boyfriend," he said. "I only said that to Jenna so she knew I was on his side no matter what."

"But you want him to be your boyfriend, right?" They

had made their way to the main building's lobby. The central elevators had a few people waiting for them. Mack wanted to keep their private talk private, so he held his brother back to finish the conversation.

"I think there's been a lot going on for him," he said.

"You mean just because you were the spoons last night doesn't mean you're suddenly both in the same utensil drawer."

Mack rolled his eyes.

"You and this spoon thing. But, yeah, I guess. I think it might be too much for him."

"It's not the right time," Finn stated.

"It's not the right time," Mack repeated.

"You need to take him on a date first. Be romantic or else he might realize you aren't good boyfriend material. No. That's smart. I understand. Good move."

Mack had started walking again, thinking the conversation was at a close, but paused at that.

"What do you mean, I'm not good boyfriend material?"

Finn held his hands up in mock defense.

"Hey, I've never seen you in action. You might have inherited Goldie's awkwardness. Remember the last guy she was with? She tried to take him to that really weird art festival and ended up in a performance art play where they got paint thrown on them."

Mack held back his laugh out of respect for his sister. It was a hard feat.

"When I take Aiden on a date, I'll make sure not to accidentally stumble into an art exhibit," he deadpanned. The elevators timed perfectly, both opening together. Mack watched two men get in one and another get into the second. The one with two men was headed down. The other was going up.

Finn started in that direction, no doubt wanting to catch a ride, but Mack stopped him once again.

This time, though, for a much different reason.

He recognized two of the men. One of them in the elevator going down had been wearing a worker's vest last time he had seen him. The one in the elevator going up was the man who had been in the car that had parked behind Mack's truck after the worker had stopped them.

The doors closed.

Everyone's here, Mack realized.

Out loud he turned to his brother and spoke quickly.

"Those are the men who came after us on the mountain. Two are going down to the basement. One is going up." Mack was already moving across the lobby to the door that led to the stairwell. The elevators at the hospital were notoriously slow. It was the only saving grace they might have at the moment. "Run ahead, and you, Goldie, and Ray get out of their way and call the cops."

Finn only had one question.

"What about you?"

"I'm going for Aiden."

That was that. No more questions or conversation. They split up the second they were through the stairwell door. Finn ran down; Mack thundered up. He knew Finn could get to the morgue before the men. Then it would be three smart adults who knew the hospital like the back of their hands. They could avoid the men until deputies came.

But Aiden and Jenna were sitting ducks.

And that was Mack's fault.

He took as many steps as he could, not breaking stride until he slammed into the fourth-floor exit. Mack still didn't stop as he turned left and ran to Jenna's hallway. Where he expected to be stopped by staff, he wasn't. He didn't have time to wonder why. Instead he didn't slow until he was at Jenna's door and throwing it open.

The room was empty.

"YOU KNOW WHAT everyone seems to overlook in hospitals?" Jenna spread her arms open wide. "The rooftops."

Over her shoulder was a view of treetops and a sliver of the town in the distance. Everything above was blue skies and sunshine. It would have been nice had Aiden not had a gun at his back since the stairs.

"No matter if you're in the city or a small, ridiculous town like Willow Creek, a hospital rooftop is just the best," Jenna continued. "Privacy with a breeze. You just can't beat that."

She was still smiling, but it was nothing like Aiden had seen before. There was an edge to it, a sharpness that wanted to cut.

Cut him, apparently.

"Why are we here, Jenna?" Aiden asked. "What do you want?"

She was wearing her hospital gown and her sling, but she was the picture of put together as she answered. It felt rehearsed, almost. Maybe it was. She tucked some of her loose hair behind her ear then nodded to the man behind him.

"Watch the door."

The man didn't hesitate.

That's when Aiden really felt it. Power.

Jenna Thompson was controlling things. What things, Aiden didn't know yet.

"What's going on?" he had to add.

Jenna took in a big breath of the fresh air. She looked at peace.

"This? This is about a little girl who decided it's better to be a knife in the back than a shield." She waved her hand at him, like a dismissal. "You don't understand, I get that. I didn't understand a lot in the beginning, either, but, don't worry, I'm here now to explain." She took a few steps toward him. The rooftop's ledge was several feet away. It made an already anxious Aiden even more so.

"See, I'm going to tell you a story, because I've always liked you, Aiden, and I want to give you a chance to make a good choice," she continued. "But, first, let's talk about the blackmail. You know, the one where our dear CEO Holloway found out that a user was having an affair and how he decided to use that against that poor, poor man." Her voice was dripping with sarcasm. "I wonder, did you ever see the actual video footage? I'm assuming you didn't."

Aiden shook his head.

"I was asked to loop footage. I didn't realize until later what it was for."

"Mmm. Sneaky." She sighed. "I figured you didn't see the actual footage or else you would have said something to me."

Aiden's eyebrow rose before he could force his facial expression to remain neutral.

Jenna didn't miss it.

"Everyone was so worried about the user that they never questioned his mistress. Who, by the way, was me." She held her hand out in a stop motion. "I know, I know. Plot twist, am I right? The executive assistant having an affair with a man right in front of her company's security cameras."

Aiden couldn't help it. He said the first thing that crossed his mind.

"It doesn't seem like the smartest move."

Jenna snapped her fingers.

"That would have been so careless of me, right? But what if I did it on purpose? What if I honey trapped the user to put him in a situation where blackmail was easy? What if, while making him fall for me, I got him front and center on his own personal home security system so the entire show was caught on camera? Would that make me less careless?"

Aiden's mind started racing.

"I would still call it a careless plan since Holloway found out."

"And what if I wanted that to happen, too? What if I knew he was keeping close tabs on me and left him a bread-crumb trail that led to my relationship as a mistress?"

She took another little step forward.

A breeze went by.

She kept going, seemingly enjoying herself.

"I know I may seem like the best company girl there is, but I actually hate two things very much." She held up her middle finger, winked and continued. "One, I absolutely despise the great and powerful Caleb Holloway. Despise him so much that I'd go around the world twice just to ruin his afternoon. Never mind his life." She held up her index finger. "Two, I think hate is a beautiful thing. Poetic. Classy. Love with nothing but consequence. Oh, and how I hate that man. So, I really hate it when the destruction of a person isn't a little dramatic. A little drawn out. A little *unnecessary*. Why hate someone if you won't really punish them?"

Aiden didn't know if she wanted an answer and, if she did, he had no idea to which question she had posed. So when she paused, he asked his own.

"So you became a mistress to trap Holloway? But why would he care if you were a mistress? Why would he care about you at all?"

Her smile melted. The pristine posture she'd been holding herself with slumped a little.

"Oh, he doesn't care about me. Just the trouble I can make. I am his daughter, after all."

Aiden felt his eyes widen.

"What? You're his daughter? But—but he doesn't have any kids."

"Mmm. Believe me, how I wish that were true." She tapped her chest twice. "But me? I'm his only flesh and blood. I'm also his biggest embarrassment. See, my mother was in fact his mistress once upon a time. After she had me, she let him know and, well, that didn't go well. We were abandoned, forgotten. Left to poverty."

Her smile came back. It was razor-sharp.

"But then a miracle happened. When that great man got into some big trouble, he found me and used me as a shield. His poor, pitiful daughter *needed* her father. Nothing bad could happen to him if anyone could hear his equally pitiful story. So I was brought to his side and kept there until the trouble calmed down. A disposable pawn. A child with nothing, who would do anything for more. After that, though? I was sent back to that nothing. Back to the shadows. There I became a secret. How lovely, right?"

Aiden paused before speaking. Jenna let him.

"Are you—are you talking about the warehouse fire?" he asked. "That's how the man who was suspected of starting it got out of trouble. His daughter."

She tapped her chest again.

"You're fast," she said. "You'd think dear old Dad would have been more grateful for my amazing performance. Crying on the spot, yelling for him. Being pitiful and loud about it. Turning the weakhearted into the shameless who simply looked the other way. But, no. Instead that father of mine threw money at me and told me to be quiet. To never speak again about how he'd *lied* about me needing him. About him needing *me*. But I—I just couldn't get over what he had done. Abandon me once, shame on you. Abandon me twice, shame on me."

"But then you started working at Bellwether," Aiden said. "Didn't he know?"

Jenna nodded.

"Not at first. He isn't really hands-on—he leaves most of his work to his vice president. That useless, spineless man who would walk off a cliff if he asked. But eventually dear old Dad figured it out." She sighed. "I put on the performance of a lifetime, again, convincing him that I just so admired what he had done with the company and that, even though we didn't have a relationship, I would be happy enough working for him." She scoffed. "He ate that up."

Another breeze swept over them. Jenna closed her eyes to enjoy it.

When she opened them again, Aiden could see rage had surfaced.

"Then I realize he had been watching me. Keeping tabs so I wouldn't ruin his life. That's how it became so easy to bait him. The man would do anything to get more power, and I picked the perfect man for an affair, because he had that and money to spare. But." Her eyes narrowed at him. "But he was a fool to bring you in for help. You, a man who had a damn heart and wouldn't simply turn the other way. You took my chance to expose him. I wanted to make him sweat. I wanted to bleed him dry. I wanted to make him suffer, then watch him die, but, *no*, you had to bring other people in to try and do the right thing."

She took several steps forward. Aiden braced for a hit, but she stopped right in front of him. Her words were low and menacing.

"Leighton started digging until he needed Bryce's help.

Then they dug so deep that they found me. And I couldn't let anyone find me. Not then, not now. Not ever."

Aiden knew then.

"You killed Bryce."

Jenna nodded.

"He wouldn't join my team, so I took him out of my game," she said. "Then I came for you next. But Leighton, bless his soul, really didn't like that."

Aiden went cold.

"What do you mean? Leighton isn't working with you?"

Jenna scoffed again.

"I sure thought I had persuaded him, but I guess he was still hung up on you." She put her hand on her hip and leaned back a little. Like she had decided relaxing was a normal thing at the moment. "Luckily, I already knew how to set him up to make everything that happened here, at the company and with you, look like an ex-lover's revenge."

That relaxation disappeared.

Then she looked annoyed.

"Even now while he's lying motionless in a hospital bed, his hired hands are finishing his last task of killing your current boyfriend…all before coming for you." She sighed. "Ah, the story will be so big that no one will even think to look for the illegitimate child of Bellwether Tech."

Aiden's fear sent him straight to his own rage.

"You're wrong if you think someone won't put the truth together," he said. "Especially if you hurt Mack and his family. This town will look for you."

Jenna wagged her finger at him.

"That's what's so great about your failed office romance. Why look for me when they have Leighton?"

Aiden shook his head. This couldn't be happening.

"You can't do this," he tried instead.

But Jenna didn't seem at all put off.

Instead, she was back to her chipper smile.

Aiden didn't know what she had planned to say next because, a second later, all hell broke loose.

Chapter Twenty-One

No one had asked why Mack had become a bodyguard; instead they had always asked what it was like. It was a strange occupation for most to get their heads around, but usually when they looked him up and down they thought it made sense for him. He was a big, strong guy. Observant. He had a thing about faces, too.

They also usually commented about him being a quiet guy. Quiet people had patience, and patience was a virtue, especially when it came to standing around usually waiting for nothing.

But Mack hadn't become a bodyguard because of his skills or personality. No, Mack had become a bodyguard because of Goldie.

It had been their father's birthday, and their mother had come to town to celebrate with them. Their mom was a nice woman, had been a kind mother, too, but after their dad had died, something in her just broke. Finn had once admitted it felt like they were always on thin ice around her, and then one day they realized she had been the one standing on it, not them. That ice had broken then and floated away with her still on it. And, though they all cared about each other, they hadn't gone after her, and she hadn't tried to come back.

Her leaving town was the reason Mack had come back to

town after college. The twins had just graduated from high school and had decided to make lives closer to home. Mack had wanted to show them that he was there, even though Willow Creek had been the last place he wanted to settle.

Goldie had known that. Finn had pretended he didn't.

Mack tried to be enthusiastic after returning, but he had become restless, aimless, too. The worst part: he hadn't realized it until one night a nineteen-year-old Goldie had come into his room with a folder in her hands.

"I want you to do a job for me," she had said. "Read through these and come out to the kitchen when you're done."

She had held it out to him with no more explanation then gone to wait. So, Mack had read through them. When he was done, he went to the kitchen.

"Are you serious about this?" he had asked, holding the folder up.

Goldie had nodded.

"If you're in, then I have some papers you need to sign." She had pointed to a stack of papers on the table, a ballpoint pen next to it. "Then we can talk details."

Mack had seen it then. Her seriousness. Her sincerity. Still, he didn't understand why her. Why him.

She had picked up on his one hesitation.

"I don't want a normal desk job, and you need to get out of this house," she had added.

It had been a simple answer, and that had been enough for Mack. He had signed the papers while Goldie explained what they meant at his side.

That was their first security contract, Mack as the bodyguard and Goldie as the boss.

Years later, their dynamic hadn't changed, and still no one had asked why he took on jobs to protect strangers.

It wasn't because he was big or strong. It wasn't because he was observant and had a thing with faces. He had done it because his sister had wanted him to leave his room.

It certainly hadn't been because he was patient.

Because, if there was one thing most people didn't know about his quiet, it was that it didn't suffer patience long.

That's why Mack didn't slow down for even an iota of time when he saw the man standing in front of the rooftop door.

Mack bulldozed up the last stairs and grabbed the man's wrist, pinned it back against his chest and slammed the man, his gun and Mack against the door with every bit of power he had.

Like Goldie's simple statement all those years ago, the simple move was more than enough.

The door exploded open, and the man yelled as he kept going backward. Mack still didn't let go. He didn't have to. He had already known the man was going to hit the ground hard. He also knew that he wouldn't be joining him.

Using his momentum and years of practice at keeping his balance in a fight, Mack used his hold on the man's arm to keep himself up while simultaneously driving the man down. Mack crouched as the man hit the graveled rooftop with a thud and crack. His eyes closed, and his body went slack. The hold he had on the gun loosened, and Mack took advantage.

He grabbed the gun and stood tall.

Mack didn't need to ask what the situation was. The second he saw Aiden standing opposite Jenna, he knew just by the man's stance who the villain was.

Mack lifted the gun and aimed it at the woman. He moved as he did so. She didn't seem to have a weapon, but when Mack was close enough, he took Aiden's arm. He pulled him back and to his left. It put him out of the sight line of the door and put Mack between him and Jenna.

"I don't know what's going on, but I need you to stand real still," Mack ordered.

Jenna's eyes were wide, but she didn't seem afraid. She did, however, comply.

"Are you okay?" Mack didn't turn, but Aiden knew the question was for him.

"Yeah. I'm—I'm okay."

"Was there anyone else with you?"

"No. They brought me up here. With the gun you have."

Mack narrowed his eyes. Again, he didn't understand how Jenna factored into what was going on, but he sure as hell didn't care as long as he could keep Aiden safe.

"The two men who went to the basement. They're yours, too?"

Jenna wasn't smiling, but there was a twitch there. She had a gun on her, but she wasn't reacting the way she should.

"It's easier to get things done when you have helpers," she said. "All *three* of them."

It was subtle, but Mack caught it. An emphasis on the word *three*.

Her eyes flashed to the left.

That's when he knew he had made a mistake.

He had missed a guy.

Mack spun around and shot at the same time the fourth man sent off his own bullet. Both hits landed, but only one of them had someone they loved to protect. Aiden screamed out at him as Mack took his hit and walked forward for his second shot.

He had never been a fan of guns, but that didn't mean he hadn't been trained to use them.

Mack pulled the trigger with more accuracy than before.

He hoped Aiden wasn't looking, but he had to watch as the man fell in the doorway. He had to make sure he was down for the count.

"Mack!" Aiden was at his side but Mack wasn't going to let him stand in front again.

"Stay behind me," he ordered.

Aiden said something, but the sound was fading.

Mack managed to turn to Jenna.

"If you run, I'll shoot."

It was a bluff but, Mack would find out later, Jenna stayed stock-still regardless.

Which was good, because for the second time since meeting Aiden, Mack slipped into the darkness in his arms.

MACK WOKE UP on a Tuesday.

It was three in the morning and raining. Aiden was lying on the couch in his hospital room with a laptop on his stomach and the work he had tried to distract himself with untouched on the screen. At first he thought he was hearing things, but then Mack gave a little laugh.

Aiden nearly fell off the couch.

"Oh, God, you're awake." Aiden was a scrambling mess but managed to make it to Mack's bedside without destroying everything in the process.

Aiden didn't know what to do once he got there, so he did what felt right.

He put his hands on either side of Mack's face and then cried.

Mack watched for a few moments before his hand pressed over one of Aiden's. He patted it twice.

"I'm okay," he said, voice hoarse.

Aiden tried to get himself together while nodding.

"You are," he assured him. "You are."

Mack hadn't been, though. Not at all. He had been shot in the chest and had a total of three surgeries. His age, his good health and the other man's slightly bad aim had been the only reasons he had survived. The man who had shot him had not.

But Aiden wasn't going to tell him all that yet.

With great effort he slowed his crying and redirected his hold on to Mack's hand.

"Everyone else is okay, too," he said. "I'm supposed to get them the second you wake up."

Mack squeezed his hand.

"Stay here. For now."

Aiden didn't say no to that.

"Only if you promise to go back to sleep if you need to," he offered instead. "You're on some pretty good meds. The doctor said you might be sleepy for a while."

Mack nodded. The movement was sluggish. He was already fighting sleep again.

Aiden didn't stand in its way. He held Mack's hand until the man's eyes closed.

The worry in Aiden's chest finally lessened.

THE NEXT DAY Mack woke up again and, this time, managed to stay awake. Aiden had walked Mrs. Cole out to her car and missed his first moments, but he walked back in to find Ray talking his head off at the foot of his bed.

"Your sister is straight feral," he said. "I mean, I already knew she was, but the second Finn tore into the morgue and we realized we didn't have time to run, she made him get into one of the empty mortuary cabinets and *shut it*. Then, can you guess what that sister of yours did?"

Mack's bed had been situated so that he was sitting up. Aiden could easily see him smile.

"Jumped on the guys?"

Ray threw his arms up in total disbelief and awe.

"She jumped on the guys!" he exclaimed. "I mean, she was strategic about it, at least, and I was there to throw some equipment at them, but honestly, if I wasn't there, I think Goldie would have been fine."

Mack chuckled.

"Not many people know that for every self-defense and fighting class I took, Goldie went with me," he said. "If I remember correctly, we even tried to get you and mortuary cabinet Finn to come with us once. You two said you were busy."

Ray was just beside himself.

"Well, let me tell you what, I have reconsidered. Goldie has made me a believer. Go ahead and put me down as a yes to every single class in the future."

Mack was more than amused. Aiden could hear laughter in his one-word response.

"Deal."

Ray finally noticed Aiden had entered and waved him over to the spot where he had been sitting.

"I'll go get the wonder twins. You stay here and make sure this one doesn't get into any trouble."

Aiden agreed, and Ray was out of the room in a flash. When Aiden looked to Mack, the man was already staring.

"Did I dream it, or did you cry on me last night?" He was teasing. Aiden teased right back.

"Most people would pay good money to have someone as amazing as me crying over them, thank you very much."

"Is that so?"

Aiden crossed his arms over his chest and nodded deeply, once.

"That's very much so."

Mack held up one hand in defeat.

"Then you'll never hear me complain about Aiden Riggs crying over me again. Promise."

Aiden nodded.

"Good."

If it were up to him, Aiden would have continued joking around. It was already hard enough keeping himself from throwing his arms around Mack in relief. But Mack was a man who didn't like being in the dark. So, when he wanted to switch back to the serious, Aiden didn't fight it.

"Tell me what's happened since I've been out."

Aiden nodded again. He dropped his hands to his lap and began his recap. He started with what Jenna had told him on the rooftop and then what happened right after Mack had been shot.

"Detective Winters was the one who showed up before anyone could get a call out of the hospital for deputies. He wasn't too far behind you, actually. He cuffed Jenna and helped me carry you off the rooftop. It wasn't until you were already being taken to surgery that the rest of the department showed." Mack was obviously surprised at that. Aiden had been, too, until the detective had explained once everything had calmed down.

"Winters said that he knew he was missing a lot of information, but the thing that bothered him the most was Jonathan Smith," Aiden said. "The more he thought about it, he believed that Jonathan had been told to go after me by someone else. So, he went to visit him as soon as the county jail opened and confronted him. Apparently, Jonathan caved. He had been paid by a man to grab and take me to a rental home in Willow Creek where I could lie low for a few days until some kind of mess was sorted out."

"You mean—"

"He was supposed to take me to Bluebird Breeze. But, instead, he had been so nervous about it all that he had gone a little overboard. He was trying to make me pass out so I wouldn't fight him. Unlucky for him, a certain bodyguard just happened to be obsessed with me."

Aiden grinned.

Mack rolled his eyes.

"On with the story there, Mr. Riggs."

Aiden laughed but then became serious again. He didn't know how to feel about the next part. He wouldn't for a long while.

"Leighton was the one who paid him. That's why Winters rushed here, especially when he realized that I was here, too. You apparently made such a fuss going up to the roof that he knew to hightail it there, too."

"Leighton wanted you to go to Bluebird Breeze," Mack underlined.

Aiden nodded. He recounted the story that Leighton himself had told Aiden two days ago while Mack had still been sleeping.

"After you left the company, I was promoted," he had told Aiden. *"I'd been working hard for years to get there, so when the CEO told me that he had learned from his mistakes, I took his word. But then it happened again a few months later. Bryce was called in to loop a video, erase some other footage and keep quiet about it. Bryce didn't like that, and instead of coming to me to talk it out, he assumed I was part of it. It wasn't until two weeks ago that I realized he was going to go public with the information. And, not only that, he was going to Willow Creek to find you to help him do it. Bryce was a smart guy, but you're the one with the better skills."*

Aiden had told him that Bryce had never gotten in touch with him.

At this Leighton had frowned so completely Aiden was almost moved to sympathy.

"I didn't want you to be involved. Even though you hacked into different databases in the name of good, what you did wasn't exactly legal. So when I realized Bryce was in town, I asked to meet him so we could talk about a way to leave you out of everything. But, when I went there, I found Jenna instead."

Jenna had made herself known as the CEO's daughter then and given Leighton the same rundown she had given Aiden on the roof, as far as Aiden could tell. Then she had given Leighton the same choice she had Bryce.

"She wanted me to help dismantle Bellwether Tech but do it her way. She had the money, she had the power, she just didn't have the technical know-how. Plus, Holloway had always been suspicious of her. She also wanted you." Leighton had shaken his head at that. *"I told her you weren't needed, but she already knew that you had been the one to find out about the blackmail. She said if we couldn't use you, she would kill you. I knew she was serious, so I acted fast. And clumsily."*

Leighton had sent Jonathan to try and take Aiden out of the equation. But then Mack had shown up. After that, Jenna had made her move with the four hired helpers she had been using for years for her own nefarious deeds.

"After Mack helped you out of that again, I had to figure out a way to separate you two. I didn't realize that Jenna had already decided to make me the fall guy."

"The laptop at Bluebird Breeze," Aiden had guessed. *"She set that up."*

Leighton had nodded.

"Then I started to build a case against her until I heard she had gone to Willow Creek. I knew she was going to tie up our loose end—you—and, since I wasn't sure where her guys were, I panicked and tried to take away the reason why I couldn't hide you until I could figure out a plan that worked."

"You were trying to shoot Mack when you came to my house. Not me."

"I didn't want to kill him, just make him stop getting in the way so I could save you."

Aiden had become angry then. Angrier than he ever had been.

Leighton didn't try to apologize.

"For what it's worth, I'm glad he's okay," was all he had said instead.

After that, Aiden had given him only one last courtesy before leaving for good.

"For what it's worth, I'm glad you're okay, too."

That was the last time he saw Leighton and, even though it hurt, Aiden felt better having gotten his side of the story.

Mack had, too.

"I guess I can't get too mad at him," he said now. "He might not have gone about it the right way, but he was just trying to protect someone he cared about. I get that."

Aiden's cheeks had burned a little at that.

Then he sighed.

"All this trouble went nowhere." Aiden took Mack's hand in his. "Caleb Holloway passed away three days ago due to his injuries from the accident. His funeral was yesterday."

Aiden hadn't known how to feel about that piece of news, either. Mack, in the moment, took it okay.

"I would have liked to talk to him," he admitted.

In the weeks to come, Mack and his siblings would talk

to Jenna while she awaited trial. There the Atwoods would get confirmation that Caleb had told his daughter he had started the fire to ruin their father. When he had realized it had instead trapped him inside, he hadn't tried to help him escape. Caleb Holloway hadn't purposely killed their father, but he had purposely not saved him. In that way, the four of them had shared a moment of true disgust for a man who had been known to the public as a promoter of safety and security and compassion. After that, none of them saw Jenna again.

But in the hospital room, once Mack had been caught up as much as Aiden could help with, the two of them had simply sighed.

"I think it would be really nice if we could not visit the hospital for a while," Aiden said. "I heard one of the doctors joke that we're starting to be frequent fliers."

Mack laughed.

He was still holding Aiden's hand.

"It would be nice to go out and see other places together, too. Maybe do something with a slower pace. I know this might be old-fashioned, but dinner and a movie might be fun."

Aiden thought he was going along with the bit, but Mack squeezed his hand. His expression softened.

"What do you say, Mr. Potted Plant?"

Heat rose up into Aiden's face, but he smiled.

"Are you asking me out on date from your hospital bed?"

Mack nodded.

"I've been told I might not be romantic, but I'll let you know, I'm impatient. I need an answer now. Please and thank you."

Aiden couldn't help but laugh.

"Call me a potted plant again and we'll see if I go anywhere with you."

Mack didn't argue, and two weeks later they were sitting front and center at the movie theater. Mack had the popcorn in one hand, and Aiden's hand in the other. Before the movie started, Mack leaned over and whispered.

"Be thankful this isn't an art exhibit."

Aiden turned his head, confused.

But Mack wasn't in the mood to explain. As soon as Aiden's lips were there, Mack's were right there, too.

The kiss was long and deep.

Aiden knew the movie must have started but, for the life of him, he didn't seem to care.

* * * * *

UNDER SIEGE

JULIE ANNE LINDSEY

Chapter One

Josi Roberts ran a hand along the side of her favorite stallion, Lancelot, proud of the big guy for his incredible patience. "You did good this afternoon," she told him. "You made a whole lot of kids smile."

The autumn afternoon had been bright and sunny, showcasing a cloudless blue sky with only a slight nip in the air. Evening, however, had come with rain. Thanks to a tropical storm off the coast of Florida, things would get worse before they got better in Marshal's Bluff, North Carolina, Josi's beloved hometown. Scattered showers and frigid gusts were predicted to continue until dawn, maybe through the weekend. That was all fine by her. She found the pattering on the stable roof and drops on her office windowpane soothing. After a long day of hard work, the breeze blowing through the open barn doors was more than welcome.

Lancelot lowered his big nose to her head and nuzzled, filling her heart impossibly further. His dark brown mane was a stark contrast to her blond, sun-bleached locks, as was his regal size. At five foot four, Josi fit easily beneath his chin, with plenty of room for a ten-gallon hat or two. He nibbled mischievously at the oversize cotton scrunchie holding the hair away from her face, and she laughed.

"Hey, now." Josi pulled back, checking to be sure he

hadn't stolen her hair tie again. "They should've named you Mischief."

He watched her with keen, all-seeing eyes as she smiled at his handsome face.

"Just one more open house event next week," she promised. "Then this place won't be so overrun for a while. You and I will both get a break."

Lancelot snorted and swished his tail, glad for the attention. Probably because he knew he was her favorite.

"Show-off," she whispered, rubbing a palm along his cheek. She made a mental note to give the other horses in her care some extra love, lest they feel slighted and unhappy.

The Beaumont Ranch, where she lived and worked, opened its doors publicly every fall in a series of preplanned Community Days events. Today's schedule, and next week's, featured the horses. Ranch hands gave introductory workshops on equine care and maintenance as well as beginners' riding lessons. People of influence and affluence in the community made appearances to donate money and raise awareness. Others came because a young person they loved needed help, likely a total life reset. Many visited because this had once been their home, where they'd reached a turning point and been given a fresh start. Those folks usually just wanted to squeeze the people who'd given them the love and time they'd needed to sort themselves out.

Josi would be one of the latter someday, she supposed, though she couldn't imagine ever leaving the ranch. She wasn't a member of the Beaumont family by blood, but they'd taken her in when she'd needed help most. At eighteen, she'd spent most of her life in foster care while her mom had repeatedly tried to clean herself up and failed. Josi had been aging out of the system fast, and no one had wanted to take in a kid who was nearly grown. Especially one so well known for rebelling over the short straw she'd drawn in life.

Somehow, none of that had fazed Mr. and Mrs. Beaumont. Instead, they'd insisted they saw promise in her, and they gave her hope—something she hadn't felt in a very long time. They'd also given her a safe place to stay, good food and thoughtful counsel on her options for the future. Then they'd offered her a job at the stables to earn some money before her birthday. Now, five years later, she still lived on the property, as the stable's manager, with no thought of going anywhere else.

Some days it overwhelmed her heart and soul to belong to a place like this and people like these. Most of the other foster kids she'd spent her rowdy teen years with had to figure things out on their own. Some joined the military. A few turned to crime or drugs. Plenty were getting by now, but it hadn't been easy, and the paths they'd taken had been hard. She was one of the lucky ones and she thought about that fact every day.

Josi grabbed the broom leaning against the wall and returned to sweeping errant bits of hay and dirt from the textured concrete floor. The cell phone in her back pocket vibrated as she worked, and she paused to pull it from her jeans.

The name on the screen surprised her. She hadn't heard from Tara Stone, the younger sister of Josi's one teenage love, in ages. They hadn't spoken on any sort of regular basis since Tara's biological brother had died a few years back, and Josi attended the funeral. A pang of guilt hit her chest. Josi and Tara had been close once. She'd loved Tara's brother, as much as anyone who'd never been loved could anyway. But Josi had checked out of their lives before Marcus died, and she'd kept her distance afterward to protect her own pulverized heart. It was selfish and not something Josi would do today, but she'd still been healing from old wounds then. Today, however, she was prepared and willing to help anyone, however she could.

Josi answered the call on a long inhale, hoping Tara wanted to share good news instead of bad. They'd lost a couple of friends from their old circle for heartbreaking reasons in recent years, and she hated to think of losing another.

"Hey, Tara, what's up?"

"Josi…" Her friend's voice was shaky and thin. Her raspy breaths gave the impression she'd been crying. "I know it's been a while, and I've got no business calling you for this, but I need a favor. I can't think of anyone else it's safe to call."

Josi's muscles tensed. "What do you need?"

"A ride. Now."

Something in the broken cadence of Tara's words set Josi's feet in motion. "Are you at home?" she asked, already slipping into her office to power down the computer and grab her keys. She wasn't even sure if Tara still lived in the same place as before. She'd shared that rental with Marcus.

"No. I'm at the Bayside Motel on Route Nine." Tara sniffed. "I made a mistake coming here, but my truck won't start, and I want to go home."

"Of course," Josi said, relieved to know exactly where Tara was and how to get there. "Are you in danger? Should I call the police first? Or are you going to be okay for about twenty-five minutes?"

A long pause stretched across the line as Josi flipped the light switch and locked the door.

"I think I trusted the wrong guy."

"Relatable," Josi said, hoping to lighten the moment.

"Just hurry."

The call ended, and Josi turned the phone around to frown at it. Nothing good ever happened at the motel where Tara was waiting for rescue, and if she was calling Josi for a ride after all this time, the situation must be bad. She couldn't help wondering whom Tara had trusted and why that had been a mistake. Did Josi know him? Had he hurt her friend?

The clatter of a falling feed bucket nearly sent Josi out of her skin. She pressed a palm to her chest as she spun in the direction of the sound.

Lincoln Beaumont, the grumpiest, and arguably the sexiest, of five excellent-looking brothers stared back.

"Goodness!" She huffed a shaky breath, struggling to calm her frantically beating heart.

He raised his eyebrows at her over-the-top response. "Everything all right?" he asked.

The gentle lilt of his Southern drawl was sweet as honey on his tongue, and the image that thought conjured left Josi speechless. He bent to swipe the fallen bucket from the ground, curious eyes narrowing when he straightened. Lincoln had been in the military when Josi came to stay at the ranch, still young and scared. Now, she was his boss, and he was slowly stealing her heart. Not that he had a clue.

After two years of working together, the attraction she'd felt upon their first official introduction had grown steadily from a hopeless crush to something more. His moss-green eyes and barely-there smile were the sexiest of icings on the sweetest possible cake. He hid his big, squishy, teddy-bear heart behind terse words and sharp tones, but she knew the truth. She saw it every day, and she was hopelessly lost because of that knowledge. Now, there was only one man for her, and he'd never know it was him.

She'd been out on a date or two in the last year, but Lincoln had silently set the bar too high. No other man would ever measure up.

Lincoln never dated. Most people couldn't seem to see past his grouchy facade, when all they had to do was look. But most folks were just too busy.

"Jos?" he asked, snapping her back to the moment.

"I'm fine." She shook off the silly, lovestruck thoughts and passed him on the newly swept floor. "I've got to run an errand. Can you lock the stable when you head out?"

"Sure, but I just finished up. You need a hand with anything?"

Her steps faltered for a moment, and she turned to stare. Lincoln had never offered to tag along with her on trips outside the ranch. And she'd never known him to drop anything, now that she thought about it. Her gaze slid to the empty feed bucket, secure in his hands. Lincoln was methodical and a near recluse. So what was he up to?

He waited, unspeaking and brow furrowed. His downturned mouth told her to walk away.

Yet he'd offered to come.

She shook her head. She was wasting time. Tara had asked her to hurry and debating the merits of an evening ride with Lincoln Beaumont wasn't doing her friend any favors. "No. I've got it, thanks."

He worked his jaw, scrutinizing her.

Josi lifted one hand in a quick hip-high wave, then turned and jogged through the stable, into the night.

TWENTY-THREE MINUTES LATER, Josi piloted her hatchback into the nearly empty parking lot outside the Bayside Motel. The rain had steadily increased as she drove, forming puddles along the roadside and forcing her wipers to work overtime. She motored past the square detached office to the large, L-shaped structure beyond. Two stories of exposed red doors faced her, each with a rusty number above a peephole, a large window next to each door and the curtains drawn on all but one.

Arriving at the motel after dark incited the worst kind of nostalgia. Josi had spent her share of time in the outdated, barely cleaned rooms, usually attending parties while the hotel manager looked the other way. The place was known for renting by the hour and a number of other practices that made it the perfect place for anyone wanting to meet privately and without a record of their time. Guests paying with cash weren't asked any questions.

She shuddered at the memories of her teen and adolescent years, and thanked her lucky stars she'd taken a different path into adulthood. She hoped Tara had too, and that her presence here tonight was an anomaly, not a norm.

She shifted into Park along the far edge of the lot, beneath the only working streetlight, and surveyed the situation. Last she'd seen her, Tara owned a rusty pickup truck significantly older than herself, but she had no idea what Tara drove these days. Josi supposed it could be any of the vehicles scattered throughout the dark lot. At least her friend would be able to see her clearly in the cone of light, despite the storm.

A flickering neon sign high overhead announced vacancies, but more than half of the security lights were out. An ice machine sat beside an outdoor picnic area and dilapidated iron grill. The pool was empty, its belly covered in fallen leaves, trash and dirt.

Josi sent a text to Tara, letting her know she'd arrived. Then she sent a follow-up asking for her room number. If she knew where Tara was, she could park closer and not have to cross the creepy lot alone while getting soaked. The thought sent goose bumps over Josi's skin. She turned a knob on her dashboard, circulating heat throughout the car.

Movement drew her eyes back to the room with the open curtains. The blue light of a television flashed against a visible wall. Two shadows appeared, then vanished in swift succession.

A nervous chill rocked down Josi's spine, and she checked her surroundings to be sure she was alone. Sheets of rain, along with the growing darkness, obscured her view and increased her anxiety. That Tara hadn't responded to her text only made matters worse.

Her friend's quaking voice came back to mind as Josi sent another text. It'd been nearly thirty minutes since they'd spoken. What if whatever Tara had been afraid of happening already occurred? What if Josi was too late?

She tapped her fingers against the back of the phone, waiting for a response, wondering if it was too soon to call the police.

A hotel door swung open across the lot, and Tara ran out. She scanned the space, her attention seeming to settle on Josi's SUV, then she darted away, moving quickly in the opposite direction.

"Hey!" Josi called, unfastening her seat belt and climbing into the storm. "Hey! Tara!" She waved her arms as the first clap of thunder split the air. Maybe she hadn't seen Josi after all, or her friend hadn't recognized her.

A second figure emerged from the room, and a flash of light on the heels of a second, more unnatural, boom ripped a scream from Josi's throat. *Gunfire.*

She stumbled back, bumping into her open car door, eyes searching the night for Tara. She was trying to understand what was happening, and how it could be real.

But Tara had vanished.

The gunman turned on Josi, illuminated in the streetlight. He extended his arm, weapon in hand, as he strode determinedly through the puddled lot in her direction.

Her phone buzzed as she scrambled back into her SUV. A single-word message from Tara lit the screen.

Run

Josi jerked the shifter into Drive. She jammed her foot against the gas pedal, spinning her vehicle in a wild half donut. She fishtailed on the wet asphalt as her tires searched for purchase, then she peeled away.

A second shot went off behind her as she swerved onto the main road, sending her cell phone onto the passenger-side floorboards. She didn't stop or look back until the Bayside Motel disappeared from her rearview mirror.

Chapter Two

Lincoln took his time after dinner with his family, lingering to help with dishes and cleanup, but keeping one eye fixed on the long gravel driveway outside the kitchen window. The Beaumonts shared dinner most weeknights and breakfast quite often as well. Even his brothers, who lived elsewhere, were known to show up for several meals a week. Whatever else was going on in any of their lives, family came first, and sitting together over food was a good way to keep the lines of communication open and flowing. Their mama had taught them that. Everyone was busy these days, but they all needed to eat, so why not break bread together?

His parents put a heavy emphasis on building strong, healthy relationships. Which meant making time for, and giving regular attention to, the people who were important to them. They'd also taught Lincoln and his brothers to engage in regular conversations, to listen more than they spoke and never to put off the occasionally necessary maintenance when cracks formed in the foundation. He was sure those lessons had made it possible for his family to grow stronger over the years and to become larger as his brothers had fallen in love, gotten married and had children of their own. Beaumonts didn't start new lives somewhere else with their spouses—they formed new branches on the ever-expanding tree.

Lincoln hadn't been much of a conversationalist for the last couple of years, but he showed up every night, and he listened. He helped when he could.

Lately he'd especially enjoyed seeing Josi at the table, her bright smile and deep dimples popping out with each bout of laughter. His family clearly viewed her as kin, and she'd accepted them wholly, long before he'd grown so attached.

Her absence tonight, coupled with the hasty way she'd left the stable earlier, had stolen his appetite. The increasing winds and sheeting rain felt like an extension of his inner distress. Maybe it was intuition. Maybe it was post-traumatic-stress-induced fear. Either way, he couldn't shake the bone-deep sensation that something was wrong.

"Lincoln," his mom said softly, a moment before moving into his peripheral vision.

He dipped his chin without making eye contact, attention fixed on the world outside.

She set a soft hand on his shoulder, as was her routine now. She'd devised the pattern following his return from the military. After 74 days spent in captivity, the honorable discharge had been a kindness. In truth, he'd become useless to the army, to his men and to himself. He'd needed time to heal, so he'd come home. And more than two years later, his mother still announced her approach and waited for his acknowledgment before touching him.

He appreciated the lengths she'd gone to in making him comfortable, but the routine wasn't necessary anymore. Not that it ever had been. In truth, the trauma seemed to have heightened his senses, making him hyperaware of his surroundings. Very few people came within ten feet of him without his knowledge.

Lincoln finished drying the plate in his hands then set it on the stack of others. "Hey, Mama." He lifted one palm to cover hers on his shoulder.

"Everything okay?" she asked. "You barely touched your dinner."

He turned to rest his hip against the big farmhouse sink, breaking their physical connection in favor of a better look at her. The threads of white in her otherwise brown hair seemed to have doubled in the past year or so. The lines around her eyes and mouth had deepened. The idea that things could've gone very differently for him overseas, that he could've missed her growing older, his nieces and nephews being born and growing up, hit like a sledgehammer to his chest. "Everything was delicious."

"Something on your mind then?" she asked, examining him with keen blue eyes.

His traitorous gaze flickered to Josi's empty seat, and he snapped it away quickly. "It's probably nothing."

"If you say so." She surveyed the cleared table. "I wonder what happened to Josi tonight."

He nearly huffed out a laugh at her casual tone and innocent expression.

His mother liked to pretend he and his brothers volunteered information, but she knew and saw everything. She just gave them the courtesy of confirmation.

"I can't say."

"Hmm. When I saw her outside the stable earlier, she was looking forward to rehashing the day over dinner. We were going to make plans for improvements on next week's event."

Lincoln's brother, Austin, appeared with their father in the archway to the family room. Austin slid into his jacket and moseyed in their direction, stopping to kiss their mother's cheek. "I saw Josi heading out as I was coming in," he said. "About an hour before dinner."

Lincoln crossed his arms. "There's nothing wrong with your hearing."

Austin grinned. "You know I hate to be left out of a conversation."

Their dad followed Austin into the kitchen. "We caught the tail end of what you were saying. That's all."

Their mama looked from one son to the other. "It isn't like her to miss a meal without an explanation. I tell her she doesn't have to keep us posted the way she does, but she insists it's a respect issue, never wanting us to worry, or to make her a plate if she knows she won't be here. Did she say anything to you, Lincoln?"

Three sets of curious eyes turned to him.

He shrugged, hoping to look more at ease than he felt, and praying the cold fingers of dread that had curled around his lungs were unfounded. "She got a call and went to run an errand."

Josi had seemed distressed by whatever was said on the other end of the line. He'd heard it in her tone and sensed it in the air halfway across the stable. He'd spontaneously offered to go with her, just in case there was trouble, and she'd looked at him as if he'd grown a second head. Clearly not an offer she was interested in, one he should probably apologize for later. Inviting himself along wasn't exactly good manners.

"What kind of errand?" his mom asked.

Lincoln shook his head. "Didn't say."

Austin examined him, probably seeing everything Lincoln didn't want to show. "If you knew that, then why're you so tense?"

"I'm always tense."

"Not like this," Austin said. "You think something could be wrong? Or is it just because—" He slid his eyes toward their mama before returning his cool gaze to Lincoln. "You know." *Because it's her*, the look seemed to say.

Lincoln fought the urge to rub the back of his neck. Fidgeting would give him away. Instead, he stared, careful to control his expression.

The Beaumonts were a military family. Everyone had served, including their mother. His brothers had all taken up careers involving surveillance and protection. Two PIs, one detective and an ATF officer. His parents ran a ranch where seeing through troubled teens' problems and into their hearts was a specialty.

Secrets weren't easily kept on the ranch.

Lincoln pushed away from the sink. "I'm sure nothing's wrong. Josi's with a friend, and I'm tired. A whole lot of folks came through this place today, and y'all know how I feel about people." He kissed his mom's cheek, clapped Austin on the back, then nodded to his dad. "I'm going to head out." He retrieved his coat and hat from hooks near the front door.

He made it as far as the porch, still threading his arms into coat sleeves, before his mother called out. "When you see Josi come in, let her know we missed her. If she hasn't eaten, she can grab a plate anytime. I'll keep one under plastic wrap in the fridge."

"Yeah," he answered, ignoring the implication that his mom knew he'd be watching for her to return safely.

He set his favorite cowboy hat atop his head and strode into the rain, refusing to turn and give the trio behind him a look at his face. He could only imagine the expression there. His thoughts were twisted too tightly to sort, and his family was sure to read in to anything they saw.

He reminded himself that the fear he felt was unfounded. That there wasn't any reason to worry until there was. And if anyone else had missed dinner, he wouldn't have been concerned in the least. Things happened. Time slipped away. People forgot things.

The problem was, as Austin had started to say, then stopped himself, that the missing dinner guest wasn't just anyone. It was Josi. And at least half of Lincoln's thoughts about her were sure to horrify his family. They likely still saw her as the broken teen they'd rescued, but Lincoln had never known that version. When he looked at the young, blond stable manager, he saw a bright, resilient, resourceful woman. Someone who'd survived enough of her own traumas to accept him and his. And he suspected that she, like he and his family, saw much more than she revealed.

He only hoped that none of them knew the whole ugly truth. He'd unintentionally fallen in love with her.

Cold autumn rain pelted his coat and hat as he crossed the darkened field toward his cabin, only a stone's throw from the stables. The small, matching structure beside his belonged to Josi.

A set of headlights swept down the nearby driveway, immediately making him change his direction. He wished, uselessly, for an umbrella to offer her when she emerged from her vehicle. There wasn't time to grab one from his home or the stables, but he could at least keep her company on the walk from car to cabin.

He stuffed his hands into his pockets and picked up the pace.

Josi's old SUV bounced along the well-trodden lane, then unexpectedly hooked a right. She bypassed the wide expanse of gravel where she normally parked and rolled around to the far side of a large outbuilding.

He followed, tension increasing as she shut off her lights.

A stream of rainwater spilled from the brim of his hat as he moved along the side of the building. It didn't make sense for her to park there, unless he was right, and she was in trouble. He half worried she'd drag a body from her trunk. A body he'd probably help hide if she asked.

Josi climbed clumsily from the driver's side of her SUV. She closed the door behind her. Light from her phone screen illuminated her worried face in the darkness.

Thunder rolled as Lincoln cleared his throat, using his mother's method to announce his presence and avoid alarming Josi, who'd yet to notice him. The storm effectively swallowed the sound.

His phone buzzed, and he reached for it on instinct. Josi raised her eyes to his and screamed a half step before colliding with his chest.

"Ahh!"

Lincoln's palms flipped up, the still buzzing cell phone in one hand.

She stumbled back, terror flashing in her eyes. She raised her phone, presumably to clobber him, before recognition dawned, then turned to relief. "Lincoln!" She launched at him, her cheek thumping against his chest. "Oh, thank goodness!"

He froze, arms still bent at the elbows in surrender.

"I was just calling you," she said, her body warm against his shirt, exposed by an unzipped coat. "I called the cops before I got out of the car, but I should've pulled over. I should've called sooner." Her teeth began to chatter as cold November rain poured over them.

Belatedly, his brain snapped back to his body, and his arms lowered to circle her.

She straightened abruptly, wiping her face and knocking

his hands away before he had a chance to return her embrace. "Sorry. I forgot you don't—" She motioned to him, then shook her head. "I didn't mean to—"

Lincoln grimaced. Of course, she hadn't meant to hug him. Why would she think that was reasonable when she apparently didn't think he…what? Touched people? "What's going on?" he asked, ignoring the pinch her impression of him caused in his core. Josi was clearly upset, possibly in danger. That was the important thing. "You called the police?" His voice roared against the storm, rougher and deeper than intended.

She'd also called him when she was clearly upset.

That had to count for something.

Rain swiveled paths over her flushed cheeks and darkened her long blond hair. Her gaze darted worriedly through the night. "Let's talk inside."

Lincoln dipped his chin and extended an arm in the direction of her cabin.

She headed for the stable.

A thousand worries filled his mind as he followed, then waited for her to unlock the door to her office and flip on the lights. She didn't appear injured, and her SUV had seemed undamaged. Both good signs.

"There was a gunman," she said, voice low and unsteady.

Tension seized his spine. "What do you mean, a gunman?" He pressed the door shut behind him, locking out the blowing wind and pounding rain. "Where?"

What kind of errand had she run?

Josi kicked off her sodden shoes and dropped her wet socks on top. "I mean there was a man with a gun. He took a shot at my friend, Tara. She got away, I think, but she's in danger now. I parked out of sight in case the guy somehow followed me." She cringed. "I don't think he did, but I probably shouldn't have come back here."

Lincoln tossed his hat onto an empty chair, then entered the attached half bath and snagged a stack of hand towels from the closet. He passed two to Josi, then ran another over his face and hair. He leaned against the doorjamb when he finished, soaked to the bone from his walk in the rain. "Start from the beginning."

Her blue eyes flashed to him, her body trembling, either due to the cold or excess adrenaline from the scare. Maybe both. "What if I led a deranged criminal here?" she whispered.

"Sit." He pointed to the chair at her back. She bent her knees and landed on the rolling seat.

Her bottom lip wobbled, and he kicked himself internally for a lack of finesse. This was why he made a good soldier, animal trainer and leader. He was firm and direct. It was also why he didn't do well in circumstances requiring a softer touch. "Look." He peeled himself away from the door and moved to the edge of her desk. "If the man who shot at your friend comes here, he'll leave in cuffs, or hog-tied, so that's not a scenario to worry about."

She nodded, wiping tears from her eyes and expelling a long breath. "Okay. You're right."

Fresh memories of her arms around his middle, and her soft body pressed to his, returned unbidden. He clenched his jaw, pushing aside the thoughts. He needed to concentrate. To get the full story about what happened tonight, then make a plan to protect her.

"You're mad," she said. "I knew you would be."

His brow furrowed. "I'm not mad."

"Tell your face."

Lincoln's hackles rose, and his frown deepened. He was

furious with whoever had shot at Josi and at himself for not being better at comforting her. But he was a doer. Not a talker. He thought she understood that. "What happened?" he asked again, more firmly now. "The whole story this time. Start from the beginning. I assume you called the police when you got home to alert them about the shots fired?"

"I called when I got home, because I dropped my phone on the floorboards tearing out of the motel parking lot," she corrected. "I was afraid to slow down or pull over until I got here."

His hands clenched into fists at his sides. He hated the fear in her eyes, tone and posture, and wished he could fix this. "Go on."

"I was supposed to pick up my friend, Tara, from the Bayside Motel on Route Nine. I didn't see her when I got there, so I waited a few minutes for her to come out. When she finally did, she was already running. A man with a gun followed and took a shot at her. Then he turned the gun on me. Tara ran off, and I drove away. I left her."

The tension in Lincoln's body ratcheted to the point of being in pain.

Someone had taken a shot at Josi, and there wasn't a thing he could do about it.

Slowly, she detailed her arrival at the Bayside Motel and the minutes that passed before her escape. She deflated when she finished, having apparently used the remainder of her energy. She lowered her face into waiting palms, elbows anchored on her knees. "She only sent one text. She warned me to run. Now she's not responding, and I have to find her."

"You texted her after calling the police?"

She nodded. "Then I dialed you."

Beyond the interior office window, horses shifted in their

stalls, probably wondering why they were being visited in the night. They likely sensed something was wrong.

Lincoln swiped his phone to life and thumbed through his contacts. "I'll call Finn."

His younger brother, a Marshal's Bluff detective, was sure to want to help. Finn and Josi were close in age. Finn was twenty-five, just two years her senior, and the two had been close during her first year or so with the family, a truth that both warmed and inspired nonsensical jealousy in Lincoln. Finn was a good man and a solid friend. It was nice that he'd been there for Josi when she'd needed someone. Lincoln had been halfway around the world.

He raised the phone to his ear and waited.

"Put it on speaker," Josi said, straightening enough to wrap her arms around her middle. "Please. I'd like to hear."

"Hey, man," Finn answered. "I was just going to call you."

Lincoln pressed the speaker button. "I'm here with Josi," he said. "You've got us both on the line."

"Ah. Hey, Jos."

She inhaled deeply, squaring her shoulders against the chairback. "Hey, Finn."

"I'm out here at the Bayside Motel on Route Nine. You know why?"

Her eyes swept to Lincoln's. "Yeah. I was there tonight."

The line was eerily quiet for a long moment, save for the muffled sound of rain.

"We got a call about a shots fired at this location," Finn said. "A witness described an SUV similar to yours leaving the scene. Said the driver was a woman with long blond hair."

Lincoln felt his eyes close. "Did they get a plate number on the vehicle?"

"No," Finn said.

Lincoln's eyes reopened as Josi groaned.

"The guy with the gun looked right at me," she said.

"But it's pretty dark out here and raining," Finn said. "Only one decent light in the lot."

"I parked under the light."

Lincoln's grip tightened around the cell phone, his protective instincts kicking into high gear. He threw the wadded hand towel onto the floor near Josi's shoes. "Anything else?"

"Not yet," Finn said. "But the night's young. I'll be around tomorrow to catch you up on anything I uncover. Meanwhile, I'd like to get a preliminary statement from Jos. Starting with what she was doing out here on a night like this."

As if there was ever a good reason to be at that place, Lincoln thought, passing the phone to Josi. The Bayside Motel was a haven for criminals, thugs and troublemakers.

"Hey, Linc?" Finn asked, as Josi's trembling fingers touched his.

"Yeah?"

"Do me a favor—stay with her tonight," he said. "And keep your phone close."

Lincoln looked to Josi, his thundering heart suddenly competing with the storm. He pressed one palm to the desk, anchoring himself against the thought of anyone attempting to harm her. He'd gladly do whatever it took to keep her safe, but she might not want him around for a whole night. Or another minute. It was never easy to guess what she was thinking.

He supposed he could camp out on her porch, if she wasn't comfortable having him inside.

"Lincoln can stay at my place tonight, if he wants," Josi

told Finn. Her steely gaze locked with Lincoln's. "He's going
to help me look for Tara in the morning."

"Good. Now tell me about Tara," Finn said.

He nodded his agreement without hesitation.

Josi set her hand over Lincoln's on the desk. The sight
of her small, thin fingers against his big, scarred mitt sent
heat through his core. And when she mouthed the words
thank you, he felt a fissure form in his long-hardened heart.

Chapter Three

Josi rolled over in bed, pulling her knees to her chest, and the comforter to her chin. Her limbs were heavy and her mind clouded as she willed herself to drift back to sleep.

Memories of the previous night returned like a landslide, making her sit her upright and kicking her heart rate into a gallop. The phantom sounds of gunshots rang in her ears. Images of Tara's panicked face as she looked directly at Josi, then ran in the other direction, hit like a slap across her cheek. Josi had assumed Tara didn't see her in the darkness and rain, but by light of day, her friend's actions read differently. As if Tara had been trying to protect her. Maybe even to lead the man away, or at least not let him know Josi was there for her. She'd even sent a follow-up text. *Run.*

Tara had done what she could to protect Josi. So where was she now?

Josi pulled her phone from the nightstand to check for messages. There hadn't been anything new since she'd fallen asleep. On the couch.

Her attention jumped to the open doorway, and her galloping heart pulled into a sprint.

Lincoln had spent the night in her cabin. And he'd…carried her to bed?

Was he still there? Asleep on her couch?

She thanked her lucky stars she'd put the laundry away. If he'd seen a stack of her underthings in the basket or her bras drying on the shower rod, she might've passed away. No need to worry about the guy with a gun.

Her feet hit the floor with a thud, and her body was in motion toward the door. She paused to check her breath against one palm, then frowned and headed for the bathroom. She needed to brush her teeth and comb her hair. At least she hadn't slept in her wet clothes. The rain had forced her to change into something dry when she and Lincoln had returned from the barn. He'd stopped at his place first to grab a dry outfit, and he'd insisted she go with him. He'd barely let her out of his sight since he'd appeared behind her SUV the night before.

Josi hurried through her morning routine as quickly and quietly as possible, taking an extra moment for lip gloss and mascara. Then she hustled into the living room, trying and failing to imagine Lincoln's long, lean frame stretched out on her couch.

Surprisingly Lincoln was nowhere to be found.

A bright pink sticky note on the kitchen countertop had a message for her, written in a tight, messy scrawl. If she woke in time for breakfast, the family wanted to see her. The request was signed with a single letter. *L*. She checked the clock, then grabbed her coat. Mrs. Beaumont likely hadn't served the meal yet. Morning chores would barely be finished by now, and Mr. Beaumont oversaw those before they ate.

Josi plunged her feet into tall rubber barn boots by the door, then headed out.

The day was cool and dreary, as expected, the ground soggy from recent heavy rain. Gray clouds skated across a bleak sky. Another storm was on the way. Hopefully, this one would be strictly meteorological and not metaphorical.

She tugged the zipper on her coat and shrank into the fabric, huddling against the wind. Her small cabin sat beside Lincoln's at the far side of the stable, making it a convenient commute to work and a several-minute walk to the farmhouse.

From the quick peek she'd gotten last night, Lincoln's place was minimally decorated. Only the necessary furniture and some framed photos. She hadn't been brave enough to look too closely, unsure how long it would take him to change clothes and return for her. It hadn't been long. Her rooms were full of books, throw pillows and blankets. All the comfortable and soothing things she'd longed for as a kid and promised herself to have in abundance as an adult. Her expert thrift-shopping skills made it possible to create magazine-worthy appeal on a stable manager's budget. Another win-win where she was concerned.

They'd discussed her experience at the motel over cold sandwiches and chips from her kitchen, hypothesizing reasons for Tara to have been there and who the man might be. Eventually, Josi had turned on the television and navigated to the local news, hoping to catch any revelations about the case. The shooting hadn't even been mentioned, and she'd apparently fallen asleep. Leaving Lincoln alone.

Based on the stacks of her favorite romantic suspense novels dotting every flat surface from desk to windowsill, her deep fascination with cowboys was no longer a secret.

She cringed.

At least he didn't know he'd been the one to kick-start that particular fantasy.

She pressed thoughts of him from her mind with a purposeful thrust, then focused on the upcoming meal instead.

She was sure Mrs. Beaumont and at least one of Lincoln's brothers had caught her staring at Lincoln in the past. They'd never said anything, but they'd definitely seen. Now that she'd spent so much time with him outside of work, even for this awful reason, she felt uncomfortably exposed. And her crush felt more like an ugly bruise.

She wet her lips, and the taste of cherry-flavored gloss nearly caused her to misstep. She rarely wore makeup and never to work. Every Beaumont at the table would notice. Some might even guess the reason. Though, probably not Lincoln, who was endlessly oblivious to her attempts at flirtation. She pulled a tissue from the pocket of her coat and wiped the shine from her lips. There wasn't anything to be done about the mascara.

Her pace slowed as another thought came to mind. If the whole family knew Lincoln had stayed at her place all night, would they have questions? Concerns?

Probably not, she realized. Josi was a full five years younger than Lincoln, and the Beaumonts still looked at her as if she was a teen in need of protecting. They'd never suspect anything inappropriate could happen between her and Lincoln. In fact, she thought ironically, her dreams that Lincoln would one day realize he was madly in love with her were probably evidence to support the fact she was still the kid everyone saw her as.

She sighed and shored up her nerves with each determined, if somewhat reluctant, step. Everyone would want to know she was okay and hear the story of the motel and gunman from her lips. They'd want to comfort and reassure her, because they were wonderful people. And that was where her thoughts should be. With Tara, wherever she was. Not on Lincoln.

The farmhouse's front door opened as she reached the

steps, and Lincoln moved onto the porch. The tiny smile she loved played at the corners of his mouth, but he quickly tamped it down.

"Waiting for me?" she teased.

He dipped his chin once, eyes narrowing. "Yeah." He shoved his hands into his pockets, the exposed skin beneath his short sleeves pebbling from the frigid wind. "I didn't want to leave you this morning, but I thought you might prefer to get ready without me hanging around. I've kept an eye on your place and the lane."

"Thanks."

The door behind him sucked open, jostling a grapevine wreath covered in faux autumn leaves and tiny pumpkins. Mrs. Beaumont hustled out. "Oh, you two! It's freezing!" She tugged her son backward and extended her free arm toward Josi. "Come inside!"

Lincoln watched as Josi allowed his mother to sweep her into the home.

She felt his eyes on her all the way to the kitchen.

"There she is," Mr. Beaumont said, greeting her with a warm hug. "How are you doing this morning? Were you able to get a little rest last night? We heard all about what happened. I expect these guys to get into harm's way from time to time, but we try to keep you safe." He motioned to Lincoln's brothers, Finn, Austin and Dean, already seated at the table. One detective and two private investigators.

Josi took one of the empty chairs, and Mr. Beaumont sat across from her.

Mrs. Beaumont and Lincoln followed, each carrying a tray of food from the counter. They placed the items at the table's center with others already in wait.

"Coffee?" Finn asked, passing a carafe in her direction.

"Thanks." She accepted the vessel and smiled at her family. Whatever else happened, she was thankful for this group.

Mrs. Beaumont lowered herself gracefully onto the chair beside her husband, and Lincoln took the seat next to Josi.

Josi fixed her attention on Finn. "How'd it go last night at the motel? Any leads on Tara?"

He shook his head. "Not yet."

"Any signs she was hit when that guy fired at her?" Josi had worried herself sick over the possibility Tara might've taken a bullet before sending that final text warning Josi to run.

"No traces of blood, but the rains were pretty heavy last night," Finn said. "My men are working the crime scene more thoroughly this morning. With a little luck, the wind didn't blow those shell casings too far. Ballistics will try to match them to the gun or another crime in the database. We can find the owner from there."

Platters of food made their ways around the table, passed hand to hand, as Finn spoke. Muffins and breads. Fresh fruits and yogurt. Jellies and jams. A lidded casserole with quiche. Another with sliced bacon and sausage links.

Josi selected toast and jam, fruit and eggs, then nabbed a slice of bacon. She filled the mug before her with coffee from the carafe and sipped gingerly as she sent up more prayers for Tara's safety.

What on earth had she gotten mixed up in that would cause someone to shoot at her? The Tara that Josi knew was quiet and a little shy. Smart and determined. Nothing that suggested she'd be in a room at a shady motel with a gunman.

Mrs. Beaumont watched Josi closely as she ate. The expression was maternal, as always, but with an edge of curiosity Josi hadn't seen before. "We were glad to hear you accepted Lincoln's offer to stay with you last night."

Josi stilled, unsure how to respond. "Finn suggested it was a good idea."

"Everyone agrees," Mrs. Beaumont said sweetly.

Josi glanced to Finn, then Lincoln. The former appeared amused. The latter, furious.

"We know how independent you are," their mom continued. "It probably felt like having a babysitter, but it wasn't intended that way."

Josi cringed at her word choice and turned her focus to her meal. If she kept her mouth full, no one would expect her to respond.

Finn forked a bite of quiche, then he set down his fork while he chewed. "Jos, you said you hadn't spoken to Tara in a long while before last night, but do you have any idea what she might've been up to?"

"None." Josi bit her lip, the faint taste of cherry still clinging there. "We haven't spoken much since her brother died." Maybe the grief had sent her into a spiral. "She apologized for calling me to ask a favor, which was odd, because we really were close once. She said she wasn't sure who else she could trust."

Finn leaned forward, eyebrows up. "Were those her words?"

Josi paused, reaching mentally backward for the conversation and for Tara's exact statement. "I think so. Why?"

Dean kicked back in his chair, coffee mug cradled between his palms. "Big difference between deciding who she could ask and who she could trust. Deciding who to ask might mean she wasn't sure who'd help if she needed it, or even who'd be available."

"You've got to know someone a little to ask for a favor,"

Austin added, running with his brother's train of thought. "You've got to know them well to trust them."

Lincoln shifted at her side, his arm brushing hers as he moved. "It goes deeper than that," Lincoln said. "If I had something I didn't want everyone to know, I could ask anyone at this table to keep my secret. They're all family. I know them all well. But I wouldn't necessarily trust any of them to keep some things to themselves."

Austin pointed his fork at Lincoln and winked, then returned to his breakfast with a hearty laugh.

Everyone else became suddenly, and equally, amused.

Josi frowned, missing the humor in the topic. "I guess if Tara had a secret she didn't want getting out, I'd be a good choice for her call. I don't know anyone in her current circle, or if she has one. And I have no connection to our old friends, if she's even still running with any of them."

Finn nodded, sobering from the joke Josi had clearly missed. "Do you know if she lost the house she was renting?"

The idea of Tara without a home soured Josi's stomach. "What do you mean?" The fear of having nowhere to live was a burden Josi had carried for many years. Especially as she'd gotten older and fewer foster families were open to taking in teens. Thankfully, Tara's older brother had returned from the marines when she'd needed him most, and he'd taken her in before she landed on the streets. Just the way the Beaumonts had brought Josi to the ranch.

"According to the desk clerk at the motel," Finn said, "Tara had been staying in that room for a couple of weeks and paying cash."

So she hadn't gone there on a whim, and not to party or hook up.

She'd been living there.

Josi felt her features bunch and her nose wrinkle. "I thought she still lived downtown, on Bay View."

Finn lifted his chin. "That's the street listed on her driver's license. I'm headed over there on my way to the station. We should probably talk about your SUV before I go."

Josi pulled the key from her pocket. "I can move it if it's in the way. I was freaked out last night and didn't want to leave it in the open."

"That was smart," Finn said. "Dad and Dean cleared out some space inside the storage building this morning. Leave the key and I'll move it in there when I leave. Just due diligence," he added. "Until we figure out who had the gun and why."

"But Lincoln said he'd help me look for Tara this morning."

Mrs. Beaumont waved a carefree hand in her direction. "Linc can drive you anywhere you need to go. And if you're with him, we won't worry so much."

Josi's lips parted but words failed to come. She'd assumed she'd do the driving, and he'd come along in case of trouble. Making him her personal chauffer was a lot more than he'd agreed to.

Lincoln wiped his mouth on a napkin, then set the cloth on the table. "I figured we'd visit Tara's work. Make a circle around town, ask a few questions. Someone has to know something that will point us in her direction."

The family all nodded, apparently in agreement with his plan.

Josi's heart swelled. Lincoln wasn't just going with her as muscle in case of trouble. He was actively partnering with her on the project.

As if she needed one more reason to be a goner for this man.

Chapter Four

By three o'clock, Lincoln had finished his work at the stable. The riding lessons were over for the day, and Josi was in her office wrapping up things on her end as well. They'd soon shower, change and begin their reconnaissance mission to garner information on Josi's missing friend. With some luck, the outing would involve the woman's safe recovery as well.

He and Josi had never left the ranch together, and it would be nice if everything went smoothly, and maybe he got to be a hero. Unfortunately, the only type of luck Lincoln seemed to have lately was bad.

Nerves coiled and tensed in his limbs as he approached the open office door, making his footfalls as loud as possible. No one liked being startled, and Josi was already, understandably, on edge.

Her eyes met his instantly, and were a little wider than usual. "I was just finishing up." She powered off her computer and grabbed her jacket from a hook near the door. "Ready?"

He nodded, watching her carefully as she moved. Coordinating his life with someone else's hadn't been a necessity in a very long time. Even growing up with siblings and the years spent in the military hadn't prepared him for this. "Should we shower first?"

Josi stopped abruptly. "What do you mean?"

"I can grab my things and take them to your cabin, or you're welcome to wait while I get cleaned up." Lincoln shifted his weight and gripped the back of his neck. "Either way, I'd like to stick together, if you don't mind."

Her cheeks flushed, and the misunderstanding became apparent.

He fought the knee-jerk urge to react. *No growling. No cussing. Or anything else that might make matters worse*, he warned himself internally. "I can wait on your porch during your shower."

Josi nodded slowly, as if struggling to come back from wherever her thoughts had taken her. Hopefully not to a place that labeled him as deeply inappropriate, or worse, a pervert. "If I promise to hurry, can we split up instead? Shower and meet back here in twenty minutes?" she suggested, averting her big blue eyes.

He considered the possibility. Hated it. But he had no solid reason to protest, and he didn't want to start their time together off-site with unnecessary tension. No need to paint himself as more of a pain in her backside than she surely already thought he was. He dipped his chin in reluctant agreement, then they made their way home to neighboring cabins.

Lincoln took a seat on her porch fourteen minutes later, freshly showered and hat in hand. The idea of being Josi's personal protector had been on his mind almost as much as the woman herself. He was responsible for her safety, which meant he had a reason to spend as much time with her as she'd allow, and no one would question it. He could ask all the questions he had bottled up without seeming nosy. He'd just be passing time. Getting to know her. Putting her at ease.

His family knew far more about Josi than he did. They loved and respected her. They'd brought her into the fold long before he'd come home.

He had catching up to do.

The door to her cabin opened, and Josi stepped out, dressed in nice-fitting jeans, sneakers and a black wool coat that hugged her narrow hips and waist. Her signature scent hit him with the wind. Coconuts and vanilla. No matter the season or weather, Josi smelled like a lazy summer day at the beach.

"Oh." She stopped short, pressing a hand to her chest. "You're here. I thought I'd beat you."

"I just got here."

She bit her lower lip, probably deciding if he was telling the truth.

Lincoln stood and pulled keys from his pocket, and she moved to his side without another word.

He could vividly remember the moment he'd met her, in the days following his return from the military. She'd talked to him when he didn't talk back. Sang while she worked. Generally made no show of being uncomfortable around a near stranger who was still half-haunted by his experiences a world away. She'd brought books to his cabin in the evenings. Bottled water and snacks during the day. She'd left both on the steps, where he would find them, but never knocked or intruded on his need for space. When he was finally ready to work, she behaved as if it was any other day.

For all those things and more, Lincoln owed her far more than a temporary position as a bodyguard. He owed her his life. There wasn't any way to know what might've happened to him if not for her presence in those early, dark days following his discharge. But he was certain he wouldn't be the man he was now without her.

Josi stole glances at him as they crossed the field, then climbed into his truck.

He started the engine and adjusted the heater. Temperatures were falling fast in their small coastal town and would likely continue to decline for the next few days, until all the storms had passed.

The radio powered on with the truck, delivering the tail end of a popular country song, and Lincoln shifted into gear while Josi buckled up.

They made it as far as the road at the end of the driveway before the station's DJ returned with news of the previous night's shooting.

Lincoln turned up the volume as he navigated the pickup onto the smooth dark ribbon of asphalt leading away from home.

"Two women were reported as targets. Security-camera footage confirms one woman escaped on foot, the other in her SUV, both were believed to be local, and the lucky driver? Josi Roberts, a stable manager at the Beaumont Ranch, a long-established haven in our community."

Josi made a small choking sound that spiked Lincoln's growing irritation.

He tapped his dashboard screen, teeth gritted as he commanded, "Call Finn."

"I know," his brother said, without greeting and before a single ring came through the speakers. "We're working to get her name removed from the story, but it's already been posted to the station's web page. Before you lose your patience with me, please remember we all love Josi, and she has you. Tara's on her own. We've got to stay focused on finding her."

Lincoln's traitorous gaze flickered sideways, seeking Josi, then he returned his eyes to the road. Had she understood the implication in his brother's words? They all loved her. Including Lincoln. Would she assume he loved her the way they did? Like a sister?

"What's wrong?" Her voice drew his gaze once more. Her bright eyes were slightly narrowed, her pretty lips in a frown. "You look affronted."

"He always looks affronted," Finn said. "I'll do what I can to fix this," he promised.

"I know," she said, dragging her attention to the screen. "We trust you, and like you said, I'm safe with Lincoln. Any leads on Tara?"

Pleasure swept through him at her words. He resisted the urge to smile. Josi's name had been leaked to the media, then announced on the local radio station and posted on-line, so he would smile after he knew she was truly safe.

"Nothing yet," Finn said.

Josi crossed her legs, then quickly uncrossed them. "It's been nearly twenty-four hours. She hasn't responded to my texts, and my calls go straight to voice mail. What does that mean? Is the phone dead? Is it off?"

"I'm working with Tech to track the device," he said. "If the phone's still on, we'll be able to narrow the search. I've got an incoming call now. Keep an eye on my brother, would ya?"

"Keep me in the loop," she said, ignoring Finn's goofy request.

The call disconnected, and Josi huffed lightly. "We should probably start with the home Tara shared with her brother. At dinner, Finn made it sound as if her address hasn't changed."

"On Bay View?" Lincoln asked, recalling the conversation clearly.

"Yeah. A yellow cottage near the cul-de-sac. I don't remember the address, but I'll know the house when I see it."

Lincoln took the next left, heading toward downtown.

"If she's not there, we can try her work, or reach out to the old friend group Tara and I shared. She might still be in touch with some of them."

"Sounds good." Both his grip and his jaw tightened. Now that her name had been leaked, his time with her felt significantly less fun, and more high-stakes.

The thin silver lining, he supposed, was that she was with him, and he was better trained, more capable and more highly motivated to protect her than anyone.

JOSI WATCHED THE familiar surroundings fly past her window as Lincoln piloted his massive truck into town. The interior smelled of fresh air, sunshine and hay. There were also hints of the spearmint gum he often chewed mixed with the aftershave he sometimes wore. His clothes and boots were well-worn and obviously old. As far as she could tell, he hadn't spent money on much of anything since his return from the military, except his truck. The behemoth was everything a cowboy could want. Big and shiny, formidable and expensive, but not just for show. The vehicle worked as hard as its owner, hauling, towing and transporting everything from hay bales to horse trailers on an almost daily basis. His priorities were clearly based on activities, and not appearances. One more thing she appreciated. Hard work rarely steered a person wrong.

She'd often wondered if Lincoln spent so many hours in motion to keep his mind busy. Perhaps to avoid the thoughts he wished he never had. That had been her reasoning once.

These days, however, she spent extra time at work because he was there.

Now she was inside his truck. And they were alone in the smallest space they'd ever shared. If only the reason for their being in this position was anything other than the search for a missing friend.

A beaded chain and black dog tag swung from the rearview mirror. She'd learned, after a quick internet search during Lincoln's early days home, that the color signified his position as a US Army Ranger. He'd barely spoken then, and she'd had innumerable questions.

The truck slowed, and her thoughts returned to the moment, eyes searching the row of older homes on each side of the road. Tara's neighborhood was blue-collar and filled with young families. Children rode bikes on sidewalks and played in the streets. No adults in sight. She supposed most of the parents in this area worked outside the home and would return after five. Meanwhile, the kids were likely fresh off the school bus and releasing seven hours of pent-up energy.

"There." She spotted the familiar yellow cottage and pointed. The home was in need of fresh paint and a little yard work, but it was nicer than a lot of the places she and Tara had lived as youths. "Grass is long."

"Finn said Tara was staying at the motel lately," Lincoln said.

He stopped at the end of the driveway, surveying the scene. No cars. No garage. No indication anyone was home. He parked at the curb and settled the engine. His keen gaze traveled over the homes, lawns and playing children.

"I'm going to knock," she said, opening her door to climb out.

In a perfect scenario, Tara would invite them in and explain what was going on. Then Josi and the Beaumonts could protect her while Finn located and arrested the gunman.

Lincoln followed her silently, his looming presence sending chills over her skin.

Whatever came at her today, Josi would be safe. It was unlikely anyone in Marshal's Bluff could get the best of Lincoln, and she had a feeling he'd protect her at all costs. He was all about completing assignments.

She knocked on Tara's door and waited, then rang the bell when no one answered. A few seconds later, she peeked through the front window. A small split between drawn curtains provided a glimpse of the tidy living room.

"What do you see?" Lincoln asked, stepping closer to her side.

She cupped her hands against the sides of her face to block the sun and help her focus. "Couch. Books on the coffee table. Framed photos on the fireplace. Looks like her stuff."

"Signs of a struggle?"

She shook her head. "Nope."

"Signs of a pet?"

Josi straightened, heart suddenly in her throat. "I don't think so." She hadn't thought of that possibility. She set a hand on his coat sleeve, moved by his concern for an animal that Tara may have had.

His gaze locked with hers for a long beat before dropping to her fingers.

She pulled back, tucking her hand into her pocket. Lincoln barely spoke. He probably wasn't big on touch either. So why couldn't she seem to stop touching him? "Tara wasn't the nurturing type," she said, redirecting his attention. "She swore she'd never have kids. Her childhood was rough. Marcus took care of her. Surviving was the real goal. She never wanted any added strings or responsibilities."

He nodded, then swept an arm outward, motioning her back toward the truck. "What about you?"

She frowned as they parted ways at the curb, him to the driver's side and her to the passenger door.

"How do you feel about strings?" he asked.

"Pets or kids?"

He lifted and dropped one shoulder before climbing behind the wheel.

She hurried to slide inside and catch his eye once more. "I love animals, and I get to hang out with the livestock every day at the ranch. It's like having a couple dozen various pets. I'd like kids too, I think, someday, but I didn't exactly have a decent role model, so—"

"You don't want to mess them up," he said.

"Yeah." Her heart fell at his words. He understood. Was it because he had a similar idea about her?

"I think the same thing about myself."

Her jaw dropped. "What do you mean? You have the perfect parental examples."

He started the engine and turned the wheel. "But I'm not the same kid they raised. Parts of me are broken that won't ever be the same."

"But they will heal," she said, suddenly sticking up for him, despite the fact he was his own attacker. "Broken bones are strongest at the points where they healed."

Lincoln lanced her with sharp green eyes, stealing her words and breath.

A round of riotous laughter drew their attention to the cul-de-sac, where a pair of boys bounced basketballs in a driveway.

He rolled slowly toward the kids and powered down his window. "Hey."

The kids advanced on the truck, lips parted in what looked like awe.

"You know the lady who lives there?" Lincoln asked, pointing to the yellow cottage.

They nodded, eyes wide as they took in the big black truck and its driver.

"Seen her lately?" Lincoln asked, voice low and thick with authority.

They shook their heads.

Josi guessed the kids to be in middle school, maybe sixth or seventh grade. Both wore ribbed white tank tops and basketball shorts. She leaned in Lincoln's direction, projecting her voice through the open window. "Does she have a dog or cat?"

"No, ma'am," the taller kid said. "It's just Ms. Tara."

Lincoln looked over his shoulder at Josi, eyes narrowed. "They talk now? All they did was move their heads for me."

She grinned, and his lips pulled into a frown.

Josi waved to the kids. "Thank you. If you see her, will you let her know her friend came to see her?"

"Yes, ma'am."

Lincoln stepped on the gas pedal and the truck rolled away before Josi could tell the kids her name. In hindsight, maybe that was best.

They left the neighborhood more quickly than they'd entered, making unnecessary turns and breaking the residential speed limit.

"Are we in a hurry?" she asked, bracing a palm against the dashboard as Lincoln took another speedy right.

Lincoln grunted. "I think we were being followed, but I lost him." He glanced at her, then back to his rearview mirror. "I haven't seen them in a couple of blocks. I'm just putting space between us now."

"We were being followed?" Josi's heart rate hiked. "Since when?"

"Since we pulled away from the curb outside her door. I noticed while we spoke to those kids."

Josi checked her sideview mirror, then angled in her seat for a better look at the empty road behind them. She hadn't seen anything unusual, other than the change in Lincoln's driving. Her stomach knotted with memories of the night before. Of a man with a gun, willing to take a shot at the back of a terrified woman already running away.

"What's next?" Lincoln asked, falling into the steady pulse of downtown traffic.

All around them, storefronts and sidewalks had been adorned with festive fall and holiday decor. Hay bales and cornstalks. Silk autumn-colored leaves and twinkle lights. Even a few early Christmas trees glowed beyond glass windows.

"Pawnshop, I think." Most people spent more time with coworkers than their families. Hopefully, Tara's coworkers would know more about where she was or what she'd been up to recently than her young neighbors. "She worked there last year. If she moved on, maybe someone will know where she works now."

Lincoln initiated his turn signal and changed lanes. "That's not in a great area of town."

"Nope." Josi gave Lincoln a fresh once-over, seeing him through a new lens. "You're going to stand out down there. Folks might even think you're a cop."

He snorted. "I look like a cop?"

"Maybe not, but you definitely look like trouble."

Mischief flashed in his eyes and his lips curved into a slow, sexy grin. "What am I supposed to do about that?"

Josi's mouth opened before she thought better of it. "I guess we need a reasonable explanation for why someone who clearly doesn't belong is in the area. Since you'll be with me, you should probably pretend to be my boyfriend."

Chapter Five

Josi's body tensed as they traveled the roads of her past, through intersections where the ghosts of street fights still sent shivers over her skin. Born to a mom with no business raising a daughter and without the good sense to give her baby to people who could protect her, Josi had lived a hundred equally awful lives before she'd been old enough to drive. Like most of her friends and foster siblings, she'd been in a dozen houses before middle school. Pulled from her mother's negligent care for temporary, emergency placement, only to be returned to her home a few days, weeks or months later. No roots. No security. Nothing of her own. Unless she counted the emotional pain, scars, neglect and trauma. All permanent gifts from her mother.

"You okay?" Lincoln asked, his voice jarring her from the dreary trip down memory lane.

"Yeah."

He probably heard the lie. Her answer had been too thin and breathy. But he didn't comment. A few blocks later, they parked outside Petey's Pawnshop.

Red block letters on the glass encouraged folks to come inside. *Get a deal! Trade stuff for cash!*

Walking the stretch of sidewalk to the door brought another wave of unwanted memories. Underage drinking. The scent of marijuana. Friends hocking things they'd stolen for money to buy more pot or beer. Petey always cut a deal, pretending he didn't know how a group of teens like them had gotten their hands on designer bags and jewelry. When Tara had come to him for employment at eighteen, he'd given her a job. Josi supposed she could thank him for that.

She was still unclear where Petey stood in the division between good and evil. Or where anyone stood for that matter.

She smoothed sweat-slicked palms against her hips and took a centering breath as Lincoln opened and held the door for her. Her ears rang and heart pounded as they stepped into the display room of miscellaneous items. Sad aisles filled with stuff people were forced to let go. Things traded for drug money, bill money, bail money, or maybe a second chance.

Things a bunch of unsupervised, lawless kids had pinched for fun.

Lincoln matched her pace, walking so closely that his arm brushed hers. Then the gentle pressure of his hand against her back caused her steps to stutter. His cool green eyes were watching when she jerked her gaze to his. "Would you prefer to hold hands?"

Josi's mouth opened, and a small unintelligible sound emerged.

Lincoln raised one eyebrow by a tiny fraction. "Don't your boyfriends usually hold your hand?"

She nodded, slammed back to the present by her earlier suggestion. She'd assumed he wasn't on board when he'd failed to respond. Then she'd promptly died of humiliation, only to be resurrected by the changing scenery outside her window and thoughts of something worse. Her life before the Beaumonts.

Lincoln's large, calloused palm pressed against her hand,

and she inhaled a shaky breath. He studied her face as he spread her fingers and slid his in between.

A thrill coursed through her as they began to walk once more.

"Well, looky here," a deep baritone boomed from the distance a moment before Petey appeared, wiping his hands on a shop rag.

If Josi had to guess, he'd probably been watching them via security cameras since they'd entered, maybe before, if the cameras out front were working.

Tattoos stretched from the short sleeves of Petey's navy T-shirt to his wrists. Similar patterns of ink climbed his neck from collar to chin. His hair was grayer than she remembered. More lines and creases had gathered on his face. He was still big. Tall and broad, but not as intimidating as she'd once imagined.

A pair of younger men in flannel shirts and jeans emerged a moment later, from the densely packed aisles.

"Petey," Josi said. "Any chance you've seen Tara today?"

"No." He shook his head. "Y'all seen Tara?" he asked, tossing her question to the others.

The younger duo smiled, shaking their heads. One dragged a hand through unkempt hair. The other scratched his bearded chin. Nothing about their expressions was friendly.

The blond man narrowed his eyes. "What do you want with Tara?"

Petey clucked his tongue. "They're friends, Dustin," he said. "Like sisters once. Doesn't she tell you anything?"

Dustin's cheeks darkened as his eyes flashed back to Josi, then climbed Lincoln from head to toe in careful evaluation. "How come I never seen you with her?"

Lincoln squeezed her hand. "She's been with me."

The air left the room as all three men stared.

Lincoln straightened slowly to his full height, and the energy around them became erratic. Something in his low tenor voice was new to Josi and, honestly, a little frightening.

"Who the hell are you?" Dustin asked.

Lincoln stared, clearly unmotivated to answer, and possibly considering how best to knock him out for swearing at him.

"He's my boyfriend," Josi answered. "I am Tara's friend. We were supposed to hang out, but I can't reach her."

Dustin didn't look convinced. "When were you going to hang out?"

Josi wiggled free from Lincoln and pulled her phone from her bag, then retrieved her call log. She scrolled to the point where Tara called her, then all the times she'd tried calling her back. "She called. We made plans. Then she just went silent."

Dustin's gaze jumped to Petey.

"You're not the only one asking those questions," Petey said. He bent forward at the waist, resting meaty forearms on the glass countertop between them. "Someone was already in here looking for her."

"Who?" Lincoln asked.

"Cops?" Josi guessed.

Petey sucked his teeth. "Nah, but they called a bit ago. They're coming this afternoon."

Lincoln's hand skimmed across her back, fingers tightening at her waist as he pulled her to his side. "Is Tara in some kind of trouble?"

The younger duo exchanged quiet words then headed for the door. They didn't stop until they were outside.

"Dustin worries about her," Petey said. "But she'll turn

up. Tara—" He chuckled, expression softening slightly. "She's tough, and she doesn't have time for boys or nonsense." He gave Josi a closer look. "You used to be the same way. Seems like a lot's changed. You've grown up nice."

Something like a growl rumbled in Lincoln's chest, and Petey straightened.

Taller than most people at close to six foot four, he was at least twenty years older than Lincoln and a hundred pounds heavier. If his plan was to intimidate, it was his unlucky day.

She stepped in front of her new boyfriend, still a little turned on by that growl and forced a tight smile for Petey. "If you see Tara, let her know I'm looking for her. If she's in some kind of trouble, I can help."

Josi turned and tugged Lincoln's arm, urging him to follow.

He stood his ground, eyes fixed on Petey far longer than was comfortable for anyone, before relenting to her silent request.

When they reached the sidewalk, a familiar voice rose from around the corner. It seemed Dustin and his friend hadn't gone far.

"She'll probably show up at Brady's tonight," one voice said. "Don't sweat it. Tara never misses a party."

Lincoln unlocked the truck and opened Josi's door. He waited while she climbed inside before rounding the hood to join her. He hadn't helped her into his ride when they'd left the farm or Tara's house. Apparently this was the Lincoln Beaumont girlfriend experience.

Add in the way he hadn't stopped touching her while they were in the pawnshop, and the protective growl… Josi would likely never recover.

LINCOLN PULLED INTO TRAFFIC, mind bucking. He hated the way the beefy pawnshop guy had ogled Josi. The two skinny punks hadn't been much better, but the older man seemed to think he had some kind of claim over her because he'd known her when she was a kid. Not only was the age difference unacceptable, and the way he looked at her completely disrespectful, but that guy also didn't know anything about Josi Roberts. Whoever she'd been when she'd last walked into that shop, it wasn't the same woman seated beside him today.

He reached across the seat between them and set a hand on her knee—he felt protective, proud and…*out of line*. His eyes slid closed a moment, then reopened to focus on the road. They were pretending to be romantically involved for the sake of finding Tara, but that pretense should've stopped when they were away from questioning eyes.

The role had just been so easy to fall into. Comfortable, natural and nice.

Now, his hand was on her knee, and it did not belong there. He locked his jaw and raised his arm, reaching quickly for the radio instead.

Josi caught his hand and settled it back on her knee. She curled small fingers around his palm and squeezed. As if touching him was the most normal thing in the world.

A barrage of hopeful thoughts took shape in his mind, and he fought the smile trying to form.

The flash of black in his rearview mirror put an instant stop to the high. The car from Tara's neighborhood was back, and it was gaining speed behind them.

Instinct kicked his muscles into gear, and he pressed the gas pedal to the floor.

Josi yelped softly beside him, releasing his hand when he pulled it back to the steering wheel. "Same car from before?" she asked, angling for a look behind them.

"Looks like it."

Lincoln powered into the next turn, and the truck fish-tailed around the corner. His vehicle easily recovered and launched forward once more, gaining speed and distance while the driver behind them struggled for control. Lincoln would've snorted at the complete ineptitude had his heart rate not kicked into an unbidden sprint, dividing his focus. He hadn't had a panic attack in months, but he recognized the signs. He intentionally kept his routines as predictable as possible, and that kept the attacks under control. Except now, he was unexpectedly calling on the offensive driving experience he'd picked up in another place and time, and his mind was filling with unwanted images of destruction.

A fervent curse slipped through his gritted teeth.

The cars and pedestrians around them became little more than blurs. His vision tunneled, and the upcoming traffic light turned yellow. Lincoln stomped on the gas, earning a series of honks as his truck sailed through the intersection and careened away.

His breaths grew shorter and more shallow as he pushed aside the intruding thoughts and focused on the moment at hand. Then his limbs began to tremble.

"Pull behind the school," Josi said softly. "No one's there."

He followed her instructions, veering into the turn lane, then onto the road surrounding Marshal Bluff High School's expansive campus. They rocked to a stop outside an aux-iliary gym.

His eyelids closed, and his chest tightened. His hands fumbled to release his seat belt. He wanted out. Wanted air. Wanted to be anywhere Josi wouldn't see him lose control, but it was already too late.

Sounds of chopper blades and gunfire echoed in his mind.

Images of his team crossing enemy lines on a recovery mission gone wrong. The realization they'd been spotted.

"Lincoln," Josi demanded. "Nod if you can hear me."

He sucked in a ragged breath that raked like claws down his windpipe. He wasn't in the desert anymore. He was home. He was with Josi. And she needed him to protect her.

"Lincoln," she repeated. "Nod."

A small clicking sound turned his head in her direction. Not a gun clip inserted. Not a hammer pulled.

She'd released her safety belt and turned on the seat to face him. Then, slowly, she moved in his direction, big blue eyes glued to his. "You see me?"

He lowered his chin in acknowledgment.

"And you hear me."

This time, he managed a nod.

"You know me?"

Adrenaline raced through his veins, gonging in his ears and causing his teeth to chatter.

"May I touch you?" she asked, voice lower and less demanding.

He cringed, hating that she had to see him like this. That he had to be like this. And that even years later, some part of him was still being tortured in another land.

Josi's small hands found his, and suddenly everything else fell away. His senses heightened, and he was hyper-focused on that single point of connection. She stroked his aching hands and peeled his fingers from the steering wheel.

"Lincoln," she whispered, softer still. "You are safe, and so am I. We are unharmed, and we aren't in any danger now."

He met her normally doe-eyed gaze, and found something fierce in her stare.

Josi raised his palm to her heart and pressed it against her breastbone.

She'd unfastened her coat to allow him access, and she moved her free hand to his chest. "Feel that? That's my heart beating fast and strong. I feel yours too. We're together, and we're okay. Count the beats. One, two, three, four…"

The cadence of her voice and the rhythm of her heart slowly carried him back to her.

"You feel my touch," she said. "You hear my voice. Can you see anything blue nearby?"

His gaze snapped back to hers. The fire he'd seen there earlier was gone, replaced with something else entirely. Not fear or pity, as he'd expected. Not even kindness or compassion. Something more like…understanding.

"Sky."

"Right." She smiled, and he did too. Because Josi saw him. Really saw him. And she wasn't afraid or upset by what she found.

"Anything red?"

"Gym sign."

"Good." She smiled. "Feeling better?"

The tension in his muscles eased and he removed his hand from her chest. "How'd you know what to do?"

She eased away by a fraction. "I had panic attacks for most of my life. Even after I came to the ranch," she said. "The animals helped me recenter when I felt myself spinning out. Before that, a friend talked me through them."

"Tara?" he asked, guessing.

"No, but she's helped me through a lot. Tara's tough in all the ways I will never be. Her brother made sure she could protect and handle herself. They both shared as much as they could of that with me."

Lincoln's rattled mind hated every possible reason Josi

had for suffering as he did. She was too good and kind to have ever been anything other than loved and cherished. "I'm sorry."

She scooted back to her seat, a sad smile on her lips. "I don't know if you're apologizing for your attack or mine, but don't. We're survivors. I'd rather deal with episodes like this for the rest of my life, thankful that I lived, rather than the alternative."

His mouth opened and, as usual, words failed.

She buckled up and turned her head to face him. "I know how the people at the pawnshop must look to you. I feel ashamed of how they look to me now. Guarded. Hard. Mean. But I spent a lifetime in that world, before yours. I was just like them not long ago, but I received opportunities they didn't. And each time I learn to do better, I try. A lot of folks don't know. Some are just stuck. I like to think everyone is out here doing their best."

Lincoln turned the truck back to the road and headed for home. "I don't care about the people at the pawnshop," he said. "And I don't know what you think I see when I look at them or you, but you're probably wrong on both counts."

"They're good people," she said, apparently still determined to make some kind of point. "It can be hard, not knowing who to trust."

"Are we still talking about the crew at the pawnshop?"

Josi turned away and dropped her hands into her lap. "I didn't know the younger guys we saw, and I only knew Petey secondhand through friends. But I know all about the parties Dustin and the other guy mentioned. Brady's bonfires are legendary."

Lincoln rolled his shoulders and stretched his neck, tipping his head from side to side. Thankful the attack had passed. He had to get ahold of himself if he was going to play bodyguard to Josi. He couldn't afford another attack. Not with a gunman on the hunt and a black sedan out there looking to give chase.

His truck picked up speed along the scenic byway.

A large setting sun painted distant waves in shades of crimson to gold, lighting the ocean on fire.

"We should eat dinner early," Josi said, pulling his attention back to her.

"Hungry?" He glanced at the clock. It was nearing dinner, he supposed. The afternoon had flown.

"Always," she said. "Plus, tonight we have a bonfire to attend."

Chapter Six

Lincoln paced the gravel outside his truck after dinner, his focus bouncing between the distant road and Josi's cabin. She was getting ready for the bonfire, where she hoped to get answers about Tara. He was sorting his thoughts. Logically, he knew he'd shaken their tail before pulling into the high-school parking lot. Whoever had followed them from Tara's home to the pawnshop had been caught at the traffic light he'd run, but that didn't mean he and Josi couldn't be found on the ranch. The local radio station had given her name and place of employment. Even if the criminals in question had somehow missed the broadcast, Lincoln, unlike his brothers, hadn't bothered to conceal his name when purchasing his truck. His job as a ranch hand generally kept him out of danger. He'd had no reason to hide and no one was looking for him...until a few hours ago. Now enough time had passed for someone with connections to run his license-plate number, get his name and his address. Lincoln's only measure of hope was that whoever had taken those shots outside the Bayside Motel was more of a civil menace than a criminal mastermind.

Then again, even the most unintelligent of thugs worked for someone.

Movement in his peripheral vision pulled his gaze from

the road to a petite and curvy figure headed his way. Josi had traded her wool peacoat and sneakers for a black leather motorcycle jacket and matching boots. Her hair was down and she'd put on more makeup than he'd ever seen her wear. Dark lashes and liner accentuated her big blue eyes. Stain the color of strawberries highlighted her cheeks and lips. She'd transformed from the literal girl next door to a vixen in the space of an hour, and the contrast caused his brain to misfire.

Worse, he had to escort her to a party looking this way. Protecting the sweet stable manager was one job. Playing bodyguard to the woman approaching him felt like a whole other level of duty, and some mixture of the soldier and cowboy within nodded smugly at the challenge.

A nonsensical, prideful refrain began in his mind and grew louder with every step she took in his direction. *My lady. My lady. My lady.*

She stopped within arm's reach, and he reminded himself not to pull her in close. Josi wasn't his girlfriend. She was his friend-friend, and also his boss.

Why did that last thought suddenly have as much appeal as those motorcycle boots?

Mercy.

"You hate the look?" she asked, guessing incorrectly. "It's what I looked like when I spent time with that group. It's what all the women at the bonfire will look like too."

He seriously doubted that.

"I can't show up looking all fresh-faced and wholesome," she continued. "They'll accuse me of forgetting who I am and where I'm from. They might even say I think I'm better than them now. Then they'll run me off." She waved a hand between them.

Lincoln caught her wrist and towed her closer despite

himself. "Josi. You look like a badass, and I couldn't care less what anyone else thinks or looks like tonight. You shouldn't either."

Her eyes widened, then her shiny red lips turned up in a smile. "Yeah?"

He forced his gaze back to her eyes. "Yeah."

"You don't hate all this?" she asked, glancing down at herself without making any effort to escape his hold. "I thought you'd scoff. Miss the wholesome girl you know."

"I don't care what you wear or don't wear," he said, the words too sharp, his voice too low.

Josi's expression fell, and she stepped back.

His grip tightened. "That's not what I meant."

She pulled free of his grip and headed for the passenger door. "Yeah? What'd you mean then?"

They locked gazes across the hood of his truck, under the thin light of a new moon.

"I meant I like you as you are," he said. "The package that comes in doesn't matter." He yanked open his door and climbed inside, hating his inability to say the right thing at the right time.

The Beaumonts had four congenial brothers. Two lovable parents. And him. The uptight, prickly one. He couldn't even blame his personality on trauma. He'd been born without a need to aspire or impress, and that had served him fine until today.

Lincoln started the truck. He didn't need to look at Josi to know her eyes were on him. He knew better than to make another attempt to explain himself. That would only make things worse. So he shifted into gear and pointed them down the driveway. "Where are we going?"

"Potter's field."

He grunted. Not a place he wanted to be tonight. Too far

from town. From the police and hospitals. No one doing anything good would be there after dark.

"You know it?" Josi asked.

"The abandoned farmhouse where the road ends?"

"That's the place." Her voice hitched with surprise, but he kept his attention on the road. "Have you ever been there?"

"In high school," he said. Those days were before Josi's time there, no doubt. He'd never been so thankful for their five-year age difference. Growing up on a ranch for troubled teens, where he and his brothers were supposed to be shining examples, had led him to a life of rebellion. He'd done a number of things he wasn't particularly proud of. Those same experiences had made him an excellent fighter. The skills had since proven useful more times than he cared to count. The military had further fine-tuned his abilities until his hands alone were deadly. He'd never use them that way. But hand-to-hand combat had proven an incredible stress reducer. It was just difficult to find anyone willing to spar.

Lincoln shot a pointed look at Josi, who continued to scrutinize him. "What?"

"I never pegged you as a partier, that's all."

He ignored the comment, having no idea what to say in response.

"Lots of people, loud music, impromptu brawling," she said. "You had to hate it. Why'd you go?"

"I liked the brawling."

She laughed, then quickly quieted. "So you were like this before?"

"Before the military?" he asked. "Yeah. This is just… me."

"Interesting."

He looked at her again, prepared to voice the thing she

wouldn't say. "You thought I was like my brothers, and being a prisoner of war made me this way?"

"Couldn't have helped," she said.

His lips quirked with humor at her tone. He smashed them flat.

"Why do you do that?" she asked. "You fight every smile that tries to grace your face. What exactly do you think will happen if someone sees you have more than one mood?"

"I don't know," he said, lacing the words with sarcasm. "They'll probably keep talking to me."

She grinned. "Like me."

"No. Not like you." He frowned, sliding into comfortable territory as they glided along the winding ribbon of road. "You keep talking to me no matter how I behave. I've never understood why."

"Maybe I like you as you are too," she said. "Regardless of the packaging." Her eyes danced with delight as she sent his previous words back to him.

Lincoln refocused on the road.

The old farmhouse appeared a few minutes later, surrounded by trucks and partygoers. Shadows cloaked the porch and yard, while an inky dome of endless starlight shone overhead. Out back, a raging bonfire blazed in the field.

He backed into the grass, close enough to escape in a hurry if needed, and already pointing toward the road. He met Josi on her side of the truck.

She stared up at him, expectant. "I appreciate how gentlemanly you are, but this crowd will see any physical distance as a lack of interest on your part or mine. That will translate into an invitation for someone else to cut in. I don't like to fight, and I don't think you should. So if you're mine for the night, we're going to have to act like it."

His eyes narrowed. "What?"

"Permission to cling?" she asked, eyebrows rising in challenge.

He opened his arms in answer, and Josi stepped up. One narrow arm curved around his back, and she molded her body to his side. When he returned the gesture, pulling her in tight, she moved his palm onto her backside.

"Okay," she said. "Let's see what we can learn."

The old farmhouse was in worse shape than he remembered, which was saying a lot. The home's white paint had nearly worn off, exposing weathered boards. The front porch had sunk in one corner, and layers of spray paint coated the open door. A deep bass sound rumbled from within. A crush of bodies filled the interior.

Josi stepped away when they reached the threshold.

A chill rushed over his skin in her absence.

She pulled his hands onto her waist as she threaded her way into the crowd. Faces turned in their direction, some smiling, others clearly stunned. Josi greeted everyone warmly. Most looked at him as if he smelled bad.

Hopefully no one would want to fight. Hurting the partygoers probably wouldn't win them any help.

"Have you seen Tara?" Josi asked, repeatedly projecting her voice above the music, a mix of country and classic rock.

Each little clutch of people shook their heads, and Josi moved on.

When they reached the kitchen, a group of presumably underage partygoers stilled and stared. A game resembling beer pong had been set up on a table made of plywood and sawhorses.

Josi addressed the group.

"Ask Brady," a glassy-eyed young woman suggested, swinging an arm toward the backyard.

"Thanks."

When they reached the back porch, she released Lincoln. "You should wait here while I talk to Brady. I won't be long."

"That's not a good—"

She shook her head. "He's a friend. See that old Jeep? The man standing in the back?"

Lincoln scanned the darkened field. A Wrangler, at least five years his senior, was parked near an impressive bonfire. The Jeep was topless, roll bars exposed, and a beefy man closer to his age than hers stood inside, holding court from his throne.

A half-dozen other vehicles circled the fire, headlights or tailgates pointed at the flames.

"That's Brady," she said. "Give me a few minutes. You can see me from here."

"What about our lack of contact being an invitation?" he asked, imagining the number of men she would attract on her way across the field.

She smiled gently. "I'll set them straight when I get back." Rising onto her toes, she dug her fingers into his hair and slid her mouth against his cheek until it reached his ear. "Kiss me," she whispered. "My neck or cheek is fine. As long as whoever sees believes it."

She lowered and looked at him, eyes heavy lidded and gaze falling to his mouth. "If that's too much we can just—"

Lincoln's mouth was on her before she finished speaking. He drew her against him with hungry arms, pressing their bodies tight.

A tiny gasp escaped her lips, and he swallowed it, licking into her as he curled long fingers in her hair.

Josi returned the kiss with fervency, her sweet tongue sliding against his in delicious, tantalizing waves.

When she finally pulled back, expression wild and eyes

dazed, he longed to toss her over one shoulder and leave the party behind. "Was that okay?" he asked, her befuddled expression failing to clear. He hadn't meant to get carried away, but damn, everything about Josi had felt so good.

She wet her lips and nodded. "Mmm-hmm."

"Did you ever date this Brady?" he asked, hating the senseless jealousy taking shape.

"Never."

Lincoln smiled. "Good, because he's watching." Along with everyone else.

Josi ran a fingertip over Lincoln's bottom lip. "I like when you smile," she said, clearly unbothered by their hot public display. "Especially when it's just for me."

If she only knew the things he'd do eagerly and repeatedly just for her.

Josi strutted away, chin high and shoulders back, a satisfied, prideful expression on her pretty face.

He tracked her with his gaze until she reached the Wrangler.

A mammoth-sized man jumped down, making her and everyone else appear tiny in his presence. Then, Josi leaped into his arms.

JOSI'S HEART HAMMERED as she clung to her one-time foster brother and lifelong guardian. He'd been the oldest kid in her first foster home, and he'd protected her from their handsy caretaker. After that, Brady had quickly become her best friend. He'd kept tabs on her, even after he'd aged out of the system, and their peers had respected his warning. As a result, she'd barely dated. Either the interested guys weren't up to Brady's standards, or they were too intimidated by him to give things a try. In hindsight, she appreciated his interference. Most of the guys on her radar had been trouble. Warning her away from them had probably saved her a lot of heartache. Brady, it seemed, had been saving her, in one way or another, for most of her life. For that, she owed him the world.

"I can't believe you're here," he said, swinging her in his arms.

"It's so good to see you," she said, eventually finding the ground with her tiptoes.

Brady released her and set his palms against the sides of her face, the way he had when she'd been lost to a panic attack. "You're just as beautiful as I remember."

"You too."

He dropped his hands to hers then raised one of her arms above her head and twirled her. "I take that back," he said when she stopped turning. "You look better than before. Healthier. Rested. Happy. Are you still at the Beaumont Ranch?"

"I am," she said, a rush of pride in her chest. Apparently he hadn't heard the announcement on the radio. Maybe the gunman hadn't either. "They made me the stable manager," she said proudly. "I take care of the horses and the riding schedule."

He crossed his arms and eyed her like the proud father or brother she'd never really had. "I never doubted that you'd be okay."

"I guess time really does change everything."

He cast his gaze around the field. "Not everything."

"Well, you're still the king, I see." She forced a brighter smile.

"Something like that." His attention slipped away, fixing on something in the distance.

Josi tracked his line of sight, then grabbed his arm before he did anything rash. "No. Hey. That's my boyfriend. He's with me."

"I saw," he said, one side of his mouth lifting in a mischievous smile. "Looks like a cop."

She laughed. "He's not a cop. He's just been in a bad mood all his life."

Brady dragged his eyes to hers, uncertainty etched on his brow. "What's his name?"

"Lincoln Beaumont."

Brady barked a laugh, stance and limbs loosening. "Dating the boss?"

"No." She bristled. "I'm his boss. He's a ranch hand."

Brady considered that a moment, then nodded, apparently in approval. "Is he good to you?"

"Very." Memories of their unexpected kiss burst into her mind and heat coiled in her core. She wasn't really dating Lincoln, but he'd never been anything other than good to her, and she was certain the treatment only got better when his whole heart was involved.

Voices rose near the fire, forcing Josi to double down on her quest.

If a fight broke out, Brady would have to leave her, and he might not have time for her later. "Before I go," she said, pulling his attention away from the disagreement. "Have you seen Tara lately? She called me last night from the Bayside Motel, but I can't reach her now."

He turned back to her, temporarily ignoring the ruckus. "What was she doing there?"

"I don't know. I went to pick her up, but someone else was there. He took a shot at her and she ran. Any idea who'd want to hurt her?"

Brady scanned Josi's face, then took another look in Lincoln's direction. "I'm not sure. I've heard whispering to suggest she was mixed up in something she shouldn't have been involved in, but no one's big on details. You remember."

She did. "Any guess about what it could be?"

He shook his head, eyes back on the fire. "Sounds like real trouble if there were shots fired."

"True."

"Is your new man in the military?" Brady asked, effectively changing the subject.

"He was." She turned to look at Lincoln.

"Ranger? Special Ops?"

"Ranger," she said. "How'd you know?"

"My brother was a ranger. I'd recognize that stance and that gaze anywhere." He chuckled. "Look at the way he's watching you. He's clearly in love. Does he have the tattoo?"

"I don't think so," she said. "What tattoo?" She'd never noticed a tattoo on Lincoln, but now that the idea had been planted, she loved it.

"They all get one," Brady said. "People don't push themselves into that league and not write it on their body." His expression turned disbelieving. "Wait. How long have you been seeing this guy?"

She stilled, realizing her error. If she and Lincoln were in love, she'd know about all his tattoos. "We're taking things slow."

Brady raised his eyebrows. "Well, I hope your guy's temper is better than my brother's. If he ever hurts you—"

"He wouldn't." Josi turned to examine Lincoln from a distance. As promised, his attention was fixed on her.

A woman screamed as the nearby argument broke into a fight.

"That's my cue," Brady said. "Tell your man to take you home. It's been good to see you, Josi, but this place isn't for you anymore. Do yourself a favor and stay away."

Chapter Seven

Lincoln met Josi at the bottom of the porch steps and hooked an arm around her waist. "Let's go."

The fight near the fire was going strong, and the man she'd been talking to was wholly distracted. So he probably hadn't noticed the handful of men who'd broken away from the pack. The group had moved toward the house behind Josi. They kept their distance, but Lincoln's instincts told him it was time to leave.

She checked over her shoulder, then took his hand. Together, they hustled around the side of the house, across the grass to his waiting truck.

He unlocked the vehicle with his fob as they approached. "Climb over."

She bolted through the driver's side and over the console without question. Clearly, she sensed trouble too.

Lincoln locked the doors as he settled behind the wheel, checking the darkened yard for signs of the men who'd been following. "You okay?" He started the engine and pulled onto the road.

"Yeah. You?"

Lincoln checked the rearview mirror, thankful for the darkness. Maybe his sixth sense was on the fritz after his panic attack that afternoon. Maybe he'd developed paranoia.

He rolled his shoulders and stretched his fingers against the steering wheel. "Better now. Did you get what you went for?"

Josi released a long, slow breath. "I did, but not because anyone wanted to volunteer information. The overwhelming lack of input tells me something's up. Maybe they no longer trust me, because I've become an outsider."

"Or?"

"Or there's a big problem no one wants to be involved in or caught talking about."

A set of distant headlights drew his attention to the rearview mirror as they motored away.

Josi turned to peer through the back window.

"Tell me more about the big guy on the Jeep," he said, determined not to overreact to the other vehicle without reason.

"He's kind of their king." She laughed softly. "More like a convoluted big-brother figure. They all respect him, and he does what he can to help them. He looked out for me all my life, but I haven't even called him since moving to the ranch. Apparently this was our goodbye."

"Goodbye?"

She took a shaky breath. "He told me I don't belong here anymore."

Lincoln set his hand on hers and offered a gentle squeeze as they rounded a wide curve.

Behind them, two other vehicles had joined the first.

Multiple people leaving a party together wasn't unusual. He might've convinced himself of the possibility if the trio wasn't gaining on him.

"Looks like we might have trouble," he said, releasing her hand in favor of gripping the steering wheel.

Josi tugged her seat belt, adjusting it across her hips as if preparing for a crash. "You've got this," she said, voice level and steady. "Last time someone followed us, we were downtown. You had to deal with oncoming vehicles, pedestrians, buildings and speed limits. This is just endless fields and open road. Plus, I've seen what you and this truck can do."

Lincoln certainly hoped she was right.

Losing a few cars on roads he'd been driving since long before he had a license wouldn't be nearly as tough as dropping a tail in traffic. And his truck was a beast. Even if the cars could catch him, they couldn't hurt his ride. His passenger was the real concern. Whatever happened, he needed to keep her safe.

Behind him, the vehicles raced forward, their collective engine growls making the world outside seem to vibrate. A small yellow hatchback darted into the opposite lane, then pulled in front of the truck, causing Lincoln to swerve. His passenger-side tires hit the loose rocks along the narrow shoulder, and the pickup wobbled before returning to the pavement. The second car moved into position at their side, facing off with nonexistent traffic in the opposite lane. The third vehicle, a dark SUV, charged forward and nudged his rear bumper gently.

Lincoln released his wheel with one hand and tapped his dashboard. Whatever happened now wouldn't be good. "Call 911."

"Calling 911," the truck repeated.

JOSI CRANED HER neck for a better look at the situation. "What do we do?"

"Stay calm," he said.

"Oh, sure." She watched the tiny hatchback, perplexed and more than a little concerned. What could the goal possibly be? Lincoln's truck was twice the size of either car and big enough to easily crush the SUV.

She could only hope the gunman wasn't in one of the rides.

Lincoln adjusted his mirrors and set his jaw. "This exercise is probably meant for intimidation."

"Well, it's working on me," she said.

The SUV behind them lurched forward again, its headlights stealing her sight and probably Lincoln's, though he didn't show it.

He relayed the details of their situation and location to the dispatcher who'd answered his call, then cited the makes and models of all three vehicles. "No rear plate on the hatchback ahead of us," he said. "No front plates on the other two."

The three cars seemed to adjust their speeds in sync, drawing closer to Lincoln's truck, closing in on them as they approached the next curve.

"They're going to run us off the road," she said, suddenly terrified for new reasons. If they got Lincoln out of the truck, things would get ugly fast. Three on one wasn't a fair fight, and one thing the people from her past didn't care about was being fair. Also, they loved to send messages.

"Doubtful," Lincoln said. "You still doing okay?"

She made a soft, noncommittal sound, certain it wasn't time to tell the whole truth. "You?"

"I'm good," he said, expression flat and gaze hard. The muscles in his arms flexed and released with each micro movement of the wheel. "Hold tight."

Before she could ask for clarification, Lincoln jerked the wheel in a sharp one-two move, cracking against the little car beside them.

The car spun out, tossing loose dirt and gravel into the

air as it left the road and smacked its back corner panel against a tree.

Josi's body jolted. Her head flopped from side to side as Lincoln recentered his truck in the lane.

"Are you still there?" the voice from the speakers queried.

"We're here," Josi called.

"What happened?"

"One of the cars left the road."

"Are they injured?" the dispatcher asked.

"I don't know. There's still someone behind us and another car—" She screamed as the truck's engine revved suddenly and the pickup dove ahead. Lincoln smacked into the rear bumper of the hatchback, the way the SUV had done to them.

The hatchback swerved wildly in response. Its headlights cut paths across the center lines before the driver overcorrected and peeled along the narrow shoulder.

Lincoln followed, the truck's big tires eating up the dirt and rocks. He hit the car again, and it shot forward, leaving patches of black on the asphalt as the driver struggled to regain control before the next curve.

Brake lights painted the night in red. A moment later, the car tore headlong into a shallow culvert at the roadside.

"Two down," Lincoln stated flatly, picking up speed in the obstacle's absence. His hard gaze flickered to the dashboard and ongoing call. "Where are those officers you promised?"

"On the way," the dispatcher returned dryly. "I'm sending a pair of ambulances now as well. Can you head toward town?"

Josi frowned as confusion set in. "Do you know one another?"

"Everybody knows Lincoln Beaumont," the older man barked. "We just thought his trouble-making days were over."

"I'm the victim," Lincoln said, a note of amusement in his otherwise flat tone.

"I've heard that somewhere before. Oh, yeah," the other man said. "From you."

Lincoln grinned. "You think if I slam my brakes he'll fly right by me?"

"Do not pull any of that *Top Gun* mess on me right now," the dispatcher complained. "There's a cruiser less than two minutes out and another pair en route. Just keep driving. Medics will follow."

The SUV ignited its high beams, and Lincoln flipped his rearview mirror, returning the light to them.

A gunshot sounded, and Lincoln steered the pickup into the other lane.

"Shooter," he stated, picking up speed once more.

In the distance, headlights and emergency flashers appeared.

"I see the cruiser!" Josi called.

Her body jerked and bent forward as the truck slowed suddenly, and the SUV arrived beside her door.

Lincoln smacked the truck against the smaller ride, just as he had the first car, forcing the SUV onto the shoulder. A mass of trees up ahead would soon stop the other vehicle, if they didn't give up on their own.

Sirens burst through the night as the cruiser barreled nearer, and Lincoln eased away from the SUV.

Josi's shoulders slammed against the door at her side as he rammed into the SUV once more.

Then the other vehicle began to roll.

"What's happening?" the man on the other end of the line demanded.

Josi struggled to breathe as the SUV rocked to a stop, tires in the air.

The cruiser angled across the road, stopping Lincoln's truck with a final whoop of the siren.

He shifted into Park and turned to her. "You okay?"

"No." Her heart beat ruthlessly against her chest. An SUV was on its roof in the field at their side. And a mass of emergency vehicles were eating up the night in their direction.

"I wouldn't have done that if he hadn't taken a shot at us," Lincoln said. "If he'd hit one of my tires at that speed, or worse, gotten a shot through the back window and into one of us—" He shook his head slowly.

Her lips finally parted, but her voice didn't come. Her thoughts were muddled, and her mouth went dry.

"Take deep breaths," Lincoln said. "I'll be right back." He climbed out and met the officer outside the first cruiser. He pointed to the road behind them, presumably relaying details about the other vehicles involved.

He returned quickly, as promised, then fished a bag from behind his seat. He unearthed a bottle of water and passed it into her hands. "Drink."

She took several long gulps before her thoughts began to clear.

"You're probably experiencing mild shock." Lincoln returned to his seat, closing the door behind him and shutting out the night. "I didn't mean to scare you."

He leaned forward, cool green eyes locked on hers, and her racing heart began to thud for new reasons. "Josi." His big hands found her face. He cupped her jaw and caressed her cheek with the pads of his thumbs. "You're okay, and I'm right here."

She unfastened her seat belt with trembling hands, causing him to release her. Then she threw herself across the console and wrapped her arms around his neck. "Thank you."

Chapter Eight

Lincoln stiffened as Josi's arms came around him. Then, on instinct, he hugged her back.

She pressed her cheek to his chest, shuddered breaths rattling her small frame.

The scent of her, warm vanilla and coconuts, encased him. Her need for safety and reassurance broke his heart, as did the fact his driving was at least part of the cause for her distress. Yet she'd turned to him for comfort, and it was nearly his undoing.

"Hey, you're okay," he whispered, lowering his mouth to her ear. Sounds of incoming sirens and loud male voices outside his window couldn't hold his attention, not with Josi in his arms. "Everyone's okay."

His hammering heart and racing thoughts slowed and tunneled until everything else fell away. "Shh." He stroked her hair and gathered her closer. "I didn't mean to scare you." He hadn't meant to do anything except keep her safe. Until the final driver had taken a shot at them, he'd been careful not to use more aggression than necessary to remove the offending vehicles as threats. But an armed assailant couldn't be allowed.

A loud knock against the glass beside his head sent Josi away like an electric shock.

Her eyes widened as they took in whoever had ruined his moment.

He gritted his teeth before turning to glare at Finn. "Hello, Detective." He powered down his window, fighting the urge to bark at his brother for no good reason.

"How y'all doing tonight?" he asked somewhat casually, given the situation.

Lincoln climbed out and closed the door. "Any ID on the drivers?"

Finn smirked, unspeaking for an extended beat, then responded. "Nope, but that vehicle was reported stolen two nights ago. The owner's going to love knowing we found it. Probably not the part where it's standing on its roof, but sometimes we have to take the good with the bad. I don't suppose you know how it got like that?"

Lincoln glanced at the scuffed paint and dented front corner panel of his truck. "Hard to say. He took a shot at us, and a few seconds later he lost control."

"Mmm-hmm. That didn't exactly answer my question, but I expected something similar," Finn said. He sidestepped his older brother for a look through the still-open window. "How you doing, Josi? You hurt? I've got an extra ambulance on the way."

"I'm okay," she said, cheeks darkening as her gaze slipped to Lincoln.

A rush of warmth slid over him, and he rocked back on his heels. "Were the other drivers hurt?" Lincoln asked.

In the field at their side, EMTs and officers guided the SUV's driver onto the grass for an examination.

"We only found one other car," Finn said. "A yellow hatchback stuck in a little culvert about a half mile back. That guy's just upset about the damage to his car."

Josi left her seat and rounded the hood to Finn's side.

She slid under his arm in an easy side hug before moving to stand with Lincoln.

He bit the insides of his cheeks to stop a smile from forming when their coat sleeves touched. She'd never treated him like a sibling, but she was starting to treat him like more than a coworker or friend. And despite their agreement to pretend they were an item, everything about their kiss had felt very real.

"Any idea who these guys are or what they're up to?" Finn asked, gaze trailing a cruiser as it crept past them, an angry-looking guy in the back seat. Presumably the hatchback's driver.

Josi stared at the car, then switched her attention to the SUV's driver, now cuffed to a gurney and being lifted into an ambulance. "Their names are Carson and Willy. That's Willy."

Finn looked over his shoulder to the man in cuffs. "Last names?"

She shook her head. "No. We were never friends. They're part of a little crew."

"A gang?" he asked.

She shrugged. "Whatever you want to call them. I steered clear."

"What do they normally get up to?"

Josi leaned against Lincoln, and his arm rose instinctively to support her. "Nothing good."

Finn's gaze dropped to the point of physical contact between Lincoln and Josi.

"I have an idea about where you can find the driver who got away," Lincoln said. "It could tell us how this set of guys are connected." The thought had occurred to him before the chase began, then slipped away when things grew dicey on the road. "I saw tattoos on a few of the men at the party that looked a lot like the ones folks involved with that bare-knuckle fight club had."

Finn's normally easy expression fell into a scowl.

"I'd start at their gym, or wherever they're training now," Lincoln said.

The fight club had been one of the town's biggest stories a few years back. Lincoln had been overseas, but news had traveled to him via his family. The ring had been successfully dismantled following the death of a local man, barely older than Finn at the time, which had wholly upset their mother, who worried incessantly about everyone.

Lincoln couldn't recall the young man's name.

"Tara had a direct connection to that club," Finn said, his voice oddly tight, eyes locked with Josi's.

Josi blinked tear-filled eyes, a soft gasp leaving her lips.

"You okay?" Lincoln asked, angling for a look at her paling face. Was she in shock? Was she going to pass out? "Let's talk to the medic at that ambulance. Ask him for an evaluation."

"No. I'm—" She shook her head and straightened. "Finn's right."

"Tara's brother—" She swallowed hard, limbs going stiff. "Marcus made ends meet by fighting for them."

Lincoln looked from his brother to Josi. They seemed to know something he didn't. "Where is he now?" Lincoln asked.

"Dead." Her voice cracked on the single word.

The brothers locked gazes and understanding passed between them. Tara's brother was the man who'd died. The reason Finn had been able to shut down the operation once and for all.

The ugly puzzle pieces shifted a little closer to one another in Lincoln's mind. "Was Tara part of that crowd?"

"She knew them, but they weren't friends. They're older than us. And her brother did what he could to keep her away from trouble."

"Like a good brother would," Finn said.

Josi nodded. "He was the best."

"Any chance she held a grudge?" Lincoln asked. "Maybe she got some dirt on them, blamed someone else for their part in his death?"

Josi swung weary eyes from him to Finn, then back. "All I know is there's nothing she wouldn't do for Marcus."

AN HOUR LATER, Josi carried a glass of iced water from Lincoln's small kitchen island to the simple brown couch in his living area. She couldn't help marveling at the contrast between her place and his. Lincoln's cabin was identical to hers in layout. The decor, however, couldn't have been more different. Where her rooms overflowed with frills and fluff, hosting every shabby-chic thrift-store find that had crossed her path, Lincoln had stuck to minimalism. If her home was adorably cluttered, his was severely spotless.

She lowered onto the sofa's edge a few steps later, her thoughts a tangled mess. "I really hope we're wrong about the fight club."

"Me too," Lincoln said, taking a seat two cushions away. "It's a hunch based on tattoos. Could easily turn out to be nothing. Finn will know more soon."

She bit her bottom lip, overwhelmed by the entirety of her day. She was accustomed to being physically exhausted at this hour, but it'd been a long while since she'd been so emotionally and mentally drained.

Despite the devotion of her time and best efforts, Tara was still missing.

"How are you holding up?" Lincoln asked. He hooked

one sock-covered foot over the opposite knee and leaned back against the worn couch. The picture of ease.

"I'm processing."

"Want to talk about it?"

She glanced at him, noticing the cream throw pillow between them, and a matching blanket over the back of the couch. Upgrades to the otherwise utilitarian furniture. Gifts from his mother, no doubt. The plush area rug beneath his coffee table was likely from her as well.

"We'll find your friend," Lincoln said.

Josi swallowed a lump of unexpected emotion. "I'm really worried about her."

"We all are."

The kind words choked Josi further, because she knew they were true. The Beaumonts didn't need to know someone to love them or want them safe.

"Your friend, Brady, didn't have any insight?" he asked, eyebrows rising as he delivered the question.

"No." Though it was hard to believe whatever caused a gunman to take a shot at Tara would fly under Brady's radar. He and Tara hadn't been close, but the goons who'd chased Lincoln's truck had been at the party. Brady had to have known them somehow. "Nothing that he shared," she amended, suddenly unsure of her relationship to the guy who'd always looked out for her before.

"What did you talk about?"

Josi set her glass on the coffee table and pulled a pillow into her lap. "You, a little."

A muscle along Lincoln's jaw clenched and flexed. "How'd that go?"

"Not great," she admitted. "He could tell you were former military. Then he guessed you as a ranger. His brother was a ranger too."

Lincoln's body stiffened the way it always did at the mention of his time in service.

"He saw you watching me and thought you looked like you were in love." She smiled to ease the tension. "He also hoped your temper wasn't as bad as his brother's—for my safety, I guess."

"I would never hurt you." The words were out of his mouth before she stopped speaking.

Josi stilled. "I know."

The tension she often felt between them suddenly increased, and Josi looked away. "You know I grew up in foster care," she said, turning the conversation to herself.

Lincoln always appeared uncomfortable when he was the topic of discussion. He hadn't asked, but since they were spending so much time together, maybe he'd like to know more about her. She'd certainly like to know more about him.

He lowered his chin. "I do."

"My mom was an addict, and I don't know anything about my dad," she said, supposing the information was relevant, given their current circumstance. "My mom's parents were flat broke and long tired of her drama by the time I was born. They were too old, too poor and too exhausted from raising Mom to step up for me when she failed. If they had, it would've meant starting all over as parents for them, and she'd have been in their lives another eighteen years. So they opted out, and every time the courts pulled me from Mom's care, I bounced around the system until they put me back. I didn't get a permanent foster placement when I was young, because she was too stubborn to give me up and not quite bad enough to lose me completely."

Josi took a slow, steadying breath and pushed on. Humiliating and humbling as it was, Lincoln deserved to hear it and know who he was protecting. "I stayed with a few nice families at first, but placements were harder to find by middle school, and I started running away. I knew Mom would pull me back into her life at the next opportunity, and I didn't want to be around when that happened. As a result, I missed a lot of school, got into fights, shoplifted food when I was hungry. Spent a little time in juvenile correction centers for that. Eventually, Mom overdosed and died. I was sixteen. No one wanted to bring a kid that age, with my history, into their nice little home. So they didn't."

Lincoln leaned forward, resting his forearms on his thighs, attention rapt. "Go on," he urged.

"With my mom gone, I returned to school. I took summer classes to make up for failed or incomplete courses. I worked hard and graduated on time. I still got in a little trouble, and I lived in my car for a while, but I survived. And I cobbled together a makeshift family of other teens in similar situations. We supported one another." She grinned despite herself. Things had been rough, but she'd done well, and life had gotten much better. "Then your family brought me here when social workers caught up with me right before my eighteenth birthday. Your folks said I could stay as long as I needed to get on my feet."

He let his lips turn up in a lazy half smile. "How's that going for you?"

"Well…" She dragged her gaze away from his mouth and was immediately drawn in by those remarkable moss-green eyes. "They even let me work with their most difficult son."

Lincoln released a small snort. "There's a price for everything."

"Now, I have a question for you."

"I didn't ask you anything," he argued.

"You wanted to," she said, hoping she was right.

Josi wet her lips and let her eager gaze slide over his arms. "Do you have a tattoo that says you're a ranger?"

His Adam's apple bobbed, and her attention moved to the long, tan column of his throat. "Why?"

"Brady said you'd have one, and I almost blew our cover when I said I didn't know."

Lincoln sat taller, searching her face for something she couldn't guess. "How'd you explain that?"

"I told him we're taking things slow." Her chest and cheeks heated at the implication she would see him without his clothes soon.

In her fake relationship.

Lincoln reached behind his head without breaking eye contact. He gathered the material of his shirt in both hands and lifted, revealing every amazing inch of tanned skin from waist to shoulders. He balled the shirt in one fist after it cleared his head, then he sat half-naked for her inspection.

She wanted to wave a hand and tell him he didn't need to do that. That he shouldn't start removing his clothes. Or she'd start removing hers, and who knew what might happen then? But her tongue stood still, and her lips didn't move. She barely remembered to breathe. The hard, flat expanse of his chest rose and fell at a steady, confident pace. His deeply defined abdominals begged for her touch. She could feel the heat of his body, could imagine his warm, soft skin against her fingertips.

A dark, puckered scar along his tapered side pushed her thoughts from sexy to concerned.

"What happened?" she asked, removing the distance between them. Her hand lifted, then returned to her lap. For a moment, she'd considered touching the marred skin, hating that he'd been so obviously hurt.

Then she remembered the game they played as boyfriend and girlfriend was limited to time spent outside these walls.

"I was shot," he said. "When my team was taken. I wish I could say that was the worst day."

Her gaze jumped to his. "I'm so sorry." For him. For his teammates. Their families.

Her gut wrenched, and she struggled to school her expression.

"My ranger tattoo is on my back." He shifted away from her, turning to expose his more severely scarred back.

Jagged ropes of raised skin crisscrossed his spine and stretched toward his sides in every direction. Cuts, she assumed, maybe lashes. And burns.

Her world tilted as evidence of what she'd heard from Beaumont family whispers became irrevocably clear.

Lincoln had endured torture.

She batted away unshed tears, refocused on the mission at hand.

In the midst of numerous scars, two black bands curled like banners in the wind. Cutouts in the ink formed letters. The letters made a single word on each line. Airborne. Ranger.

Simple, direct and to the point, she thought. Exactly like the man who'd chosen it.

"You were airborne," she said. "I didn't know." Her hands lifted to his skin. "May I?"

He shrugged, easily understanding the request.

Josi trailed her fingertips across the words, grazing lightly at first, then exploring more thoroughly when he relaxed against her touch. Her breath caught at the small gesture, and she bit her lip, fighting a smile.

"You know some of the details about what I went through," he said, voice low but steady. "My family likes to talk."

"They lean on one another," she said. "They support and comfort each other. It's more than just talk."

"So you know," he repeated. "About what happened to me."

No one had given her details, but she'd understood what a failed recovery mission meant. Knew that when the team went missing, the reason wasn't good. And she'd put the rest together on her own when Lincoln had been the only one rescued many months later when a second team had been deployed. "I know enough."

Lincoln was silent for a long while as her fingertips trailed paths over his warm skin and tragic scars. "We were supposed to return together, with one addition, the soldier we went to save."

He shivered when the tips of fingers skimmed the lengths of his sides.

"Sorry, I just—" Hadn't stopped touching him since the moment she'd begun.

She'd gotten carried away and forgotten herself for a moment.

Lincoln turned to face her, his expression unprecedentedly vulnerable. "Then you know I'm broken," he said. "I was too messed up to keep fighting, so they sent me home. And I'm too wrecked to be a decent civilian, which is the reason I still live on the ranch and work in the barn. I'm not sure where I belong, so I just try to stay busy and be useful when I can."

Josi felt her breaking heart snap, and protectiveness rose inside her. "I live here and work in the barn too, you know."

His lips quirked, fighting the small smile she loved.

"For what it's worth," she said, opening her arms and leaning in to hug him. "I think you are exactly where you belong."

Chapter Nine

Lincoln woke to the feel of warm skin against him and strands of soft, coconut-scented hair across his cheek. His eyelids flashed open to find Josi in his arms. Apparently they'd fallen asleep on the couch, then somehow stretched out to lie on their sides. Her body nestled against his. Her back to his chest, each of them facing the window across the room. He'd curled an arm over her, and she held on to it like a life raft, even in sleep.

His lids drifted shut as he recalled the long hours they'd spent together, both tired, but neither willing to call it a night. They'd stubbornly watched movies until the wee hours, talking about everything and nothing, missing the entirety of what happened on-screen.

He'd learned more about her past, devouring all the bits and pieces she'd been willing to share. And he'd told her things he rarely told anyone. About growing up on the ranch. Getting in trouble frequently. And his unending love of the seaside. They'd even made plans to ride horses on the beach after Tara was home safely. Despite all the reasons they had to be uneasy and stressed out, they'd laughed. Everything about the night had felt easy and right.

Josi was exactly who she seemed to be. Genuine and true. Vulnerable but tough. Kind to her very core. She was the type of woman he'd always hoped to meet. The sort who wouldn't judge him for his damage. Or leave him because of it.

His eyes opened once more.

Thoughts like those deeply underscored the reason he shouldn't be curled up with her. Even if Lincoln's broken pieces didn't bother her, Josi deserved so much more. Not to mention his family would probably kill him for thinking any of the things that had been on his mind where Josi was concerned.

He rose onto his elbow, angling for a look at the nearest clock. The golden hue of a rising sun beyond the window suggested they'd be late for breakfast and work, if they didn't get moving soon.

Josi moaned, and his mind formed instant images and mental lists of all the ways he could incite similar sounds.

He needed distance. Immediately.

Lincoln held his breath and tried to slip away. He could make a run for the farmhouse. The cool morning air would bring him back to reality.

She'd be safe until he returned, and he could bring breakfast. A win-win.

Josi rocked back as he tried to escape, pressing him against the couch with her tight, round backside.

Lincoln's body responded naturally, instinctively, and he grimaced as she rolled to face him on the narrow cushions.

"Good morning," she said, raising sleepy eyes up to his. "Why are you frowning already? Weren't you able to sleep?"

Her words stalled his panic and redirected his thoughts. "Actually, I did," he said, mystified. "And I never sleep." Not really. Not for more than an hour or so at a time. He hadn't in years, and he'd given up hope that he ever would again. But last night he'd slept soundly with her in his arms.

"Is something else bothering you?" she asked, settling one small palm on his T-shirt, just above his heart.

Could she feel the erratic beating?

"Hungry," he said, hoping she'd believe the lie. "Do you want breakfast?" He needed a change of subject almost as much as he needed to put some space between them. He couldn't think clearly with her body touching his from thigh to chest.

His gaze dropped several inches at the thought.

She'd changed into a tank top and pajama pants before bed.

Last night he'd done his best not to notice the way the shirt clung to her lean form, accentuating her curves. But now, pressed against him the way she was...

He met her eyes once more. He could feel the shape of her, and she could, no doubt, feel the shape of him.

A heavy knock against the door made him spring to his feet.

"Lincoln," his mom called. "I brought breakfast. Everyone awake in there?"

Lincoln crossed the room in a rush, thankful for the escape and anxious to prove he wasn't doing any of the things he desperately wanted to do.

JOSI ANGLED HERSELF UPRIGHT, dragging her fingers through tangled, sleep-mussed hair. Embarrassment heated her cheeks as she straightened her shirt and stood. She'd thought Lincoln had let down his guard enough last night for them to be comfortable now. Maybe even friends. The way he'd held her while they'd slept, and the way his body had responded to hers after she woke, made her think that maybe she wasn't alone in her feelings for him.

Then his mother had arrived, and he'd shot across the

room to greet her, unable to escape Josi fast enough. Clearly, she'd misread everything, and he was probably horrified, knowing she'd made those assumptions. Hence his wild dash to the door.

"Morning, Josi," Mrs. Beaumont said, bustling past the couch to the kitchen. She'd pulled her salt-and-pepper hair into a low ponytail, and donned a coat to protect her from the weather. Her knowing smile made Josi squirm. "I made cheesy scrambled eggs with diced garden veggies, and I packed a few biscuits with jam and honey. There's fresh fruit at the farmhouse and plenty of coffee, but I wasn't sure if y'all plan to be out and about today." She set a thermal casserole-shaped tote on the counter and unearthed the condiments from a small handled bag.

"Thank you," Josi said. "Everything smells delicious. I'm sure we'll still come around your place in a bit. You know how much I hate to miss a proper Beaumont breakfast."

Mrs. Beaumont grinned, visibly pleased with Josi's response. "Good. And for what it's worth, I know all about what happened last night," she added, tossing a pointed gaze at Lincoln. "No need for the both of you to look so guilty."

Josi stiffened as a dozen thoughts crammed into mind. What exactly had she seen? And how?

Did she know about their kiss?

"What are you talking about, Mama?" Lincoln asked, his tone a little sharp.

Mrs. Beaumont wrinkled her nose. "You must've known I'd hear. No thanks to either of you." She swung her attention to Josi, then back to Lincoln. "Y'all were chased by three cars and neither of you bothered to tell me."

"One of the drivers took a shot at us," Josi blurted, pulling her knees to her chest, and glad to look rattled for a much better reason.

"Goodness." Mrs. Beaumont pressed a palm to her collarbone, eyes wide. Maternal concern lined her pretty face. "No one told me that part. You'd better start the coffee, Lincoln."

He obeyed, casting a sideways glance at Josi on his way into the kitchen.

She hoped he didn't regret how much of his life he'd shared the night before, because she didn't want that to stop. Getting to know him and learning about his past had been wonderful and fun. Even if he didn't want her in the same way she wanted him, she couldn't bear to lose the new connection they'd formed.

"Any news on your friend?" Mrs. Beaumont asked, pulling Josi's attention away from Lincoln.

Shame slid up Josi's spine and across her cheeks. She hadn't even thought of her missing friend since waking in Lincoln's arms. What kind of person was she?

Tara's disappearance and well-being should've been the first things on her mind.

Lincoln leaned against the countertop as the coffee brewed. He rested big palms on either side of him, the usual scowl on his face. "Nothing yet," he said, answering his mother when Josi struggled for words. "But it's still early."

"You're right about that," Mrs. Beaumont agreed. "Finn's coming for breakfast at the house, so I can't stay. I've got sausage gravy cooking for the biscuits. Y'all eat up, and come over when you can. Hope everything else went okay."

Something in her tone made Lincoln narrow his eyes, and his mother's lips curled slightly in humor. She tucked away the expression before smiling politely at Josi and heading for the door. "I'll see myself out. Enjoy!"

Lincoln sighed deeply, then hung his head.

Josi grinned. Suddenly, despite the nonsensical feelings

of abandonment he'd caused by leaping from the couch, and a pinch of embarrassment over her hopeless crush, she began to laugh.

"What?"

"Your mama came to see if we were up to anything good," Josi said. "This meal delivery was a cover-up."

Lincoln's cheeks darkened slightly, but he didn't argue.

"She thinks there might be something going on between us," Josi teased, her tone low and scandalous.

"Seems that way," he said, then he turned his back on her to pour the coffee.

Not exactly the reaction she'd hoped for.

Chapter Ten

Lincoln returned from the shower as quickly as possible, only to find Josi missing and her cup of coffee abandoned on the countertop. His stomach tightened at the sight. Not because he thought she was in trouble, but because she'd been distant the moment he'd handed the drink to her. He'd been certain his mama was the cause, and he'd excused himself as quickly as possible to get cleaned up before starting the day. He'd hoped to return to a subject change.

Not an empty living room.

He reminded himself it was highly unlikely she'd been abducted from his cabin as he stuffed his feet into boots. There were few places in Marshal's Bluff safer than the ranch.

She'd probably decided to go home and get ready for her day as well.

He sent a text to confirm her whereabouts and safety.

Josi replied a moment later. As expected, she'd gone home to shower and change.

Lincoln pulled a wool-lined denim jacket from the hooks near his front door and ran a hand through his still-damp hair before heading out. The sun was bright in the sky, but there were enough clouds on the horizon to shake his hope of a full day without rain.

Green grass stretched to the horizon in all directions, occasionally broken up by livestock, outbuildings, barns and farm hands. A group of men near the stables raised their arms in greeting.

Lincoln paused then slowly returned the gesture.

"Enjoy the time off," one man called. "Looks like the rain might hold out a while today."

"Thanks," Lincoln said, projecting his voice through the distance. "Will do."

Apparently, his mama had already sent folks to handle his job today and likely Josi's too. He hadn't missed the look in Mama's eyes as she'd surveyed him this morning, noticing everything he didn't want her to see, no doubt. And Josi had picked up on her intent.

It wasn't any wonder Josi had run off at the first opportunity.

Lincoln climbed the steps to her cabin and took a seat on the porch. When she came outside, they could walk to the farmhouse together and see if Finn had any updates to share.

In the meantime, he let his thoughts wander over the case and facts at hand. Tara was gone and someone didn't want Josi asking questions. Did the drivers who'd chased them have a personal stake in the other woman's disappearance, or had they been sent by someone else? And if so, who? Petey from the pawnshop? Maybe someone he'd told about Josi's recent visit? The number of people who'd seen her asking questions was rising fast. There'd been two younger guys with Petey and dozens of folks at the party. News always spread like wildfire in small communities, especially when it shouldn't, which created a town full of suspects.

The cabin door sucked open behind him, derailing his thoughts.

"Oh," Josi said. "I thought I'd meet you back at your cabin. Or at the farmhouse, if you'd already left."

Lincoln rose to his feet. "Hope you didn't mind me waiting."

She looked away. "No. I just needed to clean up a little. Get ready for whatever today will hold."

Josi's cheeks were rosy and her lips shone. She'd added something dark to her lashes and traded her pajama bottoms for black stretchy pants that clung to her like a second skin. The hooded sweatshirt she'd paired with them barely reached her waist, and memories of her perfect body curved against him earlier returned with a heavy smack.

"You're glaring," she said, voice a little sharp. "Are you upset because I left your cabin? I knew I'd be safe coming home to get ready."

"No," he said, matching her tone. "I was just thinking."

"About?" She crossed her arms and turned on him.

"You look nice."

Josi's expression went blank. Her shiny lips parted, and she blinked.

He refused to roll his eyes, rub his forehead, or otherwise give away the internal tirade his words had unleashed. It wasn't like him to go around complimenting women on their appearances. Especially not his boss. His girlfriend, of course, but Josi wasn't that, which made the whole thing akin to a catcall, albeit a polite one.

"Thank you," she said, shocking him back to the moment. "You look nice too. I wasn't sure about these pants. I'm accustomed to wearing jeans around the farm."

"We have the day off, it seems," he said, motioning to the men leading horses into the pasture. "So no dress code."

"Then the outfit's okay?" She lifted her arms and turned in a circle. The movement raised her cropped hoodie, revealing a glimpse of tanned skin above her waistband. The pants outlined every curve and contour of her lean, toned hips and legs.

"I like it," he said.

She smiled, and something flashed in her eyes.

He'd seen the look multiple times the night before. A mischievous glint that often came with her little challenges, teases or taunts. Last night he'd devoured them. He'd even suspected she was flirting. Was she flirting now?

"Lincoln," she said, stepping closer.

A small grunt escaped him in answer.

"We should probably talk about the fact we slept together."

Lincoln barked an unexpected laugh, and her smile split, revealing a full set of straight white teeth.

"Based on the look your mama gave," she continued, "and the fact Finn's on his way, speculation will probably be making its rounds soon. We should prepare ourselves."

"Agreed," he said, willing to prepare in whatever way she wanted, as long as she continued to look at him like that. "Suggestions?"

Josi took another step forward, then rose onto her toes and motioned him to lean toward her. "What if we gave them reasons to wonder?"

His hands latched on to her hips, and goose bumps pebbled the bare skin beneath his grazing thumbs. "Was I clear about how much I like this outfit?" he asked, enjoying her little shiver. "Never take it off."

"Never?" she asked, eyes glinting once more. "You sure about that?"

Somewhere far too near, a throat cleared.

Lincoln returned his hands to his sides and glared at his approaching brother, Finn.

"Morning," Finn said, whistling softly as he crossed the final few feet to join them.

Josi crossed her arms over her middle. "Hey, Finn."

"Jo-si," he said, dragging her name into two singsong syllables. "Lincoln. What are y'all up to?"

"We were just on our way to the farmhouse," Josi said, sounding infinitely calmer than Lincoln felt. "We heard you were coming and hoped to catch you."

Finn rubbed his chin. "That's what you were doing?"

Lincoln imagined tripping him.

"Sure were," she said. "Since you're here, I guess you can tell us everything over some coffee."

"Sounds great," his brother answered, rubbing his palms together and sliding a goofy look at Lincoln.

He turned back toward his cabin and led them inside.

Lincoln started a fresh pot of coffee while Finn and Josi took seats at the kitchen island.

"Well?" Lincoln asked, setting his hands on his hips as the little appliance chugged and grunted. "What do you know?"

Finn leaned forward. "For starters, you were right when you suggested the drivers from last night still trained together. I made a few calls and confirmed they're all regulars at the Barbell Club. Same place the fight-club members all trained before."

Josi released a soft breath, and the color drained from her face. She'd lost her first love to that fight club.

Lincoln straightened, wishing he could comfort her. "You think the club is up and running again?"

Tara had already lost a brother to the group, and now she was missing. This couldn't be a coincidence.

Finn rolled his shoulders, clearly as tense as Lincoln suddenly felt. "Some folks are saying yes," he admitted, "but nothing's been confirmed. I'm working on that."

Lincoln poured three mugs of coffee and passed one to Josi, another to his brother. He raised the third to his lips.

Silence reigned as he sipped.

Eventually Josi spoke. "Marcus hated fighting," she said, voice soft and eyes unfocused. "He was a good fighter, because he'd had to be. His life was never easy. At first, I thought boxing was good for him, as some kind of release. The money didn't hurt. After a while, I realized he wasn't telling me the whole story, and the amount of money he won couldn't have been a result of anything on the up-and-up. One night he told me he was quitting, because he was hurting people. I didn't understand what that meant until all the news coverage following his death."

The fights had been brutal, and they didn't end until someone couldn't leave the ring under their own power. Most were unconscious.

"He had so much anger and pain." Josi pressed a fist to her heart. "He should've gotten help to manage the emotions. Instead, he put all his energy into protecting Tara. He was determined to shield her from everything bad in the world. On the surface, he seemed to be managing. As it turned out, he was not."

"How did he and Tara end up in the system?" Lincoln asked.

Josi pressed her lips into a tight line. "Their parents overdosed together. Marcus found them one morning when he woke for school. He was eight. Tara was four."

Lincoln set aside his mug, devastated for the entire family.

"They were placed in the same foster home until she was a freshman in high school, and Marcus aged out. He worked all sorts of jobs starting when he was fifteen. Once he was a legal adult, he petitioned the court for guardianship of Tara. Things got harder from there, because he couldn't make any real money with no formal training and only a high-school education. Then he found the fight club. Tara's grades were good, and he said he wanted her to have the future he didn't."

Josi's eyes glistened with unshed tears. "I guess he got that. At least she lived."

Lincoln set his hand on hers and squeezed gently.

Marcus had died in the ring. A blow to his head had sent him down, never to get up again. It hadn't been his first head injury that week, and according to the coroner, any physician would've forbidden him from fighting until he'd healed. But people who rely on money from an illegal fight club to make ends meet don't see physicians or take their advice.

The organization had been referred to in news articles as a bare-knuckle fight club, but according to attendees, participants weren't limited to punching. Every hit was legal, and every match was winner takes all. The amounts of money changing hands during any given fight were astronomical. The locations had changed frequently to stay off local law enforcement's radar, but eventually every secret comes to light.

"I'm sorry no one was able to help them," Finn said. "And I hate that the police weren't faster at finding and shutting down the operation."

She freed her hand from beneath Lincoln's and wiped tears from the corners of her eyes. "Let's just make sure the worst doesn't happen again."

He nodded. "I'm going to swing by Tara's place again today, talk to her neighbors, see if anyone knows where Tara might be or if they noticed a suspicious vehicle hanging around."

"We were there yesterday," Josi said. "But the kids we talked to hadn't seen her in days."

Finn's eyebrows rose. "Were you able to get inside?"

Josi frowned. "No one was home."

Lincoln met his brother's eye, understanding the question. "We didn't have reason to invade her space, so we headed over to her place of employment, then hit the bonfire."

Finn tapped his thumbs against the island's edge. "I talked to the folks at the pawnshop. Can't say anyone was very helpful."

Josi's eyes narrowed. "Did you think I'd break into Tara's place?"

Finn flipped up both palms in innocence. "No, ma'am. I trust you implicitly." His gaze drifted to Lincoln. "It's my brother who makes asking necessary."

Josi turned her focus to Lincoln. "You break into homes?"

"I can."

"You have," Finn said, tattling.

Lincoln frowned. "Only if I suspect someone is in trouble. Or when Dean and Austin are unavailable," he amended.

His brothers, Dean and Austin, ran a local private investigation company. Both were exceptional picklocks, but they were often busy. And Lincoln was better.

"Finn, cover your ears," Josi said, her wide blue eyes fixed on Lincoln. "This is weird, but I might have a key. Marcus gave one to me when we were together. I haven't thought about it in ages. I put all his things in a memory box after our split. Assuming Tara hasn't changed the locks, we might not have to break in if we want inside. If she's there, I'm sure she'll understand, and if she's not, I think she'll be glad when we find her."

"That's still illegal," Finn said, hands placed loosely over his ears. "You need permission to use the key."

"I asked you not to listen, and now you're eavesdropping," Josi said, sliding off the stool and onto her feet. "I'm going to run home and get—" Her gaze slid to Finn, then back to

Lincoln. "My library books. They're all overdue. Give me a ride into town so I can return them?"

Lincoln nodded. "Yep."

She opened the door and stepped outside. "Be right back."

Finn pointed at her retreating back. "What you're planning is called breaking and entering," he called.

"You're still eavesdropping," she repeated, pulling the door shut behind her.

Lincoln laughed, and Finn spun on him. "Did you just laugh?"

"No."

"I want to make a joke about petty crime lightening your mood, but I'm more concerned with your plan to commit a Class H felony. You aren't Bonnie and Clyde, and I'm legally obligated to stop you."

"You can always come with us," Lincoln said.

Finn pushed onto his feet. "Is that before or after you visit the library?"

"Probably before."

Chapter Eleven

Josi climbed the front porch steps to Tara's home, key in hand. She sent up prayers the locks hadn't been changed, and that maybe, Tara was hiding inside.

Behind her, Lincoln and Finn argued quietly over whether or not they should be there. Finn didn't approve of the outing but saw the validity in it, and he hadn't believed her library-book story, so he'd followed them to Tara's house.

The street was eerily silent, with all the children at school and parents presumably at work.

She froze in midstep a moment later. The front door was ajar. "Guys."

The bickering stopped, and the Beaumonts instantly bookended her, attention fixed on the problem.

Finn motioned for them to stand aside, then he toed the door open with his boot, one hand on his holstered sidearm. "Marshal's Bluff police," he called. "Anyone home?"

When no one answered, he moved into the living room.

Lincoln caught Josi by the wrist when she tried to follow. "Wait."

She fought the urge to pull away. Tara was missing. She'd been shot at, and Josi had left her. The weight of that hit hard against her chest. "What if she's here, but doesn't answer because she's terrified, or because she physically can't?"

What if the gunman had hit her that night, and she'd come home to heal? Then hadn't survived.

Lincoln released her, then moved into her path, a gentle expression on his usually furrowed brow. "From everything you told me last night, Tara's resourceful and her brother taught her well. We have to assume the best until we hear otherwise."

Finn strode back through the living room, then climbed the steps to the second floor.

Josi peered through the open door, fighting emotion and nostalgia at the chaotic scene before her. Everything from framed photos to the hand-me-down couch had been overturned since her previous visit with Lincoln. She hadn't been inside the home in a long while, but before that, she'd spent nearly every night with Marcus. Until he'd begun pushing her away. Even then, she'd blamed the fight club. Even before she'd known the whole ugly truth about the illegal matches and gambling. She'd grown close to Tara during the relationship's decline, both worried about a man they saw slipping away. Eventually, Josi had let him go. She'd stopped visiting Tara, and she'd started focusing on herself. Then Tara had called to say he'd died.

Now both Marcus and Tara were gone, and someone had destroyed their home.

Finn returned, tucking his cell phone into his pocket. "Come on in," he said. "Shut the door behind you."

Lincoln checked the street before locking up when they stepped inside. "No sign of a tail this time."

"Probably because they've already been inside and taken whatever they were looking for," Finn said. "Unless this mess was meant to send a message. Either way, crime-scene personnel are on the way to photograph and finger-print the place."

"Tara?" Josi asked, though the answer was obvious.

Finn shook his head.

Josi turned in a small circle, examining the destruction. "Do you think they found what they came for?"

"Let's hope not," Finn said. "Here." He pulled sets of blue plastic gloves from his pockets and passed one pair to Josi and another to Lincoln. "Put these on and don't touch anything."

"Why would I put them on if I don't plan to touch anything?" Lincoln asked.

Josi made her way into the kitchen, ignoring the sibling banter. A photo of Marcus with his arm around her was taped to the refrigerator. Tara had taken the shot of them outside the Barbell Club, where he used to train. Strange that she'd kept it on the fridge.

Tara had told Josi in the days following her brother's funeral that something had broken in him. He'd become detached. Emotionally withdrawn from his life. And she hated that she'd never know what had gone wrong.

Maybe she'd finally gotten an answer, and it had cost her.

"Someone was looking for something other than Tara," Finn said. "If she knew the fight club was up and running again, for example, and she wanted to bring it down, there would be a lot of money at stake."

"When they couldn't catch her," Lincoln added, piggybacking on the thought, "they might've come looking for whatever she had on them, maybe some kind of evidence, instead."

Josi blinked back tears as she looked into the smiling faces of her past self and Marcus. They could've had a great future, if only he'd opened up to her and been honest about what was going on. They should've been able to get through anything by leaning on one another, but he'd pulled away instead. Always determined to handle everything himself.

She'd loved him, but deserved a true partner, and her heart had shredded when she let him go.

She turned away from the photo with resolve. "How can I help?"

Finn cast a weary look around the space. "Let me know if you see a laptop or cell phone. Those are most likely to have traces of where she's been and who she's been in contact with recently."

Josi highly doubted that. If Tara had a secret, she'd have hidden it better than on her phone or laptop, the first place anyone would look. She climbed onto a chair instead and checked the panels of the drop ceiling near the back door. From there, she looked behind framed art on the walls and tugged grates away from vents. Then she dug into boxes of cereal, removing the bags and contents to search the space beneath.

Lincoln and Finn stopped what they were doing in favor of watching her work.

Finn approached curiously as she dropped to check the space underneath the kitchen sink. "What are you doing?" he asked, squatting beside her as she ran her hand along the backside of the pipes.

"Sometimes when you grow up in foster care, or spend too many nights at a halfway house or shelter, you learn to hide your things of value. Otherwise they turn up missing."

He stretched onto his feet and moved away. "Guess we'd better look a little more carefully."

Lincoln followed him into the next room.

By the time the crime-scene team arrived, Josi had unearthed four hundred dollars in cash, an old baggie of weed, photos of Tara and Marcus taken throughout their childhood and a journal containing a series of entries she'd written to him since his death.

She put the journal back where she'd found it and moved

on. The words were private, the pages stained with tears. Her heart broke anew for her friend's grief as she walked away.

One last trip through the kitchen drew her eyes to something she hadn't checked. A little red teapot on the stove. She removed the lid and peered inside. Nothing. Then she noticed the small key taped inside its lid.

Chapter Twelve

Later that morning, Josi curled her feet beneath her on Lincoln's couch. Finn had taken the key from Tara's teapot, and Lincoln had brought Josi home. Now, they just needed to figure out what the key unlocked.

Josi hovered a pen above a pad of blue-lined paper. She'd already scribbled several words down the center. "So far we have safety deposit box, post-office box, security box and secret lair." She groaned in frustration. So much for brainstorming ideas about the key's purpose. She moved the pen and paper to the coffee table and pulled a pillow onto her lap. "We've been at this almost an hour and all we've come up with are three basic and obvious ideas, which your brother has surely already thought of, and one desperate attempt to lengthen the list."

Lincoln's cheek ticked up. "You'll only think it's silly until we find the secret lair."

Josi tossed her pillow at him. "Stop making me laugh. I feel terrible every time I do. I shouldn't be allowed to be happy again until I know Tara's safe." It was the least she could do for Marcus. She hadn't been able to save him.

As if reading her change in mood, a mass of clouds raced over the sun outside the window, stealing the light. A distant jolt of thunder rumbled for emphasis.

"Hungry?" Lincoln asked, rising and turning for his kitchen.

"Not really." She'd been too consumed with the mystery of the hidden key to think of much else.

Behind her, Lincoln opened and closed the refrigerator and cupboards, clinking and clanging softly while she stared at her discarded, pitiful list.

It was barely lunchtime, but she was already tired. Emotionally drained and looking through the window at a world too dark for midday. The constant threat of rain since dawn seemed a perfect analogy of her life. She didn't want or need the gloomy reminder.

"It must've been hard to spend time at Tara's today," Lincoln said. "Even harder to consider the possibility the fight club is back and connected to her disappearance."

Josi released a slow, steadying breath, because he wasn't wrong.

"How are you doing?" he asked.

She twisted on the cushion to watch as he worked, his back to her, face hidden. "I don't know. Okay, I guess. Better than Tara."

The scent of chocolate rose into the air, and she turned to watch Lincoln stirring a steamy mug. Next, he shook a can of whipped topping and created a stout cone atop the drink.

"What is that?" she asked, sitting taller as he ferried the drink to her hands.

"This makes everything better," he said. "This and food."

She accepted the drink with an appreciative smile and sipped gently, her nose dipping into the whipped topping. "I can't believe I'm saying this, but you might be becoming your mama."

Lincoln swiped the pad of his thumb across her nose, removing the dot of cream. "That's quite a compliment." He returned to the kitchen, then back to her a moment later, two bowls of chunked fruit in hand. He set the bowls on the coffee table and settled a pair of forks and napkins beside them. His final trip came with a tray of sandwich halves. "I only had ham and cheese," he said. "There are casseroles in the freezer, but those take a while, and I wasn't in the mood for eggs and biscuits."

Her stomach growled at the sight of the food. "Goodness. Apparently, I'm starving."

"We didn't eat breakfast," he said, taking a seat at her side.

Josi started to argue, then remembered it was true. They'd never made it to the farmhouse, and she hadn't eaten at Lincoln's place before slipping away to shower and change. She traded her hot drink for a sandwich half. When that was gone, she made short work of the fruit. "Thank you," she said, slowing to breathe.

Lincoln stilled, fork halfway to his lips. "This wasn't any trouble."

"Then thank you for paying attention," she said. "For knowing I was hungry, even when I didn't realize it."

"You've got a lot on your mind," he said, then took another bite of his meal.

"Yes, but I appreciate you. I don't say it enough. You're always keeping watch. Of the animals. The ranch. Your family. Me."

He set aside his fork and empty fruit bowl.

"I know because I pay attention too," she said.

His eyebrows rose by a fraction. "Is that right?"

She nodded. "I do. And I like the easy, companionable work routines we have, but I really enjoyed getting to know you last night. I like talking with you."

Lincoln's expression strained.

She considered changing the direction she'd been going,

anything to avoid the pain of rejection. But she'd lost too many things to secrets and unspoken truths. Marcus was gone, and Tara was missing. Why did people keep so much to themselves? Why did those things end up hurting her?

"I can remember the first time I saw you," she said flatly. "I thought you were so handsome. You were still enlisted and visiting on leave. I knew I had to get over that before you came home, especially if you planned to stay in town like Finn, Dean and Austin."

Lincoln turned slightly in her direction. "Then I came home the way I did, silent and hurting. Probably a little short-tempered and rude."

She lifted and dropped one shoulder. "I just saw a guy processing some impossible pain. When you started working at the stable, I saw your dedication and compassion to absolutely everything, and I was hooked."

His lips parted, but he didn't speak, so she went on.

"I know you probably see me as the troubled teen I was when I got here, or even like a foster sibling," she said, and grimaced. "But that's never been the way I see you. I thought you should know."

Lincoln studied her, then leaned forward, forearms resting on thighs. "My family told me about you when you first arrived. Mama was thrilled to have another woman around. I could tell she wanted you to stay. I didn't think much more about it until I came home, then started working at the stable. To me, you were never the teen they'd described."

She smiled. "By then I was twenty-one."

"Not a kid," he said. "Believe me. I know. You're confident, smart and strong. You always say what you want to say. I envy that." He clasped his hands and turned soft green eyes to her, peering from beneath thick, dark lashes.

"What do you want to say now?" she asked, her heart in her throat.

"I'm sorry for your pain and loss."

His words were a bullet to her heart, and tears began to form.

"You loved him," he said, undoubtedly speaking of Marcus.

Josi wiped her eyes. "I did. As much as I could. I still had a lot of growing up to do, and I don't think either of us really understood what romantic love was. We certainly hadn't had any proper examples. Beyond a friendship and mutual attraction, we were two people living two separate lives. We spent our nights together as a way to refuel and escape. Then the sun rose, and we went our ways again. Wash. Rinse. Repeat. I couldn't have fathomed then what it meant to build a life with someone, not just running parallel."

"Sounds like you had an incredibly strong friendship," Lincoln said. "That love is just as deep and powerful as any other."

"Yeah," she agreed. "I see that now. What we shared was necessary and beautiful. Exactly what we both needed at that time. But it would never have been enough for me long-term."

Lincoln pulled tissues from a box on the side table and moved closer, delivering them to her hands.

She accepted and dried her cheeks. "I want a partner and an equal, not a savior or a big brother."

Lincoln leaned back slightly, as if her words had hurt him somehow. "You deserve to get exactly what you want."

"What do you want?" she asked, the idea coming into her mind a moment before flying from her lips. "A family of your own? Children?" She'd seen him with his nieces and nephews. They adored him, and he pretended to find them irritating, while indulging their every whim and desire. Because underneath all the frowns and silence, Lincoln was a marshmallow. Soft and sweet for the people he loved.

If only she was one of the lucky ones.

"Do you?" he asked, unapologetically turning the question around.

"Yeah," she admitted. "More than anything. And I want to watch my family grow. Attend graduations and weddings. Meet my grandkids. Maybe see them graduate and marry too. I want a home bursting at the seams from laughter and abundance as I grow old." She laughed and rolled her eyes. "Not too much to ask, right?"

"Not at all."

"Your turn," she said, nudging him.

"I want a good, honest life," he said. "One that makes a difference to people in need, and I want a family as united as the one I have now. I want to honor the legacy my folks have created. Whatever form that takes is good for me."

She nodded. He hadn't answered her question directly, but it was a great answer.

Her mind took an unexpected detour then, conjuring an image of the photo on Tara's refrigerator. Josi and Marcus outside the Barbell Club. It hadn't made any sense for Tara to display them as a couple after all this time.

Then something clicked, and she reached for Lincoln with a jolt of adrenaline. "I think I might know what the key belongs to."

Chapter Thirteen

Icy chills covered Josi's skin as she stepped into the parking lot outside the Barbell Club, Marcus's old boxing gym. She'd only visited the location a handful of times, and she'd regretted each. On the first trip, she'd been shamelessly ogled and catcalled, causing a lasting beef between one of the offenders and Marcus. She'd been propositioned in the lot on her second trip and opted to wait in her car after that. Her final visit had been with Tara when she'd gone to collect Marcus's personal things following his death.

The lot was nearly empty as she made her way toward the door with Lincoln at her side. The place would get busier as the day went on and members made their way to the gym before heading home from their various shifts. Hopefully, this would be the perfect time to speak with a manager or employees who knew Tara.

Lincoln opened the glass door, allowing Josi to enter the squat cinder block building ahead of him. A mechanical chime sounded overhead. Scents of sweat and some kind of food permeated the small, poorly lit space.

Josi never understood why anyone wanted to work out there. Every time she entered, she was immediately ready to leave.

A bulky man in shorts and a ripped tank top lifted free

weights before a wall of mirrors. He wore large headphones and barely spared her a glance.

In a boxing ring at the end of the rectangular space, a set of long-limbed individuals sparred with gloves and head-gear.

"Finn's on his way," Lincoln said, glancing at his phone before tucking it away. He'd called his brother from the road, letting him know what was on Josi's mind, but Finn hadn't answered. "He said he was in a meeting earlier. He'll be here in a few minutes."

"Good," Josi said, because nothing about this building's vibe had changed since her last visit, and her skin had already begun to crawl.

The weight lifter took notice as they moved marginally closer. He eyeballed them via their reflections in the mirror. The boxers stopped to blatantly stare.

Josi found strength in the fact Lincoln was with her and a cop was on the way. Then she squared her shoulders, accessed a recent photo of Tara she'd found on social media and moved toward the duo in the ring. "Hi," she drawled sweetly, hoping to look as fragile and foolish as they likely thought she was. She'd learned long ago to keep her cards close to her chest. Too often, weak men found strong women threatening and behaved accordingly. She didn't want any trouble.

"I'm looking for my friend. Have you seen her?" she asked, turning the image to face the boxers.

Unless a whole lot had changed in the past couple of years, it was unlikely more than a few women ever visited this place. If Tara had trained here, she was sure someone would remember. Hopefully, one of these three men.

"Nah," the taller man said. He looked to his partner, and the other man shook his head.

Josi turned toward the mirror and the weight lifter locked his reflected gaze on her.

He shook his head slowly, eyes narrowing. Either in answer to her question or in warning. Regardless, she'd accept the expression as a no.

Lincoln's hand found the small of her back, urging her against his side. He turned toward an open door marked Office and took her with him in that direction. "Let's see who's working."

A balding man with a barrel chest and round belly sat behind a cluttered desk. The remnants of a sandwich was lying on parchment paper beside a paper cup of coffee and open bag of chips. "Dammit," he complained, scrolling with his mouse, eyes fixed on the computer screen before him.

Lincoln knocked on the door frame, and the man turned an angry expression toward the sound.

"What?" he snapped. His features unfurled when he saw Josi, and his eyebrows rose as he took in the large man at her side. "Can I help you?"

"Hi," Josi said, trying and failing to place the man's face. He was vaguely familiar, but maybe it was the location that put the idea in her mind. "I'm looking for a friend. She might've trained here. Have you seen her?" She turned the phone in his direction, then took a step toward the desk.

"Can't say that I have," he said. "We don't get a lot of women. I'd remember."

"Are you the manager?" Josi asked.

"Dennis Cane," he said, wiping his hands on his pants. He stood and offered his hand to her, then did the same with Lincoln.

"You box?" Dennis asked, holding Lincoln's handshake a moment too long.

"I can," Lincoln said.

The man grinned. "That's what I like to hear. What are you, one-seventy? One-seventy-five? I could use another cruiserweight."

"I'm not looking to join a gym. Thanks anyway."

He hurried around the desk. "Care to show me what you've got? Maybe we can waive the membership fee."

"Why would you do that?" Josi asked, disbelief clear in her voice. Was Lincoln being recruited for the fight club right before her eyes?

His smile tightened as he turned briefly to her, then back to Lincoln. "I'm a big fan of the sport." He motioned them into the gym. "I'm not a bad coach either. Plus, boxing's a great workout. Keeps you fit. Women love that."

Lincoln kept one hand on Josi as they moved toward the ring. "I'm not interested," he said. "Isn't this the place that was associated with that fight club?"

The older man stopped short then turned on his heels. "Only peripherally, because the man who died trained here. We've been trying to shed that stigma ever since."

"So you didn't condone it," Josi said. "Were you here when that all went down?"

He scrutinized her then, and she wondered if he was beginning to recall the other version of her. One that wore leather and heavy makeup. One who'd been in love with the man whose death he spoke of so casually.

Did she remember him from those days too? Was that why he seemed familiar?

Dennis schooled his features. "He got involved in that fight club on his own. It had nothing to do with this place or anyone in it."

"Why do you think people went for that kind of thing?" Lincoln asked. "Why not just box here? Like them." He motioned to the men in the ring, who'd given up all pretense of exercise and stopped to watch and listen.

The older man crossed his arms. "I suppose some people have pain they can't deal with, and they'll do anything to beat it out of themselves. Most likely it's their demons that drove them there."

Lincoln rubbed a thumb across his bottom lip, feigning thought. "That's fair. I've got a few demons of my own."

"Exorcise them in the ring," Dennis suggested, working his unkempt eyebrows.

"I don't want to hurt anyone."

The front door opened, and the mechanical chime sounded on the heels of deep male voices. A set of men toting large gym bags slowed to stare.

Josi recognized the dark-haired man in front. He used to run with the same crowd as one of the drivers from last night. The one who'd been in the back of the cop car.

Instinct gripped her tightly and she laced her fingers with Lincoln's.

She'd never had a decent experience at this place, and today wasn't shaping up to be different.

"We should go," she whispered, rising onto her toes and lifting her mouth toward his ear.

He raised a hand in goodbye to the manager. "I'll think about the offer," he said, ending the discussion of a free membership and taking her advice without question.

Josi's heart beat painfully as they moved through the exit.

"What happened?" Lincoln asked, turning her to face him once they were safely outside.

"I recognized one of the guys who just walked in. He's friends with one of the drivers from last night. Marcus introduced us years ago and warned me to steer clear. After that, I'd notice him at parties, usually causing trouble and often with a busted lip or swollen eye. I never needed a reason to keep my distance. I don't know if he's wrapped up in what's happening with Tara, but we definitely don't want a confrontation."

Lincoln opened his mouth to speak, but his gaze landed on something over her shoulder and his face contorted in anger.

Josi spun in search of the problem and found it easily.

His pickup truck sat at an awkward angle, and the tires visible to them had been slashed. A knife still stuck into one wheel.

The veins in Lincoln's arms and neck protruded as he clenched his jaw and fists.

"Don't," she whispered, watching his internal debate. "Going inside and lashing out at those guys won't get us anywhere good. Stay with me, and let's call Finn again." Her voice quivered unintentionally on her final plea.

His eyes flickered to hers, then to the edge of the lot, where Finn's cruiser finally appeared.

Josi nearly sagged in relief. "Perfect timing," she said. "We don't even have to call."

Finn parked beside them and climbed out with an exhausted sigh. "Sorry I'm late."

"You're actually just in time," she said, pointing to the truck. "We were on our way out when we ran into a little trouble."

"Oof." He ran a hand through his hair, then tugged a ball cap onto his head. "I'll take the knife into evidence and call a tow truck. Anything else I should know?"

"I'd say this is the priority," Josi said. "A group of men arrived a few minutes before we walked out."

Part of her wondered whom she'd really saved by asking

him not to go back inside. By the look on his face, she wasn't so sure it was Lincoln who'd have been in the most danger.

Finn turned for the building. "All right. Give me a few minutes."

Lincoln's jaw clenched and released. His hands rolled into fists at his sides.

"Hey," she began. "Look at me."

Finn tipped two fingers to the brim of his hat, then walked away.

Josi faced off with the man before her. "Do you feel a panic attack coming? Or are you just really mad?"

His gaze snapped to hers, his shallow breaths making her pulse speed up.

Panic, she realized. "Everything is okay," she said. "We're together and we're safe. Tires are easily replaced, and Finn's handling the rest."

Cautiously, she placed her hands on his stubbled cheeks and pulled his face toward hers. "Breathe."

Lincoln allowed her to pull him closer. His eyes were expressive and focused. He might've been feeling out of control, but he was still with her.

She pressed a feather-light kiss to his cheek, hoping the distraction would draw him back from the brink of an attack, if that's where he was headed.

He expelled a long breath in response. He inhaled sharply when she pressed her lips to his. "Josi." Her name was ragged on his tongue. His balled fists opened and moved to her hips.

"There you are." She kissed the tip of his nose. Then his forehead.

And the impenetrable, stoic mountain of a man grew pliable in her hands. He wrapped long arms around her and molded his body against hers.

She pressed her cheek against his chest and listened as his racing heart slowly calmed. "Welcome back."

"Thank you."

"It was my pleasure," she said, smiling against the warm fabric of his shirt. "Feel free to return the favor sometime."

His chest bounced gently when he chuckled.

Josi pulled away as the wind increased, wrangling wind-blown locks. Clinging to Lincoln was a pastime she'd never quit given the choice, so it was best she not get too comfortable.

"Jos—" he began.

"All right!" Finn called, cutting him off. He reappeared outside the gym, hands on hips. "Tow truck is on the way."

"What about the guys who flattened my tires?" Lincoln asked, turning to face his brother.

"Cameras are down," Finn said. "No one inside saw it happen."

"Three guys had just walked in," Lincoln reminded his brother. "They either saw it happen, or they did it themselves. We weren't inside more than fifteen minutes."

Finn hiked an eyebrow. "A lot can happen in fifteen minutes. Going inside before you left doesn't make those men guilty."

Josi moved to Lincoln's side and slid an arm around his back, offering him a little of her calm.

Finn raised his other eyebrow at her, and she shot him her most Lincoln-inspired glare.

Finn grinned.

"What about the key?" she asked, changing the unspoken subject.

"I checked the locker room. All the padlocks in use open with a combination. No key needed here."

Finn moved his gaze from her eyes to Lincoln's.

She wondered what he found there, or what message was exchanged.

"The good news," Finn said finally, "is that the key definitely belongs to a standard lock, like someone would use to close a locker. We're on the right path, and I was able to rule out post-office and bank-deposit boxes."

Lincoln shifted, looping his arm around her back. "Still, doesn't exactly narrow the field."

"Well," Josi said, gently chewing her lip as another idea formed. "If we think Tara's disappearance is related to the fight club, we could still be right about the gym locker. Maybe we just have the wrong gym."

Finn frowned. "Okay. Run with this a little. Why hide a key to a gym locker that isn't directly involved with the fight club, assuming we're right about that much at least."

"Maybe the key belongs to her locker, not someone else's," Lincoln said. "That guy in there is looking for boxers. What if they've added women to the roster?"

Chapter Fourteen

An hour later, Lincoln's pickup had been towed, and he was back at the ranch with Josi.

Thankfully, there were plenty of other vehicles available. Unfortunately, none compared to his vehicle.

"I'm sorry about your truck," Josi said, waving goodbye to his parents as she climbed aboard a borrowed farm truck that smelled faintly of manure.

"Not your fault." Lincoln tugged the ancient gearshift into Drive and turned them toward the main road. They didn't have a plan of action yet, but they knew Tara wasn't at the farm, so they'd decided to get back into town and go from there.

Dean and Austin had offered him one of their nicer, newer vehicles, but considering his luck the past couple of days, Lincoln couldn't bring himself to accept. At least the old farm truck would be easily replaced if someone took another shot at them.

"It's at least a little my fault," she said. "The only reason you're wrapped up in this is because you agreed to look out for me."

He slid his eyes in her direction before pulling onto the county road. "Protecting you is a given. Any decent person would do the same thing."

Her cheeks reddened slightly at his words, and she looked away, focusing on the world outside her window.

Lincoln returned his attention to the road, hating how poorly the grandpa of a truck handled and how the body rattled excessively with every bump and dip of the road.

"Are you feeling any better?" she asked, still gazing through the glass at her side.

"Yeah." He couldn't believe Josi had recognized his brewing panic in the lot outside the Barbell Club. He hadn't even realized his anger was headed in that direction until she'd confronted him. More than that, he couldn't stop thinking about the way she'd chosen to redirect his focus.

Just the memories of her soft, strategic kisses made his chest swell. And she'd told him to feel free to return the favor. Had she been serious, or teasing? Definitely flirting. Right?

And she'd kissed him with purpose the night before. Maybe not completely as part of their ruse.

He stole a glance in her direction. This morning, she'd told him she thought he was handsome when they'd first met.

Not reclusive or mean, as he'd truly been, or practically nonverbal, which was also true in the early days of his return from the military. She'd been attracted to him. Was she still? It'd seemed that way more than once in the last couple of days, but these hadn't been normal days. Emotions were high, and he and Josi had been forced into continuous close proximity. More likely, his feelings toward her had influenced his perception of her kindness.

Regardless, he reminded himself, *there are more important things at stake right now*. And his feelings could wait.

A plume of smoke rose on the horizon as they neared a local dairy farm, and Lincoln eased his foot from the pedal.

"Have you ever eaten at the Davey farm?"

She straightened, eyes searching. "No, but I see the farm-hands with milkshakes from there every summer."

Lincoln made the next turn, redirecting them toward the distant barns. "There's a little building by the road with a giant smoker. They make the best pulled pork and barbecue chicken in the county. Maybe the state. I haven't stopped there in years, but I can still taste their fresh-baked corn-bread. It's better than Mama's." He shot her a pointed look. "Never tell her I said that. I will deny it to my grave."

Josi laughed. "I could eat some cornbread. And I will never turn down a milkshake. I don't care if it's barely sixty degrees today."

Lincoln chuckled. "I'm about to make you the happiest lady in town."

Twenty minutes later, they sat on an old woven blanket in the bed of the truck, with the tailgate down. Josi dunked fries in her milkshake, shivering a little with every sip, while he made short work of a pulled-pork sandwich.

Josi's expression was thoughtful as she shook the dispos-able cup. "This experience did not disappoint."

"Better than my ham-and-cheese sandwiches?" he teased.

She stilled, then smiled. "Only barely."

Lincoln looked away, fighting a grin. Around them, the sky was gray and blustery. The setting sun was sinking lower as dinnertime drew near. The fields had been har-vested, and autumn had arrived with gusto. Silhouettes of barns and farmhouses peppered the multihued horizon. Green grass. Red barns. Tiny curls of smoke rising from chimneys. "When I was growing up, kids loved to talk about how fast and far they'd go from here as soon as they had a chance. I never understood that."

"No?" she asked.

He shook his head. "I've seen a lot of this world since high school. Some places were jaw-dropping. Almost surreal. But I'm never happier than I am in this town. Sunset at the ranch is only second to sunrise at the seaside. Marshal's Bluff has both."

Josi dangled her legs over the tailgate. "Maybe we can watch the sunrise from the beach one day."

He nodded, catching and holding her gaze. "I'd like that."

She bit her lip against a smile, and he thought again of her sweet kisses.

"I've been thinking about Tara," he said, doubling down on the problem at hand.

Her expression fell. "Yeah?"

"There can't be many other boxing gyms in town. We can take her photo and stop at each. Finn's probably planning to do the same thing. Maybe we can divide and conquer."

"Tara spent a lot of time at the Y when she was younger," Josi explained, angling to face him. "We can start there."

Lincoln gathered their trash and hopped down, then offered Josi his hand. "I'll call Finn."

Josi waved him off, climbing out independently and closing the tailgate. "I'm good. Meet you in the truck."

He watched as she rounded the pickup to her door, uncertain how he'd ruined a perfectly good moment so quickly. Accepting there wasn't enough time left on earth for him to find the right answer, he let it go.

JOSI BUCKLED HER safety belt and navigated to the local Y's website on her phone. She'd been pathetically thinking of kissing Lincoln again, and he'd been wondering how many boxing gyms were in Marshal's Bluff.

She really needed to pull herself together.

Lincoln climbed behind the wheel a moment later and

gunned the old engine to life. "I sent a text to Finn. He said to let him know what we learn at the Y. He's still talking to businesses near the Barbell Club, hoping to catch whoever flattened my tires on camera."

Josi sighed as she scanned her phone screen. "The Y doesn't have boxing classes," she said. "Not even aerobic kickboxing, and they only hold self-defense courses quarterly. Should we still visit?"

He drummed his palms against the steering wheel. "Sounds like we should make a new plan. Let's get a list of places with boxing classes, then set a route to visit them that won't cause a lot of crisscrossing town. Some of the places might close earlier than others. Let's figure that into the course too."

Josi did another search. "Only six local gyms list boxing on their websites. One is the Barbell Club, so that leaves five. There's one within walking distance of the pawnshop. Two on opposite ends of the beach, one closer to the high-end rental properties, the other near Old Downtown. The last one is the farthest, but still in Marshal's Bluff. It's called Body by Bella."

"How far?"

She used her thumb and forefinger to enlarge the map. "Half an hour from here. Nowhere near Tara's home or work."

"Let's start there," Lincoln suggested. "On the chance she planned to infiltrate the fight club, she'd want to train out of sight. Maybe somewhere she wouldn't run in to anyone who'd report back to folks who knew Marcus."

Josi's stomach tightened. "I hate that this is even a possibility. What was she thinking?" She rested her phone in her lap and frowned at the windshield. "Never mind. If we're right about what she was up to, then we know exactly what she was thinking." She'd wanted to stop another fighter from dying at the hands of an illegal fight club. She might've even thought she could make Marcus proud. But she'd never had to try to make him love her. He'd never been anything other than proud of his little sister.

The drive to Body by Bella took more than thirty minutes, thanks to five-o'clock traffic.

Josi was thrilled to see the bright pink sign come into view.

Unlike the Barbell Club, Bella's had a full parking lot, and the pretty, two-story structure was painted white with murals of climbing greenery and blooms on the bricks.

Women came and went in handfuls, most carrying metal water flasks and toting yoga mats. A petite blonde held the door for Lincoln and offered a flirtatious wink.

He scowled, and Josi tried not to smile.

Inside, the space was light and airy with hanging plants and low, relaxing flute music that reminded Josi of a spa.

"Can I help you?" A brunette in her late thirties smiled from behind the desk.

"Hi. I'm Josi. I'm looking for my friend," Josi said, turning her phone to face the woman. "Do you recognize her?"

"I'm Bella," she said. "Let's see." She accepted Josi's phone and pulled it closer then smiled. "Oh, sure. That's Tara."

Josi's heart leaped. "That's right. You know her?"

"I do. She hasn't been around for her usual classes this week, but she's the best." Bella furrowed her brow. "You said you're looking for her? I hope everything's all right."

Emotion pricked Josi's eyes. Things were far from all right. "When was the last time you saw her?" she asked. "How did she seem?"

Bella's frown deepened. "About four days ago, I guess. Why? What's going on?"

Lincoln tapped his phone screen, presumably relaying the discovery to Finn. Body by Bella was Tara's gym, and likely the place where she kept a locker.

"What's going on?" Bella repeated, taking notice of Lincoln and crossing her arms.

"This is my friend Lincoln Beaumont," Josi said. "He's helping me look for Tara. She's missing."

"Missing!" Bella gasped. Her gaze darted over the busy gym, then flicked back to Josi and Lincoln. "Y'all better come back here, because I'm going to need more information."

She led them behind a welcome desk, away from the waves of incoming and outgoing ladies. Then she leaned against the far wall and nodded. "Go on."

Josi took a deep breath and explained what had happened at the motel.

Bella covered her mouth. "I knew you looked familiar."

"You've seen me?" Josi asked. Hopefully not on the local-news website.

"Mmm-hmm."

Lincoln muttered something unintelligible under his breath, then stated, "We're trying to find Tara before the shooter does, so if there's anything you can share that will help us, we'd love to hear it. We're working with local law enforcement, but we keep coming up short. My brother is the detective assigned to her case. He's on his way now."

Bella blinked—she was processing that information, or was stunned silent, Josi wasn't sure. She still hadn't answered her question. How did she recognize Josi? She was sure she'd never seen Bella before.

"We found a key," Josi said, when Bella failed to speak again. "Detective Beaumont will have it with him when he gets here. We think it might be to Tara's locker, and maybe something inside will help us know what she was up to before going missing."

Bella dropped her hand away from her lips and opened a nearby slatted door. A moment later, she raised a pair of bolt cutters. "You don't have to wait for a key."

They hurried behind her to the locker room. Bella asked the handful of women inside to step out and give her a few minutes. They quickly obeyed.

She stopped at the end of a row near the showers. "I've had a feeling something was going on with her for a while, but she always smiled and blew off my concerns when I asked." Bella lifted her cutters to the padlock in question, and it fell free. She collected it from the ground before opening the door. Inside, the same photo of Josi and Marcus from Tara's refrigerator was held in place with a large magnet. "She hung this up the day she bought her membership."

So that was how she'd recognized Josi.

"How long ago?" Lincoln asked.

"About a year ago." Bella passed Josi the lock.

"This one takes a key," Josi said, turning the lock to show Lincoln.

Bella took a seat on the wooden bench outside the lockers, still visibly shaken by the news about Tara.

"What did you mean when you said something was going on with Tara lately?" Josi asked.

"At first she was hungry," Bella said. "Dedicated. Motivated. I assumed she had some anger to work out, maybe something to prove. She was a regular from the start, using the weights and frequenting the yoga studio. She never missed a self-defense or boxing class. After a while I assumed she was fine. Maybe she'd just turned over a new leaf and realized this was all a lot of fun." She motioned around the locker room. "I've always loved fitness, so it was an easy theory to get behind."

"But?" Josi asked.

Bella wet her lips and looked briefly at her sneakers. "One day she started showing up with bruises. She had excuses, but I know what it looks like when a woman is being abused. Someone was hitting her. That was obvious. So was the fact she didn't want to talk about it. I didn't push. I wanted this to be a safe space. I didn't want her to feel uncomfortable or stop coming."

Josi looked to Lincoln and he grimaced.

"We don't think it was a boyfriend who hit her," he said.

"What?" Bella asked. "Then who?"

"We're not sure," Josi hedged. "Can you tell us more about the classes she frequented?"

Bella's frown returned. "She liked the advanced self-defense courses and cardio classes, like kickboxing, but she also sparred regularly in the ring upstairs. She was getting good before the bruises began. I assumed—"

"How long ago did the bruises begin?" Lincoln asked.

"A few weeks?" she said, guessing. "I'm sorry, but I don't understand who would hit her regularly, if not an abusive romantic partner."

The locker-room door swung open, stalling Josi's response.

Finn strolled into sight a moment later, wearing a plain black hoodie and matching baseball cap.

Bella's mouth fell open.

He flashed his badge, gaze moving over the trio. "Detective Beaumont, Marshal's Bluff PD," he said, focusing on Bella.

"Bella."

His eyes fixed on the lock in Josi's hand. "May I?"

Josi passed the lock into his hand, and he slid Tara's small key easily inside. With one gentle twist, the device opened.

Chapter Fifteen

Josi made informal introductions between Finn and Bella, then let him take over from there.

Bella appeared interested in the handsome detective's attention. Unfortunately for her, and all the other single women in town, Finn was taken. More than taken, really. He was deeply in love. All the Beaumont brothers in Marshal's Bluff had met their soul mates in the last year or so, pairing up in ways that seemed like fate. The family had a way of building relationships stronger than any armory.

Josi envied them, though she was also elated for their joy.

Everyone deserved happiness, even the grouchiest, most wonderful man she knew.

Especially him.

Lincoln caught her staring, and she turned her attention to Bella and Finn once more.

"Here." Bella pulled business cards from the pocket of her yoga pants. She passed one to Josi and another to Finn. "If there's anything I can do, or that anyone here can do, let me know. Tara is beloved. Any one of my staff members or her classmates would gladly help."

Josi nodded, fighting a burst of emotion, and moved to the open locker door.

One of Marcus's hoodies hung on a metal hook inside. A

bag of toiletries and a pair of pink boxing gloves were lying on a shelf—Marcus's initials had been written in marker along the laces.

Finn moved to her side. "May I?"

She stepped back, allowing him access, and he donned a pair of blue gloves before sifting carefully through the collection of things.

He ran his hand over the shelf and removed an envelope from beneath the boxing gloves. His focus tightened as he lifted the flap and shook the contents into the opposite palm.

"Newspaper clippings?" Lincoln asked.

Josi felt her heart break. The thin stack of articles were about Marcus's death, the fight club where he'd died. She felt the air seep from her lungs. Tara had been in so much pain, and though she'd been like family to Tara at one time, Josi hadn't visited after the funeral. She'd stayed away, licking her own wounds instead.

She'd told herself she was letting Tara take the reins, and she'd gladly visit when Tara reached out. But she was hiding and healing while Tara suffered.

Lincoln set his hand on Josi's shoulder and leaned her back against his chest.

The offering was exactly what she hadn't realized she needed. She turned and hugged him, intensely thankful for his presence, his family and his big, quiet heart.

The locker-room door opened, and a bevy of females entered, sending Josi back a step.

"I've got this," Bella said, standing and moving to meet the group. "Classes are changing. I can close the locker room temporarily, but some folks still will need to come in and retrieve their things."

Finn glanced up. "I only need another minute."

Bella hurried to corral the incomers, and Finn turned back to his work.

"Bingo." He raised a cell phone from the locker, eyes flashing. "I'll get this to the lab and see what they can learn." He dropped the device into an evidence bag, then took several photos of the locker and its contents before bagging the rest of Tara's things.

Josi hugged herself, still hating the possibility Tara had willingly put herself in the same position that had gotten her brother killed. "Do you think we're right about the fight club opening again?" She needed to know. Finn was a detective. He could be logical and objective. She couldn't stop imagining the worst possible scenario.

"We're treating every lead and theory as fact until proven otherwise," he said, sidestepping her question, something the Beaumont men excelled at.

She lowered herself onto the bench where Bella had sat moments earlier. A wave of nausea hit hard. Marcus would be utterly heartbroken if he knew this was happening. He'd designed his life around Tara's protection and happiness. Not only would he be crushed by the way her grief had festered instead of healed, but that she'd also put herself in harm's way, likely because of him.

Josi leaned forward, resting her face in her hands. "This is so messed up. What was she thinking?"

"Probably about justice," Finn said flatly. "Vigilantism isn't as uncommon as you'd think, and it doesn't usually involve crime-fighting superheroes. Usually it's just regular people who are hurting and want to do something to ease their pain, or find a deeper meaning in a loved one's death. They rarely feel any better in the end, and a lot of times they wind up in jail, hurt or worse."

Lincoln smacked the back of Finn's head.

"Hey." Finn touched the spot his brother had hit. "What?"

Josi shook her head. "You might want to work on your pep talks."

Bella reappeared, hands clasped before her and perfectly sculpted eyebrows held high. "All set?"

"Yep," Finn said, closing the empty locker and collecting the evidence bags in his arms. "Thank you."

Outside the locker room, Finn followed Bella to the welcome desk while sweaty women with curious eyes hurried inside to shower and change.

Josi and Lincoln headed for the borrowed truck.

The sun had set, leaving only a faint gray-blue glow of twilight on the horizon, and long shadows cast by short buildings over the streets and town. The headlights of an approaching car caused Josi to step aside and squint.

She blinked to adjust her eyes, but the low-slung sports car stopped several feet away, trapped in an aisle where nearly every parking spot was full. Something about the ride gave Josi the creeps. The driver was obscured by darkness and the striking glint of security lights overhead.

She hurried around the back of the truck and to the passenger door, assuring herself the driver only wanted Lincoln's parking space.

Lincoln took his time, keeping watch on the car as he approached the driver's-side door.

Then the little car's passenger door opened, and a man emerged. Tall and lean in a black leather coat and knitted ski mask, he moved swiftly in Josi's direction.

"Back off," Lincoln warned, heading toward her as well.

The man's arm snaked out and caught Josi before Lincoln reached her side. He pulled her against him and dragged her back a step, pointing at Lincoln with his free hand. "Stay back."

Josi squelched a scream. The leather of his jacket was ice against her neck. His gloved hand a vise on her ribs. A whimper escaped as the men stared at one another, Lincoln moving closer with each passing second. Her assailant could be armed. He could be the gunman. Lincoln could be shot.

"Let her go," he warned, his voice cold, eyes hot. His long-limbed body moved forward in slow, predatory strides.

Josi's eyes flickered to the building. Finn was still inside. He was armed and trained. He had the authority to arrest this man and stop her abduction. She just had to get his attention. On a sharp inhale of breath, she closed her eyes and opened her mouth. Then, she screamed.

The assailant's outstretched hand snapped back, locking under her chin and pressing her mouth closed. His long, angry fingers gripped her jaw and dug against her cheekbones. "Shut up," he hissed. "You should've left this alone," he growled. His mask-covered cheek rubbed against hers. "This is your fault. Understand?"

Her eyes filled with hot tears.

"Last warning," Lincoln said, finally within striking distance.

The car's engine revved menacingly, as if it might launch forward and crush him if he took another step.

Her abductor dragged her toward the open passenger door.

Adrenaline spiked and air whooshed from her lungs. Her body jerked into motion. A hundred self-defense lessons rushed into mind, and her limbs reacted, even when her mind struggled to keep pace. She thrust up her arms, smacking the man's ears with the palms of her hands, then she curled her fingers and yanked down on his earlobes, mask and all.

He screamed and cussed, releasing her by an inch.

An inch was all she needed.

She jerked her head forward and thrust it back, connecting her skull with his face. The crunch that occurred was bone-shattering.

His hands flew to his nose, and Josi was free.

She ran for the building, screaming as she flew. "Finn!"

Behind her, the sound of landed blows and guttural roars began.

The gym door burst open, and Finn stormed out, eyes fixed on the fight occurring behind her. "Marshal's Bluff police!" he called.

Bella pulled her inside. "I'm calling the police," she said, raising a cell phone to her ear.

Together, they watched from behind a closed glass door, as Lincoln traded a series of powerful blows with her attacker. Each man was fast and ruthless. Each hit was brutal.

"Two men in a dark-colored sports car," Bella said, presumably to whomever had answered her call.

Josi's gaze swept to the waiting car.

The driver emerged and yelled for his friend.

The distraction granted Lincoln a golden opportunity. A series of one-two punches sent Josi's attacker reeling backward before landing flat on the ground.

Finn jogged to the first man's motionless form, while Lincoln turned for the driver.

The larger man's attention ping-ponged from his fallen friend, now being handcuffed, to Lincoln, then to his car, as if he might be able to get in and drive away.

Lincoln ran at the driver, landing several hits before he returned a single blow. The fight continued full force for several long seconds. Each hit to Lincoln's ribs and torso caused an ache in Josi's chest.

Then Lincoln connected a fist with the driver's chin, and he fell like a sack of potatoes.

She shoved back through the door, running for Lincoln as Finn approached the second man with handcuffs.

Lincoln rubbed his hands, flexing and stretching the digits a moment before she crashed into him. His arms came around her instantly, lifting her slightly off her feet as he squeezed. "I'm okay," he said, breaths rushing and heart pounding against her.

Finn stood and scoffed. "I can't say the same for these two. I'll have to get a pair of ambulances out here now. I can't read them their rights until they wake up." He opened his phone, clearly put out. "It's as if they didn't recognize a Beaumont when they saw one." He offered a cheesy smile to Lincoln, then stretched out his hand.

Josi held on to Lincoln as he accepted the low five. Seeing him fight had been terrifying. She'd lost her first love that way. She couldn't bear to lose her second.

Her eyes darted to Lincoln, the realization hitting like another knockout punch.

She didn't just have a crush anymore. She'd fallen in love with him.

Chapter Sixteen

The next day was slow at the ranch. Lincoln was sore and aggravated about every scrape and bruise. He hadn't lost the fights, but he hadn't gotten the best of his opponents easily either. The men had been well trained and accustomed to winning. He saw the confusion in their eyes when Lincoln held his own. But Josi had been in danger, and that knowledge alone would've kept him on his feet and swinging for as long as it took.

No one would ever hurt her on his watch, and that would be true for as long as he had breath in his body, whether she felt the same for him or not. He'd never stop protecting her.

They'd spent the night at his place again. She'd taken the bed this time, and he'd insisted on the couch. Unlike the night he'd spent with her in his arms, he hadn't slept. Every movement and deep inhalation brought the painful reminders of his parking-lot brawls.

Now, they headed home from breakfast at the farmhouse, covered plates of leftovers in hand. As if they could possibly still be hungry. And Josi watched him as if he might break.

"Do you want me to carry one of those?" she asked, eyes wide and expression eager.

"I've got them," he said, moving his attention back to his cabin, which they were approaching. His hands screamed from effort, though the burden they carried was light. He hadn't fought without gloves in a long while, and he'd forgotten how much the pain of impact could linger in his wrists and bones.

"I wish she wouldn't send so much," Josi said. "I feel guilty when I have to throw any of it away."

He knew the feeling. His mother fed everyone with determination, one of her many ways of showing love. She'd made all their favorite dishes for breakfast, and his brothers had shown up, knowing full well what would be served. Mama was nothing if not consistent, and when someone was hurt, physically, emotionally or otherwise, she hurt too. And she did everything she could to ease that person's pain. Beginning with food.

Josi stopped in the grass between cabins. "Your place or mine?"

"Mine," he said, continuing to the door. As far as he could tell, she rarely invited anyone inside her home, and he wasn't about to invite himself.

They shed their coats and boots in the small entryway, then settled onto the couch.

She turned on the television, then navigated to the local news. "I'd hoped Finn would have more to tell us at breakfast," she said, returning the remote control to the coffee table and curling her feet beneath her on the cushion. "I hope he'll call later with an update."

"He's got four men in jail now," Lincoln said. "That's something. Two from the car chase and two from last night. I'm sure the cops are pressing them for information and using them against one another however they can. Eventually, a weak link will emerge."

"I hope so," she said, resting back against the cushions. "If they keep underestimating you, Finn will have the whole crew off the streets soon. I guess that's one way to eliminate the problem." She rolled her head to face him. "How are you doing?"

He stiffened at the reminder she thought he was delicate. "I'm fine."

"You should've let the medic check you out last night," she said. "Or at least have gone to your family physician today."

"I'm fine," he repeated, a little more roughly. He'd grown up a Beaumont. He'd spent years in the military. He knew his way around minor injuries. Neither opponent had managed to hit his face or head, and his torso was tough. He suspected a bruised rib or two, but there wasn't anything that could be done about that. And his hands were wrecked, but nothing was fractured or broken, so they too would heal with time.

"Stop saying that," she ordered. "Look at you." She reached for his hands and cradled them in hers, turning them gently for a full review. The differences were vivid and grand.

He could probably circle both of her small wrists with one thumb and forefinger. The imagery stopped him midbreath.

"Did I hurt you?" she asked, stilling her soft hands on his calloused palms.

"No." The answer was too husky, a ridiculous giveaway, and her eyes flickered to his.

He hated the dance they'd been doing. But the voice inside him insisted this wasn't the time for such discussions. Her friend was missing. Her life was in danger. Romance, or the possibility of anything like it, had to wait.

She returned to examining the bruises and scrapes on his knuckles, trailing her fingertips lightly along his skin. "Is it awful that I've enjoyed the last couple of days?" she asked quietly. "Not the reason things have been the way they are, but the parts where you and I are getting to know one another."

He followed the path of her fingers with his gaze, transfixed by their motion and the resulting rise in his pulse. "No."

"Good, because working with you taught me a little about who you are. This has been something so much better." She met his eyes briefly, then looked away.

"Taught you what?"

"Big-picture things," she said. "Like your compassion, diligence and general disposition. Talking to you the last couple of days has let me know you, and I like it. So I'm struggling to regret what's happening, because without the trouble, we might never have been more than a stable manager and a ranch hand."

Lincoln swallowed hard and pulled his hands away, rubbing them against his jeans.

She let her hands fall onto her lap. "See? Awful."

He shook his head and smiled at her pretty face. "I hope you plan to keep my secrets. You talked me out of a lot of information the other night. Some of that stuff, I've only told my brothers."

Josi's eyes widened, and he rewound his words.

"What did I say?"

"When we were at Tara's with Finn, I found a journal she'd been writing in," Josi said. "She was writing to Marcus, so I only skimmed the first entry. I put it back and didn't mention it, but maybe I should have."

Lincoln waited, unsure where she was going with this. "She told her brother everything too?" he asked, linking her new train of thought to his words.

"Not everything—not before he died anyway. But maybe

now." She pressed her lips together. "What if she wrote about the fight club, or whatever she'd gotten involved in before she disappeared. The journal might help us find her, and it could help Finn figure out where the club meets."

Lincoln leaned away, reaching for his phone on the coffee table. "I'll give Finn a call, but I think we should wait for him before we go." The place was a crime scene now, and people were coming out of the woodwork to stop their personal investigation.

"Okay," she agreed.

Lincoln passed on the theory to his brother, and Finn agreed to meet them at Tara's place in two hours.

"Two hours?" She deflated and tipped over, resting her head on the arm of the couch. "What are we supposed to do now?"

"How about a walk?" he suggested, rising and looming over her, one hand outstretched.

She accepted, allowing him to pull her onto her feet.

JOSI SOUGHT LANCELOT the moment she entered the stables. She hadn't spent much time with the stallion lately, and she missed their quiet moments. She was sure he felt the same.

Lincoln trailed her, leaving space between them as he checked on the other horses and moved things into their proper places. It was nice that the ranch had enough staff members to cover their jobs while they focused on Tara, but there was also plenty to be said for the system Lincoln and Josi had perfected months ago.

Eventually, they moved to a stack of piled hay bales outside the far door. The sky was clear and blue with no sign of rain. It would be the first time in several days. Maybe that was a good omen.

She climbed to the top and rested her back against the

barn, her boots resting on the bale below. Lincoln smiled up at her then followed. Jangling wind chimes on the farmhouse and clucking chickens in the field played the afternoon score.

"Penny for your thoughts," Lincoln said, sitting close enough to her that their shoulders touched.

"I was thinking about how lucky I was to find this place. That your parents saw something worthy and redeemable in me. And that I wasn't so damaged that I pushed them away." Because there had been a time in her life when she wouldn't have accepted their offer, unwilling to believe there was anything good in her future. But when she'd met the Beaumonts, she'd dared to hope for something more. "I feel guilty sometimes, when I see other people struggling. I wonder why I was so lucky."

"I've spent a lot of time thinking something similar," Lincoln offered, surprising her to her core.

She hadn't asked. But he'd offered. And she wondered if that was because she'd told him how much she liked getting to know him. Until the last few days, she'd rarely asked anything of him. He was so quiet, she didn't want to push or disturb his peace. Now that he'd volunteered the information, she couldn't help wondering if he wanted her to know him too. "Really?" she asked, testing the theory and encouraging him to say more.

"Sure," he said. "I think everyone asks themselves that at one time or another. Why do some people coast through life while others can't catch a break? Why do some folks have the worst parents possible, but others are handed everything they need for success? There's no logic or reason to it."

"Exactly." She leaned against his shoulder, impressed but not surprised to discover one more way she and Lincoln saw the world similarly. "What do you think the answer is?"

He sat taller, angling to look at her. "I spent weeks thinking about all this when I was captive. The best thing I could figure is that things come to us all the time, good and bad. And we have to make choices. Every day we make a thousand choices. What to eat or wear. What route to take. Who to talk to. Whether we accept or reject what's right in front of us. If we're going to settle or fight."

"I like that," she said.

"Me too. Probably because it puts the power in my hands and leaves it up to me if I succeed or fail," he said. "I've never been one to accept helplessness, but this theory works for people who fear decision making too. Inaction still leads to a result. Inaction is a choice."

Something changed in his expression, and goose bumps skittered down her spine.

"Penny for your thoughts," she said, whispering his words back to him.

His expression hardened, and his frown became something more like resolve. He raised a tentative hand to her jaw and curved one long finger beneath her chin. His moss-green eyes locked with hers and the thrill of anticipation shot through her. "The other night, when I kissed you at the party, it wasn't just for show. I've wanted to do that for a long while."

Josi bit her lip against a smile, heart soaring. "Oh, yeah?"

His gaze fell to her mouth. "I'd really like to do it again."

She angled her mouth to his, and the delicious pressure was even better than she recalled. The best part was knowing he wanted her too.

Lincoln pulled back too soon, resting his palm against the side of her neck and sliding his fingers into her hair. He searched her face, presumably gauging her reaction.

Josi relaxed into his touch. "Do you know how long I've

been waiting for you to kiss me like that?" she asked softly, breathless. If he knew, he'd probably think she was a stalker.

The surprising glint of pleasure in his eyes was enough to melt her on the spot.

The kiss that followed was hot enough to send the whole world up in flames.

Lincoln cradled her body as he explored her neck and mouth, gliding his tongue over hers in a slow, erotic rhythm that made her see stars. There was care in his touch and reverence in his gaze when he finally pressed his forehead to hers. A light swear escaped his lips, an exclamation of pleasure.

Somewhere deep inside her, the pieces of her long-broken heart knit themselves back together.

"That was—" she began, faltering quickly at a complete loss of words. And dizzy from the sheer perfection.

"Everything," he offered, finishing the sentiment for her. "Absolutely everything."

Chapter Seventeen

Lincoln's ringing phone stopped him from kissing Josi again. Before he could curse his brother's consistently terrible timing, a trio of farmhands moved into view a dozen yards away.

Josi laughed quietly as she smoothed her hair.

"Hello, brother," Lincoln said, answering the call.

"New plan," Finn said. "I'm headed to the ranch. Will you and Josi be around?"

Lincoln initiated the speaker option and leveled the phone between them. "She's with me now. I thought we were meeting at Tara's place."

Josi frowned. "What's going on?"

"Give me about an hour. I'd rather talk with you in person. See you in a bit." He disconnected and left them hanging.

"I hate when you guys do that," Josi murmured. "Y'all are the worst at answering questions."

The farmhands reached the stable, Community Days banners draped over crooked arms. The event would be back again soon, and the ranch would be filled with visitors. Not something Lincoln could bring himself to worry about at the moment.

The men tipped their hats in greeting before moving inside.

Lincoln cleared his throat, suddenly torn. Had they seen him kissing Josi?

Would news get back to his family before he could tell them himself?

What would he say?

Josi stood, knocking hay from her backside. "I guess we'd better head home and wait."

He followed her across the field at a respectable distance, hands deep in his pockets to stop himself from reaching for her.

Inside his cabin, he poured a mug of coffee and leaned against the sink, unable to think of anything other than their kisses. Josi felt exactly right in his arms. The moment had been tender, but the experience was powerful. He was certain there were parts of him that would never recover, yet he'd sacrifice them all for another kiss like that.

"Why are you in your head right now?" Josi asked, moving into the kitchen.

He cringed internally, recalling all the reasons he'd previously told himself not to act on his feelings for her. She was five years younger. Her friend was missing. Her emotions were high. His parents and brothers saw her as family.

"Coffee?" He lifted his cup with the question.

She rolled her eyes and moved in close, long hair falling over her shoulders as she relieved him of his cup. "Always dodging my questions."

He smiled as she sipped. Apparently, today's kiss had broken some unspoken boundary. He was sure she wouldn't have taken his cup before, or stood so incredibly close. The new familiarity was delicious and intoxicating. Sharing space, coffee and secrets with Josi, while handling whatever came their way, was all he needed for a happy life.

She set aside the mug and studied his expression. "Do you regret kissing me?"

"Of course not." He furrowed his brow deeply in offense. Had he said or done something to suggest as much? "Why would you ask me that?"

"Are you sure? I'm a lot younger than you, you know."

Lincoln caught the flash of mischief in her eyes and relaxed. "I'm well aware."

She slid a palm up his chest. "I'm also your boss, which is incredibly awkward."

"Maybe we should talk to HR."

She stretched onto her tiptoes and curved her arms behind his neck, pressing her body to his in a long, heartwarming embrace. "I hope they figure it out, because I really enjoyed the kissing."

A laugh broke on Lincoln's tongue, and his lips parted in an all-teeth smile. He felt silly and young. Unlike anything he'd felt in far too long.

"I know Finn's on the way," Josi said, "but I wonder if there's time for a little more..." She kissed his jaw lightly then caught his earlobe in her teeth.

Lincoln scooped her off her feet before she'd finished speaking, making her scream with delight. He set her on the counter, heat flashing in his eyes.

"So you aren't going to make me beg," she clarified, chin tipped up at him, clearly pleased.

He stepped into the space between her parted thighs. "Do I look like a fool?" he asked, dropping his mouth to her lips. "Darling, you will never have to ask me twice for affection."

She tangled her fingers in his hair and locked her ankles around his waist. The move drew a needy moan from both of them.

Lincoln kissed her deeply and slid his hands beneath the

hem of her shirt. His long fingers grazed her flat stomach, then moved up the length of her sides. When the pads of his thumbs found firm, peaked nipples beneath the thin fabric of her silky bra, he growled into her open mouth.

Josi devoured the sound, meeting his tongue stroke for stroke as she explored the skin beneath his shirt as well. Intensity climbed as they moved together, hot and greedy. When her hands reached the button on his uncomfortably tight jeans, he stepped back with a hiss of breath.

He caught her gaze and held it. "We don't have to rush," he said, the words coming in short pants. "We have all the time we want."

She removed her shirt in response.

Breath whooshed from him as he gripped her sides, taking in the sheer beauty before him.

Josi raised an eyebrow in challenge.

He pushed away the material of her bra, exposing one perfect breast, and her back arched in response. Gooseflesh pebbled her skin.

"So damn beautiful," he whispered, lowering his mouth to hers. He kissed her slowly, teasing her hard nipple with his thumb until she whimpered.

Then he lowered his head to press wet kisses against her curves.

She gasped as he closed his mouth over the tight peach bud, suckling until she called his name.

Her hands gripped the counter, one on each side of her hips, bracing herself as he lavished her with affection, affirmations and generous, heated flicks of his tongue.

Soon, her heels dug against him, pressing his jeans into the heat of her core. "More."

Lincoln's hands were beneath her, gripping her backside and hauling her off the counter. He could have her in his bed, undressed and fully sated in minutes, all without removing a stitch of his clothing. He was sure of it, and completely up for the challenge.

When they reached the darkness of his hallway, she dragged her tongue along the column of his neck to his ear. "Take me."

His doorbell rang.

His head fell forward, and he started to put her down, but she clung tighter.

She drew his mouth back to hers and kissed him slowly.

He pressed her back to the wall and willed whoever was on his porch to go away.

The bell rang again.

She allowed him to set her down. Hair mussed and lips swollen from his kiss, she ran a fingertip between nearly exposed breasts. "My shirt is in your kitchen. Can I borrow one of yours?"

He pinched the bridge of his nose, commanding his body to calm down. Picturing her in his shirt didn't help. "Take whatever you want."

"Be right back," she said, then hurried into his room without him.

Lincoln adjusted his pants and forced himself not to follow her. Instead, he turned, grabbed her shirt from the kitchen floor and tucked it into a cabinet, then went to answer the door.

Finn frowned the moment the barrier was opened. "What's wrong with your face?"

Lincoln strode into the kitchen. He needed ice water. To bathe in. "Come in."

"Are you...smiling?" Finn asked, following along on Lincoln's heels.

"No."

Finn collapsed onto the couch. He crossed his legs and set his chin in his hands, looking exactly like their mama preparing for some gossip. "Tell me everything."

Lincoln's accidental grin grew. "Stop."

"Is this about—" He pointed down the hallway, then mouthed the word *Josi.*

"Is that Finn I hear?" Josi asked, causing both men to turn in her direction. She emerged in one of Lincoln's button-down shirts with her leggings. She'd rolled the sleeves and pushed them up, as if she'd been wearing the shirt all day instead of for the past three minutes.

"Knew it," Finn whispered.

Lincoln gave him a warning look, and Finn tapped a finger against the detective shield on his belt. Lincoln rolled his eyes.

"What's up?" she asked, hiking her eyebrows as she reached the living room. "Do you have news?"

Lincoln forced his thoughts away from the feel of her in his arms. And the fact that he now had personal knowledge of what her skin both felt and tasted like.

"Nothing yet," Finn said, responding to her question. "I had to follow up on a case involving one of the guys staying on the ranch. While I'm here, I figured I'd stop by and check on you, maybe talk about Tara's case."

"Lincoln made coffee," she offered, moving into the kitchen and pulling a cup from the rack on the counter. "Can I pour you some?"

"That sounds good." He levered himself off the couch and took a seat at the island. He smiled and nodded in thanks when she delivered the drink. "I've decided to let the four guys I've got in custody go," he said. "They aren't talking."

Josi paled. "What?"

Finn lifted a palm. "They weren't budging, and I had to

weigh the lost time against progress. Tara's still missing. If she's being held somewhere, we don't have days to wait. If this was a crime where the damage was done, I could drag my feet, take the full seventy-two hours to hold them, or just arrest them and toss them in jail to await their arraignment. I don't have that luxury."

"So you let them go?" Her lips parted, and her eyes shone with tears.

"I knew you wouldn't love this path," Finn said. "Which is why I wanted to talk to you about it in person. I know those men tried to hurt you. I know you feel they pose a threat, but I'm trying something else that will benefit us both. You'll be safe, and I'll get the information I need."

Josi swung her desperate gaze to Lincoln.

"You had them tailed when they left the station," he stated.

Finn nodded. "My men are on them. They won't cause you any harm without an intervention. I'm hoping they'll shift their focus to reporting back to whoever is in charge."

"Oh," Josi said, wrapping thin arms around her middle and looking less desperate. "I guess that makes sense. I've been imagining Tara being held somewhere, alone and afraid. Wondering if she's injured. If they give her food or water. People can only go so long without water."

Lincoln moved to her side, and Josi curled herself beneath his arm. She rested her head against him and let him hold her weight. "We'll find her."

She was tough and kept her chin up, but the search for her missing friend and the circumstances surrounding it were taking a toll.

He fought the urge to kiss her head or stroke her hair. Anything to make sure she knew he had her back, and this situation would soon pass. Nothing lasted forever. Not the good stuff. And not the bad.

"What do we do in the meanwhile?" she asked, still trying to help however she could.

Finn stared at them, blinking and apparently speechless. His gaze roamed their postures and points of contact, then Josi's face and Lincoln's, before he eventually found his tongue. "I thought we'd go look for that journal you mentioned."

Chapter Eighteen

The ride to Tara's home was slow as anticipation built in Josi's chest. Too many things had happened in too short a time frame. Her mind struggled to keep up, to process the thoughts and catastrophes that never seemed to stop. Her sleep was wrecked and her nerves were shot—emotions were heightened and sharp. She wasn't over being grabbed in the parking lot outside Body by Bella. She'd need to see a therapist for years after that encounter.

In truth, she wasn't over any of the awful things happening all around her, and she wouldn't be anytime soon. Most of all she hated that Tara could die exactly the way Marcus had.

Finn was shaken as well. Josi could hear the frustration in his tone and see the unspoken emotion in his troubled eyes. Seeing history repeat itself was taking a toll on the young detective with a big heart.

Visiting the pawnshop and the party at Potter's field had taken her back to an unhappier time as well. Add in the car chases, gunman and near abduction, and Josi was definitely not okay. But for now, she had to keep her chin up and hold on to hope for good news to come.

Tara's phone call from the motel had set everything in motion. The madness wouldn't end until she was found, and whatever she'd gotten involved in was over. *The fastest way through a tough spot*, Josi thought, *is to keep going.*

Eventually Lincoln parked the borrowed farm truck in Tara's driveway behind Finn's pickup and climbed out.

Josi followed suit, meeting the brothers on Tara's porch.

Finn let them inside, then pocketed the key. "I straightened things up a little when the crime-scene team finished," he said. "The place was a mess, but nothing appeared to be stolen. Nothing obvious anyway. Her television, video games and anything else that could be turned around for quick cash are still here. Without Tara to tell us for sure, I'm going to assume whoever broke in was more interested in finding something than in removing anything."

"And you stopped by to clean up," Josi said, impressed and unsurprised.

The rooms were in one-hundred-percent-better shape than they had been following the break-in. He'd cleaned the mess, swept up broken things and neatly arranged books in stacks. He didn't know where everything went, but he'd made an effort.

Finn set his hands on his hips and turned at the waist, scanning the scene. "I didn't want her to come home to that mess, especially considering what she's already going through, wherever she is."

Josi nodded. Whether Tara was on the run, hiding out, or being held captive somewhere, coming home to a disaster would only make her feel worse. Emotion pricked her eyes and pinched her heart. "Your mama raised you right."

"She did," he agreed with a reluctant smile. "She's worried about tomorrow, trying to get every detail perfect for the next Community Days event. She's hoping y'all will be able to help, but doesn't want to ask, because she knows finding Tara and keeping you safe is more important. I told her we'd do what we could today so you could be there. I'll try to be present for as much of the event as possible, but I've got my hands full too."

Lincoln rubbed a hand against the back of his neck. "I saw some ranch hands with signs today. Before that, I'd forgotten."

Josi bit her lip. She'd forgotten too. She could hardly imagine returning to her role as stable manager, smiling for hundreds of curious visitors and nostalgic adults, while knowing Tara was still missing. She also couldn't imagine letting down Mrs. Beaumont. Not after all the family had done for her when she'd been in need. "I guess we'd better get to work."

The brothers nodded.

"Where did you see the journal?" Finn asked, fanning through a book from the pile.

She took a fortifying breath and headed for the little storage room behind the kitchen. "I'll get it."

Lincoln watched her go but didn't follow. He'd seemed on guard since Finn's arrival, but she supposed that made sense. The Beaumont family would have plenty of questions soon. Hopefully, no one would be upset by the possibility of her dating their son. After that kiss, there wasn't any denying it. She wanted to be with Lincoln, but his family was tight. She'd need their blessing, because she'd never do anything to create turmoil among people she so dearly loved. Even if that meant breaking her heart instead of theirs.

She retrieved the notebook and said a silent apology to Tara. Growing up the way she and Tara had, everything Josi did lately felt like an invasion. Yes, Tara was in trouble, and yes, she needed help. But asking everyone what she'd been up to, visiting her gym, entering her home repeatedly and going through her things felt creepy and invasive. A little like being one of the bad guys. Josi had spent a life-time protecting herself, setting firm boundaries and guarding her personal business, only to crash into Tara's life and Godzilla-stomp all over everything. Reading her personal thoughts and feelings about Marcus was officially the lowest of lows.

Josi could only hope, for multiple reasons, the words on the pages would help them find her, so the intrusion would be justified.

"Is that it?" Lincoln asked, watching carefully from the doorway.

Josi nodded, opening the thin cover and scanning the sweet notes inside. Words of heartbreak, love and loss, from Tara to Marcus. The first entry explained she'd bought the journal with hope of working through her pain by expressing it. Also, she'd hoped to retain some sense of connection to her brother by speaking to him daily. For months, the dates at the top of the page were in perfect sequence. A new entry every day. Midway through the book, the entries became less frequent, then sporadic. Sometimes two in a day. Other times only two in a week.

Lincoln moved closer and set a hand on Josi's shoulder. "You okay?"

"Yeah." She took a steadying breath.

The handwriting in the latest entries was nearly illegible, the strokes heavy and thick. A few words had been hastily scratched out and rewritten. Others circled. Exclamation points ended sentences of anger at his loss.

"She was agitated here," Josi said, tipping the journal for Lincoln to see. "In the early pages, the writing is soft and consistent. Here—" she fanned through the final dozen pages "—the script becomes less uniform, then she just starts making notes and phrases."

"May I?" Lincoln asked.

Before Josi could answer, the sound of a roaring engine turned her limbs to stone.

Lincoln darted from the room, headed back to where they'd started. "Stay here," he called over one shoulder, before vanishing around the corner.

Josi followed, the journal clutched to her chest. That sound couldn't have been good. Considering the fact she'd recently been followed and chased by multiple vehicles, she was sure she'd rather be with two strong Beaumonts than alone in the little room.

Finn and Lincoln stood shoulder to shoulder before the living-room window, curtains pulled aside for a better view of the street.

Beyond the glass, a black SUV raced forward, then braked suddenly, taking a reckless spin in the cul-de-sac where Josi and Lincoln had spoken to the little basketball players only days before. On the way back, the SUV slowed and the driver powered down the window.

Finn cursed, and Lincoln spun to face Josi.

"Get back," Lincoln ordered as his brother yelled, "Gun!"

The rat-a-tat of gunfire split the air, punctuated by a riot of shattering glass.

Josi dropped to her knees, then onto her chest behind the couch, a wild scream ripping from her lungs. Images of the gunman outside the motel sprang to mind. He'd shot at Tara, then at Josi. She squeezed her eyes shut and prayed the bullets missed everyone and everything that couldn't easily be replaced.

Lincoln's body covered hers in the next breath. His arms formed a cage of protection, his body shielding her own. "Finn!"

"I'm good," his brother returned. "Y'all good?"

Josi's body trembled as Lincoln eased upward in the fresh silence, bringing her with him. Their breathing was loud. More destruction. First a break-in. Now, a drive-by shooting. She told herself not to wonder what might be next.

"Did you get the license-plate number?" Lincoln asked.

The sound of breaking glass caused Josi to scream once more.

Her gaze jumped from the previously broken window to the Molotov cocktail that had crashed onto the coffee table. Then to the fire spreading quickly onto the couch and along the area rug beneath.

Outside, the attacking vehicle tore away with another peal of tires.

All around them, Tara's home, the one she'd once shared with her brother, was going up in flames.

Finn raced outside, across the porch, gun drawn.

"No!" Josi cried, lunging to follow. She couldn't lose anyone else to this madness. "Stop!"

Around them, flames licked over the carpet and up the wall to the ceiling, creating a barrier unsafe to cross.

Lincoln caught her at the waist and towed her toward the kitchen. The living room was already dark with smoke. "We've got to go. Finn's fine. We aren't."

Josi coughed, as if on cue, her body accepting his call.

She scanned the space, heart thundering and tears stinging her eyes. Tara's belongings would soon be gone. If she survived whatever she was going through, she wouldn't have a home to return to, and all her cherished memories would be lost. "Wait." Josi planted her feet.

Lincoln tightened his grip and tugged her into the kitchen, closer to the back door, but Josi jerked free.

"Help me!" She turned to him, forcing the journal into his hands. "I can't let it all burn. Please," she begged. "We have to save what we can."

Lincoln hesitated, his cool green gaze flickering to the photo taped onto the refrigerator. He tugged it free and pushed it into his pocket.

"The framed photos," Josi said. "And the box on the bookshelf!"

He nodded, and together, they darted back toward the flames.

Heat had filled the space and smoke billowed around them. Gentle winds through the open door and broken window fed the flames.

"Lincoln!" Finn's voice rose through the crackling and whooshing around them. "What the hell are you doing?"

Josi opened her mouth to answer and inhaled a mouth full of smoke instead. Her throat and eyes burned. She strained to see and struggled to catch her breath.

"Josi!" Finn called. "Lincoln!"

She tried again to answer but couldn't find enough oxygen.

"Josi!" Lincoln's voice echoed his brother's.

She turned to look for him. He'd been only an arm's length away, just seconds before.

Her chest tightened as her senses dulled and panic rose. Which way was the door? How had she been overcome so quickly?

Something in her distant memory told her to get on the floor. The air was cleaner near the ground. She began to crawl, wheezing painfully as she moved. Her limbs felt unfamiliar and weak. The sounds of crackling flames mixed with whooshing in her ears.

Then she was flying.

LINCOLN SWEPT JOSI'S limp body from the floor and tossed her over one shoulder, holding her tightly to his chest. The collar of his T-shirt rested high on his nose and covered his mouth. The air inside Tara's rental home was toxic, filled with smoke and whatever chemicals had been inside the broken bottle. Flames had consumed the oxygen. Visibility was nearly gone.

Josi had temporarily vanished.

Thankfully, he'd developed an uncanny ability to sense her months before. There was something about her presence that spoke to him, alerted him. And it'd only taken a moment to find her on the ground. Now, they were moments from safety, but his ability to breathe was growing precarious.

He fumbled with the dead bolt on the back door, wasting precious seconds as he wrestled with the tiny knob. The smoke had followed them, growing denser with each passing heartbeat, lightening his head and muddling his thoughts.

Then suddenly, finally, they were free.

Lincoln stumbled down the back porch steps and onto the lawn. He lowered Josi to the ground several yards away from the home, then collapsed beside her.

Crisp autumn air and the mist of fresh rain cooled his skin and face as he lay beside her, panting to regain his breath. He rolled to his side and searched her for signs of life. When her chest rose and fell steadily, he flopped onto his back with relief.

"Lincoln! Josi!" Finn rushed to them, his voice wild.

Sirens wailed in the distance.

"What happened?" he asked. "Why didn't you leave when I ran outside to get a license-plate number? You scared me half to death."

Josi coughed and pulled up the hem of her T-shirt. Instead of exposing her stomach, she revealed handfuls of printed photographs and mementos. "I couldn't fit the box," she rasped. "I had to leave it. I tucked everything I could under here."

She peeled her eyes open as the coughing jag ended, then rose onto her elbows. "I couldn't let them burn."

A pair of EMTs appeared, jogging in their direction.

"Here," Finn called, waving an arm overhead.

"Burns?" the first medic asked, lowering onto his knees beside Josi.

"No," she croaked, then broke into a fresh fit of coughing.

Out front, a fire truck roared to a stop. Emergency flashers reflected off the sides of nearby homes.

Finn sidled up to Lincoln as the first EMT snapped an oxygen mask over Josi's face. "You okay?"

"Better now," Lincoln said, examining Josi's limbs for signs of injury or trauma.

The second medic stopped before the brothers, eyebrows raised in question.

They shook their heads.

"All good," Lincoln said, earning significant side-eye from Finn. His voice had been lower and rougher than expected.

The EMT didn't move. "May I?" he asked, gaze flickering to Lincoln's arm.

He followed the other man's line of sight to a singed mark on his shirtsleeve, then suddenly felt the burn of his wound beneath. "Oh. Yeah. Go ahead."

Finn made a sour face. "Your back is worse."

The EMT circled around for a look at Lincoln's back, then opened his medical bag and got to work. Apparently, Lincoln hadn't escaped completely unscathed.

"You're hurt?" Josi asked. She held the oxygen mask away from her face with one hand.

"I'm fine," he promised, then hissed long and hard as the medic poured something that felt like acid onto his back.

Her eyes glossed immediately with unshed tears. "Lincoln."

"Put your mask back on."

She narrowed her eyes in defiance, and tears fell.

Lincoln walked away from the medic. "You need the oxygen to clear your lungs," he said quietly. "Put your mask on, and I'll let the medic finish helping me."

She snapped the mask into place with a heated glare.

Finn snorted.

The medic went back to torturing Lincoln.

"So you got the license plate?" Lincoln asked, redirecting his attention from the pain.

Finn grimaced. "No. I got the make and model, but I was too late to get anything more. The tinted glass was too dark." He reached into his back pocket and removed a small notebook. "I found this inside the clock on the mantel before the shooting started. Josi gave me the idea to look a little more closely at everywhere that might be a hiding spot."

"What is it?"

Finn opened the cover and turned the first few pages before answering. "It's a calendar. Looks like Tara's work schedule at the pawnshop, the times for various classes at Body by Bella and a third set of dates and times in red. No details."

Josi pulled off her mask again. "What do you think those mean? Fight times?"

"She hid the calendar for a reason," he said. "Fight times are my guess too."

Lincoln crossed his arms, eyes narrowed, waiting for Josi

to replace her mask. Then he turned to his brother, still perusing the calendar. "When's the next date in red?"

A smile slid across Finn's smug face. "Tomorrow night. We just need to figure out where."

Chapter Nineteen

Thirty minutes later, Lincoln held Josi's hand as they followed Finn around the house toward the trucks. She was going to be okay, thanks to a lot of oxygen and an IV. He was still fuming that she'd been in danger yet again, and he wasn't thrilled with the EMT who'd tormented him while treating his burns.

Josi gave his fingers a reassuring squeeze as they walked.

The medics had instructed them to go home, rest and stay hydrated. A solid plan. Apparently, the only safe place for Josi these days was Beaumont Ranch.

Finn stopped to speak with a group of fire officials standing in the street, arms crossed, appraising Tara's home. He'd placed Tara's keepsakes and mementos into large evidence bags and given them to another officer on the case.

Josi hadn't released the items easily, but Finn promised to return everything to Tara as soon as possible, and she'd taken him at his word.

The home came fully into view as they reached the driveway. The fire was out. The front door stood open, the window gone. Charred, tattered curtains hung askew and blew gently from the wind.

Josi stopped short of the borrowed farm truck and turned

her eyes to Lincoln. "I didn't even think about the fact you parked in the driveway."

His attention moved to the pickup, now riddled with bullet holes.

Finn grimaced from several yards away. "At least it wasn't your ride this time," he said. "You only needed new tires. This truck is toast."

Josi leaned against Lincoln and set a palm on his chest. "The important thing," she whispered, "is that we're all okay."

Lincoln focused on her words as his heart rate began to rise. He'd run from a house on fire and been calm. He'd watched her slack face while waiting for her eyes to open, and he'd remained calm. Now, a few bullet holes in an old truck caused the panic to build?

"Hey." She patted his shirt and rose onto her toes. "Look at me." Her hand slid up to cup his jaw and pull it down to her. "Remember when I was on your kitchen countertop earlier?"

His gaze bounced to hers, meeting those teasing blue eyes. The imagery she'd provided sent his energies in a whole new direction, a much nicer reason for his elevated pulse.

"Lincoln," she whispered. "Do you remember?"

He nodded, hands moving to her waist on autopilot.

"Take me home and do it again?" she asked.

"Need a ride?" Finn called, moving toward his truck, wholly unaware of Josi's mind-boggling, life-affirming request.

She laughed softly as she tugged him toward the other vehicle. "Finn can drop us off and take care of the farm truck. We'll go home and take care of each other." She winked, and he felt a smile form on his lips.

HE'D SURVIVED AGAIN with Josi at his side, and she'd stopped his panic as it had begun to swell. She'd asked him to take her home and reminded him of the ways he'd touched her. The memory was intoxicating, but instead of kissing her senseless when he imagined her in his kitchen once more, the fantasy version of himself lowered to one knee.

He pushed away the thought. They weren't even dating. How could he think of a proposal? Maybe he'd suffered a head injury along with the burns.

A short while later, the trio boarded Finn's ride after the farm truck was dragged away. Finn started the engine and waited while Josi and Lincoln buckled their safety belts. "The fire officials say they got here in time to save the structure. Homeowner's insurance will repair the damage, and renter's insurance should replace most of the lost possessions. You were a good friend to get Tara's keepsakes out safely. I just wish you hadn't risked your own life to do it."

Lincoln examined the crowd of civilian onlookers as they rolled away. Was one of them involved in the drive-by shooting or fire? Did they see or know something that would help Finn find the culprit or Tara?

"All right," Finn said, slowing at the next intersection. "It's off topic, and none of my business, but I've got to ask. What are y'all doing?" He glanced at Josi's fingers laced with Lincoln's on his thigh. "When did that start? And does Mama know or can I tell her? Because I'm always keeping secrets for this family, and when the facts come out, which they always do, I lose points for subterfuge."

Josi snorted.

Lincoln grinned.

"Well?" he persisted. "I'm starting to lose faith in my detective skills on this case. I could use a win. Give me something." His phone rang, saving Lincoln from telling him to get comfortable with another loss.

He and Josi hadn't even talked about what they were doing yet. Lincoln certainly wasn't about to have that conversation with Finn.

"Beaumont," Finn answered, clearly aggrieved. "When? On my way." He disconnected the call and pressed a button on his dash, igniting a siren and likely the new flashers he'd had installed beneath the truck's grill.

"What's happening?" Josi asked, a mix of hope and terror in her tone. "Did they find Tara?"

"No. There was an incident at Body by Bella," he said. "Bella was alone when two men in masks pushed their way inside."

FINN MADE THE drive across town to Bella's in twenty minutes. A pair of cruisers were parked in the lot when they arrived.

Lincoln offered Josi his hand, then held on tight as they climbed down from Finn's truck and followed him to the gym's front door.

Bella sat behind the welcome desk, arms wrapped around her middle and dark makeup streaks below her eyes. She straightened, then deflated as Lincoln and the others walked inside.

Finn shook hands with the officers on his way to Bella.

Josi released Lincoln's hand and jogged around the desk, arms opening to wrap the other woman in a hug. "I'm so sorry this happened to you," she said. Her voice cracked with emotion, and Lincoln suspected this hit close to home for Josi, who'd recently been attacked as well.

Lincoln longed to go to her, but forced himself to stand down, allowing her the space she needed.

"Details?" Finn asked the officers quietly.

The taller man widened his stance and checked a small notepad. "The intruders used force to push their way inside when the owner, Bella, was preparing to close for the day. Two men then interrogated her at knifepoint for several minutes."

A sob escaped Bella, drawing Lincoln's attention back to the women.

Josi passed her a tissue box from the desk and patted her shoulder.

"They kept demanding information about Tara," Bella explained. "They wanted to know how well I knew her. What she'd told me about the fight club. Who else she'd told. Who I'd told. They wouldn't stop. And they didn't believe me when I said she'd never confided any of those details. If one of my regulars hadn't forgotten this was the night I close early every week and shown up for spin class, I don't know what might've happened." Tears flowed freely over Bella's cheeks, and she wiped frantically at her face with a wad of tissues. "They ran away when she walked in, and I called 911."

The criminals had asked about the fight club. So the theory Finn, Josi and Lincoln had been working with was confirmed.

Behind Lincoln, the front door opened again.

Bella stiffened as she had before, then sagged when a pair of women blew inside.

"Excuse me," one of the officers said. "The gym is closed."

The women with puffy red hair took one look at Bella and marched past. "Oh, my glory! Who did this?"

The other lady followed. "We were just leaving the café

and saw the cruisers. We had to stop. We wanted to be sure everything was okay."

Finn scratched his head and sighed. "Everything is under control. Bella's okay."

The women turned slowly to face him, comically so. Their thinly sculpted eyebrows hiked up in challenge.

"I think we'd like to hear that from her, if you don't mind, Officer," the redhead stated flatly.

"We prefer to speak for ourselves," the other added, sounding exactly like their mama.

Finn's mouth pulled low on each side, and he cut his eyes to Lincoln, who struggled not to laugh.

The woman hustled over to Bella, and Finn locked the door, then instructed one of the officers to keep it locked when the women left to avoid further interruptions.

"It's all so awful," Bella told her friends. "I can't think straight. I don't even understand what they want from Tara or why they're badgering me. Aren't they the ones who have her somewhere? And what did they mean about a fight club?"

"Tara Stone?" the redhead asked, gaze roaming from Bella to the officers.

"Do you know her?" Finn asked, stepping forward as Josi offered Bella the entire box of tissues.

"I do," the woman said. "I'm Eileen. I take self-defense classes with Tara." Her eyebrows knitted as she considered something. "She came over for pizza one night after class and asked to crash on the sofa. She said she'd had a glass of wine and didn't want to drive home, but honestly, she barely touched the wine. Or the pizza. I could tell something was off, so I let her stay, but she didn't say a word about what-ever was bothering her. She ate a huge breakfast the next morning, showered and borrowed some clothes. I noticed a lot of bruising on her sides and suspected she might be in a bad relationship. Those kinds of men never leave marks where people will see. When they do, the women lie to cover for them." She shook her head, looking as heartbroken as she sounded. "You think she was involved in a fight club?"

"That's what we're trying to find out," Finn said. "Is there anything else you can tell us about that night or the following morning?"

"She made a phone call," Eileen said. "From my landline. I heard her telling someone named Petey that she was sorry. At first I thought it was the abusive boyfriend, but she told me she was supposed to be at work and needed to let him know she'd be late. That made sense."

"Petey," Josi said. "From the pawnshop." She locked gazes with Lincoln.

"Wait," the second woman said. "Did she have a bad boyfriend or not?"

Josi shook her head, redirecting her attention. "We don't think so. Why? Did she ever mention one?"

The woman bit her lip. "No, but it's curious, that's all."

"What is?" Lincoln asked, unable to stay out of things any longer. Josi looked ready to collapse, and the EMT had told her to rest. Attending another crime scene was the opposite of resting, and they needed to wrap this up so Finn could take them home.

"I saw her walking along the waterfront last week," the woman said. "I gave her a ride home. She was cradling one arm and hiding her face behind her hair. I didn't push, but I offered to help if she was in trouble. She refused everything except the ride, then she missed our class the next evening. I was terrified, but she was back in her place later that week. We never spoke about it again."

Josi frowned.

Lincoln could practically hear her thoughts. "Why would she be walking by the waterfront? She had a car, right?" He looked to Finn.

"The truck registered to her name was found near the Bayside Motel," he said.

Josi nodded. "She called me for a ride because it wouldn't start."

"I'm guessing that was more likely sabotage than an accident," Lincoln said.

Finn squared his shoulders and narrowed his eyes on Eileen. "Where was she when you picked her up? Exactly."

The woman blinked. "I don't know. It was dark. I was coming home from my girlfriend's house on Lighthouse Drive."

"That's by mile marker twelve," Lincoln said. "Which direction was she moving?"

"East," she said. "I think." The woman frowned. "Except that doesn't make any sense. There's nothing out there."

Lincoln nodded. "Sounds like a perfect place to hold a fight club."

JOSI HELD HER breath as she entered the pawnshop, steadying her nerves and shoring up her will to confront Petey. The older man had always intimidated her. Thankfully, no one intimidated the Beaumonts, and the two brothers accompanying her weren't in a mood to be trifled with.

She exhaled and squared her shoulders as she approached the counter. "Petey," she called.

The man appeared. He rounded the corner from a room beyond. "Fancy seeing you again so soon, Miss Josi." His smirk was rueful as he took her in. The expression flattened at the sight of the men she'd brought along. "What seems to be the problem, Officer?" he asked, clearly recognizing Finn.

"Detective," Finn clarified. "Last we talked, you had no idea where Tara Stone was or what she'd been up to in the days before she went missing."

Petey nodded, mouth uncharacteristically shut.

"I now have reason to believe you lied to me. Why would you do that? Interfering with an ongoing investigation is against the law."

"Hey now," Petey said, moving closer. "I was trying to protect the girl's privacy. Nothing wrong with stepping off the grid for a day or two. We all need a reset from time to time."

"A reset from what?" Josi asked, the earlier trepidation falling away like loosened binds.

Petey's gaze darted to a pair of men moving through the aisles to join him.

Josi recognized the duo from her last trip to the pawnshop with Lincoln.

Finn watched them closely, gaze shifting from the new arrivals to Petey, then back. "We believe the illegal fight club that led to Marcus Stone's death is up and running again. We also believe Tara knew about it and got involved somehow. If the man who took a shot at her outside the motel earlier this week gets his hands on her, it likely will not end well. So if you know something that can help us find her, I need that information. Now."

Josi sucked in a breath at the authority in Finn's voice. She'd never seen him in action this way. The difference between the often playful man she knew and the detective was drastic. Even at Bella's, faced with the shaken women, he'd been patient and kind. At the moment, he looked and sounded as if he might bust some heads.

Lincoln straightened at her side, and a smile tugged at her lips.

Petey and his friends were at a complete disadvantage.

He looked to the younger men, shifting and trading glances, then grunted. "All I know is she'd picked up boxing as a hobby, self-defense, all that. She told me she was paying homage to Marcus. I let it go. She missed some work from time to time, but never more than a day or two, and she worked hard when she was here." He cracked his knuckles and fixed the younger duo with a pointed stare. "If y'all know something more, you'd better talk. That girl's like a daughter to me."

They didn't respond.

"We spoke to someone who picked her up a few days before she went missing," Finn said. "According to the witness, Tara was walking alone at night near the harbor. Know anything about that?"

The shorter of the two guys, Josi remembered as Dustin, gave his friend an elbow to the ribs. "She could be in real trouble."

The taller guy ran a hand through his hair. "All right." He leaned against the nearby wall, as if he might need it for support. "T's been making money fighting other women," he said quietly. "That's all I know. Sometimes Dustin drives her to events."

"Where?" Finn asked.

"Why?" Petey said right after Finn.

Dustin shrugged, a look of shame on his crumpled features. "The location changes, but she pays me half of what she earns. I drive because sometimes she's too banged up to get home on her own. She knows that's always a possibility, so she plans ahead."

Petey scoffed. "Why'd she give you half if she was the one getting hurt?"

"I don't know, and I didn't ask. It was easy money. I need it, and she never seems to care about it. The rest was none of my business."

Josi felt her stomach pitch as details from the past rushed back to mind. "The fight referee won't call a winner until someone is physically unable to leave the ring. One fighter has to be out cold or too injured to continue." It was the only rule. Fighters had to fight until the very end.

For Marcus, it had been his life's end.

Imagining Tara choosing to climb into the ring, knowing what had happened to Marcus, was too much. Josi pushed aside the ideas as tears began to well once more. How awful must every fight have been for Tara? And she kept going back. Why would she do that?

"She didn't care about the money," Josi whispered, answering her silent question with the guy's words. "She was there to tear the place down."

Lincoln's strong arms circled her waist and turned her toward him, gathering her carefully against his chest.

Finn moved forward, tucking the two of them behind him. "Did you watch the fights?" he asked Dustin.

"Sometimes. It's not my thing. Gets too bloody. There are medics on hand, but they aren't very good. Tara always wanted to know who was taking the money and who seemed to be in charge. I had no idea. All the meatheads looked the same to me."

"Where have you taken her to fight in the past?" Finn asked. "The places change, but maybe there's a pattern."

Dustin used his phone's mapping system to share pins from several of the fight locations with Finn.

His expression fell, apparently not seeing a pattern.

"When was the next time you were supposed to drive her?" Finn asked.

"Tomorrow night."

He pulled the notebook from his pocket and confirmed the time. "It's a match."

Hope rushed through Josi's body. Today would be the last day of this nightmare.

Chapter Twenty

Josi bumbled her way through the next workday, sliding back into her role as stable manager while Lincoln worked with the horses and other ranch hands. Community Days on the ranch were a big deal to the Beaumonts, and she needed to keep her head in the game. Finn and his team had a plan for tonight, and members of Marshal's Bluff PD were already searching the most rural areas for signs of Tara.

In a few hours, she would be safe. The fight club would be dismantled. The perpetrators, gunmen and abductors in jail.

Josi just had to keep smiling and answering equine-related questions a little longer.

The sun shone brightly outside her office window, almost warm enough to burn away the gloom and fear from her heart. Almost. Children's laughter danced in the wind. Happy voices chatted in the stables and on the ranch grounds. She normally loved these events, but congeniality and joy wouldn't come easily today. Not until she knew Tara was safe.

Lincoln's steady footfalls echoed on the stable floor, growing significantly louder as they got near.

She turned to watch the open doorway until he appeared.

A smile tugged his lips when their eyes met. "Hey."

"Hey."

He slid inside and looked her over.

Shafts of light through her slatted blinds illuminated his tanned skin in stripes, leaving a deep shadow over his face and hiding his moss-green eyes. His boots and jeans were muddy from hoisting kids onto horseback and leading them along the preset paths he'd designed for Community Days. His cologne mixed with fresh air and dried hay in ways that made her stomach tumble.

"How are you holding up?" he asked.

"I'm okay." She shrugged. "Trying to stay busy. Keep my mind off of things. You?"

He nodded then took a step in her direction, pausing to lean against her desk. "Finn called. His men are doing surveillance along the harbor now. Things are quiet, but if this is a fight night, it'll be the last."

Josi released a long shaky breath, willing his words to be true. Finn was good at his job. He was smart and levelheaded. Tara would be safe in his hands. Now, Josi just needed to convince herself to relax.

"Dad and the ranch hands are moving the horses into the big field for a little show. Food's being lined up on the tables for lunch. You should come out and get a bite," Lincoln said.

Josi shook her head. "I don't think I can face your family or a crowd. The Beaumonts will all see through me, right down to my shaking boots. The crowd will only make me nervous."

Lincoln opened his arms and tented his eyebrows in question.

She went to him in a heartbeat, falling easily into his embrace.

Strong arms circled her, gathering her close, and she inhaled the precious scents of her personal guardian, friend and love. "Wow, I needed this," she whispered, rising onto tiptoes and snuggling deeper into his protective hold.

"Do you also need food?" he asked. "I can smuggle a couple of plates in here and have a little lunch with you."

Josi groaned at the perfection of his offer. "Yes. Please." It was as if she'd been craving his nearness and hadn't really put a finger on the need until he'd said the words. "Are you sure you can get away for a lunch break?"

Lincoln pulled back and scoffed.

"Right." She smiled. "You do what you want."

"And so do you," he assured her. "Now, what can I get you from the tables?"

A familiar country song began outside, signaling a new event and meant to move visitors in the right direction.

Josi loosened her hold on Lincoln, feeling better, if a little guilty for tying up his time. Nowhere near guilty enough to turn him down. "I would love a burger and baked macaroni and cheese, if it's out there. I've got water in here." She pointed to the mini fridge in the corner. "Maybe something sweet too?"

His mouth ticked up in a mischievous half smile and he pressed a kiss to her lips. "Be right back."

A set of gunshots exploded in the distance, and Josi's heart seized.

Then the screaming began.

"Stay here," Lincoln said. "Call 911, then Finn."

The door slammed shut, taking her view of him with it. Josi's heart hammered.

She snapped into action, grabbing her phone with uncoordinated fingers and searching for Lincoln in the mess outside her window. She took in the chaos as she dialed.

Spooked horses rose onto hind legs. Young riders fell to the ground. People scrambled to save the fallen, or ran away to save themselves. An equine stampede ran through the panicked crowd. Food tables were overturned. Truck alarms went off.

"Come on," she whispered, willing the call to connect.

"Ah, ah, ah," a low voice chided.

Gooseflesh pebbled her skin, and she spun toward the sound. The barbs of a Taser shot into her chest, jolting her silent before a leather-gloved hand covered her mouth and dragged her away.

LINCOLN SPRINTED OUTSIDE, senses on high alert and instincts kicking him into gear. "Dad!" he called, catching sight of his father on the ground near a kneeling woman and small child.

"Settle the horses!" his dad returned. "Get folks out of the way."

Lincoln changed directions, scooping a toddler off the ground and passing her to a confused-looking teen. "Take her to the porch and keep her there," he barked. "Take as many others as you can. Go!"

The teen blinked, then jolted forward, taking the hand of another child as he began to dash toward the farmhouse.

In the distance, sirens rang out. He thanked his lucky stars for Josi's call to emergency services and for the help that was on the way. Horses were gentle giants until they were afraid. Then they were frantic babies. Too large for their own good, and too dangerous for anyone unprepared.

The ranch hands slowed a few of the younger animals, then swung themselves onto the saddles. Not an easy trick, but a skill Lincoln could appreciate. Especially when those same people used the mounted horses to catch and corral the others.

A desperate wail redirected his attention to a man on the ground. He was cradling a young woman's head on his lap. Her eyes were closed. Crimson stained her blond hair, the man's shirt and hands as he struggled to slow the blood flow. A matching stain on a nearby rock suggested she'd fallen, probably from a horse, and knocked herself unconscious. "Help!" the man called, eyes searching frantically. "We need a doctor!"

Lincoln skidded to a stop two feet away. "Ambulances are en route. What's your name?"

"Frank."

"Frank," Lincoln repeated. "Who's this?"

"My daughter. Emma." The man choked on her name. "We brought her out to see the ranch. She's struggling at home, but... We thought the ranch would be good for her. She didn't want to come." He squeezed his eyelids shut, and a tear appeared on his cheek.

In the distance, the ranch hands returned several horses to a gated pen. Ambulances trundled along the gravel driveway, avoiding frightened people and exiting vehicles.

Lincoln's chest tightened unexpectedly. Images of injured soldiers flashed in his memory. Fear and tension that should've been left on the other side of the world pressed into his mind, stealing his breath and stilling his limbs.

He pushed against the intrusive thoughts, bringing better, more recent memories to the forefront of his mind. Josi speaking softly, confidently. Her small hands on his cheeks or chest. Promising everything was okay.

"Everything is going to be okay, Frank," he said, voice unnaturally low. He waved a hand high overhead, catching a medic's eye. "Talk to Emma. Let her know you're here and not to be afraid. Then explain exactly what happened to the medic."

Frank nodded and began speaking to his unconscious daughter.

Lincoln clapped the EMT on the back as he arrived. "Head injury."

The medic dropped into a squat beside Frank.

Lincoln moved on to the next set of people curled on the grass. "Wait on the porch," he told a set of young boys positioned on their knees, heads down and hands folded over top.

"A shooter!" one boy cried. "There's a gun."

Lincoln scanned the scene. Dazed people wandered the grounds, calling out to friends and family.

"That's my mom!" a second boy exclaimed, jumping to his feet.

"Go," Lincoln ordered. "All of you. Up!"

The boys stood, then ran.

The shooter, however, was nowhere to be found.

And no one seemed to have been shot.

His gaze snapped to the stable, then to Josi's office window. She wasn't there. He'd been sure she would be watching, relaying the details to Finn or a dispatcher by phone. Maybe even looking for him.

He turned in a slow circle, hoping she hadn't wandered into the chaos, where she would be vulnerable to attack. Then, suddenly, he understood.

The gunfire wasn't intended to cause harm. Each shot had done exactly what it was meant to do. And Lincoln had reacted precisely as expected.

He'd left Josi alone.

He was in motion before the thought had finished forming. "Look out," he called, dodging guests as they criss-crossed the field. "Move!"

His chest ached with effort as he leaped over abandoned bags and toppled strollers on his way to the stable. He sucked in his first full breath of hope as a familiar figure came into view outside Josi's office.

"Mama!" He slowed upon approach. "You okay?"

She nodded, eyes wide and expression aghast. "I am. I saw you in the field, and I came to check on Josi."

"Same." He nodded, pressing a hand to the pinch in his side. "She's all right?" he asked, following his mama's gaze through the open door.

"I don't know," she said. "I haven't seen her."

Lincoln froze beside his mother, gaze fixed on the empty office before them.

Josi was gone.

Chapter Twenty-One

Josi woke to harsh light and a shooting pain through her forehead. She blinked to clear her vision, trying and failing to gain her bearings.

"Be still," a rough male voice commanded.

The jostling of a vehicle slowly registered, and she struggled again to focus her eyes. "Where are we?" she croaked.

"Shut up," the man snapped. "Keep your head down."

She let the words settle in her addled mind. Why was she so confused?

She'd been in her office, watching from the window as the Beaumonts and farm hands slowed the horses and tended to the frantic crowd. She'd seen Lincoln speaking with a man beside an injured young woman.

Then—

A low groan rolled through her as she opened her eyes once more. When had they closed? Her gaze slid from the bright southern sun to the unfamiliar dashboard and interior. Black on black. Scents of heady cologne and leather.

Her throat was dry as she swallowed, her head pounded as she attempted to turn or lift it away from the window at her side.

Something hard pressed against her hip.

"I said do not move." The man ground out each word.

And Josi's heart began to race, adrenaline slowly burning away the haze of whatever had happened to her.

She tried again to remember the moments at her office window and failed.

Sirens wailed as she rocked in the unfamiliar vehicle. *Emergency vehicles*, she realized. Help was headed to the farm. A measure of relief swept through her along with choppy memories of injured guests. And a gunman.

Breath caught in her throat as the recollection of unexpected gunshots sloshed in her soggy mind. Suddenly, the hard press against her thigh took new shape, registering as the barrel of a gun.

The vehicle picked up speed as it passed the parade of ambulances and police cruisers, their sirens growing faint. Her driver released a long, laborious sigh. "I thought we'd never get away from that damn ranch."

Josi leaned herself upright, forcing her muscles to cooperate as she sat tall. The Beaumont Ranch shrank quickly in the mirror outside her window.

She rode on the front passenger seat of a black SUV, piloted by Dennis Cane, the Barbell Club manager.

His angry brown eyes slid her way briefly before returning to the road. "You just can't take a hint. Won't follow instructions. Make everything unnecessarily difficult." He jammed the gun painfully against her hip, causing her to wince.

Her body was heavy, as if underwater. "Where are we going?" she asked, voice thick and sounding foreign to her own ears.

"Somewhere you can't cause any more trouble," he said. "I've got a business to run and people counting on these fights. Your sweet little-girl-next-door look will bring a pretty penny. I can think of more than a few men who'd pay to see you taken down. A handful who'd like to do the job themselves."

"Why?" she croaked, unable to clear the gravel from her voice.

"Because you look like everything they hate in a woman." He chuckled. "And I can't say I disagree. We had to put the show on pause the last time things went sideways. I'm not ready to do that again. Taking you out of the equation should fix things up nicely."

"Again?" she asked, her mind working more quickly than her lips. Hadn't the fight club been dismantled fully after Marcus's death?

"Yeah. A lot of good men went to prison the last time. Too many. You can't even imagine the amount of money I lost while things were on hold. I won't let that happen again. They're lucky to have me at the helm."

A lot of good men went to prison the last time. But not Dennis Cane, and he had been in charge.

He pulled the gun away and rested it on his thigh.

"Do you have Tara?" she asked, a boulder of fear in her throat. "Can I see her?"

"Absolutely. You can braid one another's hair and have a little reunion before showtime. After that, you're mine."

A violent shiver rocked down her spine. Josi didn't want to know what he'd meant by that. Every possibility made her equally sick. She had to concentrate and regain her strength if she wanted to escape with Tara. Until then, she could only hope Finn and his men knew where tonight's fight would occur.

The vehicle hit a pothole, and her gaze bounced around the interior once more. A rag on the floor at her feet set off a series of rapid-fire memories.

She'd been at the window when Dennis entered her office—he'd shot her with a Taser then dragged her away. When he'd covered her mouth with a rag, the scent had been sickly sweet, then the world had gone dark. "You drugged me," she whispered. It would explain her memory loss, heavy limbs and searing headache. "You're the one who caused a panic at the ranch. You shot at Tara outside the motel." All of the week's most horrible events returned in a rush. "You sent those cars to chase us. Sent the men to interrogate Bella and try to take me."

"You know what they say," he said. "If you want something done right...do it yourself."

She rolled her eyes, and pain shot through her skull. Uncoordinated hands fumbled to pat her pockets.

"I took your phone," he said. "If that's what you're looking for, I tossed it out before we got into the truck. No one's saving you from the tower, princess. Or in your case, the dungeon."

Josi sank back against the seat, head lolling and gaze moving through the glass at her side. Familiar scenery blurred past. Shops and trees. Traffic and pedestrians. People going cheerfully about their days while she sat quietly hostage. Even if she could find the strength to scream, she was certain her body hadn't recovered enough to get away. And if she somehow managed the impossible, what would happen to Tara?

The world blinked in and out until the vehicle finally stopped, and Josi's eyes opened once more.

Dennis closed the driver's-side door with a jarring thud. Moments later, a wave of salty air crashed over her.

Something soft covered her face and she gasped.

The world went dark once more.

"JOSI." SOMEONE NEARBY spoke her name. "Wake up." Her cheek stung, and her eyelids fluttered open.

Her stomach twisted and coiled. Metallic scents churned in the dry, earthy air.

"Hey..." The voice came again, familiar this time, though brittle and thin. "You have to move," the woman said. "They'll be back soon."

Fresh panic and fear scratched at Josi's mind.

"Lincoln," she whispered, the name rolling off her tongue. Was he okay? Where was he now?

An arm locked with hers and pulled her upright, turning Josi until her head and back rested against a rough stone wall. Her bottom pressed against a cool, hard floor. Before her, a blurry figure came into focus.

Tears spilled over the younger woman's swollen cheeks and cracked lips. Her beautiful blue eyes were red with busted blood vessels. Her body was battered and bruised.

"Tara." Josi opened her arms and pulled her friend into a hug. A hot rush of tears made her vision temporarily worse.

Tara held her tight, body shaking with silent sobs.

"Are you okay?" Josi asked, hoping Tara felt better than she looked. "What happened to you?"

"Dennis," Tara said, rocking back on her haunches before falling onto the floor with a sharp cry.

"I've been looking for you since that night at the hotel. The police are too. What's going on?"

Tara glanced over her shoulder, then back to Josi, swallowing hard before speaking once more. "I overheard a few guys talking about gambling at a party. It sounded as if they were betting on fights, and I thought of Marcus. I tried to get information, but they shut me out. I worried about the possibility of another fight club, so I asked more questions. At first, I couldn't find anyone willing to talk. Then I saw a woman leaving the Barbell Club, while I was waiting for the guys to come out. I'd planned to follow them when they left, but I followed her instead. She had two black eyes and peeled away from the lot like the place was on fire. When she stopped for gas, I approached. She was discreet, but everything she said seemed to confirm my fear."

"The fight club is running again," Josi said, pulling her jumbled thoughts into line.

Tara nodded. "The woman was a single mom who'd started fighting for extra money, and it gave me an idea." Tears rolled over her cheeks as she spoke, and she hissed with pain when she brushed them away. Her hand was gnarled and wrapped with tape, and was probably broken. "I thought I could get inside and bring down the ring for good. I wanted to get names and evidence I could turn over to the police department. Especially the person in charge. If I don't stop him, the club will keep making a comeback."

"That's when you started training at Bella's," Josi said, the missing pieces coming together.

Surprise crossed Tara's face at the mention of the gym owner. "How did you—"

"We met her. She's been helping us." Josi motioned for Tara to sit at her side, and the younger woman obeyed. Josi leaned against her shoulder, willing her thoughts to clear and her limbs to regain strength and coordination.

"We?" Tara asked, tipping her head against Josi. "Not Dennis."

"No, the Beaumonts. Lincoln and Finn, mostly. Finn's a detective. The whole family has been doing what they can to help find you. And they're going to make sure this fight club comes down for the last time. We just have to help them find us when they get here." Josi looked more carefully at the dim space around them, listened to the sounds of rain against a metal roof. "Where are we?" And when had it started to rain? How long had she been unconscious?

"The old grain mill near the harbor," Tara said. "All the

money goes through here, and it's where they keep the fighters too injured to get home on their own."

Josi grimaced. "Like you."

"I don't get to go home, because they know what I was up to. I won't leave here alive."

"Don't talk like that." Anger mixed with adrenaline in Josi's heart and mind. "You will survive this. We're both leaving this place tonight. The minute I can stand on my own."

"I can't," Tara said, voice cracking again. "They make me fight every night until I'm out cold and don't get back up. Just like Marcus. My head never has time to heal. My body's broken." She pressed curled hands against her face to quiet her sobs.

Josi's arm went around her friend and pulled her gently closer. "I need you to fight one more time. Okay? Fight with me to get out of here."

LINCOLN SAT AT the kitchen table with his family, reviewing multiple security feeds from around the Beaumont property. The ranch often housed troubled teens, and that required knowing everything that went on, as well as having the ability to find kids who occasionally tried to sneak away. They'd rarely needed to review more than one feed at a time, but the system had the capability, and they'd put it to use.

Dean and Austin had shown up to help in any way they could. And like the rest of the family, they were exceptional at their jobs. Their assistance was priceless.

Now, everyone had a laptop and a security feed to analyze in the hopes of spotting Josi and the direction she'd been taken.

Lincoln's mama refilled everyone's mugs with coffee before she took a seat beside their father and linked her arm with his. He kissed her head without looking away from the feed. The simple gestures of love and support hit Lincoln in the chest like an anvil.

He hadn't dared to want what his parents had in a long time, but getting closer to Josi had brought those old dreams back to the forefront. He knew now, without any doubt, the only future he wanted had her in it.

"We'll find her," his mother whispered, reaching one hand across the table to pat his wrist.

Something hot and wet slid along his face, and he rubbed it hastily away. It took a long moment for him to realize he was crying.

All eyes locked on him as he inhaled, then released a shaky breath. "I love her," he admitted. Hating that the one woman he wanted was the only one his parents wouldn't want for him. A woman they already saw as a member of the family, and one they probably thought was way too young.

Their collective expressions turned pitying instead of the shock or horror he'd expected. His brothers shook their heads and frowned.

"About time you figured that out," Austin said flatly, returning his attention to the screen before him. "Y'all have been driving us up the wall with the goo-goo eyes and the pining for a year."

"At least that long." Dean snorted a laugh, already back to reviewing the security feed.

Lincoln blinked, too stunned to speak as he searched Finn's and his parents' faces. "What?"

"We know," Finn said, waving a hand around, indicating the whole team. "We talk about it all the time."

Lincoln pressed back in his seat. "How do you know?"

His mother made a low humming noise that sounded like a wordless "bless your heart." "Sweetie. We have eyes."

Lincoln frowned. "You're not mad."

"Why on earth would we be mad?" his father asked.

"We're delighted," his mama said. "She's strong and smart. And she seems to love you too."

"You don't see her as a part of the family? A daughter?" he asked his folks. "Or a sister?" He turned to his brothers.

Dean wrinkled his nose. "Alison, Hayley and Scarlet are part of the family now," Dean said. "That's the point, isn't it?"

Austin smirked. "What's important is that you don't see her as a sister."

Lincoln rubbed heavy palms against his face, joy mixing with heartbreak in his soul. "I can't believe I left her alone. Now, she's gone, and we don't have the first clue where to find her."

"Well," his dad said, attention fixed to the screen. "I might."

Chairs scraped over wooden floorboards as Lincoln and his brothers rose in quick unison. They moved to stand behind their parents and examine his father's security feed. Dennis Cane from the Barbell Club came into view, moving from the stable to a waiting SUV, a slumping woman at his side. He tucked her into the passenger's side and drove away, passing incoming emergency responders.

Chapter Twenty-Two

Shafts of waning daylight poured through cracks in ancient walls, slowly changing from the warm gold of an autumn day to the cool periwinkle of twilight. Wind whistled between the bricks, stirring up dirt on the cracked concrete floor. In the distance, thunder rolled.

Josi made her way around the room's perimeter, leaning against the wall for support as needed. She grew stronger and steadier by the minute, which was good, because according to Tara, they didn't have much time. She pressed her toe and shoulder to brick and wallboard, then raised a cast-off piece of metal to test the air ducts and ceiling beams.

"Once it gets dark, they'll announce the fight schedule and start taking bets. Then they'll come for us," Tara said.

Josi stilled. "What do you mean?" She vaguely remembered Dennis saying he wanted her in the ring, but Tara could barely walk. "They can't expect you to fight again tonight," she said.

Tara offered a sad smile. "They do. And I will. At least until I'm knocked out again. I just hope they don't pit us against one another."

"Never," Josi said, impossibly more horrified. She wouldn't hit anyone, especially not someone as injured as Tara. And never Tara.

"You'd be surprised what they can make us do." Tara cast her gaze to the floor, face paling with unspoken thoughts.

Josi doubled down on the task at hand. She slid the tip of the metal between slats in a vent just out of reach, then angled it like a pry bar.

The frantic shrieking of mice echoed overhead.

"They're in the vents," Tara said. "They fall out at night."

Josi moved close to the wall, peering in the direction of the now distant sounds. "How do they get in there?"

"I have no idea." Tara sagged to the floor. "I guess the vents lead somewhere outside, or at least into another part of the mill."

"Get up," Josi said, a new idea forming. Neither of them were in any condition to fight tonight, but maybe they were strong enough to follow the mice.

"What are you doing?" Tara asked, stumbling to Josi's side. Her noticeable limp and occasionally slurred speech seemed to be getting worse.

"Give me a boost." Josi moved under the vent and out-stretched her arms. "I only need a few inches."

Tara lowered to her hands and knees. "I can't balance well enough to squat, but you can stand on my back."

"Perfect." Josi stepped gingerly onto her friend, cringing at Tara's resulting whimper. She slid her fingers through the slats in the grate and tugged. Two of the corner screws fell out, landing on the ground beneath her. She worked the final two with her thumb and forefinger until they were removed as well. "Okay." Josi climbed down and set the grate on the ground. Then she offered Tara her hand. "Put me on your shoulders. I'll climb into the vent and pull you up after me."

An eternity later, when both women were past exhaustion, and night had fully fallen, Josi finally dragged Tara into the vent.

They let the mice lead the way.

Moving along on their stomachs, Josi and Tara wiggled like snakes in the cramped space, too short to rise onto hands and knees. The air was dank and uncomfortable, and the mice were only inches from Josi's face.

"I can't see," Tara said, slapping her hand against Josi's foot for the dozenth time. "Sorry."

"Me either, but we're making progress. Whatever you do, don't stop moving, and we'll be there soon," she encouraged.

"Where?"

"I don't know," she admitted. But anywhere was better than where they were and where they'd been.

Spiderwebs crisscrossed the vents, catching across Josi's face and making her want to scream. But drawing unwanted attention was something she couldn't afford. When she placed a hand in something warm and wet, she told herself not to think about what it might have been. The only thing that mattered was getting Tara to safety.

"I see light," Josi whispered, moving as quickly as possible through the metal shaft. The vent took a sharp left, but straight ahead was a way out. She reached the grate over a small office and peered inside. The room was empty, but a desk lamp illuminated the space. She slid her fingers through the metal slats, gripped the bars and pushed, but the grate didn't move. She tried again, using the full force of her arms, until the bottom corner gave way. One metal screw hit the floor with a clink, then began to roll.

In the distance, male voices registered and grew loud.

Tara tugged Josi's ankles. Her curled fingers scratched at

Josi's leg. "That's them," she whispered, the words hushed but frantic. "Stop."

Josi inched backward, and Tara made room. Seconds later, a trio of large shadows entered the little office, climbing the walls like monsters.

Dennis took a seat in the creaky office chair. "Get the girls," he said casually. "Take them both to the ring. We'll let the new one watch the other one get her teeth kicked in. I want them to regret testing me. When we toss the blonde in the ring after that, she'll be too scared to move. If she cries and begs to get out, all the better."

"Fresh meat," someone said on a chuckle. "Folks will throw money at that."

"Sure," a third man said, mild concern in his tone. "Until they're dead. Then we've got bodies to bury."

"Harbor is right there," Dennis said. "And this town needs a warning. There'll be more deaths to follow if everyone doesn't stay out of my business."

Josi pressed her lips tight against the urge to be sick.

"Let's go," he said. "I'm eager to get started."

The office emptied. It would only be a matter of minutes before the men looking for Josi and Tara realized they were gone. Additional seconds before they saw the vent's grate on the ground and knew exactly how to find them.

Josi angled around the corner, moving into the adjoining vent on her left. Tara followed. Their quiet shimmies seemed to make gonging sounds against the metal.

She paused at the next light source and reached quickly for the grate. When the cover didn't move, she backed up and carried on, eager to find a fast escape.

Inaudible voices and booming footfalls echoed in the distance beneath them, reaching up from the old grain mill to Josi's ears.

"I think they realized we're gone," Tara said, voice dazed and dreamy in a way that raised Josi's already frantic heart rate.

"We have to keep moving," she whispered. The men would be in the vents soon, assuming they could fit, or maybe they'd spread out, one in every room, waiting for her and Tara to reappear. Either way wouldn't end well. "You doing okay back there?"

Tara grunted softly, her curled hands bumping against Josi's feet as they moved.

"Another room." Josi hurried forward, pushing against the next grate. It moved immediately. A second hard shove set it free. Josi launched forward, chasing after the heavy cover, catching it by a single crooked finger before it crashed onto the concrete floor.

Tara caught Josi around her legs, torso pressed against the backs of her thighs, holding her in place as she hung, head first, over an empty room.

Tears fell from Josi's eyes, running down her forehead and into her hair as she struggled to catch a full breath. "Thank you."

Before she was ready, she reached downward, stretching toward the floor. Tara kept her from a free fall—she was trembling, but holding tight to her legs. Josi released the grate gently, careful not to make a sound, then planted her palms against the floor. A moment later, she collapsed onto the ground in a messy heap.

Tara's head and shoulders appeared above her, extended from the vent.

Josi rose to help her down.

Angry male voices filled the building, shouting threats and laments. The sounds echoed from every corner. Their footfalls pounded, sneakers squeaking against the uncarpeted floors.

"Hurry," Josi ordered, wrapping her arms around Tara as she pulled the remainder of her body free.

They stumbled and fell back with a soft thud and muted groans.

"You okay?" Josi asked, moving onto her hands and knees, then pushing upright to stand.

Tara's face was red and contorted in pain. "My hands are broken. My fingers and wrists. Ribs too, I think? Or bruised."

Josi bent to help her upright, hating that she hadn't asked about the extent of her friend's injuries sooner. It was easy to see she wasn't well, but she hadn't asked any questions. The words *I'm sorry* sat on her tongue, but there wasn't any time for that now. They needed to get out of the building. They needed to get Tara somewhere safe.

Before they reached the door, gunshots rang out. A distinct tearing of metal told the rest of the story.

The men were shooting into the vents.

LINCOLN LEAPED FROM the passenger side of Finn's truck before it'd stopped moving. He reached the Barbell Club's door as Dean pulled in behind them, Austin at his side. The lot was empty, save a single white hatchback and black truck that looked as if it hadn't moved in decades.

"Lincoln," Finn called, his truck door slamming shut, as if to underscore his authority. "Wait for me."

The lights were off inside the building. A list of hours posted on the glass indicated the business was closed.

Lincoln tried the door anyway. "Locked." He raised a fist and pounded hard, then cupped both hands around his eyes to peer inside. "This gym is open late six days a week. Today it closed early. Three guesses as to why."

Dean and Austin moved into line beside Finn, all facing Lincoln.

Dean was next to speak. "We know the SUV caught leaving the ranch on the security feed is registered to a company who also owns this gym," Dean said.

Finn had run the plate immediately.

"Is there somewhere else we can look for Dennis Cane?" Dean asked. "Maybe someone else who works here and might have answers? Some other way to cover our bases?"

Finn dragged his attention from the phone in his hand to Dean. "I don't know. I sent a cruiser to his home on our way here. The officer says no one was there. No signs of the truck in the neighborhood." He tucked the phone into his pocket, jaw locked in frustration.

Lincoln bit the insides of his cheeks to keep from screaming. He assured himself that breaking every window of the gym behind him, operated by a woman-abducting, illegal-fight-club-running criminal, wouldn't help either. Though it would be incredibly satisfying. "What now?" he asked.

The fact that Josi had been taken so brazenly from his family ranch didn't bode well for her safety. Dennis Cane had taken a major risk. He wanted her silenced.

And time was ticking.

Finn retrieved his phone, expression expectant as he looked at the device, then pressed it to his ear. "Detective Beaumont." His gaze slid to Lincoln. "That's all we need. Get the warrant." He disconnected with a smirk. "Ballistics matched casings found at the ranch to those pulled from a tree used for target practice on Cane's property. Combine that with Josi's abduction and the vehicle leaving the scene of the crime, we won't have any problem getting a warrant to search the gym and his home. Wherever he's holding Tara and Josi, we'll find them."

Lincoln stepped away, needing space to think. "What about the men you're tailing?" Lincoln asked. "Any word on them?"

Finn tapped his phone screen and initiated the speaker function. "Let's check in."

"Ramos," a deep male voice answered.

"Hey," Finn said. "Where's your guy?"

"Heading along the scenic byway. I'm a few cars back, but he's not even looking. He's been running some kind of errands all day. On the move since lunch. I'm starving."

Austin chuckled.

Finn sighed. "Have you talked to the others?"

"Yeah," Ramos said, a little more brightly. "They're moving this way. Their guys are on the byway too."

Lincoln straightened, watching as his brothers figured out what he had. "It's fight night." Everyone involved was likely heading to the location Lincoln and Finn had been searching for.

"Where are you now, precisely?" Finn asked.

"Passing mile marker eleven, out near the old grain mill."

"That's only a mile or so from where that woman found Tara walking," Lincoln said.

Finn circled a hand in the air as he turned for his truck.

The brothers raced to their rides. Within seconds, they were back in play, and Lincoln's gut said this was it. The area near the old grain mill would make the perfect location for a group to gather outside, and the mill itself would be a good place to hide a pair of hostages. No amount of screaming would be heard so far from everything and everyone else.

Minutes later, Finn slowed as he turned onto a narrow

path through the field toward the old mill. The road had
grown over with weeds and grass. In the distance, vehicles had begun to gather. He tapped the screen of his truck
and relayed what he saw to Dispatch, who assured him
that backup was on the way. Ramos and the others who'd
been tailing Dennis Cane's men took strategic positions and
awaited Finn's word.

Lincoln gripped the handle on his door, ready to jump
out again.

Finn raised one palm in warning and frowned to underscore the silent order. *Be still and stay put.*

Behind them, Dean's truck crawled to a stop as well.

Finn disconnected with Dispatch and dialed Ramos.
"What can you see from your vantage?"

"We're in the field. Just paid to park, but the money man
was tight-lipped about what I was parking to see."

"Hold your position," Finn said. "Keep me posted.
Backup is a few minutes out. We're going to take a closer
look at the mill on foot."

Lincoln opened his door and met his brothers outside.
Finn looked each of them in the eye for a long beat before
turning toward the mill. They'd all seen that look before.
Their little brother was in cop mode, and it was best to fall
in line.

Together, they flanked their leader and marched steadily
toward their target.

A sudden burst of gunfire sent them into a collective
crouch, trading looks before realizing the shots hadn't been
fired at their approach. The sounds had come from inside
the mill.

And just like that, they launched into a sprint with Lincoln leading the charge.

Chapter Twenty-Three

Josi grabbed Tara by the hand and pulled, snapping her into motion. They needed to get away from the building before the shooter realized they weren't in the vents anymore.

Tara stumbled forward on unsteady legs, knocking into a small metal trash can and toppling it onto the floor. She froze, free hand extended as if to right the bin.

"Leave it," Josi hissed. "We have to go."

They slipped through the office door and into a hallway, their shoes padding softly against the ground. Every sound was magnified in the massive, abandoned building, carrying down corridors and through the sprawling space. Thankfully, the shooting had stopped.

Josi towed Tara along, checking regularly over her shoulder.

Tara's pace slowed by a fraction with every step. Her gait grew awkward and inconsistent. She cradled one arm across her chest, wincing repeatedly, expression contorted. She was filthy and bruised from head to toe, her clothes smeared with blood.

Her normally soft hair was slick from days without a wash. And a cut on her mouth had opened and begun to bleed. How many times had Tara been carried away from the ring this week, then tossed into the cellar until the next fight? Not that she could possibly fight in her condition. She doubted Tara could even stand for long on her own. Yet the men were coming to get her.

The vents above them groaned, and Josi refocused on the escape. Tara likely wouldn't survive another fight, and neither she nor Josi would survive long if they got in front of a bullet.

"I see blood!" a male voice boomed. The sound seemed to come from the ceiling.

Had the cut on Tara's mouth opened while they were in the vents? Were they leaving a trail?

A moment later, the sound of an opening door sent them into a jog.

Tara whimpered and switched to a hop, no longer able to keep up on her more injured leg.

Panic welled in Josi as she searched for a place to hide. She pulled Tara through the next open doorway, praying for boxes or furniture to duck behind. Instead, they found themselves on a metal landing overlooking a two-story section of the mill—they were fully exposed. A dozen metal steps stood between them and the old machinery, their only chance to hide.

Beside her, Tara's hand went limp, and her body slowly slumped to the floor.

LINCOLN MOVED CAREFULLY into the old grain mill, measuring his steps while Finn took the lead with his badge and gun. Lincoln would've preferred ripping the door off its ancient hinges instead of creeping, but he knew the drill. This was a reconnaissance mission first. Tearing the place down, metaphorically, came second.

The interior was large and dank. Scents of oil and earth hung in the air. Large, motionless machinery stood before them on a cement floor. Two stories of small black-painted windows rose to the metal rafters. An office with a large viewing space faced the floor across from a set of steps that overlooked it all.

Dennis Cane stood inside the office, attention fixed on a metal landing atop the stairs. Two familiar figures sat motionless in his sights. Dennis raised one extended arm, a gun in hand. The barrel was pointed at Josi and Tara.

"No!" The word ripped from Lincoln's chest.

Dennis swung around with a start and pulled the trigger. Bang!

The Beaumonts ducked, and Dennis fled.

"Marshal's Bluff PD!" Finn called, tearing off in the gunman's direction.

"Josi's on the steps," Lincoln told Dean and Austin. "I think Tara's with her."

"Go," Austin said, nudging Dean in Finn's direction. "Cover Finn. We'll retrieve the hostages."

Lincoln broke into a jog. Numerous machines and conveyors filled the space and complicated his path. A second gunshot dropped him into a crouch.

The bullet dinged loudly off metal, indicating it had hit something close by.

Austin jumped behind a nearby machine. "I'll cover you."

Lincoln scanned the area for signs of the shooter, then continued toward the stairs. A fresh round of shots redirected him once more.

"Go!" Austin called, slipping back into view, sidearm in hand.

Sometimes belonging to a family of armed lawmen and private eyes had real perks.

A trickle of blood on the floor caught Lincoln's attention. He tracked the pattern of small sporadic dots to a wall of decrepit boxes stacked six feet high. He rushed forward, head down and body low as bullets zinged and crashed around him.

The nearby click of a cocking gun froze him in his spot. A man he recognized from the Barbell Club stepped into full view, a sneer on his face and a revolver in his hand.

The last time Lincoln had seen the man, he'd been in a boxing ring with someone half a foot taller, pretending to have no idea Dennis Cane was a killer.

"Must be my lucky day," the guy said. "You're just what we need to fish these women out from hiding. After that, maybe we'll finally see if you can box."

Lincoln appraised the man's distance and grip on the weapon. He could disarm him with a little distraction. "You lost your hostages?" Lincoln's heart soared with pride. Josi must've been terrified, but she was never a victim. He laughed, and the man scowled. "They outsmarted you, right? I mean, it probably didn't take much."

The man's expression morphed from confusion to offense, but before he could raise his gun, the wall of boxes beside them came crashing down.

A cloud of dust and grain rose into the air, and Lincoln lurched forward, knocking the weapon from the other man's hand. He shoved him back several paces, but the man bent forward, ran for Lincoln's middle and threw him to the hard ground with a bone-rattling thud.

Gunshots continued in the mill as Austin kept another shooter at bay.

It was on Lincoln to knock this one out and find Josi.

A blond blur rushed around him as he struck his opponent in the jaw and received a jab to his already sore ribs. They rolled and tussled, trading blows and each of them working to gain the upper hand.

An earsplitting gunshot froze them in place, too close to ignore.

Josi widened her stance, pistol raised overhead. "Stop!"

The man lifted his palms. Blood streamed from his nose, and one eye had begun to swell. Lincoln would've preferred that number to be two.

He winked at Josi. "Attagirl."

Silence suddenly reigned in the cavernous building, disrupted only by the growing wails of sirens outside.

"Help me get her out of here," Josi said, motioning to the pile of fallen boxes.

Tara Stone appeared on unsteady legs, hobbling and bleeding from her lips and hands. She barely resembled the photos in her home. Both wrists had been taped for fighting. Her fingers had curled into broken claws. She favored one leg and pressed an arm to her middle.

Anger over what she'd been put through boiled inside him. "Hi, Tara," he said softly. "I'm Lincoln, and this is over."

At the top of the stairs, Finn walked Dennis Cane onto the landing in handcuffs.

Across the huge room, Austin lifted his hands in victory. "Thug down."

Josi began to cry as she moved toward her friend. "Ambulances are coming. Let's get you out of here." She passed the gun to Lincoln, and reached for Tara.

The sound of another gunshot exploded and pain cut though his side. He turned his eyes to the crimson stain blooming on his shirt, then to the man seated a few feet away.

Josi had taken his pistol, but he'd clearly had another.

"Marshal's Bluff PD," Finn called, flying down the steps, gun raised. "Stop! You're under arrest."

The shooter smirked at Lincoln, but set his weapon on the ground.

Lincoln strode toward the shooter, and knocked him out.

"All right," Finn said, shoving Lincoln back. He kicked the criminal's gun away and cuffed him. "You know you've been shot, right?"

"It's a flesh wound," he grumbled, pressing a hand to his side. "I've had worse."

"I'm sure you have," Finn said, glancing back at him. "I'm worried about me. You were shot on my watch. Now, who's going to save me from Mama?"

Lincoln snorted a laugh, then swore through the pain.

The large metal door across the room opened, and men and women in uniforms filtered inside. Hurried footfalls and shouting voices raised his heart rate. A look at the wound beneath his shirt suddenly made him light-headed.

"Lincoln," Josi said, voice distant but heavy with concern.

He couldn't answer. His tongue was thick and his mouth dry, as the grain mill faded around him, replaced by ghosts from his past. Blood and chaos. Injured soldiers. Danger. Pain.

"Hey." Josi's face blurred into view. She pressed small, cool palms to his hot, stubbled cheeks. "I'm right here," she said. "We're together, and we're both okay." Tears spilled from her eyes, her voice cracking on every word. "The medics are coming. You're going to be just fine, but I need you to breathe."

He nodded woodenly, fighting to stay with her. "I'm so sorry," he croaked. "I let him get to you."

"No." She shook her head and pressed her lips to his when his body began to tremble. "Everything worked out," she promised. "Everyone is safe." She moved her hands away from his cheeks and pressed them to his side.

A roar of pain burst from his lips.

"Over here!" she called. "Help!"

Finn recited Miranda rights as medics arrived, medical bags in hand.

Dean and Austin bookended Josi, as paramedics loaded Lincoln onto a backboard beside Tara.

His teeth began to chatter with an overload of adrenaline searching for escape. "Josi."

"I'm here." She followed as they raised him onto a gurney, and she held his hand as they rushed him toward the mill's open door.

Moonlight illuminated the field full of emergency vehicles and officials.

A few yards away, Tara's eyes had gone shut.

Finn stuffed Dennis Cane into the back of a cruiser. "I'll meet y'all at the hospital," he called. "Let Josi ride with Lincoln. She's family."

The EMT nodded. He motioned to the set of open bay doors.

Lincoln's pounding heart wished more than anything that Finn's words were true. He wanted her to be a Beaumont. He wanted her as his wife.

The medic set an IV in Lincoln's arm and fixed an oxygen mask on his face once they were inside. "A little something for pain. Just breathe," he instructed.

Josi took a seat on his opposite side. "Ready," she said. "How're you doing?"

Lincoln pulled the mask away from his face. "I love you," he whispered, eyelids already pulling closed.

"I love you too," she promised. "Now put your mask on."

Epilogue

Six months later

Spring on the ranch was Lincoln's favorite time of year. There was something about the arrival of calves and foals, ducklings and every other kind of baby livestock that he absolutely loved. Not that he'd tell anyone other than Josi. It was true about friendly people getting extra attention, and the only person's attention he wanted in excess was Josi's.

He breathed in the warm evening air, admiring the remnants of a fading sunset and suppressing the mass of hope and excitement rising in his heart.

"What are you standing out here by yourself thinking about?" Josi asked. Her voice carried across the field as she made a path to his side.

They'd healed completely since their troubles in the fall, leaning on one another throughout the process. And they'd each found a professional counselor to talk to about unresolved issues in their pasts that might've otherwise stolen their joy in the future.

Even Tara was back on her feet. The doctors called her recovery miraculous, but from what Lincoln had seen and come to know about her, Tara was a fighter. He imagined there was little that could keep her down. She'd left her position at the pawnshop in favor of teaching classes at Body by Bella and seemed to be on an emotional healing journey of her own.

Best of all, her testimony had put Dennis Cane in jail for a very long time. A jury had found him guilty of a number of crimes, including kidnapping and attempted murder. They'd also found him complicit in the death of Marcus Stone. Several of Dennis's goons would remain behind bars nearly as long for similar reasons. And the illegal Marshal's Bluff fight club had finally, officially, been dismantled for good.

Josi stopped before him, smiling like she'd just been handed a prize. Blond hair hung over her shoulders in waves. The adorable sundress she'd chosen should've been illegal. Waning light backlit her sexy figure, and he imagined throwing her over his shoulder and taking her home. "Penny for your thoughts?"

Lincoln took her hand and pressed a kiss to her forehead, inhaling her sweet coconut scent. "You look beautiful."

Her mischievous blue eyes twinkled, and like every time they were this close, it felt like coming home.

His hands found the curves of her hips and pulled her closer, holding her body against his. He pressed his lips to her cheek and chin, then to the tip of her nose. When that wasn't enough, he went in for a proper kiss and took his time enjoying the stolen moment.

"Always dodging my questions," she said, a teasing smile on her lips. "But I will never complain about the way you distract me."

His lips quirked, but he fought back the smile. Josi made him happier than he'd ever dreamed of being, and each day with her had only gotten better. He was sure a lifetime with her would never be enough.

"What do you think of the dress?" she asked, stepping

back to spin in a small circle. The material floated around
her thighs. She'd topped the simple sundress with a denim
jacket and paired that with her pink-and-tan Western-style
boots.

"Stunning," he assured her. "Like the smartest, toughest,
kindest, prettiest cowgirl I've ever known."

Josi laughed softly. "I think I'll wear this more often."

The sound of tires on gravel turned her eyes in search of
the arriving guest.

"Finn," she said. "We should say hi before we head out."

"Sounds good." He bit back a grin. "I need to stop at the
stable first. We can catch Finn and my folks in a minute."

Josi turned happily on her heels and headed toward the
large stable doors. She stopped to stare at the thin stream
of light spilling along the ground outside. "Did someone
leave the lights on?"

"Yep," Lincoln said, reaching for the metal handle and
pulling it wide. "That was me."

JOSI SHOOK HER head as Lincoln pulled the doors open without unlocking them. He rarely forgot anything. To leave the
lights on and the place unlocked was completely out of char-
acter. She'd definitely tease him about that later.

Her thoughts fizzled and her mind blanked as the stable's interior came into view. Strings of bistro lights hung
in swoops from every rafter, and rose petals covered the
floor. Lancelot snuffled and grunted in his stall, locking
eyes with her as she entered.

"What is all this?" she asked, eyes and smile wide. It
wasn't her birthday, or the anniversary of anything specific
that she could recall.

She and Lincoln had been together almost six months,

but they'd already made plans to celebrate that in a couple of weeks.

He tapped his phone screen and music played softly through a wireless speaker nearby. "Lincoln. This is gorgeous. I love it! And this my favorite song."

"You approve?" He pulled her close, his earthy cologne mixing with the familiar fragrances of wood and hay.

Lincoln raised their joined hands to his chest and draped her opposite arm over his shoulder. Then they began to sway.

"I've always wanted to slow-dance in the barn," she whispered, overwhelmed with immeasurable peace and joy. "I love that you remember the things I say, and that you pay attention to the things that are important to me," she said. "I hope I can make you half as happy someday."

A gentle rapping at the door caused her to turn and see Mr. and Mrs. Beaumont approach.

"Are we too late?" Mrs. Beaumont asked.

Lincoln shook his head, never missing a step in their dance. "Join us."

His mom covered her mouth briefly, eyes glistening with emotion as his father led her over the rose petals to a little space on the floor just for them. A few moments later, his brothers filed in, their wives and fiancées on their arms. Finn and Hayley, Dean and Nicole, Austin and Scarlet.

Josi batted away tears as her heart soared. The perfection of the moment was nearly more than she could bear. How had she come to be part of this big, goofy, loyal, loving family? And how had she been so lucky as to have them love her too?

The song ended, and the couples split, stepping apart to greet one another and admire the amazing, romantic decor.

"Tara's coming soon," Finn said. "She got off work a little late, but she's on her way."

Josi frowned. "Tonight?" Weren't she and Lincoln going out to dinner?

A hush rolled over the couples, and the women began to smile.

Josi followed their collective gaze to the space directly behind her, where Lincoln rested on one knee, a black velvet box in hand.

"Josi," he said, voice steady and strong. "I love you. I want to live a life at your side. Caring for animals, people and each other. I was wondering if you might want that too."

Tears clouded her eyes as she let his words pour over her. She hadn't thought it was possible for Lincoln to feel the same way she did, because she'd never felt like this before. "I do."

He opened the box and removed a diamond ring. Then he took her hand in his. "In that case, I hope you will consider doing me the incredible honor of being my wife."

"Yes," she rasped, heart soaring and tears falling.

He stood with a broad smile and spun her off her feet.

All around them, his family hooted and hollered.

Then someone pumped up the music.

The perfect beginning to a long, beautiful life together.

* * * * *

MILLS & BOON MODERN IS
HAVING A MAKEOVER!

The same great stories you love,
a stylish new look!

Look out for our brand new look
COMING JUNE 2024

MILLS & BOON

COMING SOON!

We really hope you enjoyed reading this book.
If you're looking for more romance
be sure to head to the shops when
new books are available on

Thursday 6th June

To see which titles are coming soon, please visit

millsandboon.co.uk/nextmonth